What people are saying about …

The Secrets of the Cross Trilogy

"A wonderful tale of love, sacrifice, war, and courage, written in stunning detail. Elizabeth Musser is an amazing storyteller."

Susan Meissner, author of *A Sound Among the Trees*

"One intriguing era in France's history, one unforgettable cast of characters, and one of the best writers in the CBA today all add up to one incredible read! In *Two Crosses*, Elizabeth Musser has achieved another literary triumph."

Ann Tatlock, award-winning author
of *Promises to Keep*

"Elizabeth Musser reminds me of Francine Rivers. The characters are real, the drama is gripping, and the Spirit rises up from the grass roots of the story. You'll love *Two Crosses*."

Creston Mapes, best-selling
author of *Nobody*

"In a novel rich in historical detail, Elizabeth Musser spins an intriguing story of the lives and loves of young people caught up in the Algerian revolution to win independence from France in 1954–1962. It was a costly conflict, and we are invited to see it through the eyes of those living on both sides of the Mediterranean. Christian convictions and patriotic loyalties are put to the test, as God works His plans for individuals and nations. I enjoyed this book and look forward to reading the rest of the trilogy."

Ruth Stewart, AWM missionary for forty years to Algeria and France

"In this delightful story, the sounds, scents, and scenery of France and Algeria come alive. *Two Crosses* untangles the complicated history of Algeria's war for independence from France. You feel as though you know the characters. The surprising twists in the story never stop. As the book comes to an end, you are ready to immediately pick up *Two Testaments.*"

Margaret Haines, former missionary with over thirty years of missionary experience among the Algerians and French in North Africa during the end of the war

Two Destinies

OTHER BOOKS BY ELIZABETH MUSSER

The Swan House
The Dwelling Place
Searching for Eternity
Words Unspoken
The Sweetest Thing

THE SECRETS OF THE CROSS TRILOGY

Two Crosses
Two Testaments
Two Destinies

ELIZABETH MUSSER

Two Destinies

—— A NOVEL ——

SECRETS OF
THE CROSS
TRILOGY
III

David C Cook®
transforming lives together

TWO DESTINIES
Published by David C Cook
4050 Lee Vance View
Colorado Springs, CO 80918 U.S.A.

David C Cook Distribution Canada
55 Woodslee Avenue, Paris, Ontario, Canada N3L 3E5

David C Cook U.K., Kingsway Communications
Eastbourne, East Sussex BN23 6NT, England

The graphic circle C logo is a registered trademark of David C Cook.

The website addresses recommended throughout this book are offered as a
resource to you. These websites are not intended in any way to be or imply an
endorsement on the part of David C Cook, nor do we vouch for their content.

This story is a work of fiction. Characters and events are the product of the author's
imagination. Any resemblance to any person, living or dead, is coincidental.

Scripture quotations are taken from the King James Version of the Bible (Public
Domain) and the New American Standard Bible®, Copyright © 1960, 1995
by The Lockman Foundation. Used by permission. (www.Lockman.org.)

LCCN 2012942044
ISBN 978-0-7814-0501-0
eISBN 978-1-4347-0513-6

The Team: Don Pape, LB Norton, Amy Konyndyk, Jack Campbell, Karen Athen
Cover Design: Nick Lee
Cover Photos: Shutterstock; iStockphoto

Printed in the United States of America
First English Edition 2012

1 2 3 4 5 6 7 8 9 10

062912

This story is dedicated to my beloved mother, Barbara Butler Goldsmith. For all my life, you have modeled to me what it means to be the hands and feet of Jesus as you have reached out to those in need, "the least of these my brethren," in the inner city of Atlanta and around the world. Thank you for showing me how to give humbly and fully with no thought of what you may get in return. You are a rare and beautiful woman, and I love you.

Acknowledgments

This new edition: I am thankful and thrilled that *Two Destinies* is finally available in English! It's been a fourteen-year journey, and as with so many things in life, the Lord has taught me a lot through the waiting process. Thank you, thank you, LB Norton, my wonderful editor, and Chip MacGregor, my fantastic agent, for believing in this project for so many years and encouraging me to keep pursuing the dream of having the third book in the Secrets of the Cross trilogy in English! Thank you to Don Pape, Karen Stoller, Jack Campbell, Ingrid Beck, Michelle Webb, and many others at David C Cook for your enthusiasm for this project and your excellent and hard work. And thanks to Jeane Wynn of Wynn-Wynn Media for helping me think outside the box and come up with fresh ideas to get the word out about the trilogy. I'm especially thankful that my mother, Barbara Goldsmith, is at last seeing the novel that is dedicated to her published. She's been through two heart surgeries in the past two and a half years, and I'm so proud of her continued courage and determination.

The first edition: As I wrote this book, the Lord put His finger on some of the rough spots in my life and gave me the desire to emulate what is best in my characters—which ultimately means to be more like Jesus. My prayer is that the words of this book will reflect a little of who the Lord is, who we are, and who we want to become. "For momentary, light affliction is producing in us an eternal weight of glory far beyond all comparison, while we look not at the things which are seen, but at the things which are not seen; for the things which are seen are temporal, but the things which are not seen are eternal."

This book could not have been written were it not for the help of many of my friends here in Montpellier. I am indebted to these people:

Ian Campbell—thanks for the time you took out of your busy schedule to help me in the research. Through our years of friendship, I am always humbled and encouraged by your heart for the North African believers.

Muriel Butcher—thank you for finding answers to my many questions about what is happening in Algeria today. Your knowledge of culture and customs and your comments as you proofread these pages were invaluable.

The Algerian women who shared with me—thank you for daring to give me firsthand accounts of the war and what you have lived through as Christians in Algeria.

Dominique Fabre, the *médiateur de rue* here in Montpellier—thank you for giving me a taste of what the homeless life is really like. It made a big difference to this story.

Michèle Ausseray, Bénédicte Claron, Cathy Carmeni, and Catherine Schiltz—thanks for your prayers, your help with documents about Algeria, information about the Croix Rouge here in Montpellier and a host of other things. You are dear friends.

Trudy Owens and Odette Beauregard, teammates, soul mates, babysitters, and cheerleaders, *merci.*

And the real Rizlène—thanks for sharing your story and living out a life of faith before all of us at the Pompignane church.

And to many on the other side of the Atlantic:

My family—my parents, Barbara and Jere Goldsmith; my brothers, Jere and Glenn; sisters-in-law, Mary and Kim (welcome to the family!); and my grandmother, Allene Goldsmith, thanks for the never-ending support and prayers. Y'all are the best! And to my precious niece, Katie, thanks for sharing some of your first steps with me! You inspired the little Catherine in the book.

Valerie Andrews, Margaret DeBorde, Kim Huhman, and Laura McDaniel—thanks for using your editorial skills to give valuable insights on the novel. And as always, thanks for making the times in Atlanta so delightful.

And to the wonderful "men" in my life:

Andrew and Christopher, my sons who are growing up fast—it is a joy for me to watch your lives blossom. The way you use your creativity, humor, compassion, and love to bless me and many others makes me one proud mom! PS: Let's not fight over the laptop.

Paul, my ever-patient husband, it is such a privilege to work with you in ministry. As for my writing, you always have just the right response when I look despairingly across the desk and ask, "Can you give me a more descriptive word for *gun*?" I love you.

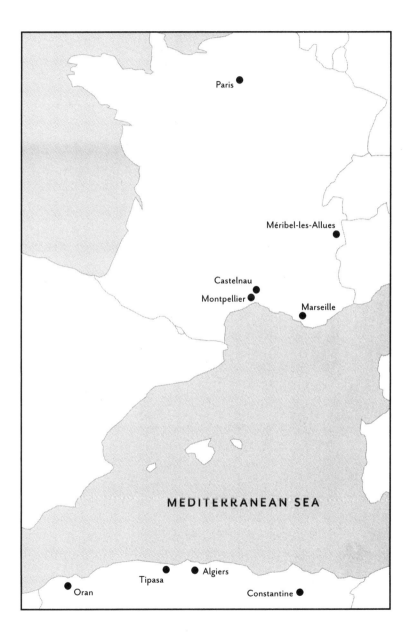

Paris

Méribel-les-Allues

Castelnau
Montpellier
Marseille

MEDITERRANEAN SEA

Tipasa Algiers
Oran
Constantine

NORTH ATLANTIC OCEAN

Paris

GERMANY

FRANCE

SWITZERLAND

AUSTRIA

Méribel-les-Allues

ITALY

Castelnau

Montpellier

Marseille

SPAIN

MEDITERRANEAN SEA

Tipasa

Algiers

Oran

Constantine

TUNISIA

ALGERIA

Glossary

Algerian War for Independence—Algerian nationals' fight for independence from France, 1954–1962.

FIS—Front Islamique du Salut, extremist militant Muslim faction that was on the brink of winning national elections in 1992 when the vote was canceled and the military installed a president.

harki—Algerian soldier who remained loyal to the French Army and therefore fought against his fellow Algerians during the War for Independence.

hijab—scarf worn by Algerian women for religious reasons; covers the hair and extends to shoulders or longer but does not conceal the face.

l'essentiel est invisible pour les yeux—quote from *The Little Prince* by Antoine Saint-Exupéry, meaning "what is essential is invisible to the eyes."

médiateur de rue—street mediator, the one who acts as a go-between for the homeless and the government.

pied-noir—a European who lived in Algeria; after Algeria became independent in 1962, most *pied-noirs* returned to France.

SDF—*sans domicile fixe*, a homeless person.

1

Montpellier, France
November 1994

Rislène Namani stepped off the bus in front of the parc du Peyrou at the highest point of Montpellier's *centre ville*. She glanced to her left, where dozens of people mingled leisurely in the wide square that was flanked on either side by two rows of naked plane trees with their dappled bark. The air was brisk but the sun high on this bright Sunday afternoon in late November. She took in a deep breath and let a smile erase the frown she'd been wearing.

She glanced around her, then crossed the wide avenue, walking away from the park and through the thick Roman arches that had earned this monument the name of le petit Arc de Triomphe. She thought it as beautiful as the one in Paris.

She turned down a side street that meandered around and opened into a small square. It too was crowded with students sitting on benches and children playing in the dirt around an ancient fountain that sprayed water from little mermaids' mouths. Again Rislène looked behind her, heart thumping in her chest.

Practically jogging now, she pushed her thick black hair off her neck, feeling a pulsing in her head, a tingling in every part of her body. Almost there!

She glanced once more over her shoulder as she stepped into

the little Café de la Paix, around the corner from the bustling little *place*.

"*Bonjour, mademoiselle,*" the barkeeper crooned.

Rislène kept her head down, her multicolored scarf twirled carelessly around her neck, and hurried to the back of the café.

He was there!

"Eric," she whispered and let the tall boy with the coarsely cropped red hair draw her into an embrace.

"Rislène! You made it!" Then his freckled face wrinkled at the brow. "No problems? No one following you?"

"No. Nazira went out with her friends for the afternoon. She glared at me the whole morning as if she knew a big secret, but she didn't try to follow me."

Now they were sitting at a little round table, holding hands, staring into each other's eyes. Eric's were a bright green. How she loved his eyes! How she loved him! She was out of breath with the thought.

They ordered two cups of coffee, and when the waiter set them on the table, the couple held each other's gaze with the steam from the coffee rising between them.

"Don't worry, Eric. We're safe. No one knows."

A faint smile spread across his thin face, and he breathed a sigh of relief. "So many months of hiding our love.... But soon, Rislène. Someday soon, I'll tell my sister. Ophélie will surely understand— why, she writes plays that are filled with impossible love stories. She'll be thrilled, and she'll help us."

"Yes, I hope she will. I know she likes me—as a student in her class, that is. I don't think she looks at me and thinks, *She'd make a good girlfriend for my little brother!*" Rislène's smile vanished, and her voice dropped to a whisper. "I'm scared about Father. He grows more fanatical each day. And Nazira is even worse. It's not the peaceful Islam I grew up with." She fumbled with a paper napkin, turning it over in her hands.

"Shh. Please. Let's just enjoy this time together." Eric grabbed both of her hands tightly.

She looked at his pale, thin fingers entwined with her dark olive-skinned ones. She loved this young man with a head filled with dreams and a heart of courage and conviction. But how complicated he made her life. Why, she wondered for the thousandth time, had she allowed herself to fall in love with a Christian, the son of two American-born French citizens?

She hadn't meant to. It had happened gradually, over the course of the past year ... when she had become a Christian too.

Eric Hoffmann watched as Rislène left the café, then he followed her out, putting a distance between them. How hard it was to hide his love for her from the rest of the world!

The Algerian beauty had stolen his heart the first night they'd met, over a year ago now. He thought of the young people gathered on the beach, the end of the summer's heat warm on their shoulders as the sun set and the lazy Mediterranean lapped at their feet.

"Meet my friend Rislène," Oumel had said, smiling broadly. "She wanted to tag along tonight and see what in the world I've been talking about." He had hardly taken his eyes off her the whole evening, while he strummed his guitar and the young people munched on *chipolata* and *merguez* sausages cooked over a makeshift grill. He'd felt his face turn red each time she glanced his way. She was so delicate, her *café au lait* skin so smooth, her eyes dark ovals that flashed pleasure and maybe even mischief, her black hair, soft and thick and full, tumbling past her shoulders …

Rislène!

Eric watched her board the bus near the Arc de Triomphe. She turned and looked his way, eyes full of love. The doors closed behind her, and as the bus pulled away from the curb, he let out a sigh of relief.

Rislène felt the tension the moment she stepped back into her family's apartment. Her mother regarded her suspiciously as Rislène hurried back to the bedroom she shared with her sister. Nazira was standing there, a wicked gleam in her eyes, holding up a small leather book.

"You're a traitor, Rislène."

Rislène's legs buckled under her, and she collapsed on her bed. "Nazira, let me explain."

"Explain!" her sister shrilled. "Yes, explain it to me, Rislène! Why are you hiding a Bible under your mattress? Explain that!"

This wasn't the way Rislène had imagined sharing her newfound faith with her sister, but it seemed the moment had been decided for her. Nazira didn't want to listen, though, and her face grew red with rage.

"We'll see what Father has to say about such beliefs!"

"Please, Nazira, don't tell him!"

Nazira gave a cold laugh. "I would never keep news like this from Father!"

With a groan, Rislène watched Nazira leave their bedroom, calling out, "Father! Father! Come quick!"

When he stepped into the room, Rislène shrank from her father's harsh gaze. Usually his deep brown eyes held a fierce pride in them for his oldest daughter. But not today.

"What is this, Rislène? What have you done?"

Rislène stood and reached for him. "It's nothing against the family, Father. Please let me try to explain what I've discovered … in this book."

His hand was swift and strong across her face, sending her reeling backward so that she fell across her bed with a sharp cry. She hid her face in her hands and whimpered, "Please, try to understand."

But she knew he would never understand. As he left the room, with Nazira behind, Rislène knew that she had just lost the innocence of her youth to the angry hand of her father.

At seven forty-five Monday morning, traffic was moving slowly along the broad avenue on the east side of Montpellier. Ophélie Duchemin frowned as the light turned red, and she pulled to a stop.

A man tapped on her window, a cardboard sign in his hand. She read the sign and shook her head, not meeting the man's eyes. These homeless people! They were forever begging for handouts at every major intersection in Montpellier. She felt a stab of guilt. Sometimes she handed them a few *francs*, but today she didn't have time to rummage through her purse. Anyway, how could she be sure this man would take the francs and buy bread instead of a cheap bottle of red wine? She couldn't help everyone on a high school teacher's salary.

Still, she wished she could offer the man something. She stared straight ahead, willing the light to turn green so she could get past this pitiful man and get to school. If she looked at him, if she met his eyes, she knew that feelings of sorrow would overtake her. The light changed. Ophélie sighed and inched the car forward as the homeless man stepped back onto the curb and waited for the next group of victims trapped by a traffic light.

Ophélie smiled at the young people who hurried into the classroom, talking among themselves. She stood and welcomed the teenagers to her French class as she did every day, challenging their intellects with an obscure quote from a favorite French author.

"Je te frapperai sans colère. Et sans haine, comme un boucher ... "

The students contemplated the quote, some leafing quickly through their literature book from which, Ophélie promised them, all the quotes came.

Finally a girl on the front row called out, "Baudelaire, *Les Fleurs du mal.*"

Ophélie nodded her approval, gave the class a half grin, and started her lecture. She was tall for a French woman, five foot seven, and slim, with long shining hair that fell past her shoulders, brown and thick. For years she had been kidded that she looked like one of the students, with her jeans and T-shirts. Even now, at thirty-eight, she could pass for a university student.

She had already begun her lecture when the door opened and a young woman of Algerian descent slipped into the classroom, her face turned down, her notebooks gathered tightly to her chest. Rislène Namani—the girl who had converted to Christianity last year, was attending Oasis meetings for teenage Muslim converts and had even started coming to church services. As she found her seat, Ophélie followed her with her eyes.

After class, Rislène waited until the other students had left before approaching Ophélie's desk. "Mlle Duchemin, could I ... could I talk with you?"

Ophélie gasped slightly, seeing the girl's bruised face. "Rislène, what happened?"

Normally Rislène's smile was infectious. But today the girl was obviously terrified.

"My father found out I've been reading the Bible."

"Oh, Rislène!" Ophélie stood and took the shaking young woman into her arms. "I'm so sorry."

"My sister betrayed me," Rislène continued. "She found my Bible hidden under my mattress." She wiped a tear and covered her mouth. "I'm afraid to go back tonight. I don't know what he might do."

Ophélie closed her eyes to think. It was a very shaky time for Algerians. The civil war in their country was threatening to spread to France. Fear could be tasted. And Rislène's story resembled that of so many others. As a young North African woman who had grown up in France, she was French in every way. Yet in the past few years, a sudden reemphasis on Islam was encouraging North African fathers to demand that their daughters wear the *hijab* and attend the newly built mosques popping up throughout France.

Rislène's danger was greater, however. She had converted to Christianity, and her father saw that as an unpardonable sin. A black eye might be just the beginning.

Ophélie held Rislène's hands and looked her in the eye. "You'll come to my apartment, then, until we can think of what to do." She touched the girl's face. The ugly bruise covered her left eye and cheek. "Come back after classes, at five. Don't worry. It'll be okay."

Rislène was cuddled up on Ophélie's floral-print sofa, snuggled under a bright-blue afghan. In the waning light, the bruise was less visible on her dark skin. Ophélie offered her a mug of tea, and she took it gratefully, holding her face over the mug and letting the steam warm her.

"It's worse than you think, Mlle Duchemin," she stated, sipping the tea.

"Please, Rislène, call me Ophélie."

"Ophélie then." She smiled shyly. "I've done the worst possible thing. I've not only become a Christian and been baptized, but …" She hesitated. "I'm in love with a Christian man. My parents will kill me if they find out. I know they will."

"Is there anyone who could talk to your parents? Have they ever met anyone from the church? Perhaps my father, M. Hoffmann, could go see them?"

"My father would not let M. Hoffmann in the apartment. I know it. Your father has already tried to speak to him once." The dark of late November came upon them suddenly as the clock showed five thirty. "But maybe Mme Hoffmann."

"My stepmother? Does your mother know Gabriella?"

"Yes, they've met before. One time Mme Hoffmann invited my mother and me over to her house for a *goûter* with other Arab women."

"Your mother was aware that you'd become a Christian?"

"Not at that time. Mme Hoffmann was simply trying to get to know some of the mothers of the Algerian girls who go to Oasis. We didn't talk religion. But my mother was very impressed with Mme Hoffmann's knowledge of Algerian customs."

"She and my father lived in Algeria for almost twenty years. They love Algeria and the Algerian people."

Rislène nodded. "Yes, yes, I know. Anyway, Mother liked Mme Hoffmann. Perhaps she could meet with her when my father is out. It would be risky, but perhaps."

"I'll speak to her then."

They dined on endive salad with avocados and bits of bacon and hard-boiled eggs. Ophélie tossed the salad gently with her own special *vinaigrette* dressing made with hot Dijon mustard, red wine vinegar, and the pure virgin olive oil that was so renowned in the region, seasoning it with garlic and parsley.

They avoided the fearful subject of Rislène's father, talking instead of words from the Gospels and then reading aloud some of Paul Verlaine's poems.

Almost shyly Rislène asked, "Can you tell me what it's like to be a playwright?"

Ophélie cocked her head, surprised.

"Some kids at the church have talked about it. They say your second play is being performed right now in one of Montpellier's theaters."

Ophélie acquiesced. "A very small theater." Then she winked at Rislène. "I like the writing," she admitted, "but I also like teaching my students and chatting with them after class. I want you all to continue your studies."

Rislène smiled. "Yes, Mlle Duch— Ophélie. We've all heard you say that many times. You don't want us to 'become another statistic in France's alarming unemployment rate. Twelve percent and rising.'"

Ophélie grinned. "Quoting your *professeur*! Well, that will certainly get you on her good side." But it was true; Ophélie hoped to inspire her students to continue their studies, to succeed.

Rislène slept peacefully in Ophélie's bed. Ophélie had given her a long T-shirt and left the girl to snuggle beneath her covers. Now Ophélie sat on the couch, her legs pulled under her, papers scattered around her in every direction, the faint smell of garlic still permeating the *salon*. From a pine-finished *étagère* crammed with every type of book as well as her small hi-fi stereo, strands from *The Golden Flute* played softly in the background, punctuated occasionally by a high arpeggio from the woodwind.

This was the way she liked to grade papers, surrounded by a type of ordered clutter, with a cup of *tisane* in her hands. And tonight, curled up and all but purring like a cat, Ophélie could practically taste contentment. Her satisfaction was full, like the moon outside her window.

Tonight the terrible loneliness that at times engulfed her, especially in the quiet after an evening of entertaining dinner guests, had not rushed upon her. Someone else was in the apartment. Ophélie had never been afraid to live alone. She liked the silence and needed time to herself. She had not tolerated roommates very well in past years. But she missed a human presence.

In her heart she knew she was waiting for a man to fill the need. It had almost worked once. Almost.

Her mind drifted momentarily to the shores of Algeria, where she had lived for a time as a child. Now the country seemed bent upon another war—a civil war. And even those Algerians who lived in France were being sucked into the iron hold of Islam that was sweeping over the once socialist state.

The flute trilled brightly a high F, the orchestra faded into silence. She marked her last paper, turned off the light, and sat in darkness for a long time, looking at the moon.

Gabriella Hoffmann hesitated only a moment before ringing the doorbell of the sixth-floor apartment. When the door opened slightly, she smiled at the middle-aged Arab woman, bowed her head, and said softly in Arabic, "Hello, Mme Namani."

"Hello, Mme Hoffmann."

Altaf Namani's smile was cold, her black eyes suspicious. She looked behind her, stepped into the hallway, and pulled the door closed. Her voice was barely a whisper. "You have news of Rislène? That is why you have come?"

"Yes."

"I cannot speak with you now. My other daughter is here. Whatever she hears, she will repeat to Rislène's father."

"When can we meet?"

The Arab woman looked around furtively. "Friday afternoon. I'll come to your house. It is where we met before?"

"Yes. Take bus number 9, the last stop."

"I remember."

"Very well. Friday then." Gabriella turned to leave, but Altaf grabbed her arm.

"She is well, Rislène?"

"Yes, very well."

"Take care of her, please. She has been very foolish."

From inside the apartment a girl's voice called, "Mother! Who's there, Mother?"

"I must go," Altaf mouthed. "No one, dear," she called out in Arabic, opening the door. "Just a salesman. You know how they are. Pushy."

Gabriella walked to the elevator. Once inside, she wiped the perspiration from her brow. That had gone relatively well.

It was ironic, she thought, that she and David had gone to Algeria to live not long after so many of the people she loved had fled Algeria for France. It was just a few years after Algeria's war for independence had concluded. Anne-Marie and Moustafa, Ophélie,

Eliane and Rémi Cebrian—these *pied-noirs* and *harkis* were building a new life in France, but she and David had felt the call to Algeria. They had witnessed the country's struggling independence, had grown to love the people, and had mastered the Arabic language.

And twenty years later, they were forced to leave.

How they had wept before their Algerian friends when the word came from the government in the spring of 1985. All missionaries out. Leave immediately.

But their work was far from over. France now housed close to four million North Africans. The hatred and prejudice had only ripened over the years. And now those who were devout Muslims were demanding that their religion be honored in France. That their daughters be allowed to wear the hijab to school. That mosques be built. Not only the culture and language, but now also the religion, once practiced privately, was becoming public, and this displeased many of the French.

Gabriella walked out into the chilly November midday with its gusty mistral. She loved living in Montpellier, just as she had loved living in Algeria and Senegal and America. So many different adventures in her life. She thought of her three sons, William, Roger, and Eric, all now grown. She and David had one grandbaby and two more on the way.

Then she thought of Ophélie, who had always been like a daughter to her. Ophélie had never married. It was a heartache that her mother, Anne-Marie, carried silently. But the world was no longer a place just for couples. There were many options for a smart, gifted teacher and playwright who loved her work. Ophélie vibrated compassion, confidence, and faith. It was a pleasure to watch her life unfold.

Still, Gabriella thought, *I too would like to see a man come into her life.*

A scene flashed in her mind and she added, *A man who would stay.*

Nazira knew that her mother was lying. The other voice in the hall had been that of a woman, not a salesman. She ran to the window in time to see a woman with long red hair leave the apartment building. Someone had come to talk to Mama about Rislène, she was sure.

She laughed to herself. Mother couldn't hide the truth from her. If Nazira waited and watched, followed her mother to the market, she was sure she would learn her sister's whereabouts.

Foolish Rislène! Converting to Christianity. It made Nazira feel sick with rage. She, who so proudly wore the hijab and attended the mosque, could not tolerate the fact that her sister had betrayed her family, betrayed her heritage and her religion. Rislène deserved to be punished.

She recalled Rislène's tearful plea when Nazira had confronted her. She had been too angry to hear her sister's explanation of why Christianity worked for her. Something about grace and salvation, and the prophet Jesus being God's son. How could Rislène believe that? All through their childhood they had faithfully learned from the Koran: Jesus was a prophet. Muhammad was the greatest of the prophets. And Allah was the one true God. Christians were heretics, worshipping three gods.

Her mother came over to where Nazira was standing. "What are you doing, dear?" Her voice was tinged with fear.

Nazira shrugged and turned from the window. "I've got some work to finish, Mother. Call me when you need help with lunch." She closed the door to her room and repeated to herself, "Rislène is a traitor. Rislène will pay!"

2

He was running out of money, but he refused to beg. The decrepit old men who sat in centre ville with a wine bottle in one hand, the other outstretched, made his stomach turn in a sort of raging pity. So did the young grizzly-bearded men with their cardboard signs: *une pièce de monnaie pour manger SVP*. Begging was not his style. At least not yet. He still had a few hundred francs stashed in his squat. *Leftover from my other life*, he thought bitterly.

He brought a hand to his face, brushing a mass of thick, tangled dark hair from his eyes. A pain shot through his arm, and he silently cursed the twisted limb. It was this hand that had put him on the streets, only this hand. He held it out in front of him and put the other one beside it. The left hand was complete, fine long fingers, soft brown hair on the back of the hand, covering what now was dried chapped skin. Why did it have to be his right hand that was sacrificed? Hadn't he lost enough without that? The thumb and the index finger were gone. The miracle, they said, was that he had a hand at all. Its skin was a smooth sort of red, almost grotesque after numerous skin grafts and surgeries. No hair grew on the back of it.

He cursed again, not the hand, but his mind, which still sought excuses. *Get on with life, Ceb*, he told himself. For over three years it had been his motto. And where was he now? On the streets, his clothes worn, his hazel eyes red from fatigue, and his skin brittle from too many nights in the cold. Once last week he had caught a glimpse of himself in the reflection of a storefront. He had stopped and stared to make sure. Yes, it was he, a homeless man in his midthirties, looking desperate and old.

Ceb turned a corner and got into line for the soup kitchen. It was run by a Catholic church in town and was open each day at noon. The rooms filled up quickly with the city's homeless, and he had learned to get there early in the morning to be sure of a meal. Today the sun was bright and the mistral nippy, and he drew his coat up around his ears and watched those closest to him. They were mostly men, but here and there a woman stood with her head down, sometimes with several children in tow.

He stepped into the warmth of the building as the line inched forward. The sound of silverware clinking against dishes greeted his ears. After receiving his bowl, he made his way into the adjoining room where all the tables were set up. A young mother held a wriggling baby in her arms, struggling to get a spoonful of soup into his mouth.

A small girl, also belonging to the woman, played in the narrow aisle between the tables, racing back and forth. She laughed as several older men reached out and patted her head. One offered her a hard candy, and she took it and popped it into her mouth before her mother could object. She ran gleefully around the room, dashing between tables and playing peek-a-boo with the other scattered children.

Ceb observed her with a hint of a smile on his lips. He turned back to his bowl of soup, taking long, slow spoonfuls, enjoying the steam that curled around his face. The girl was no older than five, about the age of Marion. Marion! The thought of the child with the brown ringlets cascading down her back and the eager eyes meeting his with complete trust made his own eyes sting. The noise in the eating hall made a comfortable din in which he could push aside unwelcome thoughts. He continued sipping the hot soup, letting it warm him.

A scream from the other side of the room interrupted his musing. "Help! Help me! My child!"

Ceb swiveled around to see the little girl collapsed on the floor, clutching her throat. Instinctively he pushed back his chair, stood up, and made his way to where the mother was shaking her child. Others gathered around, and a second woman grabbed the girl, turned her over her knees, and hit her forcefully on the back.

"She's choking!" the mother sobbed, as no amount of pushing or poking seemed to help.

Someone yelled across the room, "Call for help. The paramedics—quick!"

There in the eating hall in front of a hundred homeless people, the child was slowing choking to death, her face turning blue, her eyes bulging. Ceb fell to his knees behind her, putting his arms around her chest and pressing tightly in a Heimlich maneuver, trying to dislodge the candy that he was sure was lodged in her throat. It wouldn't come out.

Releasing her, he immediately withdrew a small pocketknife from his pants, laid the child on her back, and knelt down beside her.

"Excuse me. I can help." He nodded down at the knife.

The mother met his eyes, horrified. "You won't kill her?"

Ceb shook his head. "I must do a tracheotomy. Her passage is blocked. If I don't perform it immediately, she'll die."

"But do you know how?" she cried, grabbing his arm.

He stared at her, put a gentle hand on her shoulder. "I've done it before. Trust me." He was surprised that he sounded so confident. He turned to several men who were hovering over the child. "Please, move back and get me some clean dishtowels. And get the paramedics here as quickly as possible."

Perspiration beaded on his forehead, and his left hand trembled ever so slightly. A moment of panic passed over him. Yes, he had performed a tracheotomy, but never with his left hand.

"Please hold her still," he said, summoning two men.

He closed his eyes, as he had always done before, forcing himself to concentrate. The room grew quiet. Carefully he felt along the child's throat, found the spot, and inserted the knife. The mother screamed when she saw the blood begin to trickle. "Get her away, please," Ceb said, his voice firm, sure, calm.

For five minutes he worked deftly with his hands, feeling the pulse beating in his temples as the strong left hand compensated for the twisted right one. He watched the child's lungs fill again with air and the blue color leave her face. When the rescue unit arrived, they began first aid. A muscular middle-aged paramedic touched Ceb's arm.

"Where'd you learn to do that? A surgeon couldn't have done a better job with his scalpel on an operating table."

Ceb's heart was beating too loudly in his ears. The room was gathering in around him, suffocating him. The paramedics lifted the little girl onto a stretcher and walked her outside to the waiting ambulance.

Ceb caught the burly man's arm. "Will she make it?"

The man met his eyes, searched Ceb's face. "You don't need to ask. You know she will."

The homeless people let out a cheer, and the shrill siren of the ambulance started up. They watched it disappear down the street and then turned back to their lukewarm bowls of soup, murmuring about the stranger with the maimed hand who saved the little girl's life. They called it a miracle.

Ceb replaced the pocketknife in his pants, gathered up his coat, and disappeared into the back alley behind the soup kitchen. His hands shook violently. He could not go back. Not for a long time. But as he turned away, he couldn't help smiling, and his eyes shone with tears.

For a long time afterward Ceb lived on the memory of the small child, saw her face regain its color, felt the power of the small knife in his left hand and the power of knowing what to do with it. He moved through the streets of Montpellier in his ragged clothes with restored hope. Here something was always happening, and Ceb needed action. Before the fall from power, his action had been controlled in a way. Always the risk of failure, but never the complete freedom he now knew. He relished the freedom. And hated it.

Tonight as a bitter chill set in and a group of noisy students dispersed, Ceb began to make his rounds, as he thought of it. A homeless man, Jean-Marc, lay on the park bench across the street from the wide-open square of Montpellier's centre ville. Jean-Marc could always be found there on a Friday night, drunk and snoring, with an empty bottle of cheap wine dangling from his hand and a scrawny black dog by his side.

Ceb punched the sleeping man playfully. "Out so soon, Jean-Marc?" He pulled him to a sitting position, as the man muttered a string of indistinguishable expletives. "Too cold for you to stay here tonight. They've got a sleeping bag for you over at the *foyer*."

"The foyer is closed," the man mumbled.

"I know, but I asked them to leave one out. Come on now, buddy." He put his arm around Jean-Marc's waist, half carrying, half dragging him across the empty square with the dog following. In the shadows, the long, ancient buildings in the center of town rose beside them. Getting Jean-Marc through the back alleys to the small refuge behind the train station that offered blankets and sleeping bags in the winter months was backbreaking work. But it was work Ceb loved.

He was a self-created and self-appointed night patrol, rescuing homeless men from the cold, ensuring that they did not freeze to death on a frosty November night. To Ceb it was a game, a game of life and death, and with stakes that high, he always felt the adrenaline pumping through his body. As long as he had work to do, day and night, he did not have to think about the work he had left, the other people, the other life. Ceb didn't think of himself as truly homeless. In his mind he was a leader, a strange, charismatic savior in the side streets of a city burgeoning with tourists and students and the *nouveau riche*.

And the *nouveau pauvre*. Some of these street men had grown up good, like him, in big, comfortable villas in the French countryside. A dark shadow of sweeping unemployment was settling like a curse on every city in France. One day a job and *une situation*, as they said. The next day, nothing. Followed by a gradual dropping into despair.

The streets were littered with those who had tried desperately to hold on. But eventually the stigma of joblessness and the unpaid bills had nibbled away at their apartments and their families, eaten holes in their hopes, and left them sitting on the corner of a street, waiting for a light to turn red so they could approach each stopped car with a pitifully scrawled plea. A bit of money, please, to eat, to live.

For three years he had observed it in cities from Lyon to Marseille, until he had wandered back to Montpellier. Why? He grimaced as he helped Jean-Marc into the sleeping bag, tucked him in beside three other sleeping figures, and threw a blanket over them all.

I am not one of you, he thought, as he pulled his coat around him. His was a choice. He could at any minute pick up his life and start over. Of course he could. He made his way across town, stopping once to drag another sprawled-out man into an alleyway and pile his covers on top.

When he reached his alcove and pushed into the corridor of the old building, he was thankful for the relatively warm interior of his squat. For Ceb, as for many other homeless, these abandoned apartments served as a type of home and refuge. His fingers were icy as he pulled himself into the sleeping bag stashed in the far corner of the empty room.

Got to get enough sleep, he told himself, but the chill in his bones kept him awake. *Got to get some sleep so I'll be ready for my rounds tomorrow.*

The white two-story building behind the train station at the corner of rue Gambetta and rue d'Angoulême looked rather like a prison with its barred windows and its heavy metal door. It was, in fact, a shelter for homeless men. At ten in the morning the sidewalks in front of the building were empty.

Dominique Lefevre pressed the doorbell and waited. When no one answered, he fished his keys from his pocket and opened the door himself.

"Was that you ringing, Dominique?" came a woman's voice from another room as he stepped inside. "Sorry. I've just finished mopping the dormitories."

Dominique smiled, running his fingers through his thick black hair. "Don't apologize, Janine. I was just being lazy."

"Hmph. You, lazy? That'll be the day." An attractive woman with a wide smile appeared in the front hallway. She scrutinized Dominique, shook her head, and kissed him on his bearded cheeks. "Hard night, *n'est-ce pas*? Come on back. I'll get you a cup of coffee. *Bon sang*, you're cold to the touch!"

Dominique sat down wearily in a metal folding chair as Janine placed a cup of coffee on the table before him. He closed his eyes briefly, rubbing them with a finger. "I lost one last night, Janine," he said softly. He sniffed quickly, took out a handkerchief, and blew his nose.

"Who was it?"

"Little Kate. Remember her?" He pulled out his *sacoche*, the leather purse carried by most French men, and reached inside. "Just last week she gave me this picture." He slid it across for Janine's inspection. A slim, smiling teenager with long blond hair and wearing a floral dress stood in front of a stuccoed house.

"That was six months ago. Six months."

"Hard to believe it's the same girl," murmured Janine.

The image was a shocking contrast to the girl they knew, in her black T-shirt and ripped jeans and spiked blue hair.

"That's what six months on the streets will do to a cute kid," he said bitterly. "And now she's gone. Overdose. One of her gang found her under the bridge early this morning." His eyes clouded with tears.

"Terrible shame, Dominique."

He nodded stiffly, rose, and went into the dormitory to his right. The forty bunk beds in the dormitory were painted in bright primary colors. Any belongings of homeless men were locked in brightly painted cubicles. This morning the sheets had been stripped off, and the shelter was empty and immaculate. The men came at six in the evening, showered, ate, and slept. They were served breakfast at six thirty the next morning and put outside at seven. A week at a time was all they were allowed to stay. Such were the rules.

Dominique absentmindedly fluffed a pillow. "How many men were here last night, Janine?"

She poked her head into the dormitory. "We were full. Had several sleeping right outside the door."

He looked wearily at the beds. "I think I'm going to take a quick nap."

"Go ahead, Dominique. You need it."

He stretched out on an unmade mattress and closed his eyes. His was a difficult job, but he loved it. His official title was *médiateur de rue*. A street mediator, the link between the city's homeless and the organizations that sought to help them.

Every day was different for Dominique. Single, in his late thirties, he poured his life into his work. His deepest desire was to see the homeless reintegrate into society. He hung out in their squats, helped them with paperwork, rounded up furniture when one was lucky enough to get an apartment. And sometimes, he watched them die. Like Kate. Dead at eighteen. A wasted life. *A hellish job*, he thought as he drifted off to sleep. *But I'm not quitting. Not ever.*

3

Algiers, Algeria

At eight o'clock Thursday evening a small group of people sat with heads bowed in the den of a large farmhouse on the outskirts of Algiers. The shutters were closed, and a rifle lay underneath each window. Abdul Charfi stared at the loaded rifles, and a memory from thirty years earlier raced through his head. Rémi Cebrian, his boss and neighbor, had shaken his hand and left for the port while all of Algeria bathed in the glory of freedom from France. It was 1962. The French citizens, most of them anyway, had fled.

And now another war, a civil war, was brewing, threatening to rip through the very soul of Algeria once more. There was a soft rap on the door. A middle-aged man looked over at Abdul and raised his eyebrows, surprised.

Abdul nodded. "Don't worry; we're expecting two more. You can open the door."

A young couple entered the den, the woman's hair hidden under her white scarf. Once safely inside, she removed the hijab, her broad smile lighting up the room. "Madira," she said softly, embracing Abdul's wife.

"Yasmina, you made it," Madira returned warmly. "And Salim too. God be praised."

Abdul watched his wife as she made the new guests welcome among the others who sat on cushions on the floor. A bright-blue silk scarf covered her hair, which was pulled away from her face and pinned at her neck. She had a gracious smile, inviting, warm like a breeze from the Sahara, and eyes that spoke confidence and trust. She was offering café au lait served in pretty *demitasse* cups. The coffee's strong, sweet aroma filled the room.

Abdul counted—twelve people, including himself. He breathed in deeply, exhaled, felt relief wash through his body like the hot coffee going down. Madira was passing around a tray filled with teacakes and crescent cookies, her smile ever present.

He took his seat in the small group. "Welcome. How thankful we are that you have all made it safely." He smiled at the young couple who had just arrived. "This is Salim and Yasmina's first time among us. They are not, however, new to our Lord."

At sixty-two, Abdul was slightly stooped, his hair thick and gray. His skin was rough and wrinkled, copper in color from the sun and a lifetime of harvesting olives and oranges. He sipped his coffee, then began to speak slowly, thoughtfully. "We greet you in the name of our Lord Jesus Christ. Peace be with you."

He set the delicate cup down in its saucer, and the clink of the porcelain was the only sound in the room. The tension hung in heaviness among them. He glanced at Madira, who met his eyes and nodded.

"For some months now the rebels have threatened that Christians will be the first to be murdered when they take over the government. This has understandably caused fear among us. But these rebels have not been successful, I remind you. Do not let fear seep into your souls, my little flock. Our Lord has said, 'Fear not, for lo, I am with you always.' Therefore, tonight we will choose not to fear. We will do as we have always done. We will fight fear on our knees in prayer."

For seven years, Abdul and Madira had been head of one of the many house churches in Algeria. For many years the government hadn't bothered with the Christians. They had their hands full with extremists who wanted to make Algeria into an Islamic state, yanking the country away from any hope of democracy.

And it had almost worked. The three-year-old Front Islamique du Salut was winning the elections last February when the military stepped in, canceling the elections and naming their own president. Since that day, the FIS had lashed out with terrorist attacks. The military was fighting back, determined to squelch these terrorists. Hundreds of deaths reported and thousands of others wounded in the past months, many of these among the FIS rebels. But hundreds, maybe thousands, of innocent civilians had been murdered too.

And because the FIS was a fanatical group of Muslims who mixed politics and religion, the government now suspected any religious group of having political aspirations. Surely these Christians were backed by the West, seeking to take over and exploit Algeria's fragile freedom.

Lately stories of spies within the groups had spread throughout Algeria. One report told of a young man, a new convert, who had attended a house church for almost a year. He seemed sincere, a true believer. Months later, the leader of that particular house church was brought in by the government for questioning. Standing before this church leader was the young convert, now his accuser. No one had suspected that he had infiltrated the house church as a spy. The leader had eventually been released, but it became obvious to the Christians in Algiers that new safety precautions must be put in use.

So they met in secret, irregularly. Since Friday was the Muslim holy day, the weekend in Algeria was on Thursday and Friday, and the Christians chose these two days for fellowship too. There were no official church buildings, no official meetings. Believers traveled long distances to meet with other Christians, in groups of no more than fifteen or twenty. Their time together was the lifeblood of each worshipper. Sometimes they prayed straight through the night, and they were never sure when they would see one another again.

When time came at the Charfi home for sharing requests, different ones in the group asked for prayer. Finally Madira spoke softly, wiping her eyes. "For years you have joined us in praying for our son, El Amin. Now we have news. What we have long suspected is true. He is among the fractured FIS. We think he is very angry at us for our beliefs. He has not been back home now for several years, but we cannot be sure when he will show up. We must be extremely careful."

Abdul felt the tears well in his eyes. El Amin. His only son. For so long he had been the only child, then there had been a string of girls. Five of them. All were grown and married and followers of Christ. But El Amin single-mindedly pursued another life. His loyalty to Islam and Allah was fierce. He was ready to betray anyone in his way.

For years Abdul had accepted his son's religious differences. After all, Islam was the religion of his people. It was through Eliane and Rémi Cebrian that Abdul and his family had been introduced to Christianity, over thirty years ago. But in those early years after Algeria became independent and the Cebrians had fled the country with the rest of the pied-noirs, Abdul and Madira's faith in God had wavered. Preoccupations of caring for baby after baby took their thoughts away from Christianity.

It was only later, when their youngest daughter almost died in infancy, that they had returned to prayer and found the strength of God for their family. But by that time El Amin was a teenager, rebellious and enthusiastic for a better life, a better way for Algeria. He embraced Islam with all his adolescent energy and over the years joined increasingly fanatical groups. His relationship with his parents became strained at best, and a fragmented family resulted.

Abdul sank to his knees with the others in the room, closed his eyes, and began to pray aloud. He knew that the best place to go was to the God of heaven and to wait humbly for the answer.

✥

El Amin Charfi cursed the report from the month of November. Over a thousand wounded, many of them members of the FIS. *So be it*, he thought. If he had to die for his cause, for Allah and Islam, let him die.

In his thirties, El Amin was tall and muscular. His eyes were proud and hard, his posture erect. With his men, he was going to conquer this government and bring in a new, devout Algeria.

He was well respected by his peers and greatly feared by his four children. Jala, his wife, was obedient though strong willed, like so many Algerian women. She raised the children well, immersed them in the tenets of Islam, treated him as the Koran prescribed.

A frown crossed his face. Jala loved him terribly and feared he would be killed. His love for her was equally strong, though he never acknowledged it. Still, she knew. Ah, Jala. Beautiful Jala.

His superiors ordered more bombings, targeting innocent civilians in lazy villages. The fear in the deepest part of El Amin's heart was that someday they would discover his great, terrible secret and test his complete loyalty to them. Someday, the order from the top would come: *Destroy the farmhouse on the outskirts of Algiers—the house of your parents. They are extremely dangerous—Christians who pastor a church. Kill them all!*

A chill ran through his body. Beneath his proud allure and fierce loyalty was a small boy who looked into the face of his father and promised, "I will never betray you, Baba. Never."

❉

Rislène left the school building, waving happily to Ophélie. The bruise around her eye was barely visible today. And Ophélie had brought good news. Mme Hoffmann was meeting with her mother this afternoon. She hoped she would be able to return home soon. She was not as afraid of her father as of her sister.

As she waited at the bus stop, her smile disappeared. She glanced around, expecting at any moment to see Nazira suddenly appear out of nowhere. When the bus came, Rislène stepped inside, made her way to the back, and tossed her backpack onto the empty seat beside her. Butterflies danced in her stomach. Two more stops and then …

She got off with the parc du Peyrou on her left, walked under the thick arch and down the small side street, through the square and into the Café de la Paix. As soon as she entered the room, Eric stood from a back table.

"Rislène," he said softly. "You're okay." He kissed her on each cheek, then ran his hand across her forehead.

"Eric!" She beamed up at the tall boy. "I'm fine, really."

"Mama called to tell me."

"Mme Hoffmann called you? Does she know about us? Will she tell Ophélie?"

Eric shook his head. "Mama just wanted me to get the word out to the kids at Oasis so they could pray for you. Don't worry. Our secret is safe for as long as we wish to keep it that way." He touched her hand.

"And did she say she was meeting with my mother this afternoon?"

The young man nodded.

"It will be fine, Eric." She smiled eagerly at him as they sat down. For a while she said nothing more, content to stare. Then she reached over and ran her hand through his short, cropped red hair.

"A gift from Mama," he had commented tersely when they first were getting acquainted. "You should see the curls when it gets long." He had laughed, and his long, thin face had turned into a ripple of creases across the smooth skin, green eyes twinkling behind thick blond lashes.

Rislène giggled. "Well, if there's one thing for sure, you don't have any Arab blood in you!"

That had made him frown. "Is that a big problem for you?"

She shrugged. "For me, no. I told my mother years ago that I'd never marry an Arab.… If only you could have gotten your father's dark hair."

He feigned a hurt look. "So you don't like my hair, huh? Well, it isn't likely to change."

"I like it. I like everything about you."

Now, all these months later, she felt simply lovesick sitting with him. And afraid. "If Nazira ever finds out," she whispered, "or Father, you'll be in danger too."

"Rislène, I'm not afraid for me—not at all. But for you. We'll figure something out. I promise."

He pulled his chair closer to hers and held her in the shadows of the café. She rested her head on his shoulder, but her body was tense with fear.

"I'll take care of you, Rislène. I'll take care of you, my love."

She turned her face to his, eyes misty with tears. "I believe you. Hold me for a little longer and I won't be afraid at all."

Eric wondered what he'd gotten them into as he watched Rislène board the bus and slip away. The bruise on her face had not been totally concealed with makeup. He felt such anger pulsing in his skull at the thought of her father striking her. He could imagine himself in front of M. Namani, fist clenched, ready to punch him in the gut.

He could not let these thoughts continue.

Eric loved the Algerian people. He spoke their language and understood their culture. He attended Oasis as if his skin were the same color as his Arab friends. Started years ago by a pastor in Lodève, the Oasis groups had spread throughout France as a way for young Arab Christians to share their hopes and struggles with one another.

"You know, Mama," Eric had confided the year before, after a particularly moving meeting, "someday I'm going to marry an Arab girl. Just wait and see." He had winked at his mother playfully. Now he wondered if she had guessed the truth about his feelings for Rislène. *She* was the Arab girl he wanted to marry!

How could he protect her though? Ophélie's apartment was a safe place for now. But what next? Yes, he needed to talk with his big sister. And his parents. There was strength in numbers. Surely they would have an idea.

Anne-Marie Dramchini took a sponge and wiped off the round oak table in the kitchen of her farmhouse in Lodève. She glanced toward the phone, almost picked up the receiver, hesitated, and turned back to the sink. She washed the dishes, humming the melody of a favorite hymn.

Seen from the back, bending over the sink, she looked like a schoolgirl, slim, her long black hair swept back in a loose braid. Only as she brushed a strand of hair from her face and turned around did the streaks of gray show, as surprising as the deep lines in her face where years of smiling had left their mark. Sometimes she would stand in the midst of the spacious den, hug her arms around herself, and whisper, "Thank you, Papa. Thank you so much for this."

This was her shelter from the storm, this solid farmhouse her father had left to her thirty years ago. Here she had started over as Moustafa's wife, with little Ophélie by her side and Moustafa's mother and sisters down the hall. Eventually two Dramchini babies had been born. Now they, like Ophélie, were grown.

The urge to telephone her daughter overtook Anne-Marie. She didn't want to pry, but Gabriella had mentioned that the Arab girl, Rislène, was staying with Ophélie.

"*Allô?*" Ophélie's voice on the other line was bright.

"*Chérie!* How are you?"

"Oh, Mama—I was going to call later this morning. Have you heard that Rislène is here?" She lowered her voice. "It doesn't look too promising with her family."

"So Gabriella told me. But apparently she's going to meet with Mme Namani."

They talked for a while about the situation.

Anne-Marie hung the phone up carefully, lost in thought. Why was she so protective of Ophélie? The child was thirty-eight, of all things!

Two strong arms suddenly encircled her waist, causing her to gasp. "Moustafa, *chéri*, you scared me." She closed her fingers around his, then brushed back his short black hair.

"Calling Ophélie again?" he teased.

"I have a good reason," she scolded playfully, then related their conversation.

Moustafa released his wife and took a seat at the kitchen table, worry written across his light-brown face. "Is this girl's family devout?"

"The father and sister are."

"But Gabriella and David will try to help?"

"Yes, Gabriella has arranged to meet the mother."

"Then what makes you so afraid for Ophélie?"

Anne-Marie laughed. She could not hide her thoughts from her husband. She ran her hand through his hair. "I miss the curls."

"I'm too old for curls, my dear. Must look serious or I'll be the next one laid off at the plant."

"Shh. Surely not after all these years."

"Hard times, Anne-Marie. And you can't deny it. I'm an Arab keeping a good job from one of the thousands of jobless French. It could happen." He brushed her cheek with his hand. "Never mind that. What else is on your mind?"

"Nothing much. Just wishing the Lord would fill Ophélie's apartment with someone more permanent than a hapless student."

Moustafa stood, then bent over Anne-Marie to kiss her hair. "No worries, my love. Your daughter is a fine woman, and she doesn't seem to be complaining, does she?"

"No. Not out loud at least."

"Then leave it with the Lord. He hasn't disappointed us yet."

4

The mint tea was brewing, and Gabriella took a batch of chocolate chip cookies from the oven. The smells of the tea and the freshly baked cookies warmed the little house and calmed her soul. With her hands she smoothed her long floral dress, relishing the feel of the soft cotton with its elaborate embroidery work. Hers was a bright blue that almost matched her eyes. It was the typical garment worn by Algerian women in the home; she had not put it on for many months. Out of respect for her guest, she pulled her long red hair back in a bun and covered her head with a silk scarf. Gabriella never compromised her faith by wearing the hijab, the thick, drab white scarf that Muslim women wore as a sign of religious devotion, but as a cultural courtesy she was glad to cover her hair with a scarf.

The melody from an instrumental tape floated peacefully through the small house, and she hummed along. The sun was already low, streaming through the den's long French doors that were covered with white-dotted sheer curtains, making spots of light on the cool tile floor.

The doorbell rang moments later. Opening the door, Gabriella met the worried eyes of an Arab woman wearing her coat over a long, colorful dress. "Come in, Mme Namani."

Her guest entered cautiously, offering her hand, which Gabriella shook gently. Altaf Namani was a sturdy woman, her black eyes punctuated by thick lashes and thicker brows, her face round and pleasant in spite of her concerned expression.

"Your home is lovely. Yes, I remember how inviting it is," she said softly, as her eyes took in the warmth and simplicity of the room.

"Thank you. Please have a seat. May I get you some mint tea?"

"Oh, no. Don't put yourself out for me," Altaf said quickly.

Gabriella smiled, knowing this was merely the polite response that was part of Algerian culture. "It's no trouble at all. Everything is ready."

She brought out a tray from the kitchen, on which sat two small engraved glasses and a plate of cookies. She then retrieved another of her treasures, a silver teapot in which the tea was brewed. Holding the silver spout close to the small glass, she began to pour the tea, at the same time raising the teapot higher in the air so that the tea flowed into the engraved glass in a long, steaming stream.

"I know mint tea is usually reserved for special occasions, but I thought you might enjoy it today," Gabriella said.

"You follow Arab customs very well," Altaf commented warmly, reaching for a glass. She took a sip. "This is delicious. Just right."

Gabriella thanked her, and she silently thanked the Lord. The outward appearance was essential for the Arabs, from the way a woman dressed to how she sat—never crossing her legs—to the way tea was served. How carefully she had studied these customs over the years. If the Lord gave her the gift of meeting with an Arab woman, Gabriella did not want to spoil the encounter by offending her before they even got to discuss the deeper issues of life.

Altaf seemed relaxed, even talkative. They spoke for a while of their children, their ages and interests, while Gabriella offered her guest a chocolate chip cookie.

"Have you ever had these?" she asked. "We used to exchange recipes when we lived in Algeria. The Arab women were fascinated with our American cookies—especially the cutout ones we decorated with the children at Christmas. And I learned how to bake several of your tea crescents. Delicious."

"These are delicious as well," Altaf murmured. Then she ventured outside politeness. "Please tell me of Rislène. She is staying with you?"

"No. With my stepdaughter, Ophélie."

"Her teacher."

"Yes."

"I see. It was very foolish of her to keep a Bible in the house."

"Was it concealed?"

"Yes, under her mattress. But my daughter Nazira found it. Very foolish."

"How do you feel about Rislène's conversion to Christianity?"

Altaf turned her hands over in her lap. "I feel she is wrong. She is denying not only her religion but her culture and her family."

"You would forbid her then?"

"I? No. She has made a choice. But her father. He feels betrayed."

"Do you think he will be violent again?"

Altaf looked uncomfortable. "Violent? No. I assure you that will not happen again. But … but Rislène will have limitations on her freedom."

"She will not be allowed to see Christians?"

Rislène's mother smiled slightly, almost sympathetically. "I cannot keep her from seeing friends, you understand. But her father wishes to restrict her activities. She must not attend church."

"You understand how much it means for her faith?"

"Yes, I understand. But he will not allow it. And Nazira is more adamant than my husband. She's very angry with her sister." She picked up another cookie, took a bite, and chewed thoughtfully. "I'll come again, Mme Hoffmann. Another time you will tell me of your three gods and why my daughter has found these gods so attractive. But for now you must tell Rislène to come home." She leaned forward and smiled. It was not a forced smile; it was meant to convey trust. "Rislène is in no physical danger. Tell her to come home."

On Fridays David taught a class at the seminary where he himself had gotten his theological training many years ago. When he got home late that afternoon, Gabriella met him at the door with a smile. "It went okay," she said, answering his question before he could formulate it.

Relief spread across his face, and he pulled her into his arms and kissed her forehead. "Thank the Lord."

Gabriella relaxed, thankful as always for her husband's calm strength.

"What did she say?" David set his briefcase down in the hallway and took a seat in the den, and Gabriella related her conversation with Mme Namani.

"You look tired, sweetheart," she said. "This is weighing on you, isn't it?"

Regional director of their mission board, adjunct professor, pastor of the small Eglise Protestante Evangélique in Montpellier—her husband carried a heavy load of responsibilities.

"Gabby, I don't want to alarm you. Perhaps you've noticed it already. But Eric ..." He searched for the words. "Maybe I'm reading everything all wrong. You're the one with the intuition, but you haven't been at Oasis meetings to see ... to see how he looks at her."

Gabriella wrinkled her brow. "What are you saying?"

"I'm sure Eric cares deeply for Rislène."

"Our Eric?" she asked, dumbfounded.

"Yes, our Eric. Your youngest son."

Gabriella considered the news for a moment, then laughed. "Why in the world am I surprised that he would be interested in beautiful Rislène? He told me last year that he was going to marry an Arab girl." She sat down beside her husband. "Have you discussed their relationship with him?"

"Not yet. I had no reason to, but now ..." David rubbed his eyes wearily. "If ever the father found out ..."

"Shh, David. Don't think about it." But Gabriella knew what was running through her husband's mind. It was a potentially explosive situation. How many times had they seen it before? At best, a Muslim who converted to Christianity was banned from the family. But sometimes it was worse. There had been beatings, death threats, forced marriages. Rislène's situation was what the French called *délicat*.

Two years ago, in Lyon, a young Arab girl had fallen in love with a French Christian boy. David had visited the city several times to counsel the young couple. But in the end the family had cloistered the girl, Samira, in their apartment, threatened her, and forced her to marry an eligible Arab man. She was never allowed to attend church. Her life had turned into a nightmare. They had recently received word that she had tried to kill herself.

"You must talk to Eric, *chéri*. To see if your hunch is right, and to tell him that they must be extremely careful."

"Of course, Gabby."

It was rare that Gabriella had seen David cry, but when he had heard the news from Lyon about Samira, he had fallen to his knees and wept. How often they had prayed for her. Even now she lay in a hospital bed, with nothing but the prayers of others to comfort her.

"We must proceed carefully too, on our knees," he whispered.

They held hands and did as they had done for so many years, addressing their fears to the One who was in control.

When the phone rang from the den, Ophélie almost didn't answer it, so intent was she on beating Rislène in a game of Scrabble. "Don't you dare cheat while I'm gone!" she called out.

"*Oui, allô?*"

"Ophélie!"

"Hi, Bri! What's up?" She lowered her voice. "Did you see Mme Namani?"

She listened as Gabriella related their meeting and felt an odd disappointment when her stepmother said that Mme Namani thought it was safe for Rislène to go home. The apartment would be empty again.

"Do you really think it's safe?" she asked.

"I think M. Namani will not harm Rislène physically. But we fear what kind of pressure he may put on her otherwise."

"Forbidding her to attend church?"

"Exactly. And there's one other thing, Ophélie. Has Rislène mentioned anything else, any other reasons that she's afraid?"

"No. I mean, her conversion and baptism are reason enough, don't you think?" She paused, reflecting. "Oh, I know what you mean. Yes, she mentioned she was in love with a Christian. Is that it?"

"Yes. Do you know who it is?"

"Well, no. Should I?"

"Your father suspects it is Eric."

Ophélie sucked in her breath. *Eric!* Eric in love with an Arab girl. Yet when she thought about it, she wasn't one bit surprised.

"Your father and I thought perhaps you could talk to Rislène. Try to make her see the dangers ... how careful they must be."

Ophélie knew why they thought she should be the one to talk to the girl. They were thinking of Bachir.

"Yes ... yes. I will speak to her. But I hope she won't take it wrong. Think we've been prying, you know."

"Ophélie." It was her father's voice that came on the phone.

"Oh, hi, Papa!"

"Listen, honey. It may seem like prying, but it is of utmost importance."

She thought of Samira, whom the church had been praying for all these months. "I know, Papa. I'll talk to her. And I'll talk to Eric, too, if you want—if what you suspect is true."

"I think that would be wise."

"How soon do you think Rislène should go back home?"

"Not immediately. Would it inconvenience you too much if she stayed on through the weekend?"

"Not at all."

Ophélie felt relieved. It would give her time to discuss this with Rislène. It would also give her time to prepare herself psychologically for an empty apartment once again.

The Scrabble game was almost over, but Ophélie had saved one last word to slip onto the board. She placed three letters vertically beneath the E of the horizontal word *cacher*.

Rislène looked at the word and protested, "Hey, that's not fair! You're not allowed to use proper nouns!" Then it registered, and she looked up at Ophélie with a question in her eyes. "Why'd you spell *Eric*?"

"Why do you think?"

Rislène blushed, her light-brown cheeks growing darker.

"We need to talk, Rislène," Ophélie stated simply, kindly. "You care for him, don't you?"

Rislène was silent for a while, a frown having wiped away her initial embarrassment.

Ophélie placed a hand over Rislène's. "I'm sorry. I was too direct. That was Gabriella on the phone and my father."

"Did Mme Hoffmann talk to my mother?"

"Yes. Your mother wants you to come home."

Rislène looked skeptical.

"Gabriella doesn't think you're in danger. But you'll have to be careful, especially if … if what my father thinks is true."

"I knew he had guessed! He saw us talking after the last Oasis meeting. I mentioned it to Eric, but he just laughed." She nibbled her lip. "I love him, Ophélie. He's so full of ideas, and strong in his faith, so … wonderful."

Ophélie laughed. "You don't have to convince me. He's my little brother, you know. I think he's great." Her face grew serious. "But if your family finds out …"

"You're thinking of Samira, aren't you?"

Ophélie nodded. *And Bachir.*

"I know. I've thought of it a hundred times. We're always so careful when we meet at a café—to make sure no one follows us."

"So this has been going on for a while?" Ophélie asked, a hint of a smile on her lips.

"Yes. For a while. We really love each other, Ophélie. Is that so wrong?"

Ophélie felt a catch in her throat. "No, Rislène. No, of course not."

They placed the wooden playing pieces back in the box and folded up the board. Ophélie put the game on a shelf in the hall closet. But even as she did so, she could still see E-R-I-C spelled out vertically on the board. She offered a quick, silent prayer for wisdom.

Last night the opened hideaway bed on the sofa had felt plenty comfortable, but now Rislène sat up, the sheets a tangle at her feet, her hair damp with perspiration. The whole southern wall of Ophélie's den was one long window that gave a clear view of Montpellier by night and some of the most stunning sunsets she had ever seen. Tonight she had refused to close the *volets*, the heavy wooden shutters that adorned the windows. She had wanted to watch the vast night sky. Now in the middle of the night, only a few lights blinked.

She got out of bed and stood in front of the glass, gathering a blanket around her.

She was only nineteen, but she felt old. *Dear God, I'm so tired of this terrifying game of hide-and-seek. Is it worth it? Are You worth it?*

It was a pointless question. She might love the gangly redhead at the university, but her love for this God was even bigger. It washed through her soul and brought the strangest peace.

She leaned her forehead against the cool pane of the window and allowed herself to cry. She saw again her father's flashing eyes, heard his raised voice. She remembered his large hand hitting her with such force that she had stumbled backward, catching her balance on the bed.

She loved her father. And he was so proud of her. She was the daughter who would continue her studies, liberate the family from the heavy, stagnant role placed on its women. Her father was an intelligent man, respected in his business, forward thinking—at least until last year, when he had suddenly started attending secret meetings.

"Oh, Father, why? Why are you doing this to me?" she moaned. The tenets of Islam were demanding but simple in their own way. She had been raised to fear Allah. Perhaps that way was best. Give up Eric ... and Jesus. Then she could have her studies, she was sure. And peace. Yes, peace.

But no. The only time she had known true peace in her soul was as a Christian.

She climbed back onto the sofa bed, pulled the blankets up around her, and stared out the window. She could see the freckled, happy face of Eric, his fine green eyes blazing with his feelings for her. Then the angry eyes of her father appeared, erasing the vision of Eric. She closed her eyes tightly to wipe away the picture, but it was still there. It was not until much later, exhausted and heavyhearted, that Rislène fell asleep.

"So when were you going to tell me?" Ophélie teased, sitting on the single chair in Eric's tiny student apartment in west Montpellier the next evening. "After the wedding?"

Eric tossed a pillow at her from where he sat on the bed. "Very funny. I was actually going to tell you last night. I'm sorry Mama and Papa beat me to it. I wanted to tell you first. I figured you'd understand—I mean, you were in love with an Arab man once, right?"

He watched his sister's face drain of color as she stared at him, speechless.

"I'm sorry. I guess I shouldn't bring that up."

Ophélie recovered quickly. "It was a long time ago, and that's why—" She stopped in midsentence. "Look, Eric, I like Rislène a lot. I guess I'm not surprised that you would fall in love with her. It's just ... complicated."

"Exactly. That's why we wanted to keep things quiet for as long as possible. Rislène has been afraid of her sister ever since she became a Christian last year. It was only a matter of time until Nazira found something out." He shrugged at Ophélie. "At least the Namanis have no idea about Rislène and me."

"Not yet." Ophélie took his hands and looked him straight in the eyes.

Eric was used to his sister's intensity, but her words surprised him.

"Yes, I was in love with an Arab man once. You don't know the whole story." She looked away. "I'm sure it will be different for you and Rislène." Ophélie embraced her brother. "Oh, Eric. Please be careful. Of course Rislène can stay with me as long as she needs to. And you can come see her at my place."

"Thanks, Ophélie. It means the world to me to know she's safe with you."

"School going okay for you?" She changed subjects effortlessly, but Eric wondered what had really happened between her and the Arab man. He remembered only a vague tension in the household and his big sister in tears. All those years ago when he was just a kid.

"School is just fine—not my main worry." At twenty-three Eric was in his fifth year at the Faculté des Lettres in Montpellier. Professeur, that was his goal. "In fact, I'll steal your teaching position one day if you don't watch out!"

Now her eyes were gleaming, and the feistiness he loved had returned.

"Hmph! Not on your life. I'm a *fonctionnaire*; nothing can take away my job, and you know it. So keep your cocky mouth shut and study if you hope to do half as well as I have!"

Their eyes met, and they grinned and fell into silence.

Ophélie was fifteen years Eric's senior and had grown up in France with Moustafa and Anne-Marie while he was in Algeria with his family. It wasn't until he returned to France with his parents in

1985 that he'd really gotten to know her, but their bond and friendship had been immediate and strong. As a teenager studying for the difficult French *baccalauréat*, he'd spent countless hours on the sofa of her apartment while she quizzed him on some obscure French poet. As the nights grew late, their cram sessions usually evolved into heart-to-heart conversations and then degenerated into silly laughter and pillow fights.

Eric crossed his arms and stood, then sat back down and groaned. "I wish I knew how this story was going to end, Ophélie. I love Rislène. I want to marry her as soon as I get my teaching degree. I just hope that will be soon enough."

Ophélie gave him a nod, but her face was as pale as the new moon visible just outside the window.

As Ophélie stepped off the elevator and put the key in the door to her apartment, the door across the hall opened slightly, and a neighbor stuck her head out. "Mlle Duchemin?"

Ophélie turned around and smiled. "*Bonjour, Mme Ploussard! Comment allez-vous?* Are you and M. Ploussard well?"

The bent-over little woman came into the hall. "Yes, dear. As well as can be expected at our age. André has his *arthrite*, and last week he had another *crise de foie. Terrible!* But we're getting along." She paused. "André said to tell you *merci* for the *soupe des courges* that you brought us last week. Delicious. So like you, Mlle Duchemin. Always taking care of people." She leaned toward Ophélie and whispered, "We know you bring your students to your apartment. But …"

"Is there a problem, Mme Ploussard?"

Mme Ploussard's prominent nose was almost touching Ophélie's. "I've seen an *Arab* girl go into your apartment. Several times. When you weren't here. She had her own key!" Her eyes darted to and fro, and then she grabbed Ophélie's arm tightly. "You mustn't trust those Arabs, Mlle Duchemin! I feel it's my duty as a citizen of France to warn you. I wouldn't want anything to happen to you." Her eyes were wide as she drew one wrinkled, gnarled finger across her neck. "They'll slice you in a second. 'The Kabyle smile,' they call it. My André—he saw it all during the war."

Ophélie tried her best to suppress a smile. Mme Ploussard spent hours every day staring out of her window into the street below, watching for new tidbits of information to gossip about. Ophélie patted the elderly woman on the back and said, "Thank you for your concern. You and M. Ploussard have always been such good neighbors. But don't you worry, Mme Ploussard. I'm very careful, and this young woman needs a place to live for a while." She lowered her voice. "Family problems."

Immediately Mme Ploussard's face broke into a smile. "*Ah oui! Des problèmes dans la famille!* Poor child. Such strange customs they have! Well, then, you take good care of her, Mlle Duchemin."

Mme Ploussard scurried back into her apartment. Ophélie heard the latch on three different locks being turned. A bit paranoid, her neighbor. But Ophélie felt quite protected living under the eagle eye of Mme Ploussard.

5

She stood behind the curtain with her back to the audience, wiping the tears that ran down her face and with them, thick streaks of makeup that she had so carefully applied thirty minutes before. Offstage a voice called softly, "Janine! Ten seconds."

The curtain rose slowly. Janine Dufour could feel the eyes on her, burning questions into her soul, waiting. The theater was warm and stuffy. She didn't need to look out to know that every seat in the small auditorium was filled.

"I can't do it!" she said at last in a strong voice that died into a pitiful whimper at the end. She blew her nose and turned to face the silent crowd. "I can't do it! And I won't! Not tonight." She stooped down, picked up a broken compact, and looked at her face in the miniscule mirror.

"You look so tired, face. Who can this be? Surely not me. This is not how the script was written. Not the words I planned to say!" Gradually her voice broke from a lyrical spoken tone into a song.

"Something happened in the meantime

Changed the hope I had today

This was not supposed to happen

Happy endings were in sight

Tell me please where life went crazy."

Now she was facing the audience, letting the well-planned tears shine in her eyes. She held a soft soprano note, her arms extended to her sides, watching the blinding lights from the back of the theater.

"Tell me, who turned off the light?" As she sang the last note, a high A, all the lights in the house went out. A flute from the orchestra trilled sharply, then faded into nothingness. Janine walked off the stage.

Immediately the whole cast burst into the opening song as the lights came up on a colorful array of characters. Janine paused only a moment to watch from the wing, then rushed to her side of the stage to change for the next scene. She had only seven minutes to put on fresh makeup, change into a tightly fitting dress, and put on a wig of perfectly managed curls. Seven minutes to sweep her character back fifteen years in time.

She worked quickly. This was her favorite part in the whole musical comedy, making herself up to be a lovely young woman. She hoped the mirror would not betray her. Could the makeup still work its magic on her aging face? The sequins hid the extra pounds she'd gained in the past months. Simon, the director, had said nothing. She still had the best voice in the Midi, so what could he say?

Exactly seven minutes later Janine strutted back onstage, head held high, and broke into song. The same melody with which she had opened the program was sung more brightly, happily:

"Here I am to face my future
On the stage at first at last
I'll pull out each stitch, each suture
No one will suspect my past
Now I've made a great beginning
Now this girl has found her niche
Out of bad luck, now I'm winning
Take my rags, I'm gonna be rich ..."

By the end of her song, the audience was clapping enthusiastically. She left the stage with a smile on her face. Opening night was going to turn out just fine.

"You were wonderful, sweetheart!" Mme Dufour enthused, kissing her daughter on each cheek. "I think it's your best performance yet! Lovely play, and half of Montpellier turned out to see it. Be sure to congratulate Ophélie for us."

"Thanks for coming. Tell Papa thanks too, okay? I've got a cast party to run to. You know how it is—opening night. I'll see you on Sunday. *Bonne nuit!*"

She watched her mother leave, her small silhouette disappearing down the alleyway. Dear Mama. Always so enthusiastic, in her peculiar way. She sighed. Well, yes, the play had been a success. She wondered if they might even leave Montpellier with the production.

"Good job, Janine. You brought Emilie to life. It was exactly as I pictured it."

"Hey, don't flatter me, Ophélie!" She winked at her friend. Then, with a smile, "Did you really think it was good?"

"Fabulous! And the playwright is also the best critic, right?"

They both laughed. "Right!"

Arm in arm the two women left the theater. "How do you feel?" Janine questioned her friend.

"Scared to death. It's always the worst part for me, after the opening-night performance. Waiting to see what the critics say."

"Yeah, I know. But let's get out of here. A little celebration will take away your worries."

Ophélie shrugged. "You know cast parties aren't my favorite, but I certainly won't turn down the star of the show!"

"Anyway, Jean-Luc would love to meet you. He's been on my case for two months now. Nice guy, Jean-Luc."

"Not exactly my type, Janine."

"You're impossible. Give the guy a chance. I'd go out with him if he asked me."

"You'd go out with anybody!" Ophélie laughed, then ducked as Janine swung her purse playfully at her.

Janine regarded her friend. Why exactly they were friends still baffled her, even after all these years. Ophélie was quiet, pensive, mysterious, and childlike all at the same time. She liked dark novels and talking over a cup of hot tea with a friend. And she liked church. Janine liked parties and nightlife and being surrounded by people. It was not that she sought the spotlight, but her genial personality attracted people to her. And there in the crowd, she didn't have to deal with her solitude.

That was what she and Ophélie had in common. Solitude. Singleness. Oh, their lives were filled up with people and work and good deeds, but still, there was something that hadn't quite turned out as they planned. Their arms were made for holding babies and being held by a man. How often they had spoken of that intangible feeling of loss. Loss of something they'd never had in the first place.

Ophélie found her solace in religion at that strange little Protestant church. Janine had tried religion in its different forms. She'd occasionally attended Mass and visited the cemetery on All Saints' Day. Religion had never worked for her.

Instead she kept looking for a decent man who would take her in. Oh, she didn't have any illusions. She was pushing forty and had long ago given up any desire for marriage. All she asked for was a man who would truly care for her.

"We're here!" she said brightly, leading Ophélie down the steps into one of Montpellier's chic hidden nightclubs. The place was already teeming with people, with several members of the cast among them.

A man with long gray hair, dressed in a tuxedo, popped the cork on a bottle of champagne. "To Ophélie and Janine!" he called out over the pulsating music of the live band. He poured the champagne into a tall fluted glass, letting it bubble over the edges, then presented the first glass to Ophélie, kissing her lightly on the cheek. "To our beloved playwright, Ophélie Duchemin."

"*Merci*, Simon. Thank you. You did a great job."

Simon beamed, handing a second glass to Janine.

She held it high and cried out in her strong stage voice, "A toast to Simon! France's most distinguished director!"

Simon called out, "And to Janine, the star of the show!"

A cheer rang out in the nightclub. Janine absorbed the kisses and words of praise like a sponge. It felt so, so good.

"You were splendid, Janine."

She twirled around to see Dominique Lefevre smiling warmly from behind his beard.

"Dominique! Were you at the show?"

"Of course. I wouldn't miss the hottest play in Montpellier on opening night. Especially when my biggest helper is the star." He kissed her on the cheeks. "You look *superbe*."

Dominique Lefevre was just the decent sort of man she was looking for. She had met him last year when she began volunteering at a homeless shelter in Montpellier. He had a challenging job, working with the SDFs, as they were called: *sans domicile fixe*. Homeless, no permanent residence. She detested the term, though people meant it harmlessly. It was short and very descriptive.

But Janine saw the wasted lives, the excruciating pain, the fear and anger behind each homeless man and woman. She had a degree in social work but had long ago abandoned that career for the arts. Still, in her heart she found great fulfillment in helping these people, whom she liked to consider as in a temporarily difficult situation. Unfortunately, many times it didn't turn out to be so temporary. Like for Kate, the teenager who was found dead last week.

Those thoughts were too black for a night of celebration. "Get yourself a glass of champagne," she instructed Dominique.

He smiled and declined. "I've got a full night ahead of me. But I promise. We'll celebrate another time."

"Sounds great. Thanks for stopping by."

"My pleasure. You were really good, you know. I mean it. I was very impressed."

"*Merci*," she said softly, feeling her face turn red. "Thanks, Dominique. See you on Wednesday at the Red Cross."

"Yes, Wednesday. *Bonne nuit.*"

Dominique made his way through the centre ville, drawing his coat around him. The temperature had plummeted to below freezing during the evening, unusually cold for the south of France. The squats provided minimal warmth for those lucky enough to have them. The four shelters in town were completely full. He worried for those who lacked any type of protection. The winter months were lethal for the homeless.

He headed toward the neighborhood where the most pitiful of his clients usually clustered together. The music from Janine's play ran through his mind—a haunting melody with a strange hopefulness mixed in. The play had dealt with the expectations that society placed on people, the lack of fulfillment, the soul's constant aching for something more. Janine's character had embodied the aching soul.

Sometimes Dominique wished his life were a play, with the lines memorized and the ending foreshadowed throughout the first acts. So far his part seemed to be bad-guy-turned-good. He had lived on the streets for several years when he was in his twenties, and it had changed him forever. But the streets had been kinder back then, if that life can be kind to anyone. He had shared a hopeless camaraderie with his fellow homeless. They had protected one another. Not so now. The homeless world was one of cruel rivalry and survival of the fittest, a dark, dark play. And his role as mediator between the street people and the government was never ending.

He watched his breath materialize in the freezing air, dug his hands further down into the pockets of his coat, and pulled a black ski hat over his head. He looked like one of them, the SDFs often commented, with the worn coat and the almost hidden face. Sometimes he felt he was beginning to reason like them too.

He squinted, watching a man hauling another man across the square. He smiled sadly. Good ol' Ceb, the eternal rescuer. Of course he'd be out on a night like this.

Dominique approached him slowly. "*Bonsoir*, Ceb. Can I give you a hand?"

He picked up the legs of Ceb's drunken charge. "Where are you heading?"

"My squat," Ceb answered.

"That's still a ways off."

"Everything else is full. I've checked." There was anger in his voice.

"This is when we could use a van, on these bitter nights," Dominique commented.

It hurt him to see Ceb struggle. The man's eyes were fixed and hard, showing no feeling, but Dominique knew how much his maimed hand ached, especially in the cold.

"What do you want a van for?" Ceb asked.

"To help transport the homeless to shelters, to hand out food, soup. To go to the people, because there are so many who refuse to come to us."

Ceb nodded. "You're right about that."

They walked on, grunting occasionally from the weight of the man they carried between them, hearing their heavy footsteps on the cobblestones of Montpellier's downtown.

"Not a bad idea, about a van, Dominique," Ceb said after a while. "Soup and coffee. But you'd need medical supplies too, you know."

When they reached Ceb's squat, Dominique climbed the darkened stairway with him, the drunken man muttering to them. The room was glacial, the windows broken out and covered with filthy blankets.

"Home sweet home," whispered Ceb. "Have a seat." He motioned to the floor. They set the man down, then proceeded to pad him with old newspapers and cover him with a thick, musty blanket.

Dominique sat down on the floor and leaned against the wall, watching his breath.

"You got some food, Ceb?"

"Got everything I need, Dominique."

"I think I could get you an apartment, you know. Come to the shelter sometime. We could work on papers."

Ceb looked at him with his reddened eyes, wiped his maimed hand across his beard, and said warily, "I've got an apartment right here, rent free. I'll let you know when I need help." He pulled out an alcohol burner and lit it with a match. Then he poured water from a bottle into a dented saucepan and set it on a homemade wire stand over the burner. "You want a cup of coffee?"

"*Merci*, Ceb. That would be good."

Dominique sat with Ceb for an hour, sipping coffee and talking about their common friends, the homeless men and women in the city. He was an enigma, this Ceb. He never admitted that he was one of them. An educated man with unending energy. Dominique was sure Ceb could make it off the streets, but the man trusted no one and wanted no help. His dull hazel eyes reflected the same deep pain and disillusionment that Dominique saw on so many other faces. Somewhere, for some reason, Ceb had given up on society, perhaps almost given up on life.

Could he ever fit back in? That was the question that haunted Dominique. For every six months on the street, it took at least two to three years before a person could find his place back in the mainstream. Many never did. He wondered if it was too late for Ceb. Somehow he didn't think it was.

❈

"I'm heading home, Janine. I'm exhausted. Absolutely *crevée*." Ophélie had to yell to be heard over the sound of the band in the smoky nightclub.

"Come on, Ophélie. The night is young! It's not every Friday that you get to celebrate the opening of a play."

That was certainly true. The Friday before she had spent in her own living room playing Scrabble with Rislène.

Ophélie patted Janine on the back. "You know me. Not exactly a night owl. Give Simon my love. I'll never find him in this crowd."

Janine hurried after her, stepping out into the frigid night. "See you tomorrow for the matinee. Get some sleep."

"Don't worry about me. *You* get some sleep. *Ciao*."

She was relieved to feel the icy air on her face. Her head was throbbing and her eyes stinging from the smoke. She never quite felt she fit in the artsy world. They partied all night while she went home to prepare a Sunday school lesson for the children at church. She chuckled to herself.

But soon her thoughts turned to her conversation with Eric last weekend. She *was* worried for him. Just allowing herself to say Bachir's name in her head had brought back such hard memories.

You have to be so careful, Eric. You really never know.

She scolded herself. She was sounding like Mme Ploussard!

"You look cold, Ophélie."

The voice startled her. She spun around to see a bearded man with a ski hat pulled low over his head. She narrowed her eyes. "Do I know you?"

He laughed. "Forgive me." He pulled his hat off and shook his black hair, then offered her an ice-cold hand. "Dominique. Dominique Lefevre. I'm a friend of Janine. We work at the Red Cross together. I saw the play tonight. Very good."

"Dominique." Ophélie recovered. "Pleased to meet you. Janine has told me about you—and your job."

He fell into step beside her.

"What brings you here? Were you at the party?"

"A while ago, yes. Janine invited me. But I just got back from a trek across town. An errand."

She understood. "You must be half frozen."

"Oh, no. I'm fine. I just had a cup of coffee. You don't mind walking alone in the middle of the night?"

She laughed wryly. "It's not the best idea, but I've got my can of mace. I'm afraid I'm not much of a partyer."

"The writer needs her sleep for inspiration. Is that it?"

"Something like that. Here we are at my car. Nice to meet you, Dominique. May I drop you off anywhere?"

He peered at her, almost said something, then shook his head. "No. My place isn't far away. See you later then, Ophélie."

"Sure, maybe. Good night."

"Bonsoir."

Ophélie drove through the night, suddenly wide-awake. Janine had made Dominique out to be a sort of demigod, the savior of the street people, and now Ophélie understood why. She had mixed emotions about street people, but there was a new interest starting up that suddenly included Dominique Lefevre. If nothing else, thoughts of him would chase away the memory of Bachir, at least for one night.

6

Across the street from the high school, two men in blue overalls were raising a tall, spindly fir in front of a fountain. Several teenagers watched the procedure from their perch on a low stone wall, taunting the workers.

Rislène crossed the street, glanced at the tree, then looked behind her to make sure no one was following as she hurried to the bus stop. At five thirty, the sky was already somber, almost black. The wind whipped through the street, and she drew her wool coat more tightly around her.

She settled into a seat on the bus and sighed. For over two weeks now, she had enjoyed the safety of Ophélie's apartment, savored the good meals and the conversations at night with her teacher about her young faith. *And moments alone with Eric*, she thought with a blush. Time in Ophélie's apartment to share their thoughts and dreams, to sit on the sofa, her head on his shoulder, to walk him to the door and feel his lips on hers before he whispered good-bye, eyes all full of love.

She frowned involuntarily. But it was time to go back home. To face her family.

She had only four stops before she got off and walked a short distance to a stuccoed building with a large Plexiglas sign marked "Eglise Protestante Evangélique." There was still plenty of work to do to prepare the church for the Christmas party Saturday afternoon. She had happily volunteered to help, knowing she'd have the chance to be with her friends. And Eric. Inside the church building, she could talk with him and not worry.

She pushed open the wooden door, reflecting that this building looked nothing like what she had always thought of as a church. None of the high spires and flying buttresses that France's majestic cathedrals boasted, just several old garages that had been transformed into a small sanctuary by the hard work of individuals volunteering their time. After she'd asked several naive questions last fall, the others had explained to her that "the church" was not really a building but the gathering of believers together to worship God.

She thought it a lovely explanation. Ever since then, Rislène liked to think of the church building as the outside of a living thing, and the people were the inner workings.

Inside the physical building were three rooms. The smaller two served as a meeting place for the children on Sunday morning, what these Christians called Sunday school. The way the Bible stories were taught to the children, with pictures and games and songs, differed drastically from the lessons in the Koran she had experienced, where children memorized the whole holy book, repeating it over and over in a singsong chant.

The larger room, with a tile floor, wood-paneled walls, and comfortable chairs, welcomed the adults on Sunday morning for their worship service. The first time she had attended ten months ago, it wasn't for a service but for an informal Oasis meeting on Saturday afternoon.

"Rislène, welcome!" one of the Arab teenagers called out. "We're in desperate need of your decorating skills."

She entered the large room and grinned at the sight of two young men hanging ornaments on a fake Christmas tree.

"That looks terrible," she teased. "Let me try."

A few moments later, Ophélie entered the room, followed by Eric. "Look who I dragged in from the cold." She punched Eric playfully in the shoulder, then went to inspect the decorations. Rislène felt her cheeks burning as Eric came and stood beside her.

"How are you?" he asked. "I feel like I haven't seen you in forever!"

Rislène rolled her eyes at him. "It's been two days since I saw you at Ophélie's, silly boy! And I'm fine. But ... I'm going home tomorrow after the party." She nibbled a fingernail. "At least I think I am."

He took her gently by the shoulders. "Don't go, Rislène, if you're afraid. Wait a little longer."

"Eric, I've already been at your sister's for over two weeks." She touched his hand, looking him full in the eyes. "You know I am so thankful to be there, for the times we could be together, alone. Safe. But I can't just stay on indefinitely. It isn't making matters any better with my family. I have to face up to it."

"Then I'll go with you."

"A lot of good that would do. I'd really be in for it if they saw me with a French-American Christian!"

"They wouldn't see me."

Rislène opened her mouth to protest, but Eric cut her off.

"No, I mean it. I'll take you to the apartment but stay out of sight. You can close the shutters or something when you get inside to show me all is well."

She smiled sadly. Dear Eric. He was made to teach literature. All imagination and zeal. How could he not understand the danger? "Thank you for caring, Eric, but you know it won't work. Mama promised Mme Hoffmann that nothing will happen. We'll pray. The hand of God on me will be all the protection I need, don't you think?"

The café across the street from the Protestant church was always filled with teenagers in the late afternoon. Some sipped coffee and smoked. Others played at the four video games in the back of the room. Nazira pretended to write a letter, chewing on her pencil as she gazed out the window. Rislène was so careless! Nazira had installed herself at the café an hour ago, suspecting that her sister would show up at the church after her last class. Three Arab youths had arrived a half hour before Rislène. Later Rislène's teacher had shown up along with a gangly red-haired boy.

This was news for Father, Nazira told herself smugly. Yes, that redhead was coming to see Rislène and using the church as a cover. Their younger sister, Fouzia, had attended a meeting with Rislène several weeks ago, and she had reported that Rislène had talked at length with a red-haired boy. "I'm sure he likes her!" Fouzia had giggled with fourteen-year-old enthusiasm.

Ah, yes! A Christian boy made Rislène's story all the more interesting and the evidence against her all the more incriminating. If she were not only a Christian but also romantically involved with a Christian man, this would be the ultimate scandal. Nazira had to let Father know.

Music from the radio was interrupted suddenly with a flash bulletin. "Early this morning the bodies of two hundred people were found in a small village outside of Algiers, their throats slit. Many of the victims were women...."

Such macabre announcements from Algeria were becoming commonplace. It made Nazira's eyes well up with tears to consider it. At eighteen, she wanted desperately to do the will of Allah. But there was a tortured questioning in her soul. By her zeal for Allah, she was giving up her education, her chance for a better life. Already she had been refused entrance to her high school because she insisted on wearing the hijab to class. The French saw this as a direct threat to the Catholic roots of their country and, more important, a sign of militant Islam. They feared that the barbarous acts occurring on the other side of the sea might find their way into France. Devout, fervent Muslims were suspect.

Nazira left the café, her white veil in place. No one must know she had been here. Not yet. Not until the evidence against Rislène was strong enough to persuade Father to act.

Mme Ploussard's door flew open the moment Ophélie stepped out of the elevator. "Mlle Duchemin! Come quick!" The old woman pulled her into her apartment, shut the door, and turned the three locks. M. Ploussard was sitting in the salon, sipping a drink, but when he saw them enter, he put his glass on the coffee table and stood up shakily.

"*Mais alors!* What in the world is the matter, M. and Mme Ploussard? You both look as if you've seen a ghost!"

Mme Ploussard put her finger over her lips. "Shh. Not so loud! And not a ghost, Mlle Duchemin. *Ooh là, non!* Not a *fantôme!* We saw him plain as day. Plain as day, that handsome young brother of yours—so tall with that strange red hair all cut short and sticking up. I suppose it suits him well. He is a little pale though, don't you think? And very thin. Has he been eating enough *soupe?* You know what they say about needing your *soupe, n'est-ce pas?*"

"Evelyne! You're straying from the point," M. Ploussard reprimanded his wife. "Come sit down, Mlle Duchemin, while we tell you. Please, have a seat. And a glass of *muscat*, perhaps?"

"No, thank you. But is there something wrong with Eric?"

"Wrong! Wrong! *Mais bien sûr. C'est catastrophique!* He was with *her!*"

"What are you talking about, Mme Ploussard?"

"Your fine young brother went right into your apartment two days ago with that *Arab* girl. In the apartment together. Holding hands! *Ooh là! Ce n'est pas possible.*"

Ophélie opened her mouth to protest, but Mme Ploussard shook her head and wagged a finger at her young neighbor. "You must talk to him. Doesn't he know that French and Arabs cannot mix! *Une catastrophe*, I tell you." Then her face sagged and she sank into a worn brown leather *fauteuil*. "Poor Mlle Duchemin. I'm sorry to break the news to you like this. We've shocked you! *Ooh là là!* But we felt it only right to tell you."

"Yes," added M. Ploussard, his pale gray eyes now lively, a frown across his wrinkled face. "Our duty as citizens of France! We had to warn you. *Pour la patrie!* You must talk to him."

Ophélie stood up and took M. Ploussard's feeble hand, which was shaking slightly, in hers. She furrowed her brow. What could she say? Then inspiration came.

In a whisper she said, "Oh, I need your help. Please don't say a thing to anyone. It's a very difficult situation. No one must find out, or it would be very dangerous for Eric!"

"*Oui, oui,* very dangerous! Terrible. Such a nice boy."

"You won't say anything then? Our secret? Believe me, I am working on things."

M. and Mme Ploussard were now smiling broadly. "Ah, yes! A secret. Of course. We won't breathe a word! Not a word."

She kissed them each on the cheek as she left the apartment, listened for the locks to be bolted in place, and walked across the hall to her door. She let herself in, grinning at the thought of her elderly neighbors keeping watch over her apartment for the honor and glory of France.

She set down her purse and said, "*Liberté, Egalité, Fraternité.*" Then with a chuckle, she added, "*Compliqué!*"

Life was indeed complicated at times like this.

On Saturday, December 17, the small sanctuary at the Eglise Protestante Evangélique was filled with young people, many of them Arab. The strong aroma of mint tea brewing permeated the room. Gabriella and Anne-Marie talked together happily as they set up a table filled with Christmas confections in the small Sunday school room.

"You don't mind using your white lace tablecloth, Gabriella?"

Gabriella laughed. It was a nostalgic joke between two old friends. The white lace tablecloth was a treasured keepsake from Gabriella's mother, but through years of use at Christmastime, it had absorbed stains from coffee and tea, red wine, and even spaghetti sauce. Now the trick was to place the dessert plates on the table in such a way that the stains were not visible—a more difficult task each year.

"These stains are here to stay," Gabriella had complained at one party, years ago.

To which Anne-Marie had replied, "But what are a few stains on a tablecloth if in the process teenagers are hearing of a God who can remove the stains from their hearts?" Ever since then, whenever Gabriella brought out the treasured cloth, it made them smile.

The women surveyed the table together: a mixture of French, American, and Arab desserts on bright Christmas paper plates adorned almost every inch of available space. No stains were visible now!

"Is the tea ready, Anne-Marie?" Gabriella asked.

The two women slipped quietly into the kitchen, brought out a kettle and thick paper cups, and placed them on another smaller table. David was speaking to the young people, a brief message of the hope and promise of Christmas. It was something these young Arabs needed to hear. Their faith cost them dearly.

Eric was sitting next to Rislène. Gabriella whispered a prayer for them. She thought of the verse from Colossians: "There is no distinction between Greek and Jew, circumcised and uncircumcised, barbarian, Scythian, slave and freeman, but Christ is all, and in all."

All were equal in God's sight; Gabriella knew this. But since the relationship between an Algerian girl and her son threatened their safety, she found it hard to trust. Especially when she thought of Samira.

Give them wisdom from above. It was all she could pray.

Eric came to the front of the little sanctuary to conclude the Oasis Christmas party. His father had just finished telling the moving story of a young Huguenot who was persecuted for his faith back in the 1700s. Looking around at the faces of the other young people in the room, Eric saw their courage and zeal. He silently thanked God for them.

"Time for a few songs!" he said, picking up his guitar. "How about 'Eclate de Joie'? Page 43 in your songbook, if you need it." Eric strummed a few chords, and the kids began singing in French: "Burst into song, my soul, overflow with joy, my heart."

They sang it so sincerely. He closed his eyes as his fingers moved over the strings. Long before he'd attended Oasis or met Rislène, he had fallen in love with music and this old guitar. Playing it today and glancing out at Rislène, who smiled back at him, his heart felt full. Yes, overflowing with joy.

After they had sung four songs—two in French and two in Arabic—Eric set down the guitar. "As always, we want to hear if you have particular things we can pray about. My father shared a story of someone who suffered for his faith many years ago. We know that even now many are suffering for their faith—being killed simply because, like the Huguenots, they refuse to deny their God. Let us pray for our brothers and sisters in these persecuted countries. We think especially tonight of Algeria, ravaged by internal war, where innocent people are murdered daily."

He took a breath and felt the heat come to his face. "And I have another request. Rislène's family has found out about her conversion." He briefly related the events of the past couple of weeks, never taking his eyes off Rislène. "She feels it is time to return to her family. So would you all please pray for her safety?"

There was a catch in his throat. He tried to swallow, tried to say something else, but no sound came. He glanced again at Rislène, whose eyes were shining with love.

Dear God, protect her. Protect her.

Abdul and Madira studied the letter with concern. Could they house a Moroccan pastor who had fled his country under threats for his life? His eventual destination was France, but until money could be raised for the flight, he needed a secure shelter.

Abdul almost laughed out loud, the idea seemed so ridiculous. No one was safe in Algeria. You didn't need to be a pastor with a price on your head; you could be a housewife or a schoolgirl. Death in Algeria was not a respecter of persons.

But of course his fear was greater. Already he was seeking an alternative meeting place for their small house church. The government had said nothing for all these years. Perhaps they did not know of the existence of the little church. But El Amin knew, and Abdul felt as if he were sitting on a smoldering volcano that at any minute might spew to life, sweeping away his home, his family, and his church, covering them with the heat of his son's fanatical wrath. How could they invite a hunted Moroccan pastor into this nightmare?

"You must simply write and say it is not possible," Madira said, smoothing her husband's silver hair.

"It's not just that, Madira. We can say no this time. But the next? And the next? I detest the fear that is creeping into my heart. Where is my faith?"

He closed his eyes briefly to stop the sting of a tear. It happened, the renewed fear, every time another massacre took place. Abdul's fear was not for his life, but for his family and his flock. The thought of his five daughters, all secret followers of Christ, being abducted and butchered kept him awake at night.

"Shh, now, Abdul," Madira comforted. "God is our protector. God is in control."

But with his eyes closed, Abdul saw the grief-lined faces of veiled women and weary men walking behind the caskets of teenage girls who had been raped and murdered. And these were girls who wore the hijab and recited from the Koran. No one was safe.

"We must pray," he whispered. "It's the only peace we will know for now."

A gust of wind brought the fine Saharan sand up from the ground, stinging El Amin's eyes. He liked the windstorms of the region, so sudden and completely out of control. It was how he lived his life, and many others had learned to respect his quick temper and strategic mind. And strategy was what he needed now.

Daily reports made him curse the lack of organization in the fragmented Front Islamique du Salut. After its near victory last January, the strong militant Muslim party had lost its focus. The government's angry coup to regain power in those elections had left the FIS confused and bitter. Soon disputes had risen within the ranks until what was left was a handful of smaller militant groups, each with its own leader. And each with its own weakness.

For almost two years the police-backed government had been on a rampage of brutality, determined to halt the fundamentalists' attempt to take over Algeria. Now many of their best men were either dead or imprisoned.

El Amin squinted in the sun, admiring the turquoise sea that lapped at his feet. Here in the town of Tipasa peacefulness reigned. Here he could hear his thoughts as he carefully considered his options with the cadence of the slow-moving tide. An hour's drive from Algiers, Tipasa was often called an antique Monaco, an exotic escape on Algeria's northern shores. With its tropical scenery and ancient roots, Tipasa welcomed tourists who had money enough to pay for lodgings in the exquisite white geometrical buildings that sat on a promontory, shaded by pine trees and offering a perfect view of the sparkling Mediterranean that played at the village's edge.

In this ancient Roman city one could walk among the ruins on the other side of the promontory unhindered. El Amin liked that. The worn tier of stones leading to a Roman temple was hidden under an umbrella of mimosas. He stepped over a fallen Roman column and observed sheep grazing inside the broken amphitheater. Eucalyptus and pine trees decorated the remains of a smaller theater. The grassy area around the sarcophagi in the antiquated sailors' cemetery bloomed with daisies and gillyflowers, and everywhere the stony hillside was rough and wild.

Someday he would bring Jala here to enjoy the intoxicating beauty with him. He imagined her skin glowing as the sun's last rays inflamed the crest of cypress and olive trees, little by little plunging the golden stone into shadow.

How ridiculous to let his mind stray to such romantic notions! He was tired, and weakness came with fatigue. He would not let it master him, because after these two intruders came the inevitable: fear.

"*Inshallah*," he said aloud. If Allah wills. It was the ending note of every conversation with a devout Muslim. The will of Allah ran in his veins, a pure, fervent love for everything that Islam meant. How long had he known that his life would be guided by this fervor? Forever, it seemed. Once, as a child, he had been tempted to follow another god, a Christian god that his parents had embraced, then abandoned. But it had soon become evident in El Amin's adolescent eyes that Christianity, with its heretical three gods, was much inferior to Islam.

Why then had his parents returned to this helpless religion? Why did they now pursue the forbidden religion with the same zeal with which he pursued Islam? Anger and pity washed through him. Foolish, blind people!

He was a strong man, an important man. But he could offer them no protection, nor any to his five sisters, likewise hopelessly lost to this foreign intruder. Could they not see it? Women, innocent women who wore the white veil of Islam and obeyed their husbands, were being slain in broad daylight. What did his family think would befall them if the government discovered their covert activities? Or worse, what would his comrades do to those who betrayed Allah? They would make examples of them. Another gory warning for anyone who dared step out of the line of conduct that was demanded.

Algeria was dying another long, slow death as it had thirty years ago in its seven-year fight for independence from France. Resurrected for a time, the country was faltering. It was meant to be an Islamic state. An icon for the world to see and admire. A carefully calculated strategy was all that could save it from destroying itself in a cloud of chaos.

El Amin sat down on the steps of the amphitheater and watched the sea spray the rocks with white foam. Only a few more hours of refuge at Tipasa before he was due to report to his soldiers in Algiers. Terrorism had always been their strongest weapon—yet the thought seemed incongruous in this setting. He picked a wild daisy and thought again of Jala and his children. Then he fell on his knees, hearing in his mind the voice coming over the loudspeaker in Algiers, calling its people to prayer. He touched his forehead to the ground, facing Mecca, facing his fears, and prayed.

7

It was the twenty-fourth of December, but there was no sign of Christmas at the Namanis' apartment. No, they calmly waited for their month of celebration, Ramadan, which this year would begin February 1. To Rislène, it seemed like total hypocrisy. Most every Arab, even those who never prayed, who drank alcoholic beverages all year long or disobeyed other of the many interdictions of Islam, celebrated Ramadan as if their devotion to Allah were unquestioned and complete.

But religion seemed to be brimming over with hypocrites. She knew that most of the French called themselves Catholic, but it seemed to mean nothing in their lives. A cultural tradition. How many of her friends were completely anesthetized to organized religion? Some had New Age crystals, others saw mediums. Most were just very skeptical, philosophers ready to argue with anyone about the lack of importance of religion in a humanistic, progressive society.

That is why she had been so intrigued by the young people who attended Oasis. Their religious beliefs seemed to make a difference in the way they lived their lives. There was a freshness there that smacked of truth. And it cost them something. Every one of the kids talked of strange words like *sacrifice* and *surrender*. Those words didn't scare her off. Instead they compelled her, drew her toward these Christians like a magnet. And afterward, she had discovered the truth for herself.

Oh, the Protestant church had its own brand of hypocrites; she knew that. But this God-Man, Jesus, was personal, and she felt different because of Him. The words He spoke in the Bible were true. Oh, but they were hard! *Love your enemies. Bless those who persecute you. Rejoice when you suffer for Christ's sake.*

At times she felt a fleeting jealousy of the French Christians who had grown up in Protestant families. Belief had not really cost them much, she complained in her weak moments. Their zeal, even Eric's—and he had seen many difficulties with his parents' missionary work—was not superficial, but it was a little too light. Hers felt heavy with responsibility. Pulling her thick black hair into a tight braid, she made herself thank God instead of comparing. That advice, given by Gabriella Hoffmann months ago, had helped her more than anything else to fight jealousy and self-pity.

She admitted to God that she was disappointed she couldn't celebrate with Eric and his family, singing Christmas carols and praising God for sending His Son. In a whisper she added, "I just want You to know that it's hard to be here, with the eyes of my whole family on me, suspicion hanging in the air. But it's worth it. I'll do whatever it takes. For You."

Rislène busied herself cooking the noon meal for her large family. Her three older brothers, who still lived at home, were lounging in the den, smoking and playing cards.

"Hey, Rislène! Get the food ready quick, will you? I'm starved!" one of them complained.

Nazira and her youngest sister, Fouzia, did not offer to help. Nothing had changed during Rislène's absence. If she wasn't there to cook, Mother did it, begrudgingly. It was a duty that fell to the oldest daughter. She thought that maybe the only reason Mother had smiled when she had come home three days ago was because now someone else would do the cooking.

After the meal, she cleared the table with a sigh. She wished she had not come back. Her mother did not speak to her at all, just watched her with large, sad eyes. Her father had smiled roughly when she came into the apartment. She was still his favorite, which made Nazira furious with envy. The tension in the house was enough to suffocate them all.

When Rislène had finished washing the dishes, M. Namani called his daughter into the den and spoke to her alone. "We've been talking, Rislène, while you've been away," he began. "We're planning a trip to Algeria to see Grandmother. We leave on Tuesday."

"Everyone is going?" Rislène asked, taken aback.

"No, of course not. You and Nazira and Fouzia, your mother and I. The boys have their work. But you have the school holidays. We'll be gone ten days."

She did not dare protest but spoke the first words that came to her lips. "Is it safe?"

"Do you think we would return if it meant danger for any of you? Anyway, Grandmother's house is well protected. An army couldn't get in. And it's only for ten days. She's very lonely."

Rislène shuddered. Was her father crazy? She heard the daily accounts. No one was safe. Not even Grandmother with her wealth.

"Why do you want to go back now?" she questioned.

Father did not meet her eyes. He stared sternly at the wall, smoking a long pipe. "Grandmother is not well, Rislène. She called us last week while you were gone." These last words he pronounced like an accusation. "Everything had to be decided very quickly. It may be the last chance we have to see her."

This news came as another shock to Rislène. Grandmother, the terrible matriarch of the Namani family, the one who had groomed her sons and struck fear in the hearts of her daughters-in-law, the respected and revered head of the family, could not be dying. Rislène felt tears sting her eyes. As much as she feared Grandmother, she loved her fiercely.

"Oh, Father, I'm so sorry." She ran to his arms, and he embraced her tightly. "Of course I'll go. Don't worry. It will be a blessing to Grandmother to have us all there. You'll see. She'll be all right."

But later that night in bed, she felt sick with fear. She did not want to go to Algeria. And how could she let Eric know?

I wish I were with him tonight, Lord. I wish I were with them all. She thought of the words to "Silent Night." She couldn't hum them, because Nazira would hear from her bed across the room. But she said the words over and over in her mind. *Christ our Savior is born. Christ our Savior is born.*

The French called it the *Réveillon*. It was the family feast served on December 24, usually starting after midnight Mass and going straight through the night. More money was spent on the preparations for that one meal than for all the gifts and presents given during the whole Christmas season.

Janine Dufour loved the *Réveillon*. The last performance at the theater was December 22, giving her two days away from her work to spend with her mother, cooking. On the evening of the twenty-third her two brothers had arrived with their families. And just this morning her sister had pulled in after driving through the night from Lille with her boyfriend.

"The *bûche* will be a huge success, Mama!" she called out from the kitchen as she carefully rolled a thin, moist rectangular yellow cake, spread with chocolate-cream filling, into a long cylinder. After it had been refrigerated, she would take it out and frost it with stiff chocolate, drawing a fork's tines through the frosting and sculpting it so that eventually the cake resembled a log—a bûche. She could have bought a frozen bûche at the store. But for Janine, the pleasure was in the preparation, not just in the tasting.

Why she still longed for these age-old traditions she did not know. In spite of its reputation for wonderful *haute cuisine*, France was seeing McDonald's and other fast-food restaurants spring up throughout the major cities. And with the convenience of micro-waves and frozen food, plus the pressures of a busy career, what woman had time to spend on cooking? Perhaps this old, celebrated art of France was dying, but Janine was determined it would not end with her.

Her mother came into the kitchen in a rush. "*Ooh là!* Is it all ready? Let me see."

Together they inspected the various platters and bowls crammed into the refrigerator. The *foie gras* had been chosen from her father's friend's farm, as it was every year, the freshest goose liver around. Her mother's specialty, a *feuilleté au jambon*, was ready to be baked in the oven when they returned from Mass. Janine could almost taste the light, buttered pastry filled with creamed ham and cheese. The turkey was stuffed with chestnuts. The large old house was filled up with succulent smells and warmth. Janine felt content.

Soon it was time to herd the whole family into cars for midnight Mass. All of France went to church on Christmas Eve—never mind that they didn't set a foot inside during the rest of the year, Janine contemplated a bit cynically. They were good Catholics, and good Catholics went to Mass at Christmas. Mme Dufour was what was called *praticante*, which meant she attended Mass fairly regularly, but she was a loner in the family. Janine herself hadn't attended St. Vincent since last Christmas.

But she had been to church. Ophélie Duchemin was forever inviting her to events at the strange little Protestant church on the east side of Montpellier. This past year she had acquiesced, more out of intrigue than true interest, attending what they called a Bible study. Each week a small group of people, including several non-Protestants like herself, studied a different passage in the gospel of St. John. Everyone, even she who had never opened a Bible before in her life, was free to share an opinion on the passage. Sometimes the discussion got quite lively.

Ah, well. Tonight she was a good Catholic again. And once this nice formality was over, the meal could begin!

The Hoffmanns' house was overflowing with people. Ever since the end of the war in 1962, whenever they were in France for Christmas, Gabriella and David had spent Christmas Eve with two other families: the Dramchinis and the Cebrians. The end of the Algerian war had united them to each other and to God, and their bond of friendship had endured. Whenever possible, the three families gathered for the *Réveillon*. Over the years, their numbers had grown.

This year Gabriella expected twenty-six. It was quite a crowd for their small house, but no one minded. Until three years ago, the friends had gathered at Rémi and Eliane Cebrian's ample home in Prades-le-Lez, a village twenty minutes north of Montpellier. Gabriella's eyes misted up momentarily, but before she could succumb to sad thoughts, the doorbell rang.

She opened the door wide to admit Rémi and Eliane, laden with packages. Behind them, in another car, Gabriella saw their daughter, Rachel, arriving with her husband and children, as well as their son José and his fiancée.

"Gabriella! How wonderful to see you!" Eliane was petite and plump, her sixty-year-old face still round and cheery, her silver hair cut in an attractive style. For years Eliane had been the hostess, jolly, optimistic, and in control, loving every minute of the Christmas Eve bedlam. But her eyes were not so bright now, and the lines on her face were not only from age, Gabriella knew.

"I've been counting the days, Eliane. It's so good to see you both!" Gabriella embraced them warmly. "Oh, look at all this! You've done too much, as always."

"You know how it is, Gabriella," Eliane whispered, her voice catching. "It helps to be busy at this time of year." She cleared her throat. "Someday perhaps we'll meet again at our place. Until then, at least I can cook."

Rémi Cebrian was stocky, still muscular in his midsixties, a little round around the middle, with short, cropped gray hair. "You're a saint to have us all, Gabriella!" he said good-naturedly, kissing her on each cheek.

"Oh, no! Not at all. Here, let me take your coats. You can set the food in the kitchen and then let David get you something to drink."

As Gabriella climbed the stairs and laid the coats on her bed, she closed her eyes briefly. *Dear Lord, give us joy tonight, as we anticipate celebrating Your birth. Please don't let the memories of what we have lost crowd out the knowledge of what we have gained.*

The day's schedule had not changed much in thirty years: a mixture of traditions from France, America, and Algeria. Gabriella made cut-out cookies and let the children help decorate them. At five o'clock, Ophélie organized what was one of the highlights for the children: setting up the *crèche*, a manger scene made up of miniature *santons*. The tiny clay figurines had been collected over many years. Ophélie could remember helping her half sisters, Aurélie and Christine, carefully arrange the six-inch clay figures around the wooden barn when they were small girls. Now she observed Aurélie holding her own daughter, two-year-old Chloé, on her knees, and slowly unwrapping a tiny sheep from within crinkled newspaper.

"*Oh! Maman! Regarde ça!*" Chloé exclaimed in glee.

Aurélie laughed. "Hey, Ophélie? Remember this one? You helped me paint it."

She smiled to think of the santons they had bought unpainted and decorated over the years. Somehow they blended in perfectly with the "real" santons, those with every detail minutely painted in bright colors by Marcel Carbonel, the well-known artisan from Marseille.

Roger Hoffmann, David and Gabriella's second son, came over. "Hey, can we get in on the fun, Ophélie?" He lifted his small daughter onto his lap and began unwrapping another santon.

Ophélie had three half brothers, the Hoffmann boys, and two half sisters, Moustafa and her mother's girls. Christmas Eve was one of the rare times they all got together. She cherished the memories of the years past, the celebrations, the laughter. One by one, each sibling had married, until now only she and Eric were single. And even he had someone picked out, straight from the hand of God.

She was surrounded by family, almost overcome with thankfulness to belong to these people. She took little Chloé from Aurélie and squeezed her tight. The smell of her niece's baby hair, the feel of her silken ringlets on Ophélie's cheeks brought a deep contentment that helped to make up for all the times when her arms were empty.

David Hoffmann enveloped Rémi in a big bear hug, then slapped him on the back.

"You Americans! Always hugging!" Rémi mocked playfully. Hugs were definitely not French, but hugs had gotten these men through many trials.

"Hey, Moustafa! Rémi's here!" David called out to the small backyard where Moustafa was playing with one of his grandchildren.

A few minutes later the three men were sipping *pastis* and commenting on how much the grandchildren had grown. Rémi kidded Moustafa on his short hair.

"Long gray curls did not make me look distinguished," he defended himself. Then, playfully inspecting David's salt-and-pepper hair, he added, "You've got a few silver threads too, my friend."

They ate peanuts and the fresh green olives that were Rémi's contribution every year, the best quality, imported from Algeria.

"Montpellier's team won the big one Thursday," David commented. "Did you see it?"

"Just the first half." Moustafa laughed. He motioned with his eyes to where his wife stood talking with Gabriella and Eliane in the kitchen. "Then Anne-Marie insisted we watch her movie. You know my sweet lady—she's never been too fond of *le foot*. I always tell her she should thank the Lord we have only girls."

David nodded, tossing an olive into his mouth. "Now that's for sure. Between our three boys, Gabby says we spent our retirement fund on cleats, and all our vacation got swallowed up in tournaments!"

Small talk never lasted long between them, David reflected. Why pretend that their lives were filled with banalities when they knew differently? He put a hand on Rémi's shoulder. "How are you and Eliane doing?"

"We're okay." There was an awkward pause. "Getting here is always the hardest for Eliane. Once she's with the rest of you, it makes everything easier."

"I suppose there's nothing new to report?" Moustafa queried.

Rémi tightened his lips and shook his head. "Nothing. It's been a little rough lately with Rachel's baby. I thought maybe a new little grand-daughter would help Eliane, but ..." He couldn't finish his sentence.

"Sorry to bring it up," Moustafa said softly.

"Ce n'est pas grave." Rémi shrugged. "If I can't share it with you guys, who do I have? Christmas is always the hardest time. But then God gives hope by bringing us here."

The littlest ones stood around the dining-room table, eagerly watching the big red candle shining its light from Gabriella's homemade chocolate bundt cake. Everyone joined in singing "Happy Birthday" to Jesus. Then Gabriella and Anne-Marie and Eliane sliced pieces of cake and passed them around.

Eric smiled to himself. It was the same every year. But this year, his mind kept straying to Rislène, wondering what she was doing with her family. And wishing she were here with him.

The meal was consumed. Stacks of Gabriella's fine china, which she insisted on using every year, stood on the kitchen counter. The six grandchildren were sleeping in different bedrooms upstairs. Rachel came down the stairs, wiping a strand of hair from her face. "The baby's out, finally."

It was nearly one o'clock when the kids were finally asleep and David led the adults in a time of thanksgiving for their many blessings. Eric let his gaze fall lovingly on the people crowded in the den—his family and dear friends. All the lights in the house were off except for those on the full, sparkling Christmas tree, covered with a jumble of handcrafted ornaments added over the years. Another small light illumined the manger scene of miniature santons that the children had set up. Eric strummed his guitar softly, and the whole group began to sing.

At one point a little head peeked over the banister, bright cheeks and wide eyes, to listen to the peaceful harmonies. Roger stood with difficulty in the mishmash of bodies and went up the steps to retrieve his daughter and snuggle her in his lap while the singing continued. Eric felt God's faithfulness wrapping them up together like a blanket.

Rislène, he thought, with a catch in his throat.

The singing over, the adults rose and yawned, stretching arms over their heads, smiling at each other. As the older adults headed up the stairs to find a mattress or any empty bed, Eric stood, eyes twinkling.

"We're starting a new tradition this year, for all of you who can handle it." He winked at his mother, who was yawning unabashedly. "I've taped the old American film *It's a Wonderful Life*, complete with subtitles, and we'll be starting it up in ten minutes."

His brother William punched him playfully and said, "Not me."

"Oh, come on, William," his wife said, pouting. "It's a great movie. Don't be a spoilsport."

Soon his brothers and their wives, along with Ophélie, the Cebrian and Dramchini young adults and their spouses, were crowded around the TV, lying on the sofa and mattresses, cuddled under blankets and his mother's old quilts, watching the story of George Bailey and Clarence the angel. Eric rubbed his eyes, fiddled with the sound, and then settled into an empty chair. Looking around at the others, comfortable with their spouses, he longed for Rislène to be snuggled safely beside him.

Someday soon, he promised himself.

Late in the morning on Christmas Day, after *croissants* and *pain au chocolat* and plenty of coffee, the families made their way to the little Protestant church for the Christmas service. Many of the regular attendees were absent, scattered throughout France to be with their families. Still, there was a reverent joy, a deep, rich emotion that passed among the believers that morning as they lifted tired voices and sang familiar carols from centuries past. They sang what in their hearts they knew to be the truth. Christ our Savior is born! And they left the church building comforted.

Gabriella and David bid the Cebrian and Dramchini families good-bye. Ophélie left to be with Anne-Marie and Moustafa. But the three Hoffmann boys and their families came back to their parents' house to help clean up. They shooed Gabriella out of the kitchen, promising their mother that no china would be broken.

David pulled his wife to him and kissed her softly. "My beautiful Gabby," he said. "God has blessed us immensely with family and friends. Thank you for making this possible once again."

"It was wonderful, wasn't it, David?" She closed her eyes and yawned. Nodding to the kitchen as they listened to the boys joking together, she added, "I sure am glad someone raised those boys right."

Later in the afternoon, when the house was empty and the leftovers had been consumed, David took out a cassette tape and popped it into the stereo system. On the casing was written *50 Favorite Christmas Songs*. He had copied the songs from an old 1950s vinyl album. "Rudolph the Red-Nosed Reindeer" wafted through the living room.

"Now whatever made you put on that old album?" Gabriella asked.

But when he turned around, her eyes were sparkling, full of love, and she motioned for him to sit down beside her. It was another tradition for them, this music from a Christmas night thirty years ago, before they had dared declare their love for each other. And every year they put on the cassette to remind themselves of another aspect of their God: His faithfulness in bringing people together.

With the music softly playing in the background, Gabriella asked, "Sweetheart? Did Ophélie seem happy to you today?"

"Yes, she did. All smiles to be holding her little nieces and nephew."

"Do you think the Lord will give her someone someday?"

David smiled tenderly at his wife. "Dearest Gabby. Don't worry so about Ophélie. She's a big girl with a wonderful, full life."

"Eric missed having Rislène here, don't you think?"

"I'm sure he did. But that kid! He was having a fine time himself." He rubbed her hair playfully. "Quit your worrying, woman!"

"Just one more question, David."

"Go ahead, dear."

"Do you think one day we'll celebrate Christmas again at Rémi and Eliane's?"

David did not answer immediately. He thought of the pain in Eliane's eyes, the awkward moments during the previous day. He drew his wife into his arms and held her there tightly. With a catch in his voice he said softly, "I don't know, Gabby. All I know is that I pray that the Lord will remind them that He is a God of hope and of new beginnings."

"Me too." The music continued as they held each other, lost in their memories.

8

There was nothing particularly different about Christmas Day for the homeless people in Montpellier. Some charitable organizations offered noon meals, others gave presents to the children. It was a drop in the bucket, thought Ceb. A moment of goodwill to appease uncomfortable consciences.

"*Joyeux Noël*," a round woman in black robes had chimed yesterday as she rang the Salvation Army's bell outside of the big department store, Monoprix. At seven p.m., the store was still flooded with people hurrying to make last-minute purchases for family and friends. But by eight thirty, the streets in centre ville were empty, littered only with pitiful alcoholics strewn out on park benches.

"Merry Christmas," Ceb spat as he walked through the streets. "Merry Christmas indeed!"

The days before the holiday and the day itself were some of the busiest for Ceb. He helped take meals to those who would not come to the soup kitchen, joined Red Cross workers in delivering brightly wrapped presents to children who would otherwise have none, and spent the evenings with Dominique Lefevre distributing medicine to people who would never seek out medical attention themselves. He even roasted chestnuts on an open fire behind the place de la Comédie, Montpellier's immense open square in the heart of downtown. Many homeless gathered around the blazing warmth and mumbled verses from Christmas carols they could hardly remember.

Still, late on the twenty-fifth, there was nothing left for him to do. The meals had been eaten, the gifts opened by happy children, the hot chestnuts roasted to a crusty black and popped open with all the delicious meat inside devoured. Many of the SDFs had crawled back to their corners of the city, some drunk, others high on cheap drugs, still others lavishing their affection on their mangy dogs, their sole possessions and companions.

Ceb dreaded being alone in his squat, dreaded the memories of long-ago Christmases that would flood in once he had run out of activities to distract him. Warm fires roaring in stone fireplaces, the kiss from a lovely woman with blond hair, a cherubic little face peering into her father's eyes, eager to know if *le Père Noël* was coming. He cursed his memories, felt sick to his stomach, searched his mind for something else to do to fill the emptiness with anything besides these happy snapshots of the past.

At last he succumbed to the one numbing force that worked every time. Three years ago he had started his downward spiral by consuming bottles of cheap liquor. Some grain of decency and his immutable, ironclad will had stopped him from becoming an alcoholic early on his homeless pilgrimage. But on Christmas night, tortured by his past, Ceb had no choice. He took out the bottles stashed throughout the one-room squat, saved up for this night of need. He drank one after another, quickly, desperately at first, then slowly as his mind and senses blurred and the throbbing in his right hand disappeared and every power of reason left him. He sang old carols with slurred speech, laughing uncontrollably and then sobbing with the same lack of control. By the time he fell into unconsciousness, everything felt warm and cozy and familiar. He had escaped the past once again.

Christmas Day came and went in Algiers without even a blink to the Jesus of the Bible. If the Arabs in that fated city remembered the significance of this date for much of the Western world, they remembered it with a taste of violence on their tongues. Yet hidden throughout the immense country of Algeria, unknown to the casual spectator, were pockets of people who dared lift their voices of praise to someone other than Allah. Their voices were actually silent, even though their hearts were full. Christmas, the day when Christians everywhere celebrated the birth of God's Son, was not forgotten in their souls. It burned there, courageous and fervent, branded on their hearts, not intimidated by threats of persecution and death.

Hussein El Youssif and his family attended a house church in Algiers that sometimes met secretly in their apartment. The small group of Christians rotated between homes so that the neighbors would not grow suspicious. Keeping these meetings secret was the easy part of Hussein's work. His main mission was to ensure that Bibles and other Christian literature brought into the country arrived at their intended destinations. A wrong look, a suspicious movement, and everyone's cover could be blown.

On December 26, late at night, an old red Peugeot pulled up in a deserted mountain hideout far outside Algiers. Swiftly, without exchanging words, the driver of the car and Hussein lifted boxes out of the trunk and deposited them in Hussein's gray Citroën. Then Hussein passed the driver stacks of letters, neatly tied with twine.

They met eyes, shook hands, and drove off, each to his next destination. In this silent, secret way, the Word of God was spreading throughout many countries in the Arab world.

Hussein drove for an hour, his eyes glancing instinctively to the rearview mirror every few seconds. No one was following him tonight. He gave a sigh and thought of Dounia, waiting for him at home, never knowing where he was or when he would return. At times he wished he had been strong enough not to marry. Then he would have no ties, no one waiting at home for him, worried when he was late. But Dounia loved him and loved his God. She never complained, firmly asserting that God had chosen Hussein for this job and he must do it, as unto the Lord. So their life was full of secrets. Even Dounia did not know, could not know, how deeply he was tied to both sides of this political chaos. His friends in the government were sure he worked for them. His friends in the FIS knew beyond any doubt that his allegiance was to their fundamentalist cause. Neither suspected that this small, square man in his midforties swore allegiance to no one but Jesus.

If they ever found out, Hussein knew the terrible outcome. How often had he wondered if he should leave Algeria for a time, flee to France where he had friends to welcome him. Two of his three children were teenagers now. What life was there in Algeria, a country determined to self-destruct? But Dounia trusted God, and each night when they prayed together, she reaffirmed, "God has given us this mission."

Who would take up the call if he left, Hussein wondered. "Let me not give way to fear," he said softly. *I will not fail you or forsake you.* The words of Scripture were his only encouragement as he drove through the starless night.

Abdul and Madira received the sealed box in the early morning. A quick rap sent them to the door in time to see a gray Citroën driving away with sand spraying from its tires. Eagerly they opened the box to discover its contents.

"Look, Madira!" Abdul exclaimed, hugging his wife. "Six Bibles! And not one but two copies of the video in Arabic. And the Bible courses. Why, there's enough material here for four months' worth of course work. God be praised."

And what they found across the bottom of the box was like the feel of the blue Mediterranean on their toes in the middle of a blistering afternoon. Letters from Rémi and Eliane, David and Gabriella, Anne-Marie and Moustafa. The mail system still functioned in Algeria, but letters to anyone suspected to be Western-minded were routinely opened, read, and discarded. Likewise, Algerian Christians wishing to take correspondence courses from France found that after the first two or three responses were sent out, no other materials were received. Sabotaged along the way.

So now, Bibles and videos and correspondence courses were discreetly brought in to Algeria a few at a time, placed in the suitcases of Algerian Christians reentering the country or foreign Christians coming expressly to encourage believers. And men like Hussein delivered the literature around Algeria to those most in need.

Abdul sighed. Dear Hussein. A dark figure in the early hours of dawn delivering a package to the doorstep of an Algerian farmhouse. Such secrecy seemed normal now.

They opened the letters. Each was filled with Christmas greetings and words of encouragement, but Rémi's spoke another truth too.

No word from Samuel. Perhaps there will never be any. We hurt for you, for El Amin. Our lost sons. Surely God is near them. Surely He hears ...

Madira listened intently as Abdul read each letter out loud to her, pausing in the hard places, holding the stationery close for Madira to inspect. She had learned to read late in life, when her girls were teenagers, but only in French, and still with difficulty. Her daughters had taught her, and her first one-page letter, which had taken her four hours to write, had gone to Eliane. That was twelve years ago, when life was easier and letters came and went to Algeria with no concern. Now they went wrapped in crates of olives and accompanied by many tears.

How proud she and Eliane had been of their sons. And now, as Rémi said, they were lost. She closed her eyes and saw El Amin and Samuel when they were both just six years old, playing with toy soldiers right here in this very farmhouse. Best friends. Then the Cebrians had moved to France, leaving the house and most of their possessions with the Charfis. The little boys had told each other good-bye.

Madira had taken good care of everything in the house, ready at a moment's notice to give it back. But no pied-noirs came back after the war. The French citizens living in Algeria had fled with only a few belongings, never to return. And afterward, Eliane had insisted that Madira keep everything.

And then, ah, Madira remembered with a smile breaking across her face, the reunion! In 1974, the Cebrian family had come back for ten days. She and Eliane had laughed and talked and baked and visited all their favorite pockets of the city of Algiers, as if nothing had changed.

It was senseless to let herself remember these things. It could not change the present or the future. Only God could do that. She did not say it to Abdul, did not share with him this thought buried deep in her bosom. *On this issue, God, the issue of our lost sons, it seems You are taking Your time.* And her deepest dread she could not even admit to the almighty God. Perhaps He would never call them back at all.

Janine Dufour had performed Ophélie's play to two weeks of full houses during December. Three days with her family during Christmas had raced by, and all too soon she found herself back in her apartment alone.

This year she found the week following Christmas interminably long. After all the happy family rituals, she had nothing planned for New Year's Eve. It made her heart ache with loneliness. Oh, there were parties, but she refused to attend *those* gatherings this year. She would end up with only a terrible hangover and an even deeper emptiness.

When Dominique asked if she had any time to spare before the New Year, she had tried not to sound too eager. "Yes, maybe, to help out the homeless," she had said, carefully checking her words. Not saying to help *him* out. It was true, she cared deeply about the homeless. It was also true that she was attracted to Dominique.

So, early on December 28, she took a bus across town, getting off at the bottom of the magnificent Boulevard Henri IV. She climbed the hill, admiring the wide street that was lined on each side by naked plane trees with their gray mottled bark and the stubby branches that shot into a deep-blue sky. She stopped near the bottom of the hill and stared ahead at one of her favorite scenes in Montpellier.

Up to her left she could see a thirteenth-century cathedral's arch with its slated turret, marking the entrance to Montpellier's renowned medical school. Beyond it, a small replica of the Arc de Triomphe welcomed cars and pedestrians into the true centre ville. And to the right was the spacious parc du Peyrou, a tree-lined park with an ancient water tower and aqueduct at the end. From there Janine had often looked out on the red-tiled roofs of the city and the cathedral's tall steeples that punctured the southern French sky like needles going through bright blue velvet.

Immediately on her right, still near the bottom of the hill, was Montpellier's historical Jardin des Plantes. This garden was created by Henri IV in 1593 when students flocked to Montpellier to attend its medical school. Some of the trees that grew there were hundreds of years old. The wrought-iron gates were always locked in the early morning; the immense park that stretched over five acres did not invite the homeless to spend the night on its stone benches or find shelter behind its marble statues.

Janine turned away from the park, walking down the adjoining alleyway that led to the Red Cross facility, a low, narrow building separated from the park by a stone wall and high spiked bars. She knocked on a door. After a few moments, Dominique opened it and welcomed her inside.

"You're here bright and early, Janine!" he said enthusiastically. "*Merci d'être venue.*"

"I'm happy to help."

"It's always a bit of a problem during the holidays. So many of the staff and volunteers want to take time off to visit their families."

"That's one advantage of having my parents here in town. The rest of the family comes to us!" said Janine. "Shall I get things ready to open up around back?"

"Yes, that would be great. Can you make the coffee and handle the clothes closet? And here is the key to the showers."

Before long, a line of homeless people were coming for coffee, looking through clothes, and waiting patiently to use one of the two showers in the facilities outside and around the back. Janine found that she could barely keep up with the requests and noticed that Dominique seemed to feel a bit overwhelmed himself. She should ask Ophélie to come with her tomorrow.

Ophélie had often expressed interest, but her teaching job, plays, and church activities kept her busy. Perhaps she'd have time to help out during the holidays. It seemed like something her friend would enjoy. Or maybe not *enjoy*, Janine corrected herself. But she would give of herself happily and willingly. That was always Ophélie's style.

If Janine had thought that she would have a chance to talk with Dominique today, she was mistaken. They smiled and exchanged glances, never having a chance to sit side by side for even five minutes. But the week was not over yet.

Eric stared at the short letter in disbelief. Rislène was in Algeria! How could it be? He read the words again:

> *December 25, 1994*
> *Eric,*
>
> > *I have just found out that I leave for Algeria tomorrow. My grandmother is ill. My parents and sisters go with me. Father promises that we will be home in time to start school. I go in fear, but out of love and respect for my grandmother, for my family. I pray God protects us all. I ask only for your prayers.*
> >
> > *I love you,*
> > *Rislène*

How could M. Namani take his family to Algeria at a time like this? It was insane! He picked up the copy of *Le Monde*, read the headlines on the front page, and threw it down in anger.

Four days ago FIS terrorists had hijacked an Air France plane in Algeria, forced a landing in Marseille, and held the entire crew and passengers hostage while the French government desperately sought a solution to this newest outbreak with Algeria. Then on December 26, after futile attempts to negotiate with the terrorists, French commandos stormed the plane. The news of the shootout, which resulted in the deaths of all the hijackers, demonstrated to the whole world that France was willing to risk a bloodbath to resolve the terrorist act. The French government viewed the rise of the Islamic militant movement in Algeria as a very serious problem.

And now Rislène was there!

Eric knew the statistics: four million Muslims now lived in France, making Islam the second religion behind Roman Catholicism. Many of those Muslims were French citizens, the children of North Africans and black Africans who had come over in the fifties and sixties to do the menial labor that the French refused. Though the parents were relatively reserved about their religion, some of these children were finding their identities in the militant side of Islam.

They want it all, thought Eric. They wanted to be accepted as French citizens *and* as devout Muslims. But the French struggled with how tolerant they could be when Islam was becoming more and more threatening—as the hijacking displayed in all its gory reality.

Algeria was coming apart at the seams. And now Rislène was in that crazy country!

His first thought was to call his father.

"Papa, it's Eric. I've got bad news. Rislène has gone to Algeria with her family. It happened so quickly that she only had time to scribble me a note. Apparently her grandmother is quite ill."

David Hoffmann answered his son's grim pronouncement with a long silence. Eric knew that his father feared Rislène had been taken to Algeria only on pretext of her grandmother's failing health. And yes, this was even worse than what had happened to Samira in Lyon. She had been forced to marry a Muslim, but at least she had stayed in France.

"So what do we do?" Eric asked in a weak voice.

"We wait and we pray. Perhaps she'll be back as she believes. If not, there is no cause for panic. We have many friends in Algeria, you know. We'll have news. Don't worry, Eric. We must simply pray."

Wait and pray. Why did that impossible theme reoccur so often in their lives? Eric dropped Rislène's letter to the floor, closed his eyes, and watched the blackness. He swallowed hard, cleared his throat, and rested his head in his hands. Nothing came to mind. Nothing, except one single word. *Help. Oh God, help us now.*

As Ophélie opened the door to her apartment, her neighbor appeared in the hall, a wide smile on her face.

"*Bonjour, Mme Ploussard,*" Ophélie said, turning.

"*Bonjour, dear Ophélie!* So good to see you." Mme Ploussard walked into the apartment without waiting for an invitation. "I've brought you some *saucisses* that André made with his *potes*—you know how his friends love the *charcuterie*! Butchered three pigs last week, and *voilà!*" She held out three long links of dried sausage.

"How kind of you, Mme Ploussard. *Merci.*"

Her neighbor took a seat at Ophélie's dining-room table and began to talk. "Well, we have just been worried to death about your Eric and the lovely Arab girl. Haven't seen her for over a week! And so I wondered. Well, André said I should just come over and ask you. Are the family problems solved?"

"Well, I hope so. She's back home now."

"Ah, good, good! And your Eric? Has he come to his senses?"

Ophélie thought for a moment, then smiled. "I believe he has. I really believe he has."

"What a relief! Of course we must help those people, but there are ways to help, and then"—she showed the whites of her eyes—"there are certain things we must *not* do! You have to be so careful! *Ooh là là!*"

Ophélie helped Mme Ploussard stand up and walked her to the door. *Otherwise she'll be here all night.* "Thank you again for the saucisses."

"*Pas de quoi!* Our pleasure. What are neighbors for?"

As soon as she closed the door, Ophélie's smile vanished. Had Eric "come to his senses"? Was she kidding? He was losing his mind right now. Only two hours earlier he'd called her, nearly hysterical with the news of Rislène leaving for Algeria with her family. Oh, Eric!

She hated hearing the distress in his voice. He loved Rislène.

You were in love with an Arab man once. Yes, she had been. Bachir came to Oasis and had a very young but sincere faith.

Or so she had thought. Oh, it hurt too much to think of Bachir. How could she help her little brother? She cared for Rislène, but she felt that instinctive big-sister protection for Eric. He didn't know what had really happened with Bachir because no one had ever told him.

She collapsed on her sofa and thought of Mme Ploussard's words. *Of course we must help those people ... but you have to be so careful.* Yes, so very careful. She had learned that the hard way.

9

From the moment Rislène stepped on Algerian soil, she felt a part of her soul, deep and hidden, coming back to life. During the first few days at Grandmother's home, she soaked up this Algeria that she loved. Each summer, except for the past two, her family had spent a month at Grandmother Namani's house. Though Rislène had been born and raised in France, this was the country of her roots.

The Algerian open markets had always fascinated her. She didn't mind the smell of perspiration as bodies brushed side by side while making purchases at the market. It had a heady effect on her. The older women wore white *haiks*, long garments made of lightweight material, tied around the waist, draped over the head, and held in place with one hand. The younger women, who wanted to look attractive underneath their pleated white hijabs, found the solution by wearing colorful Pakistani balloon pants that were tight around the ankles and flattered their figures. Some daring young women even wore Western dress.

Rislène liked the tightly woven streets with their staircases climbing up into other layers of the city. She liked the quiet afternoons spent with the other women, sipping café au lait on the flat roof of Grandmother's house with a perfect view of the city spreading out below.

And the smells! The spiced fragrance of her grandmother's *couscous* and the *tagine* stew that tasted better in Algiers than anywhere else. The rich, strong, sugary aroma of brewing coffee. Even the sound of the early-morning call to prayer over a loudspeaker when the sun was still low and pink in a violet sky brought happy memories to her mind. The first few days back were like a long, refreshing gulp of clear, cool water on a hot desert day.

In spite of the internal strife, the Algerian people were still warm and hospitable, demonstrating kindness to strangers, speaking easily to one another, their conversations punctuated by their wonderful sense of humor. She even heard women joking about dealing with the police and the terrorists. That was another thing she loved about Algeria: the courage of its women, determined to fight in whatever way necessary for the good of their country.

But she could not ignore the obvious. In places, the city of Algiers resembled a battleground with shells of buildings and carcasses of bombed-out cars littering the street. She sensed that the city had drawn in upon itself and that the women wore scarves not only to show religious devotion but also to hide the fear and sorrow chiseled into their faces as they witnessed firsthand the terror of this civil war. She was very glad that her family's stay was only temporary.

The other thing that Rislène observed with an odd little tingle in her stomach was that Grandmother did not appear to be ill. She was a gruff-looking woman, thick and strong, with a slightly protruding jaw and blazing eyes. She had ruled the Namani family ever since her husband had dropped dead in the fields years before Rislène was born. She looked no weaker today than she had two years ago, the last time Rislène had visited.

"Father said you are unwell?" she had questioned that first night, kissing her grandmother on the cheeks.

"It has been a difficult autumn, my child. I'm glad you came."

"You are feeling better then?"

"Better. Yes." Her reply was ambiguous, almost defensive.

Tonight as always, Grandmother Namani motioned for her grandchildren to come to her, and she engulfed them in her long, bright-orange dress. The deep lines in her face cracked open into a smile. "It is so good to have you here, children. Allah be praised."

Grandmother Namani did not live alone. Her two eldest sons and their wives and children lived with her, the wives working in a type of docile servility. Rislène's own mother feared Grandmother, who treated her harshly. It was almost as if Grandmother blamed her mother for stealing her son away.

With slippers on, for shoes were always removed inside an Algerian house, they came into the living room, empty of furniture except for a low wooden table and several mattresses covered in dark-blue velvet. During meals, they reclined on the mattresses. At night, if the house was crowded with extra family members, the velvet covers were removed and children slept on the mattresses. On this night, after the evening meal, Rislène, Nazira, and Fouzia sat beside their mother. Their father sat on the floor in front of Grandmother Namani as she stroked his hair, her long silk scarf pulled over her head.

The tension between her mother and grandmother and the man they shared had always been there, but it had never struck Rislène as it did now. Her father's powerlessness toward his mother and his strong power over his wife … She watched their superficial communication and felt suddenly very sad.

"It's time for prayer," Grandmother Namani stated. Her son rose and left the room. Women and men did not pray together.

"You're not praying, Rislène," her grandmother scolded a few minutes later, in the same tone she used on a small child.

"I pray in my mind, Grandmother," Rislène replied.

"She prays to another god!" Nazira said harshly.

Grandmother Namani lowered her eyes, glaring at Nazira and signaling for conversation to stop.

It was true. Rislène was praying to another god in her mind. *Lord, protect me. Protect us all. Algeria is falling apart.* In spite of her prayers, deep in her soul she felt cold fear. *Protect me, dear Lord. Grandmother isn't sick. Why did we come to Algeria if Grandmother isn't sick?*

"Thanks for coming with me today, Ophélie," Janine said as they got off the bus in downtown Montpellier Friday morning.

"Of course. I'm glad to help out. But you know how things will be once school starts back up." She had come reluctantly to the Red Cross, only because Janine had begged, telling her how Dominique was desperate for help during the holidays.

Ophélie admitted to herself that seeing Dominique Lefevre was one of the motivating forces behind her yielding. She felt very uneasy around the homeless. And it wasn't just at stoplights. At least once a week someone was at her apartment door, trying to sell cheap posters or stale fruitcake to earn a few francs. As a Christian, she felt obligated to do something, but what?

The problem had gotten completely out of hand. It was a national crisis. Whole families were moving onto the streets. Many others were one measly paycheck away from a grim future. And with the lack of jobs and mounting unemployment, a solution seemed far off.

Janine and Ophélie arrived at the Red Cross complex well before eight a.m. Ophélie had expected something in disrepair; instead, the building was clean and bordered the well-known Jardin des Plantes.

"You brought help!" Dominique said, kissing Janine on the cheeks. "Wonderful. Good to see you again, Ophélie," he said softly.

"You two have met?" Janine asked, surprised.

"Just briefly, after opening night," Ophélie said quickly.

"Well, great! Then no introductions need to be made." Janine laughed. "Put us to work, Dominique."

"The doors open in fifteen minutes. Yesterday we ran out of coffee, and the shower water was ice cold by the time the last ones came. And we didn't have enough towels. I washed as many as I could last night."

They walked together into a room where clothes were scattered on the floor and wadded on top of other piles.

"This is *la pagaille*! I've never seen this room looking so … so muddled," Janine exclaimed.

Dominique smiled sheepishly. "I told you I needed you, Janine. I had too many other things to look after, and no one was watching in here."

"I'll be happy to clean up if you like," Ophélie volunteered. "Just tell me what to do."

"That would be great. Straighten up a little. When people come in to pick out clothes, encourage them to put things back. Your job isn't to be a maid. They can show a little respect. It's important that they don't just come for handouts, you understand?" Then he called back to her as he and Janine went to prepare the coffee. "And for those who can pay, it's five francs for everything but the coats. We charge ten for them."

"And if they can't pay ten?" Ophélie asked.

Dominique turned to her, smiled and shrugged. "What do you think? It's cold outside. We give it to them anyway."

She stood in the middle of the room and looked around her. Shelves lined every wall from the floor to the ceiling. Most were piled high with neatly folded clothes. But on some, shirts and sweaters had been pulled out hurriedly and other clothes had tumbled to the floor. Sweaters and coats lay in a crumpled heap, inside out where someone had tried them on and hastily removed them.

She had barely picked up a handful of fallen sweaters when the first man came into the room. "May I help you?" she stammered, suddenly feeling quite ill at ease.

He was young with tangled blond hair and crystal-blue eyes. He did not look French. "I need a coat," he mumbled, not meeting her eyes.

Indeed he was wearing only a tattered gray sweater with thin baggy pants and a pair of old boots.

"Coats are …" She looked around, feeling foolish. "Coats are right here."

He began sifting through them, taking one off its hanger, trying it on, then slowly, as if his fingers didn't work very well, hanging it up again. After a few moments he found a tan corduroy coat that wrapped around him comfortably. "Can I have this?" he asked, embarrassed.

"Of course," Ophélie answered. "Umm, normally it's ten francs for a coat, but …"

"I have it," he said quickly. He fished in his pocket and pulled out a ten-franc piece. "*Merci*," he said, with genuine warmth. "*Merci*."

Ophélie suddenly felt very glad that she had come.

She had not planned to stay the whole day, but how could she leave? The homeless had won her heart. Dominique brought back three *croque-monsieurs* from the little café-bar across the street for lunch. The toasted ham and cheese sandwiches filled up the room with a delicious smell that momentarily wiped out the stench of cigarettes and musty clothes. During the break between noon and two when the Red Cross was closed like most businesses in France, they ate, cleaned, and talked.

"Are you here every day?" Ophélie asked Dominique between bites.

"Oh, no. There's normally a staff of four people. And then all the volunteers, like Janine." He smiled at her. "*Exceptionellement*, the whole staff is gone this week. No, usually I make my rounds between the various shelters and the street. Eighty-five percent of my work takes place on the street."

Ophélie was both fascinated and repulsed by Dominique's stories. She and Janine listened for an hour as he recounted a typical day in the life of a street person.

"Our biggest problem right now is with hygiene. Many of those in the streets have dogs. These mangy beasts are their sole friends. But the dogs aren't vaccinated and carry all kinds of disease. The SDFs can barely feed themselves, yet they'll give up their meals to feed their dogs. They think of them as family! I've even heard some men talking about letting their dogs 'marry' and have pups, so they will be grandparents. It's a very twisted, fragile subculture."

Ophélie asked him the question she had wanted to ask all day. "Do you hand out money to people, the ones begging at the intersections?"

"I never give money. Ninety percent of the time it goes for booze. No, I offer to buy them a meal."

"But I can't get out of my car and take them somewhere to eat. Should I carry a *baguette* with me in the car and hand them a piece of bread at the red light?"

Dominique laughed. "You could try. If they are really hungry, they'll take it."

It was almost time to close, but several men were still picking through jeans and shirts. Janine went around the back to check the two outdoor showers and lock them up. Dominique came over to Ophélie. "I've got to go. Janine has the keys to lock everything up."

"Good-bye then, Dominique."

"Bye, Ophélie, and thanks for helping." He hesitated. "I was just thinking ... could we get a bite to eat sometime next week? Tuesday or Wednesday night, maybe?"

She narrowed her eyes. "Are you serious?"

He laughed. "Of course I am. Don't you like to eat?"

She felt her face turn red. "Sure. Sure ... um, maybe not Tuesday. I have another meeting. But Wednesday. *Pourquoi pas?* Yes, that would be fine."

"Good. I'll pick you up at your place. Seven thirty okay?" He stopped, grabbed his jacket, and added, "What's your address—oh, never mind. Janine can tell me."

"Don't ask Janine," she said too quickly. "I mean … it's easy: 30 rue des Cygnes, bâtiment C. It's the tallest apartment building on the Lez River. My name's on the door outside. Just ring and I'll come down."

"*Très bien.* See you Wednesday." He kissed her on the cheeks. "Yes, *à mercredi.*"

Ceb came out of the icy shower at the back of the Red Cross complex, clean but chilled to the bone. "Any more coffee?" he asked jovially, greeting Janine with a smile.

"Hey, Ceb. Sure. I just brewed some more. Let me lock up here, and I'll get you a cup. We'll be closing soon. Go on up and use the hair dryer if you want."

"*Merci*," he said, walking the thirty yards from the back of the building and letting himself inside. He passed the room with the clothes, heading to a small back closet where Janine kept a hair dryer. Suddenly, out of the corner of his eye, he saw something, *someone*, and stopped. "*Ce n'est pas vrai*," he whispered to himself. "It can't be." He stood there for a moment, letting his long hair tumble over his face as he dried it. Very cautiously, he watched as the woman in the next room helped an older man find a sweater.

Ophélie Duchemin.

He stood transfixed as she helped another SDF, putting several shirts into a plastic bag. She met the eyes of each forlorn man with a bright twinkle in her own. She called one by name, and for a moment, Ceb wished desperately for her to pronounce his own. To look him in the eyes and say, surprised yet thrilled, "Well, Samuel Cebrian, what brings you here? It is so, so good to see you."

But his was not a story ready to be discovered. So he quickly put away the hair dryer, feeling a tightening in his chest. Just the sight of Ophélie transported him back to his earliest memories. The house in Algiers, the wide sea, the beautiful woman who had held his head in her lap as he slept on a crowded ferry. How many times had Mama recounted their crossing the Mediterranean, their "escape from Algeria," as he thought of it, with Anne-Marie Duchemin by their side?

He saw Ophélie's fragile mother on that terrifying night and then he saw her later, at the orphanage, strong and striking with little Ophélie by her side. They were the same age, he and Ophélie, just six years old then. They had grown up, he in Montpellier, she in nearby Lodève, friends and pied-noirs. Those were the happy years. The brilliantly happy years, before tragedy had come.

He disappeared out the door, with his hair still damp and no coffee in his hands. He could not let her see him. Not beautiful Filie. He ran down the alleyway and out onto the wide boulevard, heart beating fast, clutching his mangled hand, which had begun to throb in the cold.

"Ophélie. You are here …" He could not tell if his heart was beating from fear or joy.

10

"You went to church on New Year's Day? That is not what I would have expected of you, dear," Mme Dufour said as she sliced the pork roast.

"I know, Mama." Janine chuckled. "Usually I'd have too big of a hangover. But the party was tame last night, and after all, it is Sunday."

"Janine, you are spending more and more time at that Protestant church. Don't you think that you're overdoing it a bit?"

"What do you mean, Mama?" Janine's voice was cross.

"Oh, nothing, dear. But it sounds like the place is full of pied-noirs and"—she lowered her voice—"Arabs. Such a strange mishmash of people."

"Mama! I can't believe you. You love Ophélie, and she's pied-noir!"

"Ophélie Duchemin is a dream, but she is not exactly pied-noir. She's half American, with that nice-looking M. Hoffmann for a father. And she only lived in Algeria for the first years of her life. She hasn't got that ... oh, you know ... that *mentalité*."

"What mentality, Mama?"

"Oh, they all just flock together and talk about the good old days in Algeria. It's just not the healthiest environment."

"Mama! Come on. There are all kinds of people at the church. Americans, English, French, Arabs. There are plenty of converted Catholics too, if you don't mind my saying it!"

"Exactly! Very strange. Who knows what it could be—maybe one of those dangerous cults that have come over from America. They sweep you in and then …" She lifted her eyes to the sky, leaned her head back, and dramatically placed the back of her hand against her forehead.

Mama should have been the actress, Janine thought.

Her mother continued, "And those Arabs. Goodness knows we have enough problems with them without inviting them to church! They're out to take over this country with their fanatical religion. A bunch of terrorists, Janine. Could be they're just spying out that Protestant church. You never know …"

"Mama, you're nuts."

Mme Dufour paid no attention to her daughter's remarks. She continued to slice the roast, arranging it on a platter and sticking bits of parsley in between each slice. "I think Ophélie Duchemin's a smart, nice girl, and I like M. and Mme Hoffmann as well. But you just never know! I'm warning you to be careful. Strange things come from America." She lowered her voice again. "And you know all the problems we've had with the Arabs. France is in this mess of unemployment because of them. They come over and have a pack of kids, drain the *allocations familiales.* No wonder the economy is in shambles. And as if that isn't enough, they smuggle in their uncles and their cousins from Algeria and Morocco, using one French identity card to treat the whole family's medical problems in France. For free! And who pays? Us! The hardworking French citizens. We pay!"

"Mama! That's enough for today. I'm a big girl—almost forty, remember?" Janine stood up and kissed her mother's forehead. "No one said I was going to join that church. And I'm plenty up-to-date on all of this country's problems." She glanced at her watch. "Listen, I've gotta go. I promised Simon I'd get to the theater at five for a quick run-through."

Mme Dufour set down her knife. "You mean you aren't staying for dinner?"

"Mama, I told you three days ago. I have a rehearsal."

"Oh, well," she said with an air of resignation. "Abandoned by my own daughter!"

"Good grief, Mama! Bye, Papa!" Janine called out to her father. She pecked her mother on the cheek. "See you later."

Mme Dufour shrugged. "*Ooh là.* Tell that dear Simon hello. Such a sweet man. Why he puts up with all of you in the cast, I'll never know."

"He knows talent when he sees it, Mama." Janine laughed. "*Au revoir.*"

Several young people from Oasis had decided to go skiing for the New Year's weekend. Two hours away, in the Cévennes mountains, a tiny ski station called Esperou had a man-made slope with man-made snow. It was a real letdown for an avid skier, but the perfect place for a day of fun if getting away with friends was the main objective.

Eric Hoffmann was a good skier. Very good. He'd skied in the Alps and the Pyrenees many times, and he had even skied once in Colorado when his grandfather had paid for a trip to the States. The slope at Esperou, for there was only one, was for beginners, but Eric tagged along for the fellowship. And to occupy his mind.

It infuriated him that Rislène had gone to Algeria when the country was in the midst of a civil war. Her family was always dragging her around, giving her no choice in the matter. *Typically Algerian*, he thought. He had grown up in Algeria. He knew the culture. But Rislène was French. She was nineteen, already *majeur*, as they said in France. She should be able to make her own decisions.

He pulled a ski cap over his short red hair and put on his skis. Last year he had been at Esperou with Oasis, and Rislène had put on skis for the first time in her life. How the rest of them had laughed as, skis pointing straight in front of her, she had slid down the hill screaming hysterically, as if the slope were perpendicular instead of just a gently undulating descent. When she tumbled into a pile at his feet, everyone, including Rislène, had roared with laughter until tears ran down their cheeks and mixed with the snow.

She was not a natural skier, they had agreed that day between bursts of hilarity. But at that moment he had decided that there was a lot more about Rislène he wanted to get to know. And he had.

Eric tried to imagine Rislène at her grandmother's house. She had described it so often. Grandmother Namani lived in one of the nicer suburbs of Algiers. Eric had driven through it with his parents years ago, when they lived there. Someday he would go back—perhaps he would go with Rislène to visit her grandmother. But not now. Not when daily reports from the country announced mutilated bodies from random bombings.

She'd been gone for a week. Only a few more days until she came home and they could talk about their future together, plan for it.

He'd protect her from her own family if he needed to. One thing was for certain. Nothing was going to happen to Rislène—nothing like what had happened to Samira in Lyon.

He took off down the crowded slope, laughing and chasing an Arab friend. For a few carefree hours he did not worry about Rislène. He only thought of her smile and her warm chocolate eyes.

Ophélie knew perfectly well why she had agreed to help with the meal at St. Vincent's soup kitchen. Dominique had called to see if by chance, since the high school had not started back yet, she could help. He had apologized profusely, explaining that most of the regular volunteers were just getting back from out of town.

"You and Janine have already gotten us out of a pinch at the Red Cross. Now I'm introducing you to another hot spot."

She had laughed and said yes, knowing that Janine had given him her number and feeling a bit guilty. For how many months had Janine been telling her about wonderful Dominique? And now Ophélie had a date with him.

If Janine knew about it, she gave no hint of it on that morning. They worked well together, kidding one another even as they filled the bowls of soup and offered them to the men and women.

Ophélie disappeared into the back kitchen to retrieve another large pot of soup, and when she came back out, a tall man was standing patiently next in line. He was well built, solid, with thick brown hair that had a hint of red in it. His face was covered with an unkempt beard, and the hair on his head receded, leaving a prominent fore-head that was marred by a long scar running from his left temple to the center of his forehead. There was no evidence of alcohol on his breath or in the eyes that met hers with a look of utter surprise.

When he took the bowl of soup, Ophélie noticed the man's large, strong hand. The other one, red and swollen, he held across his belly. For an instant the soft hazel eyes looked into her own, and she was struck by their extreme sadness. He mumbled "*Merci,*" his warm voice filled with kindness, then he quickly looked down at his soup and bread and disappeared into the crowded adjoining room.

Ophélie felt a weakness in her knees and a sick burning in her stomach. Surely it couldn't be …

She remembered the phone call three years ago. She had been grading papers, her feet pulled under her, listening to Handel's *Water Music* late in the evening. The phone had startled her so that she jerked, knocking papers on the floor as she rose to go into the kitchen to the phone.

"Sweethcart, how are you?" It was Mama's voice. A phone call at this late hour could only mean bad news.

"Fine, Mama. How are you and Moustafa?"

"Doing well, dear. I am …" Anne-Marie had paused. "I'm afraid we have some tragic news. Sam Cebrian and his family had an accident in the Alps. Their car crashed into the side of a mountain in a snowstorm. Annie and little Marion were killed. Samuel isn't expected to live.…"

Ophélie remembered the funeral, the two caskets, one so very small, and Samuel's obvious absence. He lay in a coma in a hospital in Grenoble. He came out of it weeks later, recovered, and then disappeared, swallowed up in a hole of anguish that no one in his family could reach. He had simply disappeared. No more Dr. Samuel Cebrian.

And now he had come back as a homeless man standing in a soup line. It had not been the face that she recognized but the voice and the kind, sad eyes.

Ophélie hesitated. Perhaps if she spoke to him, he would disappear again.

"Have you ever seen that man before, the guy with the scar and the messed-up hand?" she asked Janine.

"Oh, that's Ceb, a real sweetheart. He saved a kid's life last month, right here in front of us all. The child was choking to death, and he pulled out a Swiss army knife and performed a tracheotomy."

"Did he explain anything about himself?"

Janine laughed. "Not Ceb. He's been hanging around off and on for a few months now. He was at the Red Cross last week, the day you helped out. Goes there for his shower. Didn't you see him then?"

Ophélie shook her head. "No, no I didn't."

She continued dishing out the soup, glancing furtively into the other room where Ceb was seated, his back to her. When the last bowl had been filled, Ophélie removed her apron and excused herself. She took a bowl of soup for herself and cautiously sat down at the end of the long table. "Do you mind if I join you, Ceb?" she asked softly.

He shrugged.

"We're glad to have you here." Then she lowered her voice. "Samuel, there are so many people who care, who want to help."

He stopped eating, placed the spoon in the bowl, and reached over to touch her hand. "You won't say anything, will you, Filie?"

"Not if you don't want me to."

He smiled, relieved. "Thank you."

They ate in silence.

When their soup bowls were empty, Ophélie spoke again. "Samuel—Ceb, please. Can I help you?"

He regarded her with his clear hazel eyes. "Can you bring someone back from the dead?"

"You know I can't."

"Don't worry about me, Ophélie. I'm doing okay."

"Please." She squeezed his hand, then let go quickly. "Please, Samuel. Anything."

"How are Mama and Papa?"

"Good. Still out in Prades-le-Lez."

"And the rest of the family?"

She told him about Rachel's new baby, Catherine, and he cocked his head, listening. Suddenly he turned, his eyes darting across the room. "Sometimes I think I hear her, you know. Little Marion calling out to me. Sometimes."

"Yes." Ophélie bit her lip.

He shifted in his chair and stood up quickly. "I'll be going now, Ophélie. You remember. You won't say anything?"

"I remember." She watched him leave, then hurried after him. "Samuel, please. They are so worried. Can't I at least tell them you are well?"

"I'm not well, Ophélie. Seeing me like this would only hurt them worse."

"Will you come back here at least? Or to the Red Cross? I'll be there every Wednesday morning."

"I'll see you again sometime, Ophélie. Good-bye." He brushed her shoulder, then left the building.

She cried, standing alone in the hallway, wondering where a homeless man went. What kept him busy? His strong hands had saved another child's life, but he had not been able to save his own little girl. Yes, he was sick. Heartbroken, defeated. But he was here, in Montpellier. Perhaps with a lot of encouragement, Samuel "Ceb" Cebrian would yet go home.

"I hope you like Arab cuisine," Dominique said, guiding Ophélie through the narrow cobbled streets in Montpellier's ancient centre ville. "Here we are." He held the door open as Ophélie stepped inside an elegant restaurant.

She admired the rich tapestries hanging on the stone walls and the high vaulted ceilings. A waiter indicated the way to the dining hall, down a worn flight of stone steps.

"It's one of the oldest buildings in Montpellier," Dominique commented. "Have you been here before?"

"No, no. It's lovely." She turned to him skeptically. "It's a bit more extravagant than I expected."

He laughed, took her coat, and held the chair for her to be seated. "I didn't want you to think that all I know of Montpellier is squats and soup kitchens. Anyway, sometimes it does me good to get away from my work."

"Yes, I imagine so. And you certainly deserve it."

He shrugged. "That I don't know. But an evening with a charming woman does me good."

The spicy aromas coming from the kitchen reminded her of the times that Moustafa's mother had cooked for them. She relaxed, studying the man seated across the table. His thick black hair and beard were trimmed immaculately, and a faint hint of aftershave lingered in the air. He had the look of someone who was used to women staring at him—self-assured, the tiniest bit aloof, guarded, yet penetrating her thoughts with his soft brown eyes.

After the *entrée* was served, he raised a wineglass to toast her. "My newest and most promising volunteer." He set down the slender glass and studied her face.

She felt her cheeks reddening and was thankful for the dim light of the restaurant.

"So tell me something about yourself, Ophélie Duchemin. I'd love to hear."

She laughed and looked him in the eyes. "I'm a girl who is terrible at small talk. I can't seem to get the knack. At least that's what I've been told. But give me a book to analyze, a class to teach, a conversation to share with a close friend, and I'm at ease."

"Or a play to write," Dominique added with a smile.

"Yes, that too. I enjoy writing."

"You're very good at it."

"Thank you. What about you? What fills your hours when you aren't with the homeless?"

He looked past her, then slowly shook his head. "I can never get them out of my mind. They haunt me, Ophélie. Sometimes I think I've lost my life to them. It's hard to allow myself a simple extravagance like this dinner when I know what most of them are eating, or not eating. I run from the cruel streets to the posh offices of the government officials, pleading the cause of the homeless to stuffy businessmen who don't try to understand."

"Don't you ever want to leave it all?"

"Sometimes. But once you've lived on the streets, tasted the hopelessness, understood the rules of the road that run diametrically opposed to normal society, you can never truly get away from it."

"You've actually been one of them? A *sans domicile fixe*?"

"Years ago, yes, when I was in my early twenties. The streets were kinder then, but it changed my life."

"You got out. Surely others can too."

"Maybe. It's a long road back, and"—he set down his fork— "most of them don't have the support to come back into society."

"And if they did? If they had a family who cared?"

"Most of them are in the streets because their families have put them there. Maybe 5 percent of them have someone who cares. That may be too generous. Could be less."

"What about the guy called Ceb? What do you think of him?"

Dominique wrinkled his brow and stared at her oddly. "Ceb? Now he's a strange one. He's a smart man, was some kind of doctor, I think. Yes, maybe Ceb could leave the streets."

"I know him," Ophélie said softly.

Dominique looked up, surprised. "You know him? What do you mean?"

"He was a good friend of mine when I was growing up. We went to the same church, smoked our first cigarettes together." She blushed. "He has a family right here in Montpellier. They haven't seen him for three years. They'd do anything for him."

"You know Ceb," he said, shaking his head. "Tell me about him."

"He's a brilliant guy. Top of his class in the med school here ..." She cleared her throat. It hurt to think of the rest.

"He married Annie when he was twenty-seven; everybody loved her and was sure they were headed for success. She was a social worker with a hard job that she loved; he was an up-and-coming cardiovascular surgeon." Her eyes misted up. "There was an awful accident ..." She quickly told him the rest.

Dominique reached across the table and took her hand. "I'm sorry. I ... yes, it makes sense. He's heading home, Ophélie. He told me he's been in five other cities before coming here. Maybe we can help."

"The only problem is, he doesn't want me to talk with his family," Ophélie said. "I saw him today for the first time. He says he's dead. Samuel Cebrian is dead." She sighed heavily. "I'm sorry, Dominique. I didn't mean to bring it up. It was just so shocking to see him, so disturbing."

"Of course. Let me think about it."

They talked of other things, of their studies and of their families. "Have you ever been married?" he asked much later.

"No," she said too quickly. "No, I haven't. As soon as an eligible suitor finds out that I'm a practicing Protestant and a playwright, well ..." She laughed. "As I said, I'm not very good at small talk." She shrugged self-consciously.

"I'm in no hurry," he replied softly. "I'll look forward to finding out more."

She wanted to change the subject, but all she could think of was to ask, "And you? Have you ever been married?"

"Once. Divorced. Several other stormy relationships."

"Any children?"

He rubbed his finger around his mouth and grinned. "Hundreds of them."

She nodded. "I know what you mean. I feel the same about my students. You're trying to get your 'children' off the streets—I'm doing everything I can to be sure that mine never get there in the first place."

After dinner, Dominique walked Ophélie back to her apartment, and she wondered if he expected her to invite him in. That was not her style. Instead she simply said, "I had a wonderful evening, Dominique. *Merci.*"

"Yes, it was fun. Thanks for coming. You'll be hearing from me again, Ophélie Duchemin. As I said, I am in no hurry whatsoever." He leaned down and kissed her lightly on each cheek, brushing his hand through her hair. *"Bonsoir."* He left without another word.

For a long time Ophélie didn't turn on a light in her apartment but sat staring out at the skyline of Montpellier by night. She could barely make out the tall steeple of the church of St. Denis, reminding her of the restaurant near the church where she and Dominique had dined. Dominique was interesting, but it was not he who occupied her thoughts. It was Samuel Cebrian, the homeless man who had renamed himself Ceb.

"Filie! Come on!" He stood at the edge of the mountain, taunting her. "Don't say you're afraid!"

"I've told you, Sam, I'm not taking a black slope—it's dangerous."

"It's not dangerous, Filie. It's an adventure."

She rolled her eyes at him. His were dancing with mischief. "Everything is an adventure to you, Samuel Cebrian. You are the most reckless, fearless guy I know."

"Come on! I'll go right in front of you—just follow my tracks."

There were twelve of them at a small ski station in the Alps, youth from the church. Sam had organized the weekend outing, and all the girls had signed up—just to be with smart, handsome, gregarious Sam. They were all in love with Sam. And so was she.

She stood at the top of the slope and peered down. It looked practically perpendicular, and dotted with hundreds of moguls. "I'm not going down there, Sam."

"Of course you are! Follow me!"

And off he went. She watched him twist and turn around every mogul effortlessly. He skied halfway down the slope, stopped to turn back and yell up at her, "Come on, Filie! I'm waiting."

Slowly she pushed off the mountain, the chill of January whipping in her face. She needed to pick up speed—going too slow only made facing the moguls harder. But she was terrified, staring down the almost vertical slope. She kept her skis together, let them lift and fall over the huge bumps. Her heart was pumping in her ears. The slope was an icy mess.

On her third turn, her skis slipped, and she found herself hurtling down the slope sideways, poles flapping behind her, a scream stuck in her throat as she tried to slow down and right her balance.

"Filie!" Sam called, and then she hit another mogul and went flying, twisted, and landed smack on her side with a loud *wham*! She heard her arm crack as she fell onto it.

"Filie!"

She didn't want him to see her crying. Not Samuel. Not her best friend, the boy all the other girls were in love with. He was by her side, leaning over her, face in anguish. "Oh, Filie, I'm so sorry." His hand brushed the snow from her face, his soft hazel eyes filled with concern. He ripped off his ski jacket and wrapped it around her. "I'm going to get help. This should keep you warm."

That night at the chalet, with her arm in a cast, Ophélie watched him leading the youth in a lively discussion. How convincing he was! Their youth group had swelled and burgeoned with charismatic Samuel as one of the leaders.

He brought her a cup of hot chocolate and peered at her from those hazel eyes beneath straight brown bangs. "Will you ever forgive me, Filie?"

"You know I can't stay mad at you for long."

They stayed up half the night, as they had so many other times, talking about faith and life and love. The rest of the kids were playing a game of Monopoly. Somewhere around two a.m. Sam grinned at her, pecked her on the cheek, and said, "I love discussing things with you, Filie. You make me think. You slow me down."

Then he gave a boyish laugh, admitting, "It would never work between you and me, would it? You're too deep for me. You have another road to follow. You won't ever be a compliant wife, will you?" More laughter.

But she had cried herself to sleep that night, and it had nothing to do with the throbbing of the cracked bone in her arm. She kept repeating to herself, "Oh, Sam, I've tried to keep up with you. For all these years, I've tried. But you see, I can't. I just can't...."

Ophélie rocked back and forth, her knees drawn up to her chin. Oh, how those memories hurt. She wiped her eyes on her sleeve.

And then Sam had started his pursuit of medicine at Montpellier's renowned medical school. She had chosen Montpellier's Faculté des Lettres, and though they were both students in the same city, a distance sprang up between them. They made different friends, and in their rare conversations they began to disagree on many points that Ophélie considered essential.

The Cebrians' house in Prades-le-Lez was lit up with candles as Ophélie walked to the door with her mother and Moustafa and her two little sisters. She could hardly wait to step inside.

The house was brimming with people, neighbors, family, friends, other students. Ophélie found Eliane in the kitchen. She gave her a kiss on each cheek and asked, "Where's Sam?"

Eliane gave a shrug. "Oh, you know Sam, Ophélie. Busy, always busy, studying at the med school. But he'll be here in a little while. He promised me, and he knows better than to disappoint his mother!"

An hour later he found her sipping *vin chaud* and talking with a fellow student.

"Hey, Filie! Long time no see." His eyes were dancing. He took her face in his hands, then kissed her gently on each cheek. "You look great!"

"Sam!" She grinned at him, then pouted. "Some friend you are! I haven't seen you in months. Don't you even go to church anymore?"

"Oh, Filie! You know what med school's like. No time for anything else. But don't worry about me, Filie." He pecked her on the cheek again and gave her a quick hug. "I've missed you. No one else will dare tell me that I'm straying from the straight and narrow." He grinned again. "And I suppose you actually like your studies in literature?"

She stuck out her tongue at him.

Suddenly serious, he touched her arm. "Listen, Filie. I want you to meet someone. Wait here." He wended his way through the crowd, smiling, shaking hands with the men, kissing the women on the cheeks, and disappeared into another room.

A few minutes later he was back, holding the hand of a lovely blond-haired young woman. "This is Annie."

Annie gave a stiff smile. "Ophélie. *Enchantée.* Sam's told me so much about you." There was a look of suspicion in Annie's eyes. Then she turned to Samuel and fluffed his hair. "*Chéri*, Dr. Franck, the professor from Strasbourg, has arrived. He's looking for you." Her eyes were all full of love as she took Sam's hand and led him through the crowd.

Annie was beautiful, with brains and a heart ready to follow Samuel wherever his wild imagination led him. They married near the end of med school, and three years later had a baby daughter, Marion. Samuel worked impossible hours, pushing himself hard, fighting for a position in the competitive medical world. By the time he was in his early thirties he was *chef de clinique* and earning a wide reputation as a skilled cardiovascular surgeon. His papers were published in a few medical journals, his future looked promising, and always Annie was there beside him.

Had Ophélie been jealous of Annie? No. She had lost Samuel before Annie ever stepped into his life. And now she had found him again, in the strangest way. Samuel Cebrian, a damaged, hurting Samuel Cebrian, had stumbled back into her life. But Dominique said there was hope.

Dominique. Samuel.

Ophélie's head hurt. She crawled into bed, not even taking the time to undress, feeling completely drained. But she did not fall asleep for a long, long time.

❈

The sound of the empty kettle hitting the wall and crashing to the floor would have awakened the whole apartment building if anyone else lived there. But the place was abandoned, and Ceb was alone in his squat. He picked up the kettle, gripping the handle fiercely, his whole body shaking. He reached for a bottle stashed in a pile of dirty clothes, opened the top, and took a long chug of the rancid liquor.

"To hell with you, Ophélie Duchemin!" he yelled, grimacing as the liquid burned his throat. "How dare you come back into my life!" He kicked a rickety chair and sent it skidding across the floor.

He crumpled into a corner of the room, clutching his bottle and sobbing, "Filie. Filie. Help me." Then he cursed again and flung the bottle against the far wall, where it smashed and broke, the cheap liquor painting the wall in a dark burgundy stain. He watched it puddle up on the filthy linoleum as he drew a ragged blanket around himself. He began to shiver and vigorously rubbed his left hand over the right one, which throbbed with pain.

His parents were a short bus trip away. If he hurried, the last bus would still be running. He could knock on their door and walk back into their lives.

No, no, no! The alcohol had momentarily blurred his senses. He could never go back. He was a murderer!

So what was he doing in Montpellier? Deep down, he had known that someday someone would recognize him. Is that what he'd wanted? He was shaking again now. Sharp pain shot through his hand, through the amputated stubs of his fingers. He lived with pain every day. But he fought against panic when, like tonight, it became unbearable.

He got up and retrieved a worn leather bag from the drawer of a nightstand that he had recovered from the street. Inside were his pills. Pain pills. It was only iron discipline that kept him from taking a whole handful each day. Only because, as a doctor, he knew the outcome. But tonight he took two, ignoring the alcohol that was already in his stomach. To hell with it all. Anything to make this awful pain stop.

He crawled onto the mattress on the floor and pulled his two blankets on top. Still rubbing his hand, he began humming a tune, then singing it louder, anything to get his mind off the pain. It was the only way he survived. *"Il connaît nos défaillances, nos chutes de chaque jour. Sévère en Ses exigences, Il est riche en Son amour."*

He knows our weaknesses and our daily failings. He who requires everything of us, He whose love is so extravagant.

Gradually the pain subsided enough for Ceb to fall asleep.

11

Rislène let out a long sigh. Tomorrow she was going home! She was ready. The ten days in Algiers had been pleasant in many ways, seeing her grandmother, her aunts and uncles and cousins. Her grandmother had sheltered her from the realities of the war as much as possible. Still, so much had changed.

Not only did the Algerian people live in fear, but the countryside seemed closed and cold. More importantly, she had changed, and seeing the way that Islam was imprisoning these people saddened her greatly. The prayer times and washings and outward constraints that her family practiced were only superficial. No amount of ceremonial washing could cleanse their souls as Christ could.

She felt ashamed that she was too afraid to tell them about her faith, but she had tried before and been ridiculed. Now she held her tongue and counted the days. She knew her mother was doing the same. It was agony for Mother to be constantly under the supervision of Grandmother Namani. Ah, well, tomorrow they would both be free.

Grandmother was controlling, authoritative, but full of wisdom about life and how to live it. She epitomized the strong Arab hierarchy, with the husband's mother at the head. It was paradoxical, this country where women's rights were being continually limited, yet within the home they reigned. Their heads were covered but never their minds, and Grandmother knew what she was doing, building her family into a strong tribe. Rislène still enjoyed sitting at her feet and hearing her speak of days long gone.

They didn't speak of Rislène's differing faith. But several times Grandmother alluded to the good Muslim man that Rislène would someday marry. Rislène didn't argue.

Let Grandmother think what she wants. Soon it will be too late to stop me. Soon, she hoped, she would be engaged to a tall redhead with bright-green eyes.

"Quickly now, Nazira! Get her purse," Grandmother Namani barked. "Rislène and your mother will be back from the baths soon. Hurry!"

Nazira opened Rislène's purse, dumping the contents on the kitchen table. Out came the passport, the French ID card, the newly acquired French driver's license, the student card from her *lycée*. She handed them to Grandmother, who put the passport and ID card to the side and burned the other papers in the sink, never taking her eyes off the papers until they had curled into a fine black ash.

Ah! There it was, hidden in between two other pictures of classmates. A photo of the red-haired boy. Nazira showed it to Grandmother. "This is the Christian boy she loves."

"Foolish girl! She will forget him soon enough!" Grandmother said, examining the photograph.

Nazira's father came into the kitchen and took the passport and ID. He observed the ashes and nodded approvingly. "You understand your role, Nazira," he said gruffly. "Never let her out of your sight, you understand? Not until we can arrange for the rest of the details."

"I understand, Father. It will be as you and Grandmother wish." She could not tell them that staying in Algeria with Rislène frightened her. Not because of Rislène. No, her sister was getting what she deserved. But the war scared her to death. No one was safe, no matter what Grandmother said. She had seen the city. She had heard the daily reports. She drew her scarf tightly around her face, as if to hide from what was coming upon her.

And there was something else that maddened her. Why did Rislène matter so much? Why didn't they reward Nazira for her devotion to Islam?

I'm a good Muslim! I obey the will of Allah.

Nazira would find a way to gain the approval of her grandmother and her father. To get their eyes off Rislène and onto her.

"*Inshallah,*" she whispered. "*Inshallah.*"

They laughed together happily, walking back from their weekly trip to the *hammam*, the sauna baths where the women congregated. As their one social outing of the week, many women dressed lavishly, wearing gold jewelry and fine dresses to impress their neighbors. The elaborate rituals at the baths lasted half the day. Today was the first time that Rislène and her mother had been left alone together.

"Mother, aren't you happy to be going home?"

"Yes, my dear. Yes. But ..." She slowed her pace and caught Rislène's arm. "You must be more careful with the church. Nazira has told your father about a young man you are seeing. Is it true?"

Rislène lowered her eyes and did not speak, the happy mood broken.

"Rislène, your father is furious. Please be careful. I'll talk to Mme Hoffmann again if you wish. I want to help, but there's nothing I can do if he decides to—"

"Oh, Mother! Why does it have to be so complicated? Father and I used to be so close. But it all changed when I became a woman— you know what I mean. Everything is regulated. We are covered up and whisked into the house. It's a prison! Why can't I do what I want, like other girls my age?"

"Shh. Rislène. We'll talk again when we're home. You must understand. You may think like a French woman, but to your father you will always be Algerian and a Muslim."

Grandmother's house came into view. Rislène nodded and interlocked her arm with her mother's. "We'll talk more, Mother. For now, all I want is to go home!"

The news came like a stab in the back. Rislène screamed, lurched at her father, and slapped Nazira hard across the face.

"You can't do this! You can't! You are barbarians. All of you!" She ran to her mother. "Did you know too? What was all your talk about going home? Did you know their plan?"

"No, Rislène, I swear it!" Her mother was weeping loudly, reaching out to her daughter.

"It's for your own good!" Father yelled, holding her arms and shaking her.

"Liar!" Rislène spat. "You schemed with Grandmother. You brought me here to kidnap me—you planned it all along. I hate you!" She tried to wrestle free of his grip, but he held her almost fiercely.

"We aren't the traitors! It's you, Rislène, who have forced us to this." Father's voice was loud, angry. "Do you think we will let you ruin the family honor by converting to Christianity? You're better off here in Algeria, where you will not be tempted by false gods!"

She looked at him in disbelief. "Better off here! You don't care that this country is full of lunatics. You don't care if I'm murdered! Why don't you kill me now? Or I'll do it myself."

Father slapped her across the face. "You'll stay here until we can find a suitable man for you to marry. Once that happens, if he so wishes, there will always be room for you in France."

"Youssef! Please. Don't do this. Please, Youssef!" her mother pleaded.

Her father screamed at his wife. "Silence! Haven't you already done enough harm? It is you who raised her wrong, pitiful woman! Raised her to think too broadly!"

Rislène was used to these violent reproaches between her parents. Everyone knew that the Koran taught that a girl who argued with her father had been spoiled by her mother.

"Rislène will marry an Algerian! She will never marry a Frenchman, and if she even thinks of marrying a Christian—" He tore the photograph of Eric into shreds before Rislène's eyes. "You will not ruin the family name! You will obey your father!"

He left the room, slamming the door behind him, while Rislène's mother whimpered miserably with her daughter. Rislène looked at her and felt she would throw up. Her mother, large and ample under her bright robes. Her mother, effaced and fearful in front of her husband and mother-in-law. Such it had always been and always would be. Her sole responsibility was to raise her children, and now one was straying miserably.

Her mother had six children, the first three sons. Producing boys first and thus preserving the family's honor was her one good deed in the eyes of Grandmother Namani.

Rislène thought of her uncle Hamid's first wife, Inas, the mother of three girls. In the Family Code, it was stipulated that her husband could leave her for a younger woman who could give him sons. He had done just that, forcing Inas out of her apartment. She had had no choice but to take her three daughters to her parents' small apartment and beg them to take her in.

Father came back into the room, ignoring the pleading eyes of his wife. "You stay out of it!" he said gruffly to her. "It's not your decision. It has already been decided."

Rislène gazed at her father through blurred eyes. It was a nightmare. How had she not seen it? But it had all happened so quickly. If only she had had time to talk with Eric or Ophélie or Mme Hoffmann, they would have warned her not to go to Algeria. They would have told her how dangerous it could be.

Now she was stuck. Kidnapped by her own family, with Nazira watching her every move. And even if she could get away, where could she go? She had nothing to prove that she was born and raised in France.

She began to shake violently. Grandmother knew how to keep her imprisoned. There was no escape.

"Mother!" Rislène screamed. "Mother, help me! Don't let them do it!" She threw herself into her mother's arms and sobbed.

A few minutes later, Grandmother gave her a cup of tisane. "Drink this, Rislène. It will calm you."

"I don't want to be calm!" she yelled, knocking over the teacup. The hot liquid burned her hand as the cup splintered on the tile floor.

Unperturbed, her grandmother took another teacup and filled it with steaming brew. "Drink it now!" she said firmly.

The herbal tea went down easily. Gradually Rislène's screams and sobs turned into a soft whimper as she watched her father, mother, and youngest sister leave the house with their luggage.

"Help me!" she cried feebly again and again until whatever drug Grandmother had put in the tisane took over, and she was led into a bedroom. She collapsed on the cot, still mumbling, "Help me. Oh God, help me."

Somewhere around five a.m. a loud, muffled sound broke the stillness outside. Rislène pulled herself awake, feeling groggy and confused. Where was she? Then she remembered, and immediately the weight of all the Muslim laws descended upon her. Always before, she had considered them as strange laws that didn't affect her. She lived in France, and her father was not a particularly devout man. How could she have been so blind, so stupid as to ignore his building rage? Not to mention Nazira's ever-present eyes? Why had she not been more careful? She sank onto her cot, every limb feeling so extremely heavy.

So she was to be condemned to the life of an Algerian woman. She thought of her three older brothers. They had been spoiled, even in France. They had always had the best rooms. They had the liberty to stay out late and sleep in, something no girl was allowed. Slavery. That was the future promised to an Algerian woman.

At least Mother had never lived in Grandmother's house for more than two months at a time. And at least Mother had married for love! Yes, Father could be cruel, at times even violent, but he loved his wife. The Family Code ordered that this never be shown in public. And no arguments between women should bother the ears of the men, even if it was between his wife and his mother. That was not a man's business! How could a man say that his wife was right and his mother wrong? Impossible! She had seen her father on several occasions help her mother at their home in Montpellier. But never here in Algeria. A wife should not think she occupied any important part in her husband's life. It simply was not done.

That was what Rislène hated about her culture. Nothing was said, it was simply understood. The silence shouted unwritten rules from every Algerian home. *It is not done that way.* The terrible silence and oppression of the Algerian women made her tremble. And now she was one of them.

Rislène remembered hearing whispers about an older cousin who was married to an abusive man. But when the cousin fled with her small child to her parents' house, they refused to let her in. "A good wife always stays by her husband, no matter what happens." That was her parents' reply.

The Algerian law had been revised in 1984 and now imposed stricter rules on women than they had previously known, making women's rights a backward-moving agenda. Although in the market-place there was a so-called equality between men and women, in the family, women were not allowed to leave the house alone.

If a young woman did not marry, it was a terrible disgrace to the family. A professional woman who wanted to live independently was often rebuked, considered a woman of low morals.

Polygamy, though restricted by law, was not forbidden; one of Mother's Algerian friends had been forced to let her husband take a second wife. She could have refused, because the law insisted that the first wife must give her accord, but at fifty years old with no skills and barely able to read, where could she go if her husband divorced her?

There were many marriages between French and Algerians, but most were between French women and Algerian men. The children coming from these mixed marriages were considered Muslim and therefore belonged to the *oumma*—the vast Islamic community of the world. So when one of these mixed marriages broke up, the Muslim father often sought revenge, wanting to raise his children within the Muslim family. How many times had Rislène heard whispers of children being taken from France to Algeria, "held" there by not only the Muslim father but also by the whole community.

All the most frightening stories came back to her, smothering her, making her shiver inwardly as Nazira woke and Grandmother called from outside the barred door, "Time for prayer, girls."

Prayer. Forced prayer. Appearances mattered more than reality, but everyone knew the reality too. It was like what Jesus said in the Bible, Rislène thought. The outside of the vase was clean and shiny, but everything inside was rotten and smelly. Did Islam, could Islam clean the inside of the vase? Could it offer freedom? *No!* she told herself. All it offered was a gleaming exterior and a forced bending to a set of rules. And a silence that screamed out to a world that was too deaf to hear.

The entire village was a pile of smoldering ashes and fumes of burning flesh. All of the inhabitants of the tiny town an hour south of Algiers had been slain. The men had been decapitated, and several of the women's bodies hung from the roof of a burnt-out building. The children's bodies … El Amin could not look at the pitifully contorted faces without seeing his own children there. His jaw was set and firm, his eyes steely hard. But his stomach churned, a mixture of nausea and bubbling anger.

This was not the work of the fractured FIS. This latest atrocity had the handprints of the government all over it. The annihilation of a whole village. It was not his men who had done this. Or perhaps it was.…

Who would dare report it, and to whom would their cry go? Reporters, especially foreign ones, were targeted for murder. Several had recently lost their lives. When the word got out about this latest atrocity, as it eventually would, his men would be blamed. But it really didn't matter. The power play would continue. Already every Algerian citizen was quaking in his boots. There was no rhyme nor reason. Whole families were massacred. And the poor, terrified population swore allegiance to whoever threatened the loudest at the time.

El Amin swallowed hard, his nostrils flaring. He walked to the woods, rummaging through the trees and decaying leaves for other bodies. At least that was what he appeared to be doing. He had to get away from the sickening smell.

"Sir!" One of his men ran up beside him, his eyes shining with excitement. "No one left, sir!" He was barely more than a boy, this young activist.

"Yes, I know." El Amin's voice betrayed no emotion.

"Shall I help you look for other bodies?"

"No, return with the others. I'll be there shortly."

It was a game to his young charge: the civil war, the terrorism, the gruesome killings. El Amin remembered when he had felt the same way. When murder had brought a rush of adrenaline.

Now he felt only repulsion and anger. He was exhausted. That was all. Tomorrow the butchery would make sense again. *Inshallah*. Was that not why he and his men fought this civil war? Allah's will was that Algeria be a fundamentalist Islamic state! His superiors had stated not long ago, "Either it will be an Islamic state, or we shall die!"

He remembered as a child the Western dress worn by many of the younger women. Now none dared leave the house without being covered from head to foot.

Ah, Jala, you are safe. And the children. Safe for now.

His oldest child was a daughter. At the time of her birth, it had been a terrible shame and shock to his young pride. Now at twelve, Fatima was beginning to bud, and her beautiful black eyes broke her father's heart. No one could see it in his rigid gaze, but at night El Amin sometimes woke in a sweat. Young girls no older than Fatima were being kidnapped and taken to the militants' mountain hideouts. He had watched his men take part in gang rapes, heard the screams, seen the terror in the young girls' eyes, which eventually was replaced by a glazed, death-like stupor. Many did die. And at night he dreamed that Fatima was one of them.

And always, all the blame fell on him, on his men. Yes, they committed barbaric crimes in the name of a *jihad*, but the government's security forces were responsible for equally heinous crimes in the name of combating fanatical terrorism. Thousands of men had disappeared into Algerian prisons for unnamed political reasons. They would never have a trial. Many were tortured and killed. And no one was ever sure what happened to them.

His men were not the only terrorists in this war, thought El Amin, as he turned back to the lifeless village. He did not stop to inspect the carnage. He called his men to follow, and he left with the stench of burning flesh still in his nostrils.

12

Ever since his chance meeting with Ophélie the week before, Ceb lived his days in a sort of nervous excitement. On his return to Montpellier, deep down he had known that sooner or later someone would recognize him. That it had been Ophélie, he surmised now, was more of a blessing than a curse. If there was one person in all the world he trusted to keep her word, it was Ophélie Duchemin.

Beautiful Filie! Night after night he relived his adolescence. It was a relief to jump far back in his life, skipping over the tragedy, delighting in his teenage memories as if nothing had come between that time and the present, as if it were all one smooth flowing river, continuing purposefully on its course downstream.

Filie. Dear friend.

They had shared so much, and the bond had never been broken in all their teenage years by any type of physical intimacy. It had always been for him something better, purer in all its platonic pleasure.

"Anyway," Ophélie liked to say, "I want to be friends, I mean really great friends, with the man I marry." And then she had laughed that soft, singing laugh that sometimes made goose bumps run down his arms.

When he had started med school, she had warned him, in her clear, frank way, not to forget his faith. "You're too smart to be left on your own," she had teased. "You need God to give you that restraining liberty...."

But he had ignored Ophélie Duchemin and every other voice of wisdom from his youth. Action was Samuel's favorite game, and at med school he kept himself in perpetual motion. Classes, studies, debates, and Annie. He had fallen for her and fallen hard. In his third year, they decided to live together. Annie made him laugh. She was on the same fast track as he was, smart, determined, and beautiful. And yet often at night, as she fell asleep in his arms, he wondered, *Are you my friend?* And he never really dared to let her see into his soul.

He pulled himself to his feet, cursing the memories that now overshadowed recollections of a carefree adolescence. If he let himself think of these things, of Annie and med school and the faster and faster moving track that they raced on, exhausted and yet filled up with thinking that this was the right one, well then, the track would eventually crash into the side of a snow-covered mountain.

He ran his hand over his chapped face, feeling suddenly dizzy. He needed something. A drink? No! More pain pills? Yes, maybe it was that. His hand had begun to throb miserably.

No! Not pills. He sank back onto the mattress and pronounced the word, "Filie." If only he had a phone in this godforsaken squat, he would dial her number and listen to her sweet voice. What Ceb needed was a friend.

"Have you heard the news, M. Dominique? I'm a grandpappy!"

"*Félicitations, Jean-Marc!*" Dominique said, patting the homeless man on the back.

"Well, don't ya wanna see the grandbabies?" His red-tinged eyes shone with pride.

"Of course I do. Wouldn't miss it for the world."

"No more sleeping on a park bench for me, M. Dominique. I've found a squat. And just in time! Got me a place for Lassie and the babies." His smile revealed a row of stained, uneven teeth.

Dominique followed the feeble man through the back alleys of centre ville that he knew so well and inside an abandoned squat. In the corner a thin dog with drooping eyes and matted black hair lay on a pile of bloodstained sheets. Seeing Jean-Marc approach, she wagged her tail weakly.

"There you are, *ma belle*. Papy's come to help you now. And look here. I've brought M. Dominique to see the babies. Your first visitor."

Dominique knelt beside the mutt and watched five tiny, fuzzy heads pulling voraciously at the mother's teats. "A fine brood, Jean-Marc," he whispered. "I know you're proud."

"You bet I'm proud! Me and Antoine, we worked it all out months ago. Matched up our kids, planned the wedding and all. Didn't take no time at all for the five grandbabies to get here." He squatted down beside the dog. "Lassie, she's a fine dog." He looked over at Dominique. "I hate to ask you this, in front of her and everything, but I don't have much more food for Lassie these days. An' now with the babies ..."

Dominique put a hand on Jean-Marc's shoulder. "*Ne t'en fais pas, mon ami*. We'll find something for Lassie. Don't you worry. Have you got any warm water to clean her up a bit?"

"Oh, sure. I'll heat up my burner over there. Got me a couple bottles of good water at Monoprix. Yessir. I was just gonna do it,

M. Dominique." He scratched his chin. "You wouldn't be able to stay and help me a little, would you? I know how busy you are and all, but—" He giggled like a schoolboy. "I haven't ever had the pleasure before of delivering babies!"

Thirty minutes later Dominique had finished attending to Lassie and the pups. He took the bloody sheets with him, stuffing them into a plastic bag. "You come by the foyer tonight and pick up some clean ones, Jean-Marc," he advised, as he left the grizzly man in his squat.

Lassie, he thought sadly. There was nothing in the half-starved black mutt that even remotely resembled the elegant collie for which she was named. Dominique wondered if Jean-Marc's Lassie would survive long with those five pups. He brought out a small spiral notebook and jotted down *Food for Lassie,* then tucked it back into his coat pocket.

He glanced at his watch. Thirty minutes until the appointment with the mayor's adjunct to talk about getting a van to help with the homeless. He wondered if Ceb was home. His squat was only a half block away. If Ceb really had been a surgeon, as Ophélie said, maybe he'd have an idea about teaching the SDFs a little canine hygiene. It was worth a try.

Ophélie Duchemin had not been far from his thoughts since their meal together last week. An exceptional woman, classy, with a good dose of humility mixed in. He liked her frank honesty and her penetrating questions. They had not talked politics or religion, he thought with a chuckle. But he had the feeling that no subject was taboo with Ophélie, if she found it mattered to someone.

He had not called her back. No need to rush, he reminded himself a half dozen times throughout the week. And Janine seemed to think that Ophélie would be helping out at the Red Cross on Wednesday mornings. Tomorrow. He could manage to drop by at some point.

The squat was on the second floor of the shell of an apartment building. Ceb's was the only intact room in the whole place. Dominique knocked on the door.

"Who is it?"

"Dominique."

The homeless man opened the door.

"Sorry to bother you, Ceb. Have you heard the news about Jean-Marc's dog?"

Ceb's face broke into a smile under his crusty beard. "Did she have her pups?"

"*Oui*. Five of them. I just went by." He motioned down to the soiled sheets in the plastic bag he was holding.

"Dog doing all right?" Ceb asked, his expression clouding over.

"She's pretty thin. I'll see what I can do. We don't stock many cans of dog food at the Red Cross, but when any comes in, it's gone in a flash."

Ceb went over to a makeshift nightstand and opened a drawer. "Here," he said, handing Dominique several coins. "I know I can trust you. Use this to get some stuff for that dog. Don't want her dying or anything, or any of those pups. It's all Jean-Marc has."

Dominique regarded Ceb. "You don't want to get the food for him yourself?"

"*Non*. It's best for him not to know I've got cash."

Dominique nodded. "I understand." He licked his lips. "Listen, Ceb. You seem to have some good medical sense. I was wondering what you'd think about talking to the men about their dogs. It's getting to be a bad problem. Could you say anything to them? Any precautions?"

Ceb raised his eyes and met Dominique's. Ceb's were soft hazel, sad with a hint of arrogance behind the sorrow. It had taken all of Dominique's street smarts to know how to approach these SDFs, to show them he had something to offer without coming across as condescending. He hoped Ceb could tell he was sincere.

Ceb shrugged. "You're right. It's a problem. I don't know. I can give vaccinations, show them a thing or two. But I'm no vet." He stared out the window. "You're the one with the connections, Dominique. If you could find a vet with some outdated vaccine—still usable, you know—I'd be glad to give the shots."

"Thanks, Ceb. I'll let you know what I find."

"Oh, and Dominique." He stopped the mediator before he got to the door. "If you find any free medicine for people, you know, I could help there, too."

On an impulse, Dominique held out his hand. Ceb grasped it hesitantly. "Thanks."

Eliane Cebrian rocked the baby back and forth, back and forth, listening to the sound of the chair's wooden blades on the linoleum floor. Little Catherine slept peacefully in her arms. Eliane closed her eyes, unable to gaze at the soft, cherubic face without seeing the face of another baby there. Her daughter had thought that it would do her good to help with the little one, and Eliane had readily agreed. On Tuesdays and Thursdays, while Rachel worked, Eliane cared for baby Catherine.

But after only two days of babysitting, Eliane was almost certain that it was a mistake. Not that she was too old to care for a baby. No, little Catherine took long naps and cried infrequently. But holding a tiny baby girl in her arms did not erase the memories of the other baby girl she had held. On the contrary, it seemed only to accentuate the pain.

Marion. Her first grandchild. Samuel's daughter. How she missed that little girl, her exuberant squeals, her grown-up vocabulary and teasing mind. So like Samuel when he was a child. The pain in Eliane's chest seemed almost physical, tightening, tightening. She breathed slowly. *Angoisse*, the doctor had assured her. Her heart was fine, but deep heartache that manifested itself as a physical pain was normal after a terrible shock.

Annie and little Marion killed in an automobile accident. Samuel in a coma. Samuel fighting for life. Samuel gone.

Lord, please, stop these thoughts!

During the first year after the accident, Eliane had called Annie's parents regularly. Their pain was even greater than hers, she had reasoned. She had tried to do what was right. But all they shared between them were memories of what had been. Eventually she stopped calling, and the only communication between them now was a superficial card offering *Meilleurs Voeux* for the New Year. She had sent such a card off yesterday, dreading the last sentence that she had penned. *Still no word from Samuel. We pray that he is safe and well....*

Did God even hear her anguished prayers anymore? She had begun to wonder. A long sigh escaped her lips. You just never knew what turns life would take, and grief was such a long process. She often wondered, with a stabbing guilt, if it would not be easier to go on with life if she just knew that Sam were dead. Instead she lived with an aching hope that someday, somehow …

Baby Catherine stirred in her arms, and Eliane stood slowly, carrying her to the cradle and carefully placing her on her side, with several small blankets rolled up behind her to keep the baby from sleeping on her back. Special instructions from Rachel. Things were always changing, Eliane thought with a sad smile. She remembered her pediatrician's adamant advice to have the babies sleep on their tummies. That was almost forty years ago.

Ah, yes, times had changed. Eliane sat down in the rocker and no longer tried to suppress the tears that rolled gently down her lined face. She dabbed them with a cloth diaper that she had draped over her shoulder. Samuel. Her firstborn. He had gotten too much too soon. Everything was fast for Samuel. And it all came so easily. Studies, sports, friendships, awards. Why was it that parents pushed their firstborns so? Had it been her fault? Rémi's? Of course they were proud of his accomplishments, but they had tried to teach him balance and wisdom.

I think some children are just born reckless. It's their destiny to make their mothers prematurely gray. Gabriella had written that once, referring to her own eldest son. Never had a word been more truly spoken. Samuel was born reckless, and it had caught up with him three years ago in the Alps. She thought of him in the hospital bed in Grenoble, a mass of bandages, lying in a coma. She had been the one to see his eyes flicker open, she the one to answer his faint question—"Annie? Marion?"—with a slow shake of the head. She the one to hold his left hand when the doctor showed him the mangled right one.

Oh, but motherhood was cruel! And now she was the one who day after day stared aimlessly out her window in the spacious villa in Prades-le-Lez, imagining that one day Samuel would come trotting across the field behind the house, that boyish grin on his face, adventure shining in his eyes. And while she watched, she felt the fervent faith that had walked her through so many other trials drying up in her soul. Even Rémi could not get to her.

They all thought it would bring me back to life to hold this baby. They didn't say it, but they thought this little girl could replace Marion. But, Lord, You give us the capacity to expand our hearts to love more and more people. And when You take one away, she can never be replaced. The part of my heart that loved Marion and Annie and my Samuel, it is still open and raw. Nothing will fill it, Lord. Nothing this side of heaven.

She stood again and, holding the railing of the cradle, watched through blurred eyes the rise and fall of Catherine's tiny chest.

When the alarm clock buzzed at seven forty-five, Ophélie turned it off and pulled a pillow over her head. Then she remembered. The Red Cross. Ugh. What on earth had made her give up her one morning to sleep in? Street people, that was what. Samuel. Dominique. Just thinking of the two names made her head ache.

She pulled on a pair of black leggings and a thick green turtle-neck that hung halfway to her knees. She turned her head upside down and brushed her hair vigorously, then threw it back behind and secured it in a heavy barrette. She washed her face, stared at it in the mirror, and laughed. "You hypocrite! You're going to put on makeup on your day off just because you might see Dominique. Or Sam …"

Life had been easier a few weeks ago. Or had it? Before Ceb and Dominique, there had been Rislène. *I wonder when she gets back from Algeria*, she thought with a frown. School had started last Thursday with no sign of her student. Dear Eric was terribly worried, and so were Papa and Bri.

And so am I.

Poor Rislène, so young in her Christian faith and now, smothered by her family's faith. Just like Bachir all those years ago.

As Ophélie was waiting for the elevator to come to her floor, Mme Ploussard peeked out of the door across the hall. "*Bonjour, Ophélie!* Leaving so early this morning! My goodness. No school on Wednesdays. Whatever gets you up so early?"

Ophélie took a deep breath and smiled at her neighbor. "Homeless people, Mme Ploussard. I've gotten rid of the Arab girl, and now, wouldn't you know it, I've got a string of homeless people to look after. But don't worry! *Ne t'en fais pas!* I won't bring them back here." The elevator door opened, and as Ophélie stepped inside, she turned and added, "Yet."

She had just enough time to see the startled expression on Mme Ploussard's face before the doors closed and the elevator started its downward descent.

When she walked into the building, one look from Janine told her that her friend knew all about her date last week with Dominique.

"So, I convinced you after all to give up your day off," she quipped, adding, "or perhaps it wasn't me at all."

"Hey, Janine, I'm sorry. I didn't know what to say to him."

Janine flashed Ophélie her best stage smile, batting her eyes. "Never mind," she said dramatically. "I'll get over it. Just promise me you'll invite me to the wedding."

"Silly girl!" Ophélie scolded, and they both laughed. Then she sobered. "Look, Janine, I won't come again if it bothers you."

"What! And turn down a much-needed volunteer? Look, I've been helping out Dominique and company for almost a year now. If he had wanted to ask me out, he would have gotten around to it by now. I'm not dumb...." She smiled. "Just hanging on to hope."

At the midmorning coffee break, Dominique stopped in to chat. "Hey, girls!" he greeted them enthusiastically. "Good to see you both." He kissed them both on the cheeks, but his eyes lingered on Ophélie.

He glanced down at his spiral notebook, filled with his scribbled penmanship. "Janine, I talked with the mayor's adjunct earlier today. Sounds like we may get that minivan to do rounds at night, hand out soup, allow us to penetrate the deepest parts of the city."

"That's great, Dominique," Janine replied. "I'm happy for you."

He laughed. "Well, nothing's in the bag yet. Lots of red tape first."

After fifteen minutes of chatting, he rose. "Gotta go. I have a special delivery to make." He picked up a plastic sack filled with cans.

Ophélie peered into the bag. "Dog food?"

"Yes, indeed! Dog food for Lassie and her pups. Good ol' Jean-Marc has become a grandpappy!"

Ophélie looked bewildered for a moment, then said, "Ah, yes. I remember what you told me on my first visit."

Janine winked. "Just another quirk of the homeless culture. Poignant and sweet."

Ceb waited until Ophélie came out of the Red Cross building and stepped onto Boulevard Henri IV. "Hello, Filie," he said softly.

She looked around quickly and didn't seem to recognize him under his bright-red wool hat. Then her face broke into a relieved smile. "It had to be you," she confided. "No one else has ever called me that."

Ceb nodded. *"I'm calling you Filie whether you like it or not,"* he had said to her so long ago. *"You may have the name of Shakespeare's tragic heroine, but I won't let you take life too seriously."*

They walked automatically into the Jardin des Plantes, and it almost seemed natural.

"I'm really glad to see you again, Samuel." She scrunched up her nose. "Do you want me to call you Ceb?"

"Yeah, that would be good," he mumbled.

"Would you like to get a bite to eat?" she asked awkwardly. "I'd be glad to buy you a sandwich."

"No, thanks. I'm fine." His hands were buried in his pockets.

He knew she didn't know what to say, and no words came to his mind. They wound through the park in silence. It was enough. Someone to walk with, someone beside him. He breathed in the frosty air, closing his eyes briefly. Something felt so right.

They made a circle and came back around to the front gates. "I guess I'll be going now," she said softly.

He looked down at her, met her eyes, and smiled warmly. "Thank you, Filie."

She stood on her tiptoes and kissed him softly on each cheek, brushing his unkempt beard with her lips. "*A bientôt, Ceb.* I'll see you soon."

He watched her leave, touched his cheeks, and felt a warm flood of human affection piercing him way down inside. Just a touch. The touch of another human being. It was too much, too close, threatening, soothing, painful. *Filie,* he thought as he turned back into the park. *My friend.*

13

Eric sat on the faded couch in his parents' house, biting his lip, turning his hands over in his lap. He had stopped by for lunch, and now that the food had been consumed, it was time to talk.

His mother called from the kitchen. "Eric, would you like some coffee?"

"Sure, Mama," he answered unenthusiastically. Then, shaking his head, he said slowly, "Papa, we've got to do something. She should have been back last week. She's missing classes. You've got to admit that something is wrong."

His father sighed and nodded.

He's trying to keep cool so I won't worry, Eric thought. *But he's really worried too.*

"Eric, I know you've been counting the days for Rislène's return. I won't say I'm not alarmed. I am. On the other hand, Ramadan will be starting up soon, and you never know. Maybe the Namanis decided to stay in Algeria for their holy month."

"So what are you suggesting, Papa? That we do nothing? You know as well as I do that they're holding her there. Her family took her to Algeria to keep her there. And in the middle of a civil war. It's insane!"

Gabriella brought in cups of steaming coffee and set them on the low table in front of the couch. Eric watched his parents, saw the worry lines on their faces, the tears just behind his mother's eyes. It frightened him to see their concern. His father was a man of intellect and reason. He also had an uncommon amount of knowledge of the Muslim world.

Papa knows it's hopeless.

"Sweetheart, I don't think your father means that we will do nothing. But you know the customs. We must proceed slowly, carefully."

Yes, they were thinking of the Muslim customs, but he knew they were also thinking of Samira, the girl who had tried to kill herself. Rislène was tough and realistic, he told himself. *Then why in the heck did she agree to go to Algeria?* He rubbed his forehead with his long fingers, then ran them through his short, cropped hair.

"Okay, then. Tell me what I'm supposed to do," he said defensively.

"Get the Oasis group together for prayer. Let them know the situation. I'll go by the Namanis' apartment, just to see ..." His mother looked worriedly at his father.

"Yes, it's time for you to go for a visit, to see if anyone is home." David stood and walked over to his son, placed a hand on his shoulder. "Please don't think I'm not concerned, Eric. It's just that there are many things at stake. After your mother checks on the Namanis' apartment, I'll write to Abdul and Madira. It's not hopeless. Think of all the impossible things we've seen God do in the past."

Eric gave a half smile and took one last sip of coffee. "Thanks, Papa, Mama. But I want you to know that if things don't start moving quickly, I'm going to start moving on my own. I'll go there and get her. I swear I will." He said it almost defiantly and felt the color rise to his cheeks.

His father regarded him soberly. Then as Eric stood with them, they engulfed one another in a bear hug. After a moment they bowed their heads and did what Eric had done with his parents for twenty-three years. They prayed.

※

When the phone rang at the Hoffmann house, Eric had just left for class at the university and David had gone to his office across town. As soon as Gabriella picked up the phone and heard the hysterical voice on the other end, she felt a chill run through her body.

"Mme Hoffmann, I must see you!" Altaf Namani cried. "Rislène! Rislène was left in Algeria with her sister. Why, why did she dishonor the family? Youssef and his mother will never let her come back."

"Mme Namani, slow down. Explain it all to me," Gabriella said, forcing herself to remain calm.

"I'm calling from a phone booth. It's the first chance I've had. If Youssef knew … I will come to see you."

"When would it be possible?"

"Today. Now. Can you see me now?"

"Yes, yes, of course."

"I'll be there immediately." The line went dead.

Gabriella hung up the phone, unnerved. It was a quick answer to prayer. She didn't need to go to the Namanis' apartment; the woman was coming here. But her news of Rislène confirmed all of their fears. It made Gabriella's eyes sting. A stack of lunch dishes sat in the sink, but she didn't even glance into the kitchen. Instead she seated herself on the couch, closed her eyes, and let the tears come.

Lost children. It caused a flood of memories to wash over her, just hearing the pain in Altaf's voice. It reminded her too much of Eliane's grief-filled questions as she waited day after day, year after year, for news from Samuel. Or of Madira, whose son, El Amin, was involved in a militant group that was ravaging Algeria's villages. Lost children. In whatever way it happened, the mother's heart was broken.

When David arrived home that night, Gabriella told him of her meeting with Mme Namani. "The woman is beside herself. She's livid and terrified and everything in between. She blames us for 'converting' Rislène, and she's just as angry with her mother-in-law and husband for resorting to such a devious scheme. But the main thing is, she's desperate. And I think that if we can offer her a way to bring Rislène back, she might be willing to help."

David sighed. "I've written to Abdul."

"And now you'll put the letter in the bottom of a suitcase?" She interlaced her arms around his neck and kissed him on the top of the head.

David touched her hand and gave it a squeeze. "Yes, you know that phoning or faxing is too dangerous."

"And what you're asking is more dangerous still, isn't it? 'Abdul, do you have anyone who can find out where Grandmother Namani lives and help get Rislène to a safe place?'"

"Exactly. And I know the man for the job."

"Yes, I imagine you do," she said, watching as David pulled the letter out of his briefcase and sketched a Huguenot cross in the upper left-hand corner of the envelope.

Seeing the cross, with its thick sides turning inward like four arrows pointing to the center of a target, reminded Gabriella of all the times in the past that David had used this symbol as a code when helping those in need. He added the figure of a dove, dangling from the bottom arrow, to complete the drawing.

"And if Abdul says yes?"

"I'll send someone—or maybe go myself—to bring Rislène back to France."

"Eric is determined to go," she whispered.

Gabriella watched her husband bury his face in his hands, let out a sigh, and then turn those deep-set dark eyes on her. "I know Eric is ready to take the risk, even eager. But I can't let him walk into the nightmare on the other side of the Mediterranean."

"You did the very same thing all those years ago."

David stood and went to the window. She went beside him, looking out from the den at a few brittle leaves on the sidewalk.

"Does history repeat itself then? And can you tell me, my Gabby, why the wild, unrestrained things from our past can influence our children in a way that none of our wise words can? Is it something subconscious, passed from generation to generation?"

"Shh, quit all this reflection! Eric loves Rislène, and he'll do anything to make sure she's safe. I certainly don't want him to go, but I understand his love." She led her husband back to the couch, pushed him down, and climbed into his lap. "So we are going to pray and see how God answers."

She sounded calm and sure of herself, but Gabriella knew very well that Eric would make his own decision. And if David didn't come up with another plan of action, and fast, they were going to lose their son to a country that knew no pardon for its own people, much less for a tall, lanky redhead bent on a rescue mission made up in his wild imagination.

❈

"El Amin! You're home!" Jala gathered up the children, calling, "Baba's home! Come see! Baba is home." She raced out of the house into the small yard of scruffy bushes and threw herself into her husband's arms.

"Jala!" he said softly, burying his unshaven face in the nape of her neck and then lifting her off the ground. "Jala," he said again, almost scolding her.

She knew he did not like any show of affection outside of the house. But it had been so long. Almost two months since she had seen him. Two months of daily reports of killings, two months of wondering if he would be caught by the police and sent to some dungeon to be tortured for the rest of his life. *Oh, El Amin. Oh, Allah! Why this life?*

They were in the kitchen now, the three girls crowded around their father, eager for a touch, a favorable look. Only their son, eight-year-old Mehdi, hesitated, forcing himself to stand erect, reserved and brave. "Hello, Baba," he said at last, extending his hand.

"Hello, Mehdi," El Amin said, pride shining in his eyes. "Have you taken good care of your mother and your sisters?"

"Yes, Baba, we are all well."

The approving look from his father filled the boy up to overflowing. Jala saw it and thanked Allah that El Amin had returned home in a better humor than last time. Perhaps he would stay for more than a few days.

After the children were put to bed, he came to her with the mischievous gleam in his eyes, reaching out and putting his strong arm around her small waist, pulling her tightly to himself. She felt the passion in his movements, but there was something more. The tenderness was gone, the soft words. He came to her like a ravaged beast or a brutal madman.

She pushed him away, her eyes gleaming as well. Her fierce love for him and deep repugnance for what he did collided in her mind. "El Amin!" she whispered intensely. "You will not treat me like one of the girls your men drag to camp to play with and then murder!" The anger in her own voice shocked her. "I'm not a plaything to appease you! I'm your wife."

They faced each other, his fury equal to her own, but she was not afraid. In public she played the submissive wife. But she was strong, as all Algerian women had to be, strong behind their veils and the crushing laws, strong in devotion to Allah and to her husband, and strong in her mind. El Amin would not beat her, of that she was sure. He loved her wildly, but many a husband who loved his wife also did not hesitate to beat her. No, El Amin would not beat her because he knew she would leave. She would pack up the children and go to France in a moment's time, because more than her devotion to Allah or to El Amin, Jala was devoted to life. Life for the children and life for herself.

She watched her husband regain control of himself. His face softened.

"You must not accuse me of these things, Jala. You know they aren't true. I'm faithful to you." He approached her cautiously now.

"Perhaps," she whispered. "But you have seen things that torment you and transform you. You must not become a beast, like the rest of them. Believe in what you do, but it must never overpower you, El Amin. Never."

Now she held his hand, led him to their bed, sat down beside him, and softly stroked his face. "Never give in to it. Never."

He met her eyes and nodded, then took her into his strong arms.

"Hussein! You're home at last!" Dounia's light-brown arms enveloped her husband's waist. As she rested her head on his thick chest, he smelled the fragrance of her hair. This trip had taken him away for over a week, and he felt drained and so very weary.

"The children are well?" he inquired.

"Yes," she answered, a slight frown crossing her face. "They are all fine. But, Hussein …"

"What is it, Dounia?"

"Malika's friend, Fadia, was taken two days ago. We all fear the worst."

Hussein's heart, already heavy from several extremely trying days, felt heavier still. Little Malika, his thirteen-year-old daughter! Fadia was a close friend. And he knew what Dounia's dire words *we fear the worst* meant. Young girls were disappearing by the hundreds, kidnapped and taken to terrorists' camps in mountain hideaways where they were repeatedly raped and eventually killed. He closed his eyes to shut out the horror. Better that their throats were slit and death come quickly. Every father in Algeria quaked in his boots for the fate of his daughters.

He led his wife to the kitchen table, kissing her gently on her hair. "Fix us some tea, Dounia. We must remain calm. I'll go see the children. Then we'll all pray together for Fadia and for so many others."

Dounia nodded. He knew the knot in her throat was every bit as tight as the one forming in his. He couldn't swallow. He breathed in deeply before leaving the kitchen and going down the hall to the bedrooms in the back of the small apartment. He knocked softly on a door that stood ajar, then entered to see Malika sprawled out comfortably on her bed, reading, while little Zohra played on the floor. For that instant, there was such an air of lightness, such calm, that he could have believed they were any family, living peacefully in any town.

Malika turned and saw her father first. "Papa! You've come home. Oh, Papa!" She hopped off the bed and ran into his arms, her little sister close behind.

Kedar, his tall, handsome son with the warm olive skin and curly hair, stepped into the room. "Papa!" he said. "You're back."

Hussein soaked in the warmth of his children as they wrapped themselves around him like a thick, well-worn coat. For tonight, they were all together and safe. For tonight. It was all he could ask. One day at a time.

The next morning a knock on the door brought a mournful woman covered in a long black veil to their home. "They found her," said

Fadia's mother, unable to meet their eyes. "Her throat was slit, her hands clasped as if in prayer. Perhaps Allah answered our prayers. She will not suffer anymore."

They led the stricken woman into their apartment, closed the door, and then took her in their arms.

14

Rislène shuddered as the night fell and the streets rang with the call to prayer over the loudspeaker. How many days had she been locked up like an animal in a zoo, pacing, pacing back and forth with nothing to do but eat and sleep under the watchful eye of Nazira?

If only she could read her Bible! Or write! But she had no Bible, every pen and pencil had been confiscated, and the only book she was allowed to have by her bed was a copy of the Koran. Did Eric know she was stuck in this godforsaken place? Had Mother sought help? Surely she would try to get her out.

Nothing to do, no way to get even a note to anyone, no privacy to pray or just to bawl her eyes out. *God! It's too hard! I'm not prepared for this.*

It hit her like a slap across the face, the sudden revelation. *But you have been prepared, My precious daughter.*

Was that God's voice? Had He spoken out loud? She turned to look at Nazira, who was reading nonchalantly on her bed. No audible sound had been uttered. But in her heart, what was this sudden burning welling up in her being? This sudden strange peace? *O Lord, forgive me!* she prayed. *You haven't left me. You haven't.*

It had come to her quickly, so surely that it left her whole body tingling.

She *had* been prepared.

A memory from the second Oasis meeting she'd attended, not long after the beach outing where she met Eric, came back to her in minute detail.

Fourteen young people sat in a circle in the small sanctuary of the Eglise Protestante Evangélique. Eric was leading the meeting, and again Rislène found herself attracted to the tall redhead who looked so out of place among the Arab youth and yet whose eyes sparkled not only with love for God but also for her country and her people.

"Tonight we aren't going to sing or have a Bible study," he was saying. "Tonight we're going to pretend we're in Algeria, meeting in a secret house church."

Heads nodded enthusiastically.

"Remember, you don't have Bibles!" Eric instructed as the group huddled together. "No Bibles, so what do you do?"

Rislène listened, fascinated, to the different answers the youth volunteered:

"We'll see what verses we can remember by heart."

"Yes! And we'll write them down."

"And words from praise songs, too. But we won't sing out loud ..."

"... just in our hearts."

"Exactly!" Eric encouraged them. "And you may be surprised at how much you remember when everything is taken away."

Rislène had watched silently, wide-eyed, as different youth recited parts of Scripture or paraphrased one of Jesus' parables or whispered the refrain from an old hymn. Another youth was jotting down the verses on a piece of paper. After about thirty minutes of brainstorming, four pages were filled, front and back.

"That's exactly what happens in the underground church," Eric said. "So we should be serious about memorizing Scripture. Someday we may be deprived of our Bibles.…"

Rislène gave a lot of credit to the French school system that Scripture memory came easily for her. To survive in the tough French schools, children mastered early on how to memorize. Every child began learning poetry in kindergarten, and their repertoire increased throughout the years. Not only poetry, but also grammar rules and history and passages of literature. That skill had made learning Scripture a pleasure for Rislène.

Now she too knew many verses by heart, ones she had learned in the past year. She did have the Word of God with her! No, she couldn't write it down as they had done at the Oasis meeting, but she could think about it.

She sat on her bed and recited Scripture in her mind, shocked by the overwhelming joy and peace it brought. She stopped on a verse in Isaiah, repeating it again and again in her mind: *I will lead the blind by a way they do not know … I will make darkness into light before them and rugged places into plains.*

Much later, Rislène drifted off to sleep on her cot, hearing Eric's voice say again, *"You may be surprised at how much you remember when everything is taken away."* Yes, she was surprised, and oh, so very thankful.

Grandmother Namani and her granddaughters watched in numbed silence as TV reporters recounted the death toll for the month of January. Hundreds of lives lost. The fear was that with Ramadan approaching, the terrorists would see this as an excuse to increase the killings.

All of Algeria feels as numb as I do at this minute, thought Grandmother Namani, turning off the television and pulling her scarf tight around her large, puffy face. The war was making it very hard to carry out her plans for Rislène. It was not safe to go out in the streets, making contact with other important Algerian families difficult.

She needed to make arrangements for Rislène as quickly as possible. She was not dumb; she knew Christians would come looking for her granddaughter sooner or later. The country was crawling with them, hidden, unseen. Planning a wedding in the midst of the terrorism would present quite a challenge, but Grandmother Namani was used to challenges. Life was one continual uphill battle, to please Allah, to please men, to hold the family together, to keep the honor. She had never complained. Algerian women were strong and smart. She knew what she was doing.

With a strict glance at Nazira and Rislène, she left the room, letting herself into her small office and closing the door. She had narrowed the choice down to three old respected families, all from the right part of town, the rich neighborhoods of Algiers. It would not do to bring Rislène to Algeria just to have her marry a Muslim man beneath her family!

She smiled sadly, thinking of Hamid, the young boy who had stolen her heart almost fifty years ago. Hamid, so handsome, so perfect in every way. Except one. His family was not originally from Algiers. Dreams dashed, a broken heart, a marriage to an unknown man who was twice her age. A man who had keeled over dead in the fields, leaving her as a young widow with nine children to raise.

But times had changed. She would find Rislène a young man, in his late twenties, a good man. A frown punctuated her heavy, creased face. Karim's family was rich, but she suspected the young man of violence. He was not a part of the terrorist groups, but rumors spread quickly. Yassir, the son of another wealthy neighbor, was a few years older but had a stable job, if anything could be considered stable in this country.

She picked up the phone to make a call. Arranging marriages was not as commonplace as in former times, but usually, with the promise of good money and good bloodlines, things could be negotiated. And with Rislène, she had another trump card to play. French citizenship. Many a man could be enticed by the promise of easy admittance to France. Why, the whole country would flee across the Mediterranean if it were possible! Yes, get Rislène married and let the couple return to safety in France.

How in the world she would put on a wedding was another matter. Food supplies were running short in every store in town. Last month it had been impossible to find onions. Before that it was the grain for making couscous. Well, if it wasn't as elaborate a wedding as in times past, little matter. The important thing was that Rislène be married. Quickly.

With God's blazing revelation came a resolution in Rislène's heart. She *would* write her own Bible. And she knew just how to do it. Her only privacy was found in the tiny bathroom. There she could lock the door, close the cover on the toilet, and write her verses on squares of thick pink toilet paper. If only she could find something to write with. Anything would do, if not a pencil, a tube of lipstick or perhaps, yes, perhaps an eyeliner. Nazira had lots of makeup. That would be Rislène's mission and the subject of her prayers. *Dear God, help me find something to write with.* And if she did, that same pink toilet paper could hold a message for Eric.

No, that was impossible! Her mind worked through the potential of finding help. Was there not someone, one of Grandmother's grandchildren perhaps, who could smuggle a letter for her? Impossible, impossible.

For nothing will be impossible with God. She smiled. She knew that delicious verse, located smack at the beginning of the gospel of Luke. Nothing was impossible for God. That was the truth. She would not let that cold, desperate feeling slink toward her like an enormous python with its smooth scales and its winding body, wrapping itself around her and slowly squeezing her to death. No! She would not give in to fear. She had her verses. She had her God.

"Come on, Rislène, it's time for market." Nazira's voice was dry, emotionless.

Love your enemies, pray for those who persecute you....

She winced and forced her own voice to sound light. "Oh, good! I'm dying to get outside. Aren't you, Nazira?"

Her sister shot her a surprised glance. Up until now their communication had been icy. She shrugged. "Yeah, I'll be glad to get out of this room."

Rislène turned to her sister. "Oh, Nazira, would you mind lending me some of your makeup? I have nothing! Grandmother took all my personal items, you know. Please? Just an eyeliner pencil? I feel so wretched. And look at you, you look great."

Nazira's face broke into a sudden smile. "I do?"

"Of course you do. Look at yourself in the mirror." She marched her sister to the bathroom, and they peered together into the mirror over the sink.

"I guess it's not too bad," Nazira laughed. "And you're right. You do look awful. If you'd quit your crying, your eyes wouldn't always look so puffy and red."

"Please, Nazira …"

"Well, okay. Wait right there for me." She ran back into the bedroom and emerged moments later holding three long eye pencils. "Take your pick—black, brown, or blue."

"Black will be great!" Rislène fairly shouted.

Nazira smiled smugly, then opened her other hand. "And here, you can have the mascara too. It's almost empty, but if you want it …"

Rislène grabbed it quickly. "Want it! Oh, Nazira!" She hugged her quite spontaneously. "Thank you! Thank you! I won't cry any more. I promise."

"Well, fix your eyes then. But hurry up! Grandmother's waiting for us."

Eyes lined and mascara on, Rislène called out to her sister, "I'm just going to the bathroom. I'll be right there." Quickly Rislène locked the bathroom door, fell to her knees, and carefully tore off the paper. With the cover of the toilet down, she began to write the verse from Isaiah on the pink paper. *I will lead the blind ...* It was slow, but it worked. "Thank You, Lord," she whispered when the first verse was written. She stood up suddenly. How long had she been in there?

"Rislène? Are you coming?"

She folded the toilet paper and slid it into the pocket of her skirt. She unlocked the door, stepped into the hall, and then remembered. *Flush the toilet!* She could feel the blush on her face as she joined Nazira and her grandmother in the entrance hall moments later.

"What's the matter, Rislène? Are you unwell?" Grandmother narrowed her eyes.

"I don't know. I felt weak all of a sudden." She touched her forehead, which was clammy. "I'm fine now."

"Then let's get to market. The early morning is the safe—" Grandmother stopped midsentence. "There are fewer people at this hour. Shopping will go more quickly."

Nazira and Rislène exchanged glances. Nazira pointed to Rislène's eyes and nodded her approval. "You look better," she whispered.

"Thanks. I couldn't look worse, that's for sure."

The girls pulled the white hijabs over their heads as they left the house. It still surprised Rislène on each trip to the market to see how many women were veiled, many more than in the previous years. Some hid behind long white silk handkerchiefs, keeping everything except their eyes from others' view. Rislène wore her veil as an outward sign of acquiescence. But in her heart she ripped it off, ripped off the layers of tradition that imprisoned these women. *God, I wear this veil,* she said in her mind. *But I pray to You. They can't stop me from praying to You!*

January in the south of France was full of surprises. One week the sun baked the land with temperatures nearing the midsixties, the next found temperatures plummeting as the mistral rushed down the Rhône Valley, causing Southerners to wrap their scarves tightly around their necks and duck their heads as they walked into the wind. Ophélie pushed forward up Boulevard Henri IV without making much progress. She gathered her long hair behind her and stuffed it under her coat.

Another Wednesday where every atom in her body had begged her to stay in bed. It was only her sense of loyalty that convinced her to head out in the biting early morning, catch a bus, and go to the Red Cross.

Her thoughts were jumbled. Rislène had not come back from Algeria. Every day her prayers went up to God for her courageous student. What had they done wrong? Why hadn't she pushed Rislène to stay with her? Why had they thought, had *she* thought, the girl would be safe with her family? Had she forgotten what happened to Bachir all those years ago?

Eric's thin freckled face grew thinner and paler by the day, and the sparkle in his green eyes had turned to a somber stare. Would

Papa let him go to Algeria? She could not imagine her brother in that country. But what could her father do anyway? Eric was an adult.

She stepped inside the Red Cross building, relishing the warmth that greeted her. *I'm a hypocrite*, she thought. *Who am I coming to help? The homeless or myself?* Sometimes, after spending a morning at the Red Cross, she felt overwhelmed, the task at hand too large. She wanted to draw herself away from the suffering in front of her eyes.

So why did she come here? Not for Janine and not for Dominique. When he had called last night to ask her out again for this Friday, she hadn't been a bit surprised. Yes, of course, she'd love to go.

So no, she wasn't helping with the homeless for him. She'd be seeing enough of him anyway. The thought made her smile, then frown. *And then I'll have to bring up the subject of faith, and that'll be the end of that.* She felt pretty sure that Dominique did not need God. He *was* God to the street people. Long ago she had learned the hard way what it was like to get romantically involved with someone who did not share her values and faith.

You'd understand … you were in love with an Arab man once.

Eric had said it so casually. He did not remember the horrible heartache, the scandal. Was she still carrying Bachir around in her heart? Too painful, much too painful to admit it right now. She had let herself fall in love with Bachir when Sam had chosen Annie. It was as simple as that.

She walked into the room with the shelves of clothes. Everything was in order. Janine had already started the coffee. The line of home-less men and women was forming. *I'm coming because I want to help out. I want these people to make it back into society.* Then she admitted it to herself, *I'm coming here because I have found a long-lost friend who needs help. And, God, I don't want to lose him again.*

But Ceb did not stop by the Red Cross that morning, nor was he waiting for her outside at noon. Convinced that he was waiting somewhere, Ophélie went into the Jardin des Plantes, strolling past the ancient statues and the carefully trimmed cypress, peering at the lily pads on the pond and wondering if any frogs dared confront the bitter cold.

She found a bench in the sun, sat down, shivering, and took a sandwich from her backpack. But too many faces from the morning played through her mind, pitiful faces, scruffy, lean faces with dull eyes. Her appetite left. Setting the foil-covered sandwich aside, she rummaged through the pack until she found a pen and notepad. Awkwardly, because she was wearing gloves, she began jotting down ideas for a story. Several characters took shape in her mind. Strong characters with worn clothes and smoldering thoughts. It pleased her that her creativity was returning. A lot of time had run by since she had last written something more than a grocery list or a lesson plan.

When a hand touched her on the shoulder, she jerked back, startled, and let out a soft cry. She looked up to see Ceb peering down at her with his soft hazel eyes, his brow wrinkled.

"I'm sorry to scare you, Filie. May I sit down?"

Her heart was beating wildly, and it made her blush. "Of course." She gathered her writing pad and sandwich and scooted to the end of the bench. The backpack fell off the front. "Oh, bother," she stammered.

"I'll get it," he said, touching her hand briefly as he reached down for the pack. When he sat down beside her, he was grinning like a boy, like *the* boy she remembered from another life.

"I thought I'd find you here."

"Yes, well, it was so nice out—" she began lamely, embarrassed. Then they both broke into laughter. "Actually I'm freezing to death."

"Me too." The way he said it touched her heart.

"Oh, what the heck, Sam ... I mean, Ceb. I might as well just say it. I came in here because I was hoping to see you."

"That's why I came too, Filie." The red ski hat was pulled low on his brow, covering up the long scar. It looked as if he might have trimmed his beard. And those eyes. "Could I take you up on the sandwich and coffee you offered last week?"

"Of course!" she said too quickly. Why did her heart keep beating that way, as if she were a schoolgirl and this destitute man were her biggest crush? She breathed deeply. "You're in luck! I brought you a sandwich ... just in case." She fumbled through the backpack and handed him a foil-covered baguette.

"Thanks. Do you mind if we walk while we eat?"

"Sounds great." She noticed that his hands were covered with wool gloves, and that pleased her. *Maybe I just don't want to see his blemished hand*, she thought, then couldn't imagine why.

"There's a little café halfway up the avenue. We could get a coffee there," Ceb suggested.

"Sounds great," she said again, and then felt foolish. It wasn't like her to speak in repetitive monosyllables.

They wound back through the Jardin des Plantes, pushing their ham and cheese baguettes out of the foil little by little and chewing on them in silence. For some odd reason, Ophélie had the strongest urge to put her hand on his arm and lean into him. Instead, she munched on her sandwich, and they walked out of the park and up the wide, tree-lined avenue.

�֍

Ceb kept on his tattered coat, even inside the warmth of the café. He didn't want Ophélie to see that he was shaking like a dry leaf in a fragile breeze. And it wasn't from the cold. He felt a rambunctious excitement churning within him. That same wild drive that he had known all his life had pushed him this morning, like the forceful mistral, to the Jardin des Plantes, intent on finding Ophélie.

And now she sat beside him in this smoky café. He knew the bartender and waiters well, for he came in almost daily. Sometimes he bought a coffee, more often he just sat and stared. No one ever bothered him. But today he felt different, almost like ... like what? Almost like a kid out on his first date. *Maybe this is what it feels like to start over*, he speculated. Suddenly he realized that Ophélie had been speaking to him.

"Sorry. What'd you say?" His voice sounded too gruff.

Ophélie smiled. "Nothing. I just asked if you'd had a good week. Silly question, I guess."

"No, not at all. Not every week is the same, Filie. Some weeks are better than others, and this was one. I took care of a litter of pups. Cute little things." He stared into the distance and saw Jean-Marc's proud eyes in his mind, felt the pleasure of holding one of the little runts in his hand, the warmth and pulsating heartbeat in that little life.

In a fog, he heard Ophélie asking, "How many puppies?" Her voice seemed so far away.

He removed his red ski hat and shook his long hair, then rubbed an idle finger around his eyes and picked at a chapped spot under his beard. Slowly he turned his eyes to her and shook his head again. "I'm sorry. You'll have to forgive me, Filie. I'm not used to being with anyone." He smiled sheepishly. "I've kind of forgotten my manners."

Her eyes never left his. That was good old Filie. Intense.

"Now what were you saying?"

Another of her soft smiles. Not pitying. Patient, maybe, as if she were explaining some metaphor to a student who couldn't quite grasp it. But not condescending either. Well, that was good.

"How many puppies are there?" she repeated.

"Oh, yes, the puppies. Five of them."

Silence. They sipped their coffee. Then, leaning his head back, he took a last gulp of the hot brew and set the cup down noisily in the saucer. Quite unexpectedly, he found himself clasping Ophélie's hand, and with an intensity that matched her own, he said, "Tell me about Mama. And Papa. Tell me about everyone and everything. I'm ready to hear."

They stayed at the café for two hours, never noticing the men and women who came and went. Ophélie marveled at the way Samuel sat beside her and just listened. Occasionally she saw his attention wander away, like a little boy who suddenly got sidetracked by a big crane or a shiny fire truck. Then he'd come back around and laugh, that same infectious laugh she'd loved in the past.

It almost spooked her to look into his chapped, bearded face, now lined with scars, and see a hint of his youth still there. The way one eyebrow lifted in a circumflex when something surprised him. The large black pupils of his eyes with the light-brown circle around them that blended outward into a soft heather green. The way today the whites of his eyes were truly white and lively. And his broad gestures when he did at last talk, how he leaned closely to her and touched her shoulder, intimately, completely unaware of invading her space, caught up in his description of an event from high school.

The longer they talked, the more familiar he became, his language more polished, not the street roughness, but the erudite ease of earlier years. *Maybe it is possible*, Ophélie told herself. *Maybe Samuel can come back.*

Then as suddenly as it had begun, it was over. Ceb grabbed his ski hat and yanked it down on his head, fumbled awkwardly with his gloves, and stood up. He looked at her with an expression of panic. "You did say you'd pay, didn't you, because today I don't have a *centime* on me."

"Of course I did, Ceb." He was already out the door while she was still rummaging through her purse for change. She threw it on the table and hurried after him. "Well, good-bye, Ceb. I'll see you next week then."

He turned around, looking relieved that she had caught up with him. "*Oui, bien sûr.* I'll see you then." He raised his eyebrow again and bent down awkwardly, as if to kiss her on the cheek, then straightened up, embarrassed.

Ophélie pretended not to notice and quickly brushed his beard with her lips. "*Alors à mercredi*," she whispered. "See you then." She watched him turn and walk away with the hint of a smile forming at the corner of his mouth.

Then suddenly he turned and called back to her, "*Merci*, Filie. Thanks. I mean it. Thanks."

Thank you, Samuel. Thank you for daring to come back. She wished almost furtively that she did not have to wait until next Wednesday to see him again.

15

The letter was marked *urgent* with Abdul Charfi's name on the envelope. Usually there was no conversation between Hussein and those to whom he delivered his information. But that penciled drawing of the Huguenot cross in the upper left-hand corner made Hussein hesitate as he handed the letter to Abdul. For a brief second, they were each holding a corner of the envelope. Their eyes met, his questioning, Abdul's solemn.

"Can you stick around?" Abdul inquired, almost pleaded, with only the sound of the wind whistling through the sand to disturb the peaceful night.

Hussein nodded.

"Come in." Abdul motioned to the door, then closed it quickly after both men were inside. Hussein rubbed his hands together impatiently, stamping his feet on the tile floor. It always shook him up to step inside Rémi Cebrian's old farmhouse. This was where he had literally stepped into that crazy old trunk thirty years ago, and the bent graying man who stood before him now had stood before him then, too. He had stooped and grunted with Rémi and David and lifted the trunk with Hussein inside into the old Renault. And that was how Hussein had been smuggled to France.

Of course at the time his mission had been one of death, and neither Rémi nor David nor Abdul had suspected that he was far from the *harki's* orphaned son that he pretended to be.

Hussein cleared his throat. Ah, well. Everything had changed, and then perhaps nothing had changed at all. It made him smile briefly. He was still smuggling and being smuggled, still appearing to be that which he was not. Condemned to an enigmatic existence. No, he corrected himself. Not a condemnation. As a boy, he had had no choice but to obey orders or be murdered with so many others.

And yet, Lord, I am still obeying orders, and the risk is still death. It is costing me everything I have and am. But there was a difference, and it made his choice easy. Before, he had obeyed out of fear. Now, it was love that compelled him.

"You were right to stay, Hussein." Abdul broke into his thoughts as he pointed to the letter. He smiled, patting Hussein on the shoulders. "This message is for you, too."

Hussein nodded. Once again, some things never changed. And David Hoffmann knew how to get his attention in a way no one else could. A Huguenot cross, the symbol of another smuggling operation at the end of the French-Algerian war, was still the silent signal that Hussein's help was needed in a very specific way. In no letter or fax or book or Bible would anyone in Algeria ever find his name written. But in pockets of Algiers and villages throughout the country, needy believers held documents and books and Bibles and letters with pencil-drawn crosses on them. It meant the mission had been tough and that Hussein had handled it.

Without a word spoken or written, the symbol said, *I need you, Hussein, and I have confidence in you as I do in no one else. This is dangerous and important, and you are the man for the job. My prayers are with you and your family. Thank you for risking death so that others can discover life. God sees. With admiration and love, David.*

"What do you think?" Abdul said at last, after giving Hussein time to read the letter.

"Tricky. And that's just so I don't say *impossible*. If David is right, this Namani woman lives in a fortress, surrounded by loyal, doting family. And you better believe they're all hunting for a husband for this girl. If they succeed in marrying her off, there is absolutely nothing we can do, besides pray for her."

"Any way of getting her a message?"

Hussein pursed his lips. "All I can say is that we'll need someone to watch the place. See if the girl ever leaves the house."

Abdul nodded. "I see." The older man rubbed his chin thoughtfully. "How much damage has been done to that neighborhood?"

"I don't know. I'm sure they feel safer up there on the hill, but we all know that no one is safe."

"So what is your suggestion, Hussein?"

"My suggestion is that you do what you are very good at, Abdul. Get your people to fast and pray. I'll check the place out. Once we have an idea of the situation, I'll let you know what to tell David. But in my opinion, he needs to send someone over who will take the girl back to France. I can't leave. You can't. Too dangerous. I can try to get her to a safe place outside the city, but someone from France will have to take over from there.

"We'll also need to make a passport for her, so get David to send a picture. And tell him to prepare someone to come over. Someone with a cool head who isn't afraid of blood. Someone who can speak Arabic would be the best." He slapped Abdul on the back. "Why don't I just say it? David's going to have to come back for this one. I don't see any other way."

It wasn't that Hussein never thought of them. He thought of them all the time. Prayed for them with Dounia, wondered how they were doing. And Abdul and Madira were always kind and eager to share any news that they received from the Hoffmanns, the Cebrians, or the Dramchinis. How he had relished reading their Christmas letters. It didn't matter that his name was never once mentioned. It couldn't be. But it was understood.

He had seen David and Gabriella when they lived in Algeria. They had welcomed him home after his eight years of absence from his native country. They had even tracked down his mother and reunited them in secret. He had shared many wonderful meals and prayer times with the Hoffmanns and their boys. And he had even seen Rémi and Eliane and their kids when they came to Algeria for a visit in 1974. He had introduced them to Dounia, his new bride.

But Anne-Marie and Moustafa he had never seen again, or Ophélie. His foster family. Not in twenty-four long years. Only his soul could say how much he missed them at times. How he longed to sit in that old farmhouse in Lodève, with the Cévennes mountains outside and the fire in the fireplace and his feet stretched out, resting on that old trunk that had smuggled Moustafa to France, a twin to the trunk that had been his prison and his way of escape.

He was not one bit surprised that Ophélie was a playwright. She had the biggest imagination and the sweetest soul of anyone he had ever known. She'd been his kid sister for those eight years in Lodève. Ophélie. The mystical little girl whom he'd almost murdered in cold blood. The child who had saved his life, for it had been her love for him that had changed him.

A pain shot through his chest, something so deep and pure that he invited it to stay. It was really because of Ophélie that he had come back to Algeria. When she was fourteen and he twenty-two, his love for her had crossed the bounds from brother and sister to something else. He wanted Ophélie Duchemin with his whole heart. How he had begged God to make it possible, promising he could wait ten years if it were necessary, if only God would give him Ophélie.

He remembered asking Moustafa to tell him every detail of his love story with Anne-Marie. Although he would never admit it, Hussein could relate to the loyal, pure love that Moustafa had felt for Anne-Marie when they were children. He understood how the love had become romantic, and why Moustafa had pursued Anne-Marie for so many years, until God had answered his prayers. Moustafa and Anne-Marie's story had given him hope.

But certain things in life really were impossible. And for Hussein it was impossible to stay in the same house, under the same roof with a beautiful, budding teenager who was supposed to be his sister but whom he longed to have as his wife. And so he had made the hardest decision of his life. He went back to Algeria, to work among the Christians there. No one had suspected the real reason. Anne-Marie and Moustafa had seen it as appropriate for him to return to the country of his origin, especially since Algeria's economic and political situations had grown more stable.

He had bawled like a baby when he told them good-bye. He could still feel Ophélie clinging to him, her hot tears mixed with his as she kissed him hard on each cheek. Her love for him had been every bit as fierce as his for her, but hers remained as a sister for her brother. And she seemed to have known with a terrible foreshadowing, as she had seemed to know so many other inexplicable things in her life, that they would never see each other again, never have anything at all to share except their prayers.

There were tears in his eyes as Hussein drove through the Algerian night and called on the God of the Bible to give him courage for another mission. God had healed his heart and given him Dounia. And he loved her with his whole being. Pain and blessings, deep wounds and healed scars, and, thank heaven, a God who could make sense of it all.

Jacqueline Dufour pulled a pale-blue wool suit off the hanger in her closet and got dressed for Mass. Her husband snored peacefully in bed, and years of experience had taught her that no amount of noise would wake him if the question was about going to church. It didn't matter anyway. The important thing was for her to be at Mass.

She spent almost twenty minutes putting on her makeup, wistfully remembering all the years when her skin never had a wrinkle. She'd been well past forty when she used her first cream to cover up the imperfections that now stared back at her with a vengeance. She found her matching purse and let herself out the door.

She was petite and attractive and very well read. She loved the symphony and the opera and, of course, every one of Janine's plays, even if several had been a bit off color. Janine! Now that was the child she would pick this morning to bestow her prayers upon. Goodness, did Janine give her enough to worry about.

Janine had never married, and now she seemed more desperate than ever. Jacqueline corrected herself. No, not desperate. That was the problem. Janine didn't seem desperate. She had this new control and calmness that bothered Jacqueline. It was that Protestant cult, drawing her in, hypnotizing her, feeding her ideological lies about "the Truth."

Oh, the people were nice enough. She had met Ophélie and the Hoffmanns and several other families in the church. But that was another problem. They were almost too nice. If they would just leave her daughter alone!

She parked her car by the curb, a hundred feet past the small stone Catholic church. She walked briskly to the door, nodded politely to several other parishioners, crossed herself, and took a seat on a hard wooden pew. She welcomed the silence. Not like what she'd heard about those noisy Protestant services with pianos and guitars, a flute and even a drum, for heaven's sake. And none of the warm fuzzy treatment that the Protestants called fellowship. What a silly word! Church was for adoration and solemnity between the worshipper and God, with a little help from the priest and Mary.

When Mass was over, she left the edifice, eyeing disdainfully a little band of Arabs who stood further down the road near a soccer stadium. *Ooh, là!* She had to admit that she preferred the Protestant churches to the mosques that were springing up all over France. Made her blood run cold to think that *they* were imposing their religion on France. Stealing good jobs, ruining the social services with their broods of kids, and making Montpellier one of the cities in France with the highest amount of violence. Barbarians! That was all she could say about them. And no chance of their going back overseas. It was inhuman to read of what those Algerians were doing to each other. Absolutely made her blood curdle. She just refused to read any more of it!

Jacqueline arrived home at precisely noon, pleased at the aroma that filled the house from the roast she had put in to cook before she'd left. She leaned forward to kiss her husband's forehead as he pored over the Sunday paper. "Well, dear, that's done."

"Yes," he grunted. "One thing you can cross off your list. *Went to church.* Should be enough to appease the gods for another week."

"Georges! Really. You are such a cynic." She rolled her eyes and scooted past him into the kitchen, whistling contentedly to herself.

"Simon! *Coucou!* Simon. I'm here. Sorry I'm late." Janine hurried through the backstage, searching for the director. "Simon! There you are! Whatever is the matter?"

The energetic director with the gray ponytail was sitting at a little table and nursing a drink, a disapproving look on his face. His scowl was not altogether convincing as he motioned with his eyes for her to sit down.

Uh-oh, thought Janine. *The play's off.* "Bad news, huh?" she asked, taking a cigarette and offering one to him.

"*Ah, oui.* But not what you think. Nothing about the play. Sales are still strong." He flashed her a sympathetic smile. "Just a little concerned about the star of my show." He tapped his watch. "Where have you been?"

"Oh, Simon, what's it to you? How many times have I been late before?"

He rolled his eyes.

"Okay, okay, don't answer that. But I'm here now." She took hold of his hand and watched his eyes, as gray as his hair, studying her intensely. To Janine, Simon was like a benevolent uncle. He was everything her father wasn't. Enthusiastic, kind, sensitive, concerned. And very, very talented.

"Do you want to tell me where you were?"

She reddened. "Why in the world does it matter? I was at church of all things! I left before the service was even over. Don't start telling me now that it's a sin to go to church!" She laughed nervously.

"Your mother is worried about you."

"Oh, come on, Simon. What else is new? Is she hiring you to be a private detective on the side? Good grief. It's Ophélie's church, you know. Remember her? Sweet Ophélie, the playwright? I kinda remember that you like her."

Simon cleared his throat and sipped his pastis. His smile was strained. "Ophélie is great. A little strange, but great. But I can't have my star getting involved in some cult with my not knowing what kind of demands they'll impose on you. I have to be able to count on you, Janine." His eyes were apologetic. "You know I hate to say this."

Janine stood up, feeling her anger mount and the color rise in her cheeks. "Simon! What kind of garbage has Mama been feeding you? It's not a cult. I can do what I want. Nobody's forcing me to do anything. I go because I like it." She was pacing back and forth, puffing furiously on her cigarette, feeling like a character in a play.

She stopped abruptly. "Look, I'm sorry I was late. It won't happen again." She sat down heavily, crossed her slim legs, and pouted.

Simon leaned over and kissed her lightly on the cheek. "Janine, you know me well enough to know I won't let myself be influenced by silly hysteria. Still, you have to be careful." He took her hand. "Look, this isn't your director talking. This is good ol' Uncle Simon who loves you like his own kid. Be careful, Janine, please."

"I appreciate your concern, but you've got it all wrong. Sometime I'll have you over so you can meet some of the people. Would you do that for me?"

"Sure." He straightened up, a twinkle back in his eye. "Now that that little bit of unpleasant business is over, we have a rehearsal. You've kept a lot of people waiting."

Janine stuck out her tongue playfully, knowing full well that she and Simon were the only ones in the theater. She wondered now if he had called this special rehearsal at eleven thirty Sunday morning just to check up on her.

People were getting panicked about cults. In this Catholic country where no one went to Mass anymore and everyone was having their fortune read, lots of weird ideas were circulating. Bad news from the States, where most of those things started, had spread to Switzerland and France. Collective suicides. Stories of brainwashing. Now many so-called churches were being investigated.

Her anger subsided. Yeah, it wasn't completely off base, her mother and Simon's concern. But they were wrong about the Eglise Protestante Evangélique, of that she was sure. She admitted that the place scared her a little. But not because of an eerie trance-like subservience forced on people. On the contrary, it scared her because the people there seemed so convinced that God was real. And their faith smacked of truth.

Ah, well. Time to forget church and concentrate on learning a few lines for a new play Simon was considering.

"Let's get to work!" she said, almost impatiently. "It's past noon, and I'm starving." Her stomach rumbled its agreement.

"Don't you worry. I told your mother you'd be home by one fifteen." He winked. "And you won't be late, because she's invited me, too."

16

The dog looked half dead to Dominique. Her ribs could be counted easily as she lay on her side, eyes glazed, almost oblivious to the puppies that tugged at her teats and whimpered pitifully.

Jean-Marc paced across the narrow squat, rubbing his hands together and moaning. "We gotta do something, M. Dominique. Gotta save my Lassie."

"How long has she been like this?"

"Just last night, she took to looking so weak and sad. Didn't eat any of the good food you brought for her. That's why I came and got you. I'm sorry to bother ya so early, but she's all I got."

Dominique surveyed the room that smelled strongly of dog excrement and urine. Filthy sheets were spread across the floor, some wadded in the corner. The place was bitterly cold. And the puppies, barely two weeks old by Dominique's calculations, looked hopelessly undernourished. Lassie's black fur was matted and her eyes crusted over. She didn't even have the strength to wag her tail as Jean-Marc approached.

Dominique remembered that he had not gotten the vaccine for the puppies. It was simply a matter of finding time to go by the veterinarian's to pick it up. Now the whole lot of them might die. He thought of Ceb. "I'll be back, Jean-Marc. Keep her warm."

He left the squat, turning down a side street. He did not relish waking Ceb this morning, and it had nothing to do with the puppies. It had everything to do with Ophélie Duchemin. The two evenings he had spent with her had been—how could he describe it? Refreshingly different. Yes. She was very intense in a fun sort of way. There was an air of confidence about her mixed with the artist's fear that her works would not be understood. She didn't seem to have anything to hide, and yet he was sure she held a thousand secrets in her soul.

On the other hand, she made him a little uncomfortable. She didn't hesitate to ask him tough questions, and she didn't mind leaving his silence to speak for itself. He was rarely at a loss for words, but with Ophélie last Friday evening there had been several awkward moments when he did not know what to say. It made him want to see her again all the more quickly. To explain himself.

He had reached Ceb's squat and hesitated before climbing the flight of stairs. He sensed in Ophélie a deep affection for this homeless man who had once been her close friend. What did it matter? Was he really feeling jealous of an SDF? Yes, he was ... jealous that Ceb already had Ophélie's respect, her concern, her friendship. Dominique knew it wasn't really a choice between him and Ceb. Her concern for Ceb consisted of wanting to help out a friend in need.

It's silly to be jealous. Take your time, Dominique. Ophélie Duchemin isn't going anywhere. She's interested in you too.

They had touched on religion Friday night, and he had been surprised at her casual references, casual in the sense that her faith was a very integral part of her life. She wasn't threatened by his questions. She had laughed and said, "Now that's a good point. I'll have to think on that one." Her voice held no judgment. So why did he feel that really getting to know Ophélie was just out of reach?

Dominique knocked hard on the door. There was a shuffling sound, a mumbled "Who is it?"

"It's Dominique. Sorry to bother you so early, Ceb, but Jean-Marc's dog is dying. I thought you might be able to help."

A moment later Ceb opened the door as he pulled on an old wool sweater and zipped up his jeans. "*Bonjour*," he said, holding out his left hand. "I'd offer you some coffee, but it sounds rather urgent."

Dominique watched Ceb fumble with the zipper on his oversized coat. They took the steps two by two and jogged through the little side streets of Montpellier's centre ville. Soon the city would wake up as the sun poked its rays through the dark sky, but for now all was quiet. The garbage trucks had not started their rounds, the *boulangers* were busy rolling out dough behind locked doors, the smells of the baguettes and *gros pains* not yet escaping from their shops.

The men turned in the dirty alleyway toward Jean-Marc's squat, a tiny studio hidden between a video store and a card shop. Ceb hurried up the steps.

"Ceb! Thanks for comin', *mon pote*." Jean-Marc smiled. Then he lowered his voice. "She's mighty poorly, Ceb."

Dominique watched Ceb bend gently over the dog, listening to her heartbeat. He pulled something out of a cracked leather black bag and dabbed it on the dog's tongue.

"She's completely dehydrated, Jean-Marc. Those puppies are taking more than she's got to give. They can't keep nursing her." He stroked the dog's pointed nose and spoke softly to her.

"But the puppies'll die if they stop nursing, Ceb!"

Ceb turned to Dominique. "We'll need some milk and a way to heat it. And a bunch of eyedroppers. Any way to get all that?"

Dominique rubbed his forehead. He had a day full of meetings and a lot of desperate men to look after. "I can try," he said.

"No, you've got enough on your hands," Ceb stated, to Dominique's surprise. "What's today anyway?"

"It's Wednesday."

Ceb's face broke into a wide smile. "That's what I thought. I know someone who will help, Jean-Marc. You keep Lassie warm. And here." He handed Jean-Marc an empty syringe. "Keep getting water into her mouth, like this. And keep those puppies off of her till I get back. Give me a couple of hours. What time is it?" He used the stump of his thumb and a finger on his right hand to push back his coat sleeve and see his watch. "Almost six. I'll be back at ten, Jean-Marc. With help."

"Thanks, Ceb. Thank ya, M. Dominique. It means the world to me, ya know. Lassie is all I have." He was still repeating the same phrase when they left him.

Back in the streets, teeth chattering, Dominique bid Ceb goodbye. "What's your idea, Ceb?" he asked, suspecting the answer.

"I'm going to ask Ophélie to help. Do you think they can spare her at the Croix Rouge?"

Dominique's smile was forced. "You'll have to ask them. Good luck, anyway, and thanks." He hurried across the place de la Comédie, rubbing his hands together. The day had started early and promised to be long, but all he had on his mind right now was Ophélie Duchemin.

When Ophélie reached the Red Cross building a little before nine, head down, scarf wrapped tightly around her neck, she almost ran into Ceb. She stepped back and gave a little startled cry. "Ceb!" She could not hide her surprise or her pleasure. "You're getting good at giving me a fright."

She was relieved to see the brightness in his hazel eyes, the look of anticipation on his face. Once again, she thought she saw the winsome teenage Samuel just behind his eyes.

"I need your help, Filie." He took her hand as if it were the most natural thing in the world. "Is there any way you could skip the Red Cross this morning? Six, no make that seven lives are at stake." The urgency in his voice was only thinly covered by the excitement.

Samuel has a challenge, she thought to herself. Samuel Cebrian had always needed a challenge to spur him on.

"*Bien sûr, Ceb.* Hold on and let me just tell them that I'll be out for a while."

She found Janine and whispered the news. "I don't know what's up, but I think it's really important to Ceb. Can you make it without me?"

Janine grinned. "You're almost irreplaceable, but not quite." She winked at Ophélie. "Go on with your friend."

Ceb was pacing nervously by the entrance to the Jardin des Plantes. He flashed her a smile when she reappeared. "*Merci, Filie.* Now we've got to hurry."

He grabbed her hand again, and she followed him quickly, telling herself it was a small victory. Samuel was pulling her along, as he had always done before.

They bought milk at the *épicerie*, a plastic bag filled with tiny eye-droppers at the *pharmacie*, and a small heating appliance at the hardware store. At every stop Ophélie volunteered to pay, and each time Ceb refused. "I brought along some cash," he said. There was a control to his voice and an enthusiasm to his steps that kept Ophélie running after him all morning.

"Here we are," he said, indicating a run-down apartment squeezed in between two shops. "Have you ever been in a squat?"

"No," she said cautiously. "No, I haven't."

He flashed her a grin. "Well, welcome to my world. We're going to Jean-Marc's house. And remember, the dog's name is Lassie. She's like his kid."

"Lassie, right. And there are five puppies." She stopped, reflecting. "But I thought you said seven lives were at stake."

"That's right. Lassie, the pups, and Jean-Marc. Jean-Marc, for sure." The way he stared at her made a tingle run down Ophélie's spine.

The little room was frigid, and the cold in the air was the only thing that kept Ophélie from vomiting at the sharp odor of urine and filth. Her eyes burned.

First, Ceb boiled water and sterilized the eyedroppers. Then he poured the milk into a dented saucepan and heated it over the small appliance. As he did this, Ophélie and Jean-Marc took the puppies into their laps. The floor was icy, but she preferred not to sit on the soiled sheets.

Ophélie managed to hold two of the pups on her lap. They sniffed and pushed at her hands with their wet snouts, making her giggle. "Hey, now wait a minute. A little patience. I'm new at this." Laying the puppies on their backs in her lap, she dipped the eyedroppers in the warm milk. The puppies sucked on them vigorously.

Jean-Marc wrestled with a third pup while the other two, unattended, whimpered in protest. "*Du calme, mes petits,*" he said, chuckling. "Your turn will come."

"What are their names?" Ophélie asked, but Jean-Marc didn't answer. She observed the homeless man. He was terribly thin, his skin a callused bark that was different from Ceb's. She thought his eyes must be a perpetual red. His breath smelled of alcohol and cigarettes, but that didn't bother her. These things she had gotten used to. The filthy apartment and the bitter cold, though, these troubled her. And the fact that Jean-Marc's sweater was practically in rags.

"You know, Jean-Marc, there are some really warm sweaters at the Croix Rouge. You should come over this afternoon and pick something out. I saw a red one that would look great on you."

He looked at her inquisitively, then smiled. "Really? Yeah, I've always liked red." He glanced over at Ceb. "How's Lassie?"

Suddenly Ophélie realized that Ceb had been dangerously quiet.

"She's weak, Jean-Marc, but I think I can pull her through. But you've got to keep the puppies off of her. We'll need to keep them in a cage." He looked at Ophélie. "Do you think you could find a cage for them?"

Ophélie thought for a moment. "*Oui!* I've got some friends who kept rabbits. Had to give them away because their little boy was allergic. They might donate a cage to the cause. I'll ask."

"That's great, Ophélie."

"Yes, it is. *Merci, mademoiselle.*" Jean-Marc inclined his head.

"And what are these puppies' names?" Ophélie asked again.

"I haven't named 'em yet. I guess I just was afraid ..."

"Well, you better start naming them, Jean-Marc," she said, patting his hand and noticing the blue veins and the dirty fingernails. "Lassie's puppies have to have names."

Ophélie and Ceb talked for half an hour, standing in the alley outside Jean-Marc's squat. Ophélie's teeth were chattering as she asked, "Ceb, why don't you come to my place, have a shower and some soup? Something to warm you?"

"No, I'm fine." His response was curt.

"I mean it. I've kept you talking, and now you're freezing."

"Ophélie, you're the one who's freezing. I'm used to the cold. It doesn't bother me anymore." He was rubbing his hand.

"What about that?" she asked, motioning with her eyes.

"Yeah, my hand hurts more in the cold. But I'm used to that too."

Ophélie glanced at her watch. "I've got to get back to the Red Cross. But I mean it, Ceb. Please. Meet me there at twelve thirty."

He shrugged and mumbled, "*On verra.* I'll see."

Ceb relished the steam that misted up the bathroom mirror and hung like a thick fog in the air. It felt so incredibly good, and immediately he wished he had not come. His weekly showers at the Red Cross, outside in the cold, didn't give him any reason to linger in the steam. He pulled the blue towel that Ophélie had given him around his waist. It felt soft and fluffy with a smell of womanly care, like his towels had smelled with Annie. It was hell to remember. Every smell, every texture, even the steam around his face blasted him in the gut, taking away the appreciation and settling on him like a sickening disease.

His heart was racing as he fumbled for the razor that Ophélie had placed on the sink. He wiped the towel over the mirror to clear it. His left hand was trembling, and he knew he could never manage to shave. He quickly pulled his old, dirty clothes back on and opened the bathroom door, relieved to feel the cooler air as he stepped into the hallway.

His eyes took in the apartment. The living room and dining room were combined into one long, airy room, with French windows occupying the whole southern side, giving a spectacular view of Montpellier. Ophélie had decorated the other walls with several modern prints and one oil painting of a child on her mother's knees. There was a sofa in a floral pattern and two overstuffed chairs that matched the sofa. Several large and happy green plants tumbled their way into the room from corners and bookshelves. It was a comfortable room with a touch of sophistication, inviting, warm.

He wanted to run.

Ophélie came from the kitchen, a wooden spoon in one hand. "Already out?" she asked brightly. "I'll have lunch ready soon."

"No, I can't. It's very kind, but ..."

"What is it?" Ophélie's face fell.

He felt a stabbing guilt and knew he could not disappoint her. "I'm sorry. I'm sorry, Filie." He wrinkled his brow, measuring every word. How could he make her understand that her kind intentions felt like a blow to his gut? "It's just that everything here is so clean and comfortable and like, like it used to be *chez moi*. You can't see it, but it is the difference in night and day to me." He whispered through a catch in his throat, "It hurts ..."

Her eyes filled with tears, and she set the spoon on the kitchen counter and leaned against the wall, shaking her head slowly from side to side. "Forgive me, Ceb. It was really stupid of me to think that with a snap of my fingers, I could make everything okay for a while. I'm so sorry." She met his eyes. "What can I do to help you? Tell me what you need, Ceb. I promise I'll listen, but you have to tell me, because I'm not doing a very good job of guessing."

Again the feeling of wanting to embrace her, to hold her tight against his chest, engulfed him. The smell of olive oil and garlic and the look in the eyes of this lovely woman enticed him. He walked into the salon and slumped into a thickly stuffed chair. "What I need, Filie ..." He stopped, afraid to say it, swallowing hard, wondering if she could really comprehend. "What I need is a friend."

Over a lunch of salad and fresh pasta with pesto, they remembered so many things. He predicted the music she would play before she turned on the CD player. He teased her about the way she set the table *à l'américaine* and how she still said grace before meals. "You haven't changed, Filie. Still the same sweet girl."

But everything had changed for him. He knew she was watching his hands, seeing the right one curl unnaturally around the fork, grasping with the three fingers clumsily. He slurped his food quickly, as if he were still at the soup kitchen, feeling suddenly very self-conscious.

Ophélie was telling the story of her Arab student who had been kidnapped by her family and forced to stay in Algeria. Then she changed the subject. "Guess what I'm reading right now with my students?"

He set down his fork and studied her. There was a hint of laughter behind her question. "Tell me, Filie."

"*Le Petit Prince*. You remember Saint-Exupéry's story, don't you?" A defensive tone crept into her voice, as if she were afraid that he did not.

"Remember? How could I ever forget?"

Their eyes met again, and in unison they whispered, "*L'essentiel est invisible pour les yeux.*"

A chill shot through Ceb, and he looked down quickly, pushing a few strands of pasta to the side of his plate. *Oh God. That sweet memory, how it hurt!* It was a quote from *The Little Prince*, a novella about a little boy who traveled to an asteroid and discovered a world that held the depths of the human soul. *What is essential is invisible to the eyes.*

It had been their secret code, a proof of their tight bond of friendship, that theirs was something profound, past physical attraction, a meeting of the souls. Eventually they had shortened the sentence to just one word, *l'essentiel,* and every time one of them pronounced it to the other, it opened a whole invisible universe to them both.

He looked up, embarrassed by the sudden silence, unable to think of anything else to say, confused and overwhelmed by the array of emotions he had allowed himself to feel in the past few hours.

Everything seemed a blur as he sat staring at Ophélie, hearing, like a throbbing in his head, *l'essentiel est invisible pour les yeux. L'essentiel.* What is essential …

He felt suddenly claustrophobic. He needed to get out of this apartment with this delicate, tenderhearted woman who wanted only to make things better.

The wind was whipping around the apartment building, and rain pelted the window. Ceb pushed back in his chair and said, "I'd better go."

"Don't go yet, Ceb. It's horrid out there. You can stay here, even spend the night if you want." She felt her cheeks turn crimson and added, "That old sofa makes a fine bed. Rislène slept on it for over two weeks. And Eric's always staying over before exams."

"You've been kind, Filie. I can't get used to such comfort. I've got a little place to keep me dry."

His sudden change of mood frightened her. "Are you sure? There are so many people who want to help. Your parents would do anything—"

"I don't want to talk about them today," he snapped.

"Yes, I know. I'm sorry." Ophélie hesitated. "But you're different, Ceb. You can get off the streets. Dominique has said—"

"Dominique! So you talk to Dominique about me?"

Shocked, she said defensively, "I volunteer with him, Ceb. You know that. And yes, we talk."

"And dear Dominique, the savior of the street people, thinks that there's a chance for good ol' Ceb. How touching."

"Ceb! You know he's not like that. He gives his life for those in trouble. He understands. He was on the street before."

"I don't need to be reminded of all the laureates of our *médiateur de rue*. Talk to him all you want, Ophélie." He pronounced her name coldly. "He seems like he'd be a good guy for you."

"Ceb! Stop it. All I care about is helping you. Getting you off the streets. Can't you see? We just care about you!" Why was he turning her words against her?

"Touching, Ophélie."

"Why go rushing back into the rain and cold? You can at least be warm for one night. Let me give you that."

"And what would your neighbors think if they saw a wild man like me leaving your apartment tomorrow morning? What would that do to your reputation?"

She saw anger surging inside him, like water pouring into a sinking boat. He stood.

Rising also, she braced her hands on the table and leaned across toward him. "Ceb! Why are you saying that? I don't care what people think. Why won't you let me help you? You said you needed a friend."

He looked at her almost savagely, his eyes hard and menacing. "And what if I need more than a warm bed, Ophélie? What if I need you? Would you care that much?" He took her arm and pulled her toward him. "What if that is what I need?"

His hand was strong, tight on her arm, cutting off the flow of blood. And his look was not of a friend. Afraid, she slapped him hard across the face, and he released her immediately.

Her voice quivering, she said, "You'd better leave, Ceb. You're right. I can't help you." She didn't want him to see her crying. "Go on. I'm sorry I've made things hard on you. I didn't mean to."

He gathered up his coat, rubbing his face as he glared at her. He was someone else. Not Samuel Cebrian. How stupid she had been to try to re-create something from long ago. He went out the door without a word.

"Mlle Duchemin, are you all right in there? Are you safe? I just saw a wild man leave your apartment. A wild man who looks like"— Mme Ploussard lowered her voice—"an SDF. Homeless! Just as you said—first the Arabs and now the homeless are after my sweet neighbor...."

She ranted for a full five minutes until Ophélie at last called through the door, "Everything is fine, Mme Ploussard, but I am so very tired. I must take a nap."

Ophélie curled up on her bed and allowed herself a long cry. Eventually she slept, and when she woke, her face felt tight and dry. She went into her den and peered out toward the center of town. It was still raining, but less forcefully. Somewhere in that maze of intricately woven buildings, a homeless man was cursing her existence. A deep sadness settled on her. At that moment feelings of self-hatred, of naïveté and senseless romanticism pelted her spirit, like the rain against the window.

"Idiot!" she seethed. "You're nothing but an idiot! Did you think you could save him?" Then she turned her anger to the Lord. *Why, God, did You bring him back into my life? Why? To torture him? To tempt me to care? Or just to mock me, reminding me of how hopelessly impossible I am with my simplistic ideas?*

It scared her to let the questions come, because eventually she turned the conversation away from the Lord and back on herself, analyzing and accusing and wishing somewhere deep inside that she could just disappear. It was all too complicated. Every time she let herself care about someone, it seemed, she was left with a gaping wound in her heart.

She opened an old wooden trunk, encased in black wrought iron. This was the trunk that had brought Moustafa out of Algeria, and Mama had given it to her when she had moved into her first apartment. Now Ophélie used it as a sort of hope chest. *Hope chest,* she thought sarcastically. *Yeah, right.*

Reaching her hand down through the quilts and memorabilia, her fingers found a small glass bottle. Ophélie pulled it out and cradled it in her hands. The bottle was long since empty. It was white with a sloping, delicate contour and a pink opaque top. Across the white glass, written in a pink cursive, was the name of a perfume, *L'Essentiel.*

On Valentine's Day when she was seventeen, Samuel had presented her with the perfume. She could still see his hazel eyes twinkling at her from under his brown bangs, his embarrassed grin. It was just a bottle of cheap perfume, but she had treasured it like nothing else. She had felt understood. Profound and simple, everything had been communicated in that one word: *l'essentiel.* That was the kind of love she was looking for.

She had kept the bottle long after it was empty. For years it sat on a shelf in her room, collecting dust. Then, after Samuel married

Annie, Ophélie had placed the empty bottle in this old trunk and forgotten about it.

But every once in a while the memory of the little bottle would come back to her, especially when she taught *The Little Prince* to her students. The quote that she and Samuel had shortened to a word had expressed not only a depth of human emotion but also their faith, the vibrant belief that they had shared as teenagers. To them, on the brink of adulthood, that was the meaning of life, the whole point. They held something invisible and strong and, yes, essential, in their hearts, something that gave them a *raison d'être*.

Ophélie's faith had emerged intact and strong, even after all the philosophy classes and late-night conversations with friends who believed only in themselves. God had proved Himself faithful hundreds of times throughout her life. But things had turned out differently for Samuel.

She placed the perfume bottle back inside the trunk, wrapping it within an old quilt and closing the top. "*L'essentiel est invisible pour les yeux,*" she whispered again with a stinging in her heart.

17

Dounia sliced the yellow gourd carefully in half, emptying out the seeds. There. She placed a square of folded toilet paper in the hollow gourd, then secured the two halves back together with a touch of glue on one side. Kneeling down, she called her youngest child to her. "Zohra, today you and I are going to another market to do the shopping."

"I can go with you today, Mama?" The six-year-old's voice was filled with excitement.

"Yes, today I need you with me. You remember that Papa has brought us news of a girl named Rislène?"

Zohra nodded solemnly.

"And he said he must try to help her get back to France? Where she wants to be?"

Zohra nodded again.

"Well, I need you to help me get a message to Rislène."

The little girl's eyes grew wide with surprise and then pleasure. "Me? Papa wants me to help?"

"Yes, yes he does."

At that moment Hussein came into the room and knelt down beside his daughter. "Yes, my little one, I need your help. Mama will tell you just what to do. She will stay with you all the time. But you will be the one to talk. Do you think you can do that for me, Zohra, if we tell you exactly what to say?"

"Oh, yes, Papa! Oh, yes!" She buried her face in her father's neck and gave him a contented hug.

Dounia felt her throat constrict. Bringing her children into Hussein's business did not please her, but they had prayed and decided this was the least conspicuous way. The note from David Hoffmann had been specific. *Hide the message in a gourd, a yellow gourd, for Rislène. She'll recognize the significance.* Hussein had located the Namani house and observed that the grandmother took her granddaughters to a busy market early each morning.

Dounia gathered her coat and scarf and took Zohra's hand. As they left the house, she explained to the child what she must do and placed the gourd in Zohra's small hands.

* * *

Grandmother Namani listened carefully as the man on the other end of the line explained his wishes. A slow smile crept onto her lined face. So, the deal could be closed. She had found a husband for Rislène. The only inconvenience was the timing. Ramadan started in five days. Muslims fasted from sunrise to sunset. They might ignore the tenets of Islam throughout the rest of the year, but every Muslim respected Ramadan. A wedding ceremony during the holy month was out of the question.

It would be much better to have Rislène married next week before anyone from France started causing problems. Ah, well, Grandmother Namani knew how to play the game of cat and mouse. Hamid, the son she had named secretly after the boy who had stolen her heart, lived in another corner of Algiers. He could keep Rislène and Nazira hidden at his home until the wedding took place. No one would ever think of looking for Rislène there.

Hamid lived closer to the more dangerous parts of Algiers. A few bombings had been reported nearby and several teenage girls had disappeared. But it was the wisest precaution. Rislène must go to Hamid's.

Rislène added a new verse or refrain from a praise song to her stash of toilet paper each day. Some she hid within the pages of the Koran. Others were neatly tucked in the pockets of her skirts and folded in the back of the chest of drawers. She felt an unexplainable joy well up in her each time she added a verse to her collection. Sometimes in the middle of the night, a verse of Scripture would come to her. Nazira's bed barricaded her door, so she simply kept repeating the verse throughout the night, until she could find an opportunity the next morning to slip into the little bathroom and write it down. She had long since used up Nazira's eyeliner and last week had ventured to ask her sister for another. Now this one was almost gone too, and she did not dare raise suspicion.

"Nazira," she said nonchalantly, "do you think Grandmother would let me buy some makeup for myself at the market?"

Nazira rolled her eyes. "Why do you suddenly care so much about how you look? Found a Muslim man who interests you?" she said slyly.

Rislène ignored her sister's jab and decided to talk to her grandmother herself.

An hour later, wearing colorful long skirts, with hijabs covering their heads, the girls stepped out into the cool morning air, following their grandmother to the neighborhood market. Amid the merchants selling fruits and vegetables, clothing and household wares, Rislène found a stand displaying makeup. She fumbled through a pile of eyeliner pencils and quickly picked out three, the longest ones with the darkest shades, as well as a small sharpener. She held out the *dinars* for the merchant to count.

As he handed her the change and the pencils, Rislène felt a tug on her skirt. People were always running into each other in the crowded markets. She paid no attention and tucked her precious treasures inside a small bag.

Again there was a tug, this time more persistent. She looked around crossly. A little girl, no more than six or seven, peered up at Rislène through black eyes.

"Excuse me, miss? Look at these pretty gourds I have for you." Smiling brightly, she held out two gourds, one a deep red, the other a shocking yellow. "They aren't expensive. Please, miss."

Rislène always felt a wave of pity for the beggar children. She bent down, shaking her head. "I'm sorry. I don't have any more money. But you're right. They are very pretty."

The child's imploring eyes were shining with tears. "You must take them, miss. Please take them!"

A chill ran through Rislène as the child met her eyes.

The little girl's lip quivered, and she said again, weakly, "Please. I picked them just for you. You are so pretty ..." Her voice was barely a whisper. "Rislène."

Shocked, Rislène took the child by the shoulders. "What do you want?" she asked almost gruffly.

The girl's expression did not change. "Just to sell you the gourds, that is all."

Then it hit her. A yellow gourd! The teens at the Oasis meeting had pretended to smuggle a message to other clandestine Christians in a yellow gourd! Dizzy and confused, Rislène looked around.

Nazira was two feet behind her. "Who are you talking to, Rislène?" she asked suspiciously.

"Just this poor child. Do you have a few *dinars* so I can buy her gourds? She is so desperate."

"Good grief!" Nazira said disgustedly. "I'm not wasting any money on gourds."

The little girl licked her lips and handed the bright yellow one to Rislène. "Don't you have any money at all?" she asked hopefully.

"Here, will that do?" Rislène gave her the few pieces of change left over from her purchase.

Looking extremely relieved, the child deposited the gourd in Rislène's hand and smiled. "Oh, thank you, miss. I'm sure you will like it." And she disappeared into the crowd.

Carefully Rislène placed the yellow gourd in the bag with the eye pencils, her hands suddenly filled with perspiration. Was she going crazy, or had she heard the child pronounce her name?

"It's time to go, girls," Grandmother Namani called. "Hurry up!"

In spite of her stern tone, Grandmother seemed pleased today, humming to herself. It relieved Rislène to see her in a good mood. Perhaps Grandmother would relax the surveillance, the tireless eyes of Nazira or one of Rislène's uncles or aunts, following her every move. Perhaps somehow she could scoot down one of these alleys and escape. Every time she left the house, Rislène watched streets and directions, listening intently for any information that might give her an idea of where the French embassy was located.

But now the question of the gourd occupied her mind. Could it really hold a message for her? And from whom? Could it possibly be that someone in Montpellier—maybe M. Hoffmann—had made contact with a friend in Algiers? As she walked behind Grandmother and Nazira, Rislène felt inside the bag, letting her fingers examine the rough surface of the gourd.

Once in the house, she calmly went to the bathroom, locked the door, and took out the hard-rind inedible fruit. Although it appeared to be unblemished, when she pulled on each end, it came apart. The inside had indeed been hollowed out, and a small scrap of paper lay in the interior. Hands trembling, she unfolded it.

> *Working on your escape. Friend of Hoffmanns.*
> *If you can write a note, return to the market and*
> *give it to the child. Someone is coming to get you.*
> *Keep hoping. God be with you. Flush away the*
> *evidence.*

She almost laughed out loud as she gripped the paper in her hands and closed her eyes. *Thank You, Lord! Thank You!* She threw the scrap into the toilet and flushed it. She wasn't the only one who had found the benefits of toilet paper! Her heart was pounding fiercely. Where could she conceal the gourd? Hiding toilet paper was one thing, but this? As she held each end in her hands, turning them around, it came to her. Of course!

"Rislène? Are you ill, child? Come out of there!"

"Coming, Grandmother!" she called out, stepping from the bathroom. She wondered if her face was as bright red as it felt. She wiped her sweaty palms on her skirt, took off the hijab, smoothed her hair, and went into her bedroom.

Nazira hurried after her. "Why do you take so long in the bathroom? Are you meditating in there, or what?"

"I'm sorry, Nazira," she replied. "But look! That poor little girl gave me this gourd! I'm going to cut it open and hollow it out! It'll be the perfect place to keep my eye pencils, don't you think?"

Nazira rolled her eyes. "Right, keeping your eye pencils in a vegetable. You're strange, Rislène. Strange."

Rislène followed Nazira into the kitchen, keeping her eyes turned down. They must not see how they were shining. No, under no circumstances could Grandmother and Nazira see that, all of a sudden, Rislène's eyes were filled with hope.

Seated on the colorful cushions in the living room, Rislène scrutinized her grandmother carefully washing her hands with water. These ceremonial washings, repeated day after day before prayer, were rich in symbolism for Muslims. Each drop of water that fell to the ground was a tiny purification, a cleansing of sin. Again and again the drops fell, mandatory drops to anyone who hoped for salvation. Water. Water.

She watched her grandmother in a daze. Christians used water symbolically also. She recalled her baptism last summer in the chilly Mediterranean. She could hear M. Hoffmann's voice, so strong and clear, calling out to the group of Christians gathered on Carnon beach.

"Baptism is an outward symbol of an inward faith." She remembered the chill of the water as M. Hoffmann leaned her backward, submerging her entirely in the salty sea. She remembered her heart racing wildly, the thrill of identifying with believers from the past and present. She remembered thinking that centuries ago other believers had been baptized in this wide sea. A feeling of unity with them had swept over her, and then the piercing realization that she was clean, pure in God's sight.

Baptism hadn't purified her. That had happened on the same beach months earlier when she had prayed with several Christian friends. How she had cried as she dared to hope that this faith was real. But then the baptism had sealed it in her heart. In the icy water she felt clean and pure, felt the water wash over her, felt the goose bumps as she came out of the water to the applause of the small group of believers. Eric had strummed his guitar, and they broke into song. *"Je louerai l'Eternel de tout mon coeur ... " I will praise the Lord with my whole heart.*

Grandmother put away the wet towel and began to pray. Rislène suddenly felt a deep sadness. No amount of external washing, no matter how often it was repeated, could save a soul. It was empty. She wanted to scream it to her grandmother.

Instead she closed her eyes, her head covered with a bright-blue scarf, and began to cry. It was the deep release of emotion, the hurt for her family, the hope of escape, the gratitude for a faith that was real. Tears spilled onto her folded hands as she prayed in her mind.

By sunset the letter was ready, written hurriedly on the pink toilet paper with the new dark-blue eyeliner. Rislène had feigned stomach cramps to allow her time in the WC without arousing suspicion. Indeed her face was pale, her hands quivering as she wrote.

Dear friend of Hoffmanns! Please come quickly!
My grandmother is planning my marriage to a Muslim
man. There is no possibility of escape except if I run
away when we go to market. But I must know where
to run. Rislène

She folded the note and placed it in the Koran. Tomorrow at the market, she would hand it to the child. Then Eric would have news.

The idea that she might soon be free gave Rislène permission to think of the future ... of Eric. How she loved him. She allowed herself to recall all the times they had huddled in the Café de la Paix, sharing coffee and secrets and dreams. And stolen kisses. Eric was a musician and a visionary and a man of faith and courage. Mostly, he was hers. He loved her too!

She admired his energy and enthusiasm, his respect for his parents, and the way M. Hoffmann seemed also to respect his son's ideas. The easy, close relationship they shared made her long to speak openly with her own parents. What was her mother thinking, at home in Montpellier? And Father? Did he miss his daughter? She wanted to hate him for what he had done to her, but she could not. The emphasis on family honor had been drilled into her since early childhood. She had loved that tight-knit feeling, even if it had limited so much of her freedom. No, she could not hate her family. Even Nazira, who had betrayed her, seemed less threatening now.

I want both my family and my faith, Lord. But it was impossible. If God delivered her from this forced bondage, if she secured her freedom through marriage to Eric, she doubted she would ever see her family again. Rislène knew of another girl who had married a Christian, and to this day, many years later, she had no contact with her family.

Is the Lord worth it? Are you worth it, Eric? What kind of life will we have?

Nothing was easy. Nothing! And why did she let herself hope? It was not time to hope. It was only time to pray.

"I can't wait any longer! I'm going to find her!" Eric's green eyes shone fiercely. "Papa, don't try to stop me. It's been a month since she left. Anything can happen in a month!"

"We have word, Eric. Hussein is working on the arrangements. He knows where Grandmother Namani lives."

"Good! Then I can buy my tickets. I can leave tomorrow! Tell Abdul to expect me soon."

David shook his head. "Eric, it has to be carefully planned …"

"And while you are carefully planning, Rislène may be married and never have a chance to escape. No, I'm leaving. I'll feel a whole lot better just being in the same country. Here in France I'm helpless."

David struggled to reply calmly. Eric had been named after Gabriella's little sister, Ericka, who had died in Africa at the age of six. Gabriella's love for her sons was deep and wide, with no favoritism, but David knew the special attachment she had for her youngest and the way she worried for him. With Eric, everything was either black or white. He approached life with a tremendous zeal and sensitivity, in many ways like his half sister, Ophélie.

But he was not the one for a rescue mission into the pit of hell. David was the one to go to Algeria, and he must somehow convince bright, sensitive Eric that the decision was not due to lack of trust. David had learned where his strengths lay and where they didn't. But Eric was young, still testing his wings, longing to prove to his family and the world where he fit in behind two successful big brothers.

"Eric, I know how you feel. I was in an amazingly similar situation once, you know. So maybe my words will sound hypocritical. But I just don't think you are the one for the job."

"There you go again, Papa! I'm too young, too naive, always too *something*. You and Mama can't keep protecting me forever. Papa, I love her. If you understand me so well, can't you see how absolutely maddening it is to do nothing while I'm imagining the worst for her?" He paced around the room. "Look, Papa, I'm twenty-three years old. You can't stop me from going. I'd rather go with your blessing, but whether I have it or not, I'm going."

David watched the color rise on his son's pale face, covering the freckles on his cheeks and continuing up to his hairline. When Eric felt this strongly about something, it was useless to argue with him.

"I hear what you're saying, Eric. You're right. I can't force you to stay put. But will you please grant me one favor? Spend some time praying about this decision, because it isn't just Rislène's life at stake, or yours. A wrong move could endanger the whole secret church in Algeria." He met his son's eyes. "Please think about it."

Eric's green eyes were flashing. "Don't you think I've been praying about it all these weeks?" He turned quickly and left the office.

A feeling of pressure settled on David as if a vise were slowly being tightened around his head and chest. Something had to give. He knew what Gabriella's reaction to his going to Algeria would be. Tears. *You're not twenty-four anymore, David. Please …* But if the choice came between himself or his son, she would agree that David should be the one. Both father and son knew the language and the city of Algiers, but David had experience.

Get packing, David. He couldn't hope for Eric to wait any longer. He shook his head slowly, rubbing his deep-set eyes. And, no. He didn't blame his son. For the love of a woman, many a young man had run straight into the mouth of hell.

It was just like being a prisoner on death row. The security, the fear, the forced departures. But it was worse. Rislène's family was betraying her again. Excitement and hope had come plummeting to the ground, smashing through her dreams.

"Why are you moving me? I'm fine here with you, Grandmother! I don't even know Hamid. Please let me stay here, Grandmother! Please." She could not conceal her tears, her deep despair. Hamid lived on the other side of Algiers. How in the world could she get a message to the little girl from there? It was out of the question to come back to this market.

She felt like vomiting, and clutching her stomach, she ran to the bathroom.

Nazira grimaced. "You and your stomach, Rislène! Get over it, why don't you? Grandmother said we'd be better off there!"

Inside the small bathroom Rislène burst into tears. *I can't do it! I'm going crazy, God. Why do You let me get my hopes up just to crush them?* She could not stop crying. She blew her nose, flushed the toilet, and went to the sink to wipe off her face. A piece of toilet paper had stuck to her hand. She stared at it for a long moment. A piece of toilet paper. That was how God had spoken to her two weeks ago, the thing that had convinced her to keep going. And the gourd was proof from this morning. Surely He would not abandon her now.

She gathered up the Koran, the gourd, the hijab, and her clothes with all the pieces of toilet paper hidden inside, plus the note she had written for the little girl. A piece of toilet paper was sticking out from within the pages of the Koran. As she quickly opened the book to push the pink ply back in, her eyes fell on the verse she had written. *Be strong and courageous! Do not tremble or be dismayed, for the Lord your God is with you wherever you go.*

Holding the verse in her mind and her few possessions to her chest, she followed Nazira through the kitchen and out to Hamid's waiting car.

18

Ophélie had wrestled with her thoughts for three days, cried, prayed, written in her journal. Nothing seemed to help. She woke in the night seeing the laughter behind Ceb's hazel eyes turn to anger and then something worse. She felt her hand hitting his bearded, chapped face. He needed help, but she was not the one to give it. She cared too much, and now she felt that all the tiny steps of progress she had made with him in the past weeks had been erased, like the chalk on her blackboard at the end of the day. Start over from scratch. But how?

She opened one of the French doors from her den and stepped out onto the balcony that ran the length of the room. The railings were lined with window boxes filled with geraniums. Ophélie liked their bright, vibrant color. The wind whipped around the side of the apartment building, sending splashes of water into the air as she tipped a can and poured water into each planter.

In spite of the wind, the sun was strong, and Ophélie lingered outside on this late Saturday morning, picking a few dead blooms from the fluorescent pink flowers. With a little fertilizer, lots of water, and some pruning, these geraniums did well all year long. Once in a while she would bring them in for the night, if the temperature was predicted to drop below freezing. But that rarely happened in Montpellier. The flowers flourished because of their position on the balcony. The morning sun warmed them throughout the year. They were happy.

Watering and pruning. Ugh. She had the feeling God was doing just that in her life. She'd been trying to rescue Samuel Cebrian, to play God in his life. *I was wrong, Lord. Too impatient to wait on Your guidance. But I will listen now.*

Long ago she and Sam had followed God together, argued theology, prayed late into the night for their friends. Now he was as withered as the crisp pale-pink petals she held in her hand. Could he be vibrant Samuel again? How could he bloom in the middle of downtown Montpellier with a bunch of homeless men as his friends? Didn't God have a better idea?

Where there is no guidance the people fall, but in abundance of counselors there is victory. She had tried to handle this in her typical solitary way. Would talking to Gabriella about Samuel be an act of betrayal? He had asked her to keep his secret. But her efforts were not working. How could she let him slip away when help was literally just around the corner?

A rush of wind picked up the dead blooms from her hand and spilled them out into the air. She leaned over the balcony and watched the petals travel six floors down, falling arbitrarily onto the pavement.

Ophélie let herself into the house with a key, hearing Gabriella call from upstairs, "I'll be down in just a sec!" There was a comfort in the Hoffmann house that brought a feeling of peace to Ophélie. Her stepmother knew how to make people feel welcome and cherished. Ophélie had observed her for years, wanting to imitate her actions. But she was not an extrovert, like Bri. She was reserved and thoughtful, like her mother, Anne-Marie.

She fingered the large wooden Huguenot cross that hung in the entranceway of the Hoffmann home and pulled her own cross out from under her blouse. Thirty-two years ago her mother had left her this cross as a symbol of protection, a promise that they would one day be reunited. And while Ophélie had waited for news of her mother, this cross had bound her heart to a beautiful red-haired young woman who wore the same gold replica around her neck. As a teacher and writer, Ophélie identified strongly with the rich symbolism in the Huguenot cross. She had often reflected on each aspect of it.

Gabriella came down the stairs and kissed Ophélie warmly on each cheek. "Studying the cross, Ophélie?"

"Just thinking. Remembering the day on the beach at Carnon, when a terrified little girl found a redheaded friend who wore the same cross."

Gabriella hugged Ophélie tightly, as if she were still a scared, lonely six-year-old. "I will never forget that day when God brought our lives together, *chérie*. How could we know of all the blessings to follow?"

"Yes, the way God brought our paths together was a great blessing," Ophélie stated. "But sometimes it's hard to know if it is really God who has brought a person into your life. And if He has, what you're supposed to do about it."

"Dear Ophélie. What is it that is heavy for you today?" Gabriella gently squeezed her stepdaughter's shoulders.

After a long sigh Ophélie said, "What I need to tell you, Bri, is rather bizarre. And I'll be compromising a confidence to say it ... but I need advice." Ophélie leaned against the wall of the stairway. "Do you have time for a walk on the beach?"

"All afternoon, Ophélie. I'm in no rush."

They made the fifteen-minute drive to Carnon beach in silence. Suddenly Ophélie doubted her motives for telling Bri, doubted her loyalty to Samuel. But when they parked beside the dunes and got out of the car, the rush of winter wind that blasted her face was like a force to propel her forward. She locked arms with Gabriella, walking along a narrow, sandy path that led between the dunes and out to the beach. The tide was low, and the whole expanse of beach empty of people. The strong wind brought gusts of the fine, dusty sand into swirls at their feet.

"Brrr. It's freezing!" exclaimed Gabriella. "Just like that day so long ago."

The women smiled at each other, letting the wind push them along, watching the sea glisten as if covered with tiny jewels as the sun touched its surface.

Ophélie breathed in deeply, filling her lungs with the fresh sea air, feeling somehow stronger. "Someone I care about is hurting," she began. "There are people who could help him, but he doesn't want help. And I've promised him I would say nothing. I've tried hard to help, but somehow what I have to offer is not what he needs." She paused. "Finally I did what I should have done in the first place. I asked the Lord to direct me." She smiled. "And so here I am, Bri. Needing your advice. If I say nothing, I'm afraid he will fade into the background again. Disappear. I don't know what to do."

She watched Gabriella's face change, how her eyes were first sympathetic, then questioning, then startled.

"Samuel?" Gabriella pronounced softly.

"*Oui, c'est lui.*"

"God be praised," she whispered as a smile spread across her face.

Ophélie tried to smile, but the relief she thought she would feel did not come. There was a deep ache, a twisting inside, the way she felt when she was overcome with guilt. She brushed the hair from her face. "I shouldn't have told you. It was wrong. There is nothing you can do."

Gabriella took her hand. "Ophélie, how long have you known about this?"

"Since just after Christmas."

"Where is he?"

"He's on the streets. He's an SDF, Bri." It came out in a whimper, and Ophélie's eyes filled with tears. "He lives in a squat and spends his days watching out for his homeless friends and their dogs."

"Is he well?"

"He doesn't look good. And his hand is a mess. I think he's in a lot of pain." In her mind she saw Samuel rubbing the hand vigorously in the cold outside Jean-Marc's squat.

Gabriella bent down to pick up a clamshell that the sea brought to her feet. "Ophélie, it sounds like God put you in Samuel's path for a good reason. Sometimes we wander so far, and we are too ashamed or too proud to come back. We need a lot of help, even if we say otherwise."

"I hope you're right, Bri. I think he's trying to come back. After living on the streets in several other cities, he returned to Montpellier. Dominique says that is a positive sign. He says—"

"Dominique? Who is Dominique?"

Ophélie blushed, then let out a long sigh. "I guess I should start at the beginning. A lot has happened in the last month."

By the end of Ophélie's recounting of her tale, the two women were chilled to the bone and decided to get a warm drink at a café in the beach town of Carnon. They found a spot in the sun, sheltered from the wind, looking out onto the harbor where the masts of fishing boats mingled with those of sailboats. The harbor was crowded with beautiful floating vessels, but the shops and cafés were practically deserted.

"I never come here," Ophélie commented, ordering a *thé au citron*. "It really has quite a bit of charm."

"I'll have the same as she," Gabriella said, squinting up at the waiter. Then she turned to Ophélie. "Yes, it's peaceful here at this time of the year, before all the tourists invade." She fished her sunglasses out of her purse.

The waiter brought a pot full of steaming tea and set down two cups with a slice of lemon in the bottom of each. Ophélie reached for her purse even as Gabriella did the same. "Bri, please. Let me treat you for once." Her stepmother acquiesced, and Ophélie handed the waiter the change.

They sipped their tea in silence, watching the seagulls dipping up and down in the water. A gull flew toward them, landing a few feet in front of the café, cocking its head and looking at them.

Finally Ophélie asked, "Does faith always involve suffering? Does healing only come through pain?"

"Are you thinking about Samuel?"

"*Oui.* I understand that God must teach us humility and total dependence on Him. But even for me it's hard. And how in the world can I help Samuel understand that God can use such deep hurt for good?"

"You can't, Ophélie. Trying to give spiritual answers for another person's tragedy falls on deaf ears. Or enrages. I have found that all I can do is to trust God as I live out the pain in my life and pray that God will reveal Himself to another in his own trials. It is wonderfully freeing, you know. Giving it back to God. He's big enough."

Ophélie smiled. "You're right, of course. Pretty basic stuff. But somehow I'm too close to see it."

"Basic doesn't mean easy, Ophélie. And it sounds as though maybe your heart is involved."

"My heart? No. Samuel is just an old friend whom I care about." Even as she said it, she felt a softness in her voice. "But I think it would be all right to tell Papa about him. Anyway, I don't expect Sam to be talking to me anymore."

"And Dominique?"

"Dominique is perfect, except for that same old issue of faith. I don't really want to see him anymore either. What good will it do to get emotionally attached when I know it can't work?"

Gabriella shrugged, her lips hinting at a smile. "I don't know the answer, but I *can* understand. After all, I wrestled with those same questions many years ago."

"Yes, indeed you did, with dear Papa." Somehow, that thought eased the tension she had been feeling.

"I will pray for you, Ophélie. God's ideas are always better than mine." They left the café and ambled along the harbor. "In any case, thanks for a wonderful afternoon."

When Gabriella got home from the beach, David was already there. "And where have you been, my Gabby?" he teased. "I tried to call you from the office."

"I've been out with Ophélie."

"Really?" He sounded pleased. "How is she doing? I need to call her."

"She had some very interesting things to relate. You'd better sit down."

David looked at her suspiciously as he took a chair.

"She's been volunteering with her friend Janine at the Red Cross once a week. During the Christmas break she recognized a man in the soup line."

"Who was it?"

"I'll give you one guess."

David shrugged. "No idea." Then he narrowed his eyes, looking skeptically at his wife. "Samuel?"

"Exactly."

"Are you kidding? Samuel Cebrian is in Montpellier? How is he?"

"He's on the streets, *chéri*." She let the announcement sink in and saw pain etch itself on her husband's brow. "He's been a *sans domicile fixe* for three years, going from city to city. Now he's made his way back to Montpellier. Ophélie's been trying to convince him to go back home. Without any success, apparently. She's sure he could make it back into society, but he refuses any contact with his family."

David circled his mouth with his long fingers. "So Samuel Cebrian is back. Praise God. I wonder if he would agree to meet with me?"

Gabriella studied him. "What are you thinking, sweetheart?"

David shook his head. "I don't have the faintest idea. But I always felt that Sam and I understood each other. Surely we can help some way."

"You should talk to Ophélie about it. Go have a drink with your daughter. It's been a while, *n'est-ce pas?*"

The Faculté de Médecine, across the broad avenue from the Jardin des Plantes, was located in one of the oldest buildings in Montpellier. Originally a Benedictine monastery, the edifice was an extension of St. Pierre's. The cathedral sat at the bottom of a steep incline, its facade boasting a fourteenth-century arch joining two thick turrets that thrust themselves into the azure Mediterranean sky. Ceb stood outside the medieval structure, looking down at the cobbled stones in the little *place* outside the imposing buildings. On Saturday mornings students were sleeping in, and the plaza was almost empty.

He walked up the incline to the medical school entrance and contemplated the bronze statues of LaPeyronie and Barthez, two renowned professors from the seventeenth and eighteenth centuries. Ceb hesitated for several minutes before at last pushing open the heavy door and walking inside. He blinked as his eyes adjusted to the dark interior. This was where his love of medicine had culminated. Five years of study in the most respected medical school in France.

The Anatomy Museum was found by winding through various hallways and climbing a flight of stone steps. Open to the public free of charge, the museum also welcomed medical students from all over Europe to observe its amazing collection of nineteenth-century cross sections of the human body. How many times as a teenager had he lost track of time in this room, standing transfixed before the organs of the body displayed in their glass boxes? He had known then what his life's calling would be.

During the long years of medical school he had sometimes made his way here, slipping inside near closing hour and once again staring at the cross sections. He had his own cadaver at the med school, immersed in formaldehyde, and he knew every organ in that body, every vein and artery and how they worked. He had thought that the human body was the most masterful, complex creation that God had thought up.

Ceb shrugged and entered the large one-room museum, immediately caught again by the beauty of the green-specked marble walls and the regal marble columns. Near the ceiling, framed portraits of some of history's most famous professors hung against the yellow wall. Underneath these were frescoes of women in Grecian dress representing the many varied contributions that women had made to the world of medicine, often unacclaimed in the previous centuries. The museum contained thirty-six wooden shelves enclosed in glass. Their size varied from two to six meters in length, and the display boxes on the walls reached clear to the ceiling.

Ceb moved slowly through the vast room, as fascinated as he had been on his first visit by the jars of formaldehyde containing fetuses at all different stages of gestation. Even at three weeks, the human form was visible. Another wall held row upon row of human skulls and skeletons, from the fetus stage through the adult form. These skeletons had been donated to the museum by people who valued the study of the human body for the development of science. During the 1800s, these organs, presented in all different forms, were the only way medical students had of understanding the functioning of the human body. Dissection was forbidden by the church.

Vitrine 5 had always intrigued him the most. Inside the cubicle were waxed copies of the human heart. Several real hearts sat in bottles of formaldehyde. He had memorized each one and dreamed one day of operating on this beating organ that sat so still now inside its glass case. But today he did not linger at the heart. Instead he moved to Vitrine 1. This window box displayed the skeletons of human hands. There were also wax figures showing the veins, arteries, and muscles of juvenile and adult hands. Just seeing the replicas made his own right hand begin to throb. Why did it have to be this hand, the one that worked so feverishly to dissect, to hold the scalpel?

He wished he had not come. The last time Ceb had set foot in this place was a spring day four years ago. He had brought his Marion, almost five, into this museum and told her stories of his past. She had listened, enthralled, her wide brown eyes staring with amazement at the displays of the human body. He remembered the pride and deep joy that had welled up inside as he held his daughter's small hand in his. She hadn't flinched at the graphic displays, and he had imagined her some day using her sharp mind to discover yet other unexplored fields of science.

His throat went dry, and he felt a sudden panic, a need for sun-light and air. Why had he come back to this city of memories? That life was gone. Buried on a mountain in the Alps. So why was he standing here, in the middle of a room overflowing with memories?

He stared down at one of the wax cadavers and saw the white lifeless face, so still and pale, transform into the image of his dead wife. Sweat broke out on his brow. He turned and ran out of the room and through the maze of hallways until he stumbled out into the blinding light of day, tripping on the cobblestones. In the small open square, with the huge cathedral looking on, he vomited beside a palm tree. His skin felt clammy all over, his head was swimming, and he thought he would keel over. He lay down on a low stone wall and pulled his arms around his head to shelter his eyes from the piercing sun. Let the few tourists who passed by shake their heads, if they noticed him at all. Just another wino, sleeping off a night of liquor.

19

Saturday afternoon was dedicated to the dogs. A veterinarian in downtown Montpellier had donated a box full of vaccine to Dominique, and Ceb had promised to help. By three o'clock a group of homeless men and women stood obediently in line in a small side street of centre ville. As Ceb administered the shots to their dogs, Dominique passed out cups of coffee and croissants, a gift from a woman at the *boulangerie* next door.

Ceb had slept on the stone wall outside the Faculté de Médecine for almost two hours, feeling weak and disoriented when he woke. But then another emotion flooded his being almost at the same time. He had a job to do! He couldn't be late. He had wolfed down a piece of ham on a baguette before meeting Dominique at the appointed spot. He didn't want to faint in front of his friends.

Now, holding the syringe in his hand, he pushed back the matted fur of a motley brown shepherd and inserted a needle. "There you go, *ma belle*," he said, patting the dog's side and smiling up at its grateful master.

After an hour and a half all the dogs had been vaccinated, and there were still half a dozen shots left in the bottom of the box.

"Good work, Ceb," Dominique said, shaking his hand forcefully. *"Merci."*

Ceb nodded, a grin on his face. "My pleasure."

That was the truth. How could he explain the thrill of holding the syringe, of knowing that this tool was being used in his hands to impart health? Could Dominique understand that? Yes, Ceb reasoned. This man had seen enough to understand.

"Have a cup of coffee and a croissant," Dominique said, motioning for Ceb to sit down at a small, round table outside the boulangerie. "You must be tired."

"Thanks," Ceb muttered. He accepted a steaming cup of liquid and bit into a warm croissant. "I haven't had one of these in a long time."

"Ceb, you've got a lot of knowledge about medicine. Where'd it come from?" Dominique probed.

Ceb reflected, unsure how to respond. Finally he said, "It came from Montpellier's renowned med school and years of practice in these hospitals."

"Really?"

"*Ah, oui,*" he answered. "You don't have to act so surprised. My bet is that Ophélie Duchemin has already told you all about me."

Dominique lifted his eyebrows. "As a matter of fact, she did say she knows you. Grew up with you, I believe."

"That's right. A delightful woman, Ophélie. You should get to know her better, Dominique." His voice was hard, sarcastic.

Dominique pressed on, seeming not to notice. "She said you have family around here. People who'd be willing to help."

"Help do what? Get a surgeon with a screwed-up hand back into practice? Not likely."

"Ceb, come on. A guy like you could do a hundred things."

"I like this job. I've got free rent and enough patients to keep me busy for years." He stood up abruptly. "Thanks for the coffee, Dominique. I've got to be going. I promised Jean-Marc a house call. I have just enough shots left to take care of Lassie and those puppies."

He made his way to Jean-Marc's squat through the busy alleyways of downtown Montpellier. On this Saturday afternoon people mingled on street corners, browsing and shopping. The place de la Comédie was overflowing with students and lovers sitting at cafés. The nippy morning air had turned into a magnificent afternoon, warm and inviting.

Once inside Jean-Marc's squat, Ceb wrinkled his nose at the rancid smell. The puppies were growing fast. They whimpered and tumbled over one another inside a large metal cage that took up one corner of the squat. "Great cage, Jean-Marc. Where'd you get it?"

"Aw, you know full well where I got it. From that pretty Miss Ophélie. She brought it by the very next day. She's a nice lady. Sat on the floor and helped me feed the puppies." He grinned sheepishly. "We named 'em all, Miss Ophélie and me. 'Course it was mostly her idea. She said that puppies of someone as famous as Lassie should have really dignified names."

To hear Jean-Marc speak so warmly about Ophélie stung Ceb's heart. She had come back to this infested squat for the love of an old alcoholic and his dogs. And what had Ceb done for her kindness to him? Yelled at her, threatened to wound her forever. He couldn't bear the thought and reached into the cage, pulling out a wriggling red pup. "Who is this one?"

Jean-Marc scratched his head. "That little fellow? Let's see. Oh, yes! He's Jean Valjean. Ha! Even I know about Jean Valjean! That poor man who spent years in prison for stealin' a baguette."

Jean-Marc patted Jean Valjean on the head, and the puppy wriggled his whole body with pleasure, licking Jean-Marc's hand.

"I told Miss Ophélie that I thought they should only have French names, but she's a stubborn one. Over there's Hamlet, ya know, from M. Shakespeare. Well, that was okay by me, because Miss Ophélie said that Hamlet was a prince."

Ceb gave Jean Valjean his shot, and the puppy yelped in protest.

"It's gonna be all right, you little fellow. Come here to Papy." Jean-Marc consoled the puppy while Ceb reached in the cage for the black furry creature called Hamlet. A low growl came from the other side of the room, and Lassie, baring her teeth, approached feebly.

"Don't ya worry, *ma belle*," Jean-Marc said, quickly putting the puppy in the cage and going to Lassie's side. "He's not hurtin' much. It'll be for the best, my girl. I swear it."

"You'd better hold her there," Ceb warned. "I'll get this over with quickly."

After Hamlet came the only girl in the bunch, called Cleopatra, because, Jean-Marc said, she was beautiful, mean, and completely in charge of all her brothers.

Ceb chuckled at the explanation.

"Now this one, the brown one with the black paws, Mlle Ophélie was bent on namin' Saint-Exupéry. Ya know, the man who wrote that little book, *Le Petit Prince*? She said everyone loves Saint-Exupéry 'cause he wrote such wonderful things. But I said Saint-Exupéry is a mighty long name for a pup, so I jus' call him Saint X.

"And the last one, kinda reddish black, well it's obvious that he's the runt of the litter, so Miss Ophélie said he needed a 'specially dignified name." Jean-Marc chortled. "So we're callin' him Le Petit Prince, himself."

A chill ran up Ceb's spine. Saint-Exupéry and Le Petit Prince. Ophélie Duchemin was always up to her magic, giving hope and meaning to the most pitiful creatures. And he was quite sure she had chosen those last two names not only for Jean-Marc. She knew he would hear of them too, and remember.

He administered the last shot to Lassie, who bared her teeth again. He stroked her matted fur and noticed with relief that her eyes were livelier than when he'd seen her on Wednesday.

Jean-Marc grinned. "These are mighty fine pups, don't ya think, Ceb?"

"Good-looking animals, that's for sure. And Lassie's beefing up a little too." He shook Jean-Marc's hand and left the squat, smiling as he thought of the proud, stained-tooth grin of Jean-Marc, as Hamlet, Jean Valjean, Cleopatra, Saint-Exupéry, and Le Petit Prince rubbed their wet black noses into the callused palm of his hand.

It was late afternoon, the sun already low in the sky. Ceb had one more appointment to fill before dark. He walked past the fish market that had closed at noon. The smell of tuna and anchovies still permeated the air. Bright pansies, primroses, and cyclamens sat outside a florist's shop, while inside the owner wrapped a dozen red roses in plastic and curled a ribbon with her scissors. People seemed to be in a hurry to make their purchases and get home. Home.

Winding up and down ancient stone steps, Ceb made his way deliberately through the centre ville. It pleased him to peer in the windows of the sequestered shops in cobbled alleyways that no car could travel down. How in the world these shops stayed open had always mystified him. Designer clothes were installed in a niche of a room with a vaulted ceiling, an architectural treasure tucked into a hidden part of the city. A well-known art gallery was housed in an eighteenth-century foyer with a domed roof that let in the light of the Midi. In the same building, tiny winding steps led down to a wine cellar, what the French called a *cave*, which was reserved for special wine tastings for the art gallery's most prominent customers. Annie's favorite pottery store that sold signed plates by potters from Provence was right around the corner, a cozy cubicle boasting its original fourteenth-century stones with an *atelier* in the back, the door so small one had to duck to enter it. Across the street, what had been his and Annie's favorite wintertime restaurant, with specialties of cheese fondue and *raclette*, occupied the restored remains of an ancient scullery.

They were all there, old and new restaurants and shops, mingled together in a type of labyrinth with an eccentric charm that delighted townspeople and tourists alike. Somehow these shops survived. They had established their clientele. That was how the business world worked, a good reputation and a ready clientele. He had known it as a surgeon. Ceb grimaced and thought of the SDFs lined up in the street with their dogs. Now his clientele was vastly different. Yet he felt a similar responsibility to them and a deep satisfaction when he performed a service that mattered. More than ever, he wanted what he did in life to matter.

The church appeared as if out of nowhere, tucked in a picturesque square across the street from a *crêperie* and a store selling watches and jeans. It was hard to have a good view of its structure, even standing on the opposite side of the small *place*, for its steeple rose in gothic style high above the surrounding shops. Much smaller than St. Pierre, this church, Notre Dames des Tables, dated back to the eleventh century, shortly after the first mention of the city of Montpellier in the history books.

Ceb let himself in the church door and sat on a hard pew near the front of the nave. The altar was covered with astonishing sculptures from the Rococo period, and the ceilings were painted with fat cherubs by someone from the Rubens school. To the right of the altar, in one of the cathedral's six alcoves, was a painting of the wooden cross where Christ hung, arms outstretched, a crown of thorns on his head. Drops of blood and sweat had been painted in such a way that Ceb felt if he reached out to touch the canvas, he might truly feel them, wet and warm.

He stared at the painting and thought of the way he and Ophélie used to boast, *The Protestant cross is empty. We serve a resurrected Christ!*

But today as he sat in the cool interior of the church, he was glad he could see Christ hanging there. He was glad he could see the pain on His face and the nails piercing His hands. His hands were ruined too. His hands that were used for healing.

"But Your suffering had a purpose," he whispered suddenly, shocked to hear his own voice, shocked that he had walked so resolutely to this strange place. He had not prayed in many years. That was not to say that he hadn't had conversations with the Almighty. After the accident he had screamed at God, dared Him to show Himself, told Him that He was a weak, pitiful God and that he hated Him.

Yes, those were the last words he had pronounced to this Savior who hung on the cross before him. Ceb rested his face in his hands, and with eyes wide open he said, "I used to believe You were real and good. Now I only have an aching emptiness inside. If You are real, do something. I can't and I won't. But if You're God, be big enough to prove it to me again. That's all I ask."

The sun set outside the cathedral, but Ceb did not move from his seat on the pew. He felt lethargic, stuck in his place. One thought kept inching its way into his conscience: *Ophélie Duchemin was the best friend I ever had.*

And she hadn't changed. She still wanted to be that caring, sincere friend. He smiled sadly. Poor Filie. How she had tried! Why had he let himself be enticed into her apartment last Wednesday? Hadn't he known it would be his undoing? Had she expected him suddenly to shed his homeless clothes and be Dr. Samuel Cebrian again?

Get real, Filie! He cursed her under his breath and felt his cheeks grow hot with anger.

She had been scared of him that day. Genuinely scared. Why had she insisted he shower at her place? Everything was going okay until then. Nice and gradual. Did she know that a week earlier he had seriously considered slipping into a phone booth and dialing his parents' number? Had Dominique heard behind his sarcasm today how very much Ceb cared about Ophélie Duchemin and how jealous he was that Dominique Lefevre was just the right kind of guy for her?

Ceb wanted to cry. He wanted to hold her in his arms and sob. He needed to feel the touch of another human being, the vitality and pulse, the warmth of the skin, the smell of her hair. The smell of that silly perfume that she had worn every day for a year in high school.

L'Essentiel est invisible pour les yeux. That was so very true. *Ophélie. Come back, please! I need you. I can't do it. I don't have the strength.*

Suddenly he added a postscript to the prayer he had prayed a few moments earlier. *If You are real, God, bring Ophélie back to me.*

"You have absolutely no appreciation for modern literature!" Ophélie scolded, a tone of exasperation in her voice. She held out a typewritten paper and pointed halfway down the page. "I guarantee you the prof won't accept what you say here about Proust and Colette! It'll sound like heresy to him! You give nothing to back up your presuppositions."

Eric shrugged. "*D'accord.* So it isn't my best thought-out work. My mind is on other things. Give me a break, will you?" He snatched the paper from her hands. "I've gotta go."

"Hey, wait a minute, Eric." She grabbed his arm as he stood up from the chair in his studio. "Look, I'm sorry. I know things aren't easy right now." She put a hand on his shoulder. "Do you want to talk?"

"No!" he snapped, then reconsidered. "Well, maybe." He began pacing back and forth across the tiny studio. "Papa is driving me crazy! What has been done to help Rislène? Nothing! But he refuses to let me go to Algeria. It's the same old thing. I'm not the guy for the job. I'm sick to death of hearing it! It's not like we can't guess what's going on. For all I know, she's already married by now. Anyway, I'm leaving on February 4. I've got the tickets." He laughed dryly. "I have to go through Morocco. All the airports in Algeria are closed."

He stopped and pointed a finger at Ophélie. "And you know what else makes me furious? Now Papa is heaping a bunch of guilt on me, saying that if I go to Algeria, I could be putting the whole Christian church there in danger. Does he think I'm the enemy or what? I know what's going on over there. The secrecy, the terror. I know that city like the back of my hand. Abdul and Madira can show me around. And Hussein. What is Papa's problem, anyway?"

Ophélie waited for Eric to turn his head toward her. Then she looked him in the eye and said, "His problem is that he doesn't want to lose a son. His problem is that he loves you, Eric, and there is absolutely no way he can be totally objective. He's afraid for you. People are getting blown up all over the place. Throats slit for fun. And foreigners are especially targeted these days. You've read the papers."

"But I love Rislène! I'd rather risk my life to find her than sit here cramming my head full of Proust and Colette while the person I want to spend my life with rots in Algeria!"

"I understand you, Eric. It's a crazy situation."

"Papa says he understands too, because he was in a similar situation in the other war. Well, has he forgotten what he did? He took a ferry to Algeria at the worst possible moment and almost got his head blown off. But God protected him. He's said it a hundred times. Does he think that God won't protect his son? It's pure hypocrisy!"

"It's pure love, Eric."

"Oh, shut up!" He stopped in his tracks, saw the tears well up in Ophélie's eyes. "I'm sorry, Ophélie. I'm taking out my anger on you. It's not your problem."

Silent tension hung thick in the room for a moment. Then, more calmly, Eric asked, "So what do you think I should do?"

Ophélie wiped her sleeve across her face, reflecting. "Call Papa. Ask him to come over tonight with Bri. Let's get everything out. I think he's working on a plan, Eric. Give him a chance to explain it all. Then make your decision."

Eric's bright-green eyes flashed as he considered Ophélie's suggestion. "Okay, I'll do it," he said sulkily. "On one condition." He went to the phone, picked up the receiver, and held it out to her. "You make the call."

The play was still selling out at the end of its seventh week, a very good sign for Ophélie Duchemin's future as well as for the troupe. The cast seemed to grow more into their roles with each show, and tonight had been no exception.

"Whew! I'm glad we have two days off," whispered Janine hoarsely. "The old voice is about gone!"

"You're my hero," exclaimed Simon, giving her three forceful kisses on the cheeks and a long embrace. "You pulled it off in spite of the flu." He felt her forehead. "You're burning up! To bed with you, Janine. I'll drive you home."

She didn't protest as he helped her out the back of the small theater. After collapsing in the passenger seat of her car, she handed the keys to Simon. As they drove away, she leaned her head against the window and fell asleep.

Simon did not like to pry into the lives of his cast. His policy was not to interfere unless the actor's personal life began messing up his professional one. Janine liked a party as much as anyone else, and she had seen her share of the fast lane, but Simon knew he could count on her. He watched her sleeping now and thought of the way she had sung her heart out with a 104-degree fever.

Musical comedies were beginning to make their way back in France, and Janine had what it took to capture the audience. He had worked with her over the years and had always been impressed with her ability to adapt to such vastly contrasting roles as Marie Antoinette and a prostitute from *Les Mis*.

Yes, Janine was special to him, like the daughter he never had. She had needed a father figure fifteen years ago, fresh out of school. Her degree in social work set aside, her hope was the stage. Both he and Janine had done okay.

What bothered him was her involvement in this strange little Protestant church. Simon had spent three dreadful years in a parochial school as a child, and anything that smelled of religion scared him. Hypocrisy. And worse than hypocrisy was the death-like grip cults had on unsuspecting people. He knew Janine's weakness, her longing for relationships.

Tomorrow was Sunday. He would investigate the little Eglise Protestante Evangélique for himself.

"Home again, home again," he said softly, helping Janine out of the car and handing her the keys. "I'll check with you tomorrow. Have you got what you need?"

She laughed. "You know me, Simon. Drugs! I've always got plenty of drugs." She gave him a feeble wink.

He waited until the light came on in the window of her apartment, three stories up, and walked away to hail a taxi.

Finding the church was no problem, although the stuccoed building did not in the least resemble the fine cathedrals of France. The only distinguishing trait was a large Plexiglas sign marked "Eglise Protestante Evangélique" attached to the exterior, looking out on the busy avenue in front of the church.

Simon glanced at his watch. Ten forty-five. Drat. He'd meant to be early. His gray hair was combed neatly behind his ears, and he had chosen a conservative green dress shirt stuffed into a pair of designer jeans that were in turn tucked into a pair of silver-streaked cowboy boots. Simon Clavier was a man with *panache*, as the French said. He was used to making striking entrances.

But today he preferred not to be noticed. He could hear singing coming from the interior as he slipped through the narrow wooden door into what seemed to be a classroom. The walls were covered with scenes from Bible stories, and he remembered hearing that Protestants had a Bible-teaching hour for the children during the church service. But at the moment, the room was empty. All the noise came from the other side of the door.

He pushed it open and was startled to see a room brimming with people who were standing and clapping as they sang a very contemporary melody, accompanied by guitars, a piano, and yes, he was sure he could hear the trills of a flute coming over the heads of the worshippers. A smile involuntarily spread itself across his face. Some church!

Finding a chair on the very back row, Simon silently counted heads when the priest motioned for everyone to regain their seats. A group of children sat on benches close to the front. The musicians were huddled in the area to the left of the pulpit. And over sixty adults occupied almost every chair in the rest of the room. He reasoned that he was lucky to have found a seat.

The chairs pleased him too. Not the hard pews from his schooldays, where he had sat for hours reciting the liturgy. All he had gotten from those mandatory services was a sore backside. Now the priest, who did not look very priestly at all, dressed in a maroon crew neck sweater and, of all things, a pair of jeans, was dismissing the children to what he called *l'école du dimanche*. Sunday school! What a clever title. Out they trotted obediently. But Simon gleefully observed that one blond-haired boy of about seven was tugging on the pigtails of a smaller girl. Here were children with what the French called *du caractère*. He liked that, remembering the pigtails he had pulled in his day.

He was so busy watching the children that he noticed Ophélie too late, when she had already turned toward him as she led the children into the adjoining room. Eyes wide, she silently mouthed *Simon!* and was gone. Ah well, his cover was blown. He ran his fingers through his shoulder-length hair as he had a habit of doing when practice wasn't going very well. Blast it, Ophélie! Now he'd have to think up some excuse.

He had to admit there was a certain warmth of spirit in this service. Or maybe it was just plain old warmth, with all these bodies crowded in a small space. In any case, he was pleasantly surprised. He didn't know what he had expected. People mindlessly chanting some foggy religious rite? These people smiled and sang with a sincerity that stung his heart. Only once did he feel a chill run down his back. It was when the *pasteur*, for now he remembered the Protestant term, had opened up the program for the worshippers to take turns praying out loud.

Most of the prayers were simple, beautiful really. Until one woman, caught up surely in an excess of emotion, began to cry and pray and mix her words. *Aha!* he thought, suddenly pleased, like a private detective uncovering a clue at last. Fanaticism. He expected the whole church to burst forth in a cacophony of bizarre tongues, as he'd heard happened in some churches. Instead, the jeans-clad pastor left the pulpit, stood by the distraught woman with a hand on her shoulder, and whispered in her ear. Within moments she quieted down, and other individuals took their turn at prayer.

A few moments later the pastor announced the end of the free-for-all praying and began the sermon. Sermons were notoriously long and dry as a two-day-old baguette, and Simon prepared himself for the worst. The pastor asked his parishioners to turn to a passage in the Bible. Amazingly, pages ruffled and flipped. Most everyone seemed to have a personal copy of the Bible. All different shapes and sizes. Drat! If he'd thought about it, he could have rounded up one from somewhere.

The young woman seated beside him passed him her Bible and looked on with the young man on her other side. Simon noted with relief that she had already found the desired passage, and he did his best to look serious as he followed the miniscule print. He didn't fidget during the whole thirty-minute sermon. In fact, he found the pastor eloquent, his words sprinkled with anecdotes from life that even brought laughter at a few points. When this man pronounced the benediction to conclude the service, Simon silently slipped out of his seat. He didn't want to get caught by what looked to be a crowd of friendly people.

Fortunately, Ophélie's class must have been meeting in another room of the small building, because she was nowhere in sight. He left without speaking to anyone, relieved in many ways. That church was not a cult, of that he was sure. He was glad he had come and glad he could get away before any of their religion rubbed off on him. In his hurry he almost ran smack into a bearded man standing in the alleyway beside the church, listening intently, as if he were afraid to go in.

"*Pardon*," exclaimed Simon cheerfully. The man just nodded. SDF, thought Simon, with a touch of compassion. Poor guy. *Now there's a place for you. I'm sure someone inside might be able to help you with your problems.*

20

It was almost Ramadan, and then the markets would be empty in the mornings. Why did the beautiful girl called Rislène not come back to see her? Zohra felt that she had failed her father. She had wanted so terribly to make him proud. Once again she ventured with her mother into the crowded market, observing the veiled women who cautiously picked at the vegetables and fruits. She stood in the same spot as she had for the past four days. But no Rislène.

A heavyset woman with a deeply lined face caught her attention. Zohra had seen her the day she had given Rislène the gourd. Yes, surely this woman was Rislène's grandmother, the one who kept the poor girl a prisoner in her home. Papa had told her the story.

Zohra tapped the large woman on the back. "Excuse me, ma'am."

The older woman's round face looked pudgy and swollen because of the tight hijab that kept any hair from showing. She glanced crossly at Zohra. "What do you want?"

"I'm sorry, but aren't you the mother of the pretty girl who bought a gourd from me last week? She looks so much like you."

Immediately the woman's face softened. "Her mother?" She even smiled. "No, I'm her grandmother. Why?"

"She was so nice to me. And she said she would buy another gourd. I was sure she would come back." Zohra looked up at the woman. "Is she ill?"

"Rislène, ill? Oh, no. She's just … away. Surely someone else will buy your gourds, child."

Zohra shook her head sadly, her black curls wrapping around her neck. "No one. Will Rislène be back before Ramadan?"

"Oh, no. She'll not be back, child. Not during Ramadan. You'd best sell your gourds to someone else. Go on with you now."

"Thank you, ma'am." The women were squeezing around her, making purchases. Zohra hesitated, then asked, "Wouldn't you like a gourd for yourself? They're pretty decorations."

"No gourds for me. Now good-bye."

It wasn't much, but Zohra could at least tell Papa that Rislène was away and would not be coming back during Ramadan. She wondered if that news would help.

Rislène loved her people and her culture. She felt a great sadness as the holy month approached. She thought of her mother, so faithful, so sincere, so good. The Islam that Rislène had learned at home was moderate and full of beauty and respect. It held none of the fanaticism. And yet what good was it? Imposed fasting. Rislène had never understood this rite, one of the five pillars of the Muslim's faith. What good did it do to deprive yourself of food and drink during the daylight hours of one month? Did this forced discipline appease Allah? Yet a great community spirit surrounded Ramadan. Virtually all Muslims, devout or not, took part.

And just yesterday, Grandmother had come to Uncle Hamid's house and spoken of Rislène's upcoming marriage to a fine Muslim man. How Grandmother's face had beamed with the news. Rislène's stomach was in knots just thinking of it. Married to a Muslim here in Algeria!

Oh, Mother! Don't you care? And Eric. Are you coming for me? Is anyone coming for me? Please, God, get me out of here.

The yellow gourd sat by her bed. Hidden away in her uncle's house, with Ramadan about to begin, Rislène had no hope of going to market with Grandmother, no hope of seeing the little girl again. But somewhere there was hope. She could feel it in the depths of her soul like a faraway drum, gradually coming closer, its cadence regular and planned. Yes, surely God had a plan.

"Do you want to go to the market?" Nazira asked. "Uncle Hamid said we can go with his wife and kids. They'll spend a fortune on food today, getting ready for parties every night after the fasting."

"Yes! I'd love to go!" Rislène almost shouted. Anything to get out of this house. She did not like the way her uncle looked at her with a smirk on his lips, as if he knew a joke that he would not tell. But she knew it too. A Muslim husband. It was almost a reality. That was the pitiful irony. Yes, the joke was on her.

Madira filled her basket with oranges and olives and headed for the market. There was hope in her heart. During Ramadan, the Muslims ate and celebrated late at night after breaking their fast at sunset. It was the ideal opportunity for Christians to meet in homes without arousing suspicion.

The market was crowded, but the mood somber. Everyone knew that the terrorism was likely to increase during the holy month. Threats had ricocheted off tongues like bullets off the rooftops, and people were moving with caution. Madira thought with anxiety about the phone call from David Hoffmann, spoken in carefully coded language. Eric was coming to Algiers to bring the girl Rislène home. Giving David the good news that Hussein's daughter had successfully made contact with her did not change the rest of the story. Rislène had not been seen again. What had happened? A leak? Everyone was uneasy.

Madira's olives were well-known at the market and sold quickly. As she reached behind her to place another basket on the table, she glimpsed a young woman wearing a typical white hijab. She had a beautiful, delicate face with thick black eyebrows posed almost dramatically over her large, lovely eyes. She stood beside another girl, picking through a booth filled with makeup. The other girl, perhaps a sister, called out, "Rislène! Come on!" And the first girl looked toward her with sad black eyes.

Rislène?

The news had been that Rislène was "away." Moved to another house perhaps? No one watching the Namani residence had seen her for several days. Madira had only a moment to react. She had seen a picture of Rislène, but with her head covered, it was hard to tell. Still, Rislène was not that common a name.

"Olives! And oranges!" Madira called out loudly. Then she remembered what Dounia's daughter had offered Rislène. "And gourds! Bright-yellow gourds!"

The young woman twirled around, seeking the speaker offering gourds. She met Madira's eyes, looked disappointed, and almost turned away.

"Beautiful gourds, *mademoiselle*. Come and see."

The girl approached hesitantly.

"God be with you," Madira said softly. "Did you receive a yellow gourd from a little girl?"

The young woman nodded, eyes wide.

In a voice softer than a whisper, Madira spoke quickly. "My name is Madira; I'm a friend of the Hoffmanns."

Madira! Rislène mouthed the word without making a sound. Her eyes lit up. "I've heard of you. We pray for you."

"Shh. Where are you staying?"

"My uncle's house. Twelve rue de l'Italie. It's very near."

"Rislène! Come on!" the other girl called out.

I've got to go. Again Rislène mouthed the words, her eyes filling with tears.

"Don't worry, Rislène," Madira said softly, touching the girl's sleeve. "God has put us together this morning. He will work it out. I will be here from eleven till two every day during Ramadan. If you get a chance to come again, I'll have information."

"Oh, thank you. Please get help!" The girl's voice was low and desperate. "My grandmother has arranged for my marriage to a Muslim. It's not to take place until after Ramadan, but she may change her mind."

The fear was so apparent on Rislène's face that Madira added boldly, "Someone is coming to get you, Rislène. Go in peace. It won't be long."

To Jala, who stood in line at the post office in the heart of Algiers, it felt like an earthquake. She heard an incredible roar, and then the ground beneath her began to shake. Screams erupted from everywhere. Leaving her letters on the counter, she fled outside with other panicked pedestrians, away from the crumbling buildings. She saw the glass in the windows of the buildings across the street shatter and crash to the ground. Something sharp ripped into her cheek and arm. She looked down and saw streaks of blood.

Some people screamed hysterically, others moaned quietly as blood puddled up around them. Jala bent beside a woman who had lost her left leg, trying to offer comfort in spite of the nausea that rose in her own throat. Her eyes blurred, and she was aware of a terrible stinging sensation in her legs. From a state of semi-consciousness she heard the shrill of ambulances arriving and thanked Allah again and again that none of her children had been with her this morning. Then she fainted.

Jala awoke in the hospital, groggy and disoriented. Her arms and legs were bandaged, and the scene at the post office flashed in her mind. She felt no pain and wondered for a terrified moment if she had lost a limb, remembering the grotesque sight of the woman beside her in the street. No, wrapped in white, they were there, both her arms and both her legs.

El Amin. Where had he been this morning? She struggled to remember, but of course she never knew of his whereabouts. She pushed from her mind the thought that one of his men might have been responsible for this morning's terrorism.

A nurse approached her bedside, and Jala mumbled, "What happened? It was some type of explosion, wasn't it?"

"A car bomb went off right in front of the police headquarters. Latest reports say thirty-eight people were killed. All civilians. And over two hundred and fifty hurt. You were very lucky, *madame*." The nurse shook her head and scuttled out of the room.

Later in the day Jala heard that the bombing was the most deadly terrorist act since the violence began in 1992. And it had occurred barely before the official start of Ramadan. Already the public had feared a bloody holy month. It was certainly starting out that way.

By late afternoon Jala persuaded the nurses to let her go home. She had several deep gash wounds that they warned must not become infected. They urged her to stay the night.

"You don't understand," she stated firmly. "My children are alone. I must get back to my children."

The nurse simply nodded and said, "*Inshallah*."

Jala made her way through the long corridors, limping between families crowded around rooms of loved ones, shutting out the sounds of hysterical weeping. Her thoughts were for her children. And deep down, she had a sickening taste in her mouth. El Amin was in the middle of the violence. What would he do when he discovered that his wife had been a victim of the terrorism?

Forty prayer guides sat on David's desk beside a stack of loose papers and books. He picked them up, left his office, and went into the sanctuary where the special prayer meeting was to be held. Happy faces greeted him, Arab faces, French faces. He began to distribute the pamphlets.

"As we have done for the past few years, we'll use this guide to pray for the Muslim world. Each page represents a day during Ramadan and requests prayer for a different country."

These explanations, so familiar, normally rolled off his tongue, but today the words felt thick and stiff. He saw Rislène in his mind, crying out to him for help. His conversation with Eric Saturday night at Ophélie's apartment came back to him. His son had controlled his temper, had shown him the plane tickets dated for February 4, and had announced that he was going. No amount of talk had dissuaded him. He could not even fly directly into the country. Ever since the hijacking, all air and boat travel to Algeria had been suspended. Eric would fly to Morocco and get into Algeria by car.

Dear God, David prayed. *How can I keep him from going? Show me what to do.*

"Most Muslims practice fasting from sunrise to sunset during the month of Ramadan. This is one of the five pillars of the Muslim faith …"

Ramadan. The Algerian authorities expected the terrorism to mount sharply during this month.

David cleared his throat. "While in ordinary times Muslims are encouraged to observe a voluntary fast, during Ramadan it becomes obligatory. The fast of Ramadan is probably the most widely observed Muslim religious rite …"

David took a long breath before concluding his explanation. "The last ten days of Ramadan are considered as greatly blessed, and in particular the twenty-seventh night, called the Night of Power, which is the night in which the Koran was revealed to Muhammad. For many pious Muslims, this period is marked by a special spiritual intensity where they will spend nights in prayer and in reciting the Koran.

"It is precisely during this time that Christ has often revealed Himself through visions to Muslims. We have numerous testimonies of these occurrences. Please never underestimate the power of prayer in the lives of Muslims ..."

The group split into smaller clusters of two and three people, and for the next two hours they prayed for many specific requests. David was not a bit surprised when Eric rose to share his prayer request.

"Please pray for Rislène." His voice cracked with emotion. "We have received word of her location, and believers in Algiers will be trying to get her to the safety of the French embassy. I'm leaving on Friday to meet up with Abdul and Madira. I ask for your prayers for this trip, for safety for Rislène, myself, and the Algerian believers." He glanced at his father. "I in no way wish to jeopardize the house churches in Algiers."

There was a stunned silence. *Eric was going to Algeria! Now?* David read the questions on his friends' faces. *How could you let your son go at a time like this?*

David cleared his throat. "Eric knows how I feel about the trip. I would prefer to be the one to go. But as we have talked, I see his determination." He could not say anything else.

Reading the anguish on his face, the believers bowed their heads. The prayers flowed easily, fervently, deeply for another hour. And when silence filled the room, nobody wanted to leave, even though the hour was long past midnight.

"Do you not care, Youssef, that your daughters are in this country?" Altaf held out the copy of *Le Monde* to her husband and pointed to the grisly headline. "Please, Youssef. Bring them back. Better a Christian daughter than a dead daughter!"

His hand was swift and hard. The blow to her cheek sent her reeling, and she tumbled onto the couch. She did not cry out, but glared at her husband ferociously.

He held out his finger toward her, shaking it. "Never say that again, Altaf! Do you hear? Never! Unless Rislène marries a Muslim man, she *is* dead. Do you understand? My mother has arranged the marriage. It will take place immediately following Ramadan. Can you not even wait a few weeks to get your daughter back alive!" He stormed from the room and out of the apartment, slamming the door behind him.

Altaf picked up the phone and dialed a number. "Mme Hoffmann," she whispered, her eyes trained on the door. "Can I come to see you? Yes, it's urgent! I'll be there in half an hour."

She put the receiver back in place, let out a long sigh, and went into the kitchen. She would have a nasty bruise, but perhaps, with a little ice, the swelling would not be too bad. She did not want to call attention to herself when her heart was breaking for her daughters. Holding the ice to her bruised cheek, she pulled her hijab around her and left the apartment.

She reached the Hoffmanns' house thirty minutes later and was ushered quickly inside by Mrs. Hoffmann.

"Mme Hoffmann," Altaf said with a tremor in her voice, "this is not the Islam I grew up with. Terrorism has no part in that Islam. It is not what I learned from the Koran. Our religion is one of community, devotion, and purpose. It celebrates family. This fanaticism is tearing my family apart."

Altaf cleared her throat and took a deep breath, feeling her body begin to relax in the comfortable surroundings of the Hoffmann home. "I have not been allowed to talk with my daughters. Youssef calls his mother every few days for news, but I am not permitted to speak with them. So I must know if you have news of Rislène."

"We know that your daughters are both healthy. We know also that your husband's mother has planned a marriage for Rislène to an Algerian Muslim."

"And what are you going to do?"

The red-haired woman seemed reluctant to answer.

Impulsively, Altaf took her hand. "I will not say anything to anyone. Only please, get my daughters out of that country. Please. I will pray that Allah gives you ideas and strength to follow through. And I will help you! Tell me what to do, and I will help. I'm waiting for my daughters. Please."

Mme Hoffmann came forward and enveloped Altaf in her arms. It felt good to be able to cry.

21

The week crawled by. To chase away the worry and fear, Ophélie spent much time in prayer. Rislène, Eric. *Please, Lord, have mercy!* And Ceb, *No, no, it has nothing to do with my heart,* she had assured Gabriella. *Ceb is just a friend fallen on bad times. A friend I care about.* But that wasn't the whole truth. Ceb was someone she loved.

There. She had admitted it. She loved Ceb. No, she *cared about* Ceb, but she *loved* Samuel Cebrian, her long-ago best friend and confidant, her devil's advocate. He was the one she loved.

Her head throbbed, her nose ran, and her throat felt swollen and sore. An *angine*, the doctor had pronounced two days ago, giving her a round of antibiotics. Rest and plenty of tisane, he prescribed. So why was she forcing herself out of bed this morning? She should just call the Red Cross and say she was sick.

She couldn't do it. She longed to see Ceb, to tell him she was sorry.

She got to the Red Cross an hour and a half late, her entire body rebelling at every step. Janine took one look at her and backed away. "Ophélie, you look awful. What's up?"

"Just a bad cold," she said hoarsely.

Janine touched her forehead. "You've got a fever. Are you taking anything?"

Ophélie nodded. "Antibiotics."

"Sounds like what I had over the weekend. Get home and get in bed, girl! What in the world brought you here?" Janine didn't give her time to answer. She flashed her a sympathetic smile and said, "Men, *n'est-ce pas*? Neither of them has been here this morning."

Ceb did not come at all. Ophélie wasn't surprised. Her pride kept her standing at the gate of the Jardin des Plantes, refusing to go in. She looked toward the stone gazebo bordered by flowering shrubs. It was empty of young lovers on the chilly first of February. She considered taking a stroll around the immense park before heading home, and at once she felt a stab of guilt. Last week she had told the Lord that He was in control, that she wouldn't try to arrange things anymore. And now, with a 102-degree fever, she was hunting for a homeless man. She turned away from the Jardin des Plantes and walked down the avenue toward the bus stop.

Then she remembered the puppies. She'd promised Jean-Marc that she would check in on them. It made her smile weakly to think of the puppies with their heroic names. Something about Jean-Marc broke her heart. It was the way he seemed so childlike and naive, as if his years on the street had softened him on the inside even as his body took on the appearance of an elderly man. She was sure that his dogs helped him blot out all the pain in his life. Despite her fever, she had to visit him.

Ten minutes later she climbed the steps to his squat, marveling at the ease with which she now entered into this hidden universe of Montpellier. Only weeks ago she had not known that these places existed. She knocked on the door.

"Just a minute," Jean-Marc called out. He opened the door, blinking at her. "Mlle Ophélie! I knew you'd come. I've been waiting for you. I fixed you a pot of tea."

The stench repelled her, and she forced herself not to make a face. "*Merci, Jean-Marc!* How are Jean Valjean and Hamlet and Cleo and Saint X and Le Petit Prince?"

"They're doing great. Ceb came by a few days ago and gave them their shots. That sent 'em to howling." He reached into the wire cage and stroked the runt's red fur. "But they got over it pretty fast."

"Good. That's really good." A lump had formed in her throat at the mention of Ceb.

Jean-Marc grinned at her from behind gray shaggy eyebrows. His skin had the look of used sandpaper. The intensity of his blue eyes was diminished by the red lines surrounding the blue. Behind his smile he looked feeble and very, very tired. It suddenly occurred to Ophélie that she had no idea of his age. Was he forty-five or sixty?

"Do ya like the tea?"

"Tea's great, Jean-Marc. Thanks." She had forgotten the squat's overpowering smell and the frigid air in the room. Both rushed back on her now, and she wished she hadn't come. She lowered herself to the floor beside the wire cage and reached inside. The puppies nipped at her hand playfully.

"You feelin' okay, Miss Ophélie?" Jean-Marc poked his head down, his eyes wide and innocent. "You don't look like you're feelin' so good." He frowned. "Could I get you some more tea?"

"No, I'll be fine, Jean-Marc. I just have a little cold. I wanted to come for a quick visit. I'll be leaving soon."

"Oh, I'm sorry you're feelin' bad. I wish you could stay." He scratched his head. "Say, did ya notice my sweater, Miss Ophélie? I followed your advice! I went down to the Red Cross yesterday and got this red sweater, just like you said!"

She managed a smile. "Good for you, Jean-Marc. You look very handsome in it." Ophélie leaned her head against the cage. Before she realized it, she had nodded off.

A knock on the door brought her out of her sleep, wondering momentarily where she was. Her eyes focused on Jean-Marc.

"Now who in the world is that?" he muttered, sounding rather pleased with the prospect of another visitor.

Ceb stood at the door with a plastic bag in his hand and a funny expression on his face. "Ceb, how good of you to stop by!" Jean-Marc giggled like a little boy. "Come on in! And look who's here! Miss Ophélie." He cleared his throat and scratched his beard as if he were trying to remember his next line.

Ophélie suppressed a grin. She had a hunch this meeting had been set up ahead of time.

"*Ah, oui! Ça y est.* Do you two mind if I step out for a minute? I've got some business to do. But I trust you. I'll leave Lassie and the pups in your care."

"Sure, you go on, Jean-Marc," Ceb said. "We'll keep things under control. But don't stay away too long." He winked at the homeless man.

With Jean-Marc gone, the room felt suddenly much too big. Ceb stared at Ophélie sheepishly, neither of them able to pronounce a word. From a corner of the room Lassie whined. The puppies clambered on top of each other. Ophélie pulled her hand out of the cage and felt thankful for the noise of the puppies, filling up the awkward silence.

Ceb set his bag on the Formica table, which wobbled under the weight. He dragged the only two chairs in the room, unmatched and rickety, to the table. "*Bonjour, Ophélie,*" he said with difficulty.

She sat up, closed the wire door, then looked at Ceb and felt her lips spread into a smile. "We named that one Le Petit Prince," she said, pointing to the red runt.

"I know. Jean-Marc was quite proud of those names."

Ophélie shrugged.

"Are you hungry? I thought maybe you hadn't had a chance to get anything after your morning at the Red Cross."

She pulled herself to standing, feeling a wave of dizziness come over her. She reached for the chair, her brown eyes filled with questions. "Did you plan this with Jean-Marc?"

"Yes, kind of." He rubbed his hands over his face, absentmindedly letting one finger trace the groove of the long scar across his forehead to where it got lost in his thick brown hair. "I wanted to apologize for what happened last week." He took an unopened bottle of wine out of the plastic bag and stared down at it. "I won't make excuses. But I am truly sorry. And I thank you for caring, for trying to help." His words sounded stilted and rehearsed, and though he stood not two feet from her, he seemed a million miles away.

"You're welcome, Ceb. I'm sorry too. I was so naive. I didn't really try to understand how it might make you feel. It was wrong."

"Would you like a sandwich?" He emptied the contents of the plastic bag onto the table. A baguette, a package of vacuum-packed ham, and several cheeses, freshly cut from the *fromagerie* and neatly wrapped in waxed paper, tumbled out. He placed the bottle of wine beside the baguette.

Ophélie approached the table and examined the label on the bottle. Faugère, *carte noire*, a good wine from the region. It had been her favorite. Her head was throbbing insistently. When she unwrapped the cheeses, her eyes filled with tears. Tomme de Savoie, Beaufort, and Pyrénées. Did he really remember all her favorites, or was this a strange coincidence? And if he remembered, what was he trying to say?

She felt dizzy again and rested her arms on the wobbly table for support. The smell of the cheese collided with the damp, moldy odor and the stench of dog urine. "Ceb," she said, "it is all so very kind." The room began to spin around her, her knees buckled, and she cried out, "Samuel!" before she fainted.

No more than thirty seconds had passed from the time Ophélie passed out in his arms until her eyes flickered back open. But to Ceb, a lifetime might have run by. In those precious seconds as he held his cold palm on her forehead, he spoke to her softly. "Filie. Wake up, Filie. Are you all right?"

He almost wished she would stay as she was, unconscious in his arms, so that he could observe her without embarrassment. Her long mahogany hair fell over her shoulders and onto the cracked linoleum. A baggy black sweater hung down almost to her knees. Ceb thought she looked like a child, lying there across his lap, her face turned to the side. He saw in her profile the small, delicate nose, the high forehead and graceful cheekbones, now dotted with perspiration. Her brown lashes, long and thick, were closed across her face. Without thinking, he leaned down and kissed her on her cheek, caressing her hair. "Filie. My beautiful Filie."

It took him almost an hour to get Ophélie from Jean-Marc's squat to the bus stop and then across town and into her apartment, but he enjoyed every minute of it. He was at his best in the role of a doctor, he told himself, as he bent down over Ophélie who was now cuddled on her couch, wrapped up in a heavy blanket. Ceb searched through her medicine cabinet and found the prescribed antibiotics. He heated a cup of water in the microwave, punching the buttons with an ease that scared him, reminding him of his former life. He found the teabags in a colorful tin above the sink.

"You should never have gone out today," he scolded in his most professional voice. "Your physician should put you on sick leave. You need rest." He brought the tea to her, setting it on the coffee table and removing the thermometer from her mouth. "Almost 103, young lady."

She shrugged, then leaned forward and took the mug of tea in her hands. "Thanks, Ceb," she whispered hoarsely.

For some reason he felt pleased to have brought her home on the bus, she leaning on him, helpless and weak, as he walked her to her apartment. It was the love of control, the need to feel in charge, the need to help. For the first time since his path had crossed Ophélie's a month ago, he had something to give her.

She tried to converse with him as she sipped the tea, but it was obvious she was only being polite. "Hey, Filie, you don't have to entertain me. Get some sleep," he said softly.

"I'll try. It's just that my mind is on so many things. Remember I told you about Rislène in Algeria?"

Ceb nodded.

"Eric's decided to go get her. I'm so worried for him. He leaves in three days."

Ceb rubbed his hand absentmindedly. "Not a great place to be going right now. He should wait here for her."

"He can't! He loves her. He's willing to risk his life. You know Eric. The idealist."

"Yeah. He's a good guy, your little bro. You should find somebody else to send. Somebody who's got nothing to lose, nobody to care about."

"That kind of person doesn't exist, Ceb."

"Sure he does. There are a hundred of us downtown. Good ol' SDFs. No one cares about us, and we don't care about anyone."

"That's not true, Ceb! Why do you say things like that?"

He saw that his words hurt her, so he shrugged and stopped talking.

She fell asleep on the couch, but he didn't leave the apartment. Instead he wandered through each room, observing her life. She had lived in this apartment for years, but until that disastrous visit a week ago, he had never been inside. Annie had been jealous of Ophélie. He had felt it the first time the two were introduced. He had spoken too often of his old friend in those first months with Annie. And then, not wanting to hurt Annie, he had distanced himself from his childhood friend, seeing her only during family get-togethers with the Hoffmanns, Dramchinis, and Cebrians.

Once after Annie had moved in with him, Ceb had wanted to call Ophélie, to ask her opinion. He needed to know what Ophélie thought of her. He had dialed the number on a night when Annie was studying late at the library, but on the second ring he had hung up. What did he expect her to say?

But he missed her, missed their friendship and easy conversations, missed her questioning mind. Annie lived on another level.

Not superficial, that wasn't fair. But she didn't ask herself hard questions. She was just much less complicated than Ophélie. He had missed Ophélie's constant probing ... and at the same time he had felt relieved.

His mother had discreetly brought up the subject one day. "Have you and Annie made any plans?"

"No, Mama. We're just seeing what it's like to live together." That had hurt his mother, but she had never lectured him about it. Instead she had asked, "And what about Ophélie? I guess you don't see her anymore?"

He loved his mother. He had always been able to discuss things with her. Looking out from under his brown bangs, he had declared, "Ophélie's a great girl, Mama, but you know we've never been anything but friends. And anyway, she expects too much of me. Life would be hard work with Ophélie Duchemin. She wouldn't let me get away with anything."

Hard work, yes, he thought now, standing in the middle of her bedroom with its wicker furniture and the wooden trunk sitting at the foot of her bed. But he had found out that any relationship was hard work, and with Annie, sometimes he had wondered if he wasn't missing out on something more.

He turned toward a wicker bookshelf that displayed framed photos, memorabilia, and a few hardback classics. He picked up a picture of the Dramchinis and Hoffmanns with all the children and grandchildren huddled together. Ophélie's two families. The picture must be recent, he reasoned, noticing that two babies had been added to the clan since he had last been with them. Life went on in spite of his absence.

On another shelf, beside photos of Ophélie with members of the acting troupe, was a picture of his parents laughing beside David and Gabriella. He stroked the glass frame with a finger and felt a tear on his cheek. It startled him to see how his mother's face had aged and how gray her hair was. It wasn't like Eliane Cebrian to let herself go.

Why, Mama? he wondered, and knew the answer instantly. She wore grief on her face. She was in mourning for Annie and Marion. And for him. *He* had aged his mother! Had he been so wrapped up in his own grief and self-pity that he had forgotten the effect the accident had had on others, on the ones he loved? He felt suddenly ashamed.

There was a phone by Ophélie's bed. He could call them. He *should* call them. The temptation was strong. He reached for the phone, picked up the receiver, and held it to his ear for a long time. No, he couldn't call them yet. Not until he was sure what he would say, what he wanted to do. He replaced the receiver.

He left her bedroom and went into the tiny second bedroom, which had been transformed into an office. The desk was overflowing with papers. On the wall Ophélie had hung the publicity posters from her two plays. Two tall *étagères* were crammed with books and scrapbooks. He sat on the floor and removed an old photo album. Across the front she had written in calligraphy *Younger Years*. He opened it and saw Ophélie's face as a teenager smiling back at him. Ophélie with Anne-Marie and Moustafa, Ophélie with Hussein, that strange Arab kid who had lived with them for years.

Actually, we became good friends, Ceb thought, turning the page. Ophélie with David and Gabriella and her half brothers, Roger,

William, and Eric the baby sitting on her knees, his bright-red hair sticking out in all directions. Ceb chuckled lightly. He remembered looking through this scrapbook many years ago.

And then on the next page there was a picture of Ophélie in bell-bottom jeans, her arm interlaced with his, her head tilted, resting on his shoulder. Their mouths were open in a fit of laughter. Ceb touched the plastic and examined the yellowed photo. They were about seventeen, and he had a child's plastic stethoscope around his neck. Underneath the photo Ophélie had written "Dr. Sam!" in capital letters.

He stared at the picture of his teenage self. His hair was long and straight, his face tan from the sun of the Midi, and he was wearing cutoff jeans. His had been a bright, confident face with clear hazel eyes and the beginnings of some soft fuzz on his upper lip. Ceb touched the scar on his forehead and closed the album. He could not let himself remember all these things. He could not!

He came back into the den and knelt down beside Ophélie, wanting to kiss her again. Last week this apartment had screamed at him to leave. Now every bone in his body was begging him to stay. He sat down in one of the overstuffed chairs beside the couch and watched her breathing peacefully. She had always been so independent, with her strong convictions and her depth of character. A guy needed to feel he had something to offer in a relationship, but Ophélie had always seemed in control, with that calm inner strength, sure of her faith.

"You never needed me, did you, Filie? I don't think you ever really needed me until today." He bent over and kissed her on the forehead, but she did not awaken.

The buzzer sounded twice, waking Ophélie with a start. She struggled to her feet, surprised to see Ceb stretched out in an armchair, himself waking from what must have been a nap. She lifted the receiver from the intercom. *"Oui?"*

"Sweetheart, it's Papa."

"Papa! Hi!" She had completely forgotten that her father was stopping by this afternoon. She glanced at Ceb, who was shaking the sleep from his eyes. "Come on up," she said, pressing the button that opened the door downstairs to the apartment building.

Her heart beating hard, she turned to Ceb, feeling the flush on her face. "It's my father. He promised to come by this afternoon. What do you want to do?"

He looked completely baffled.

"He knows about you, Ceb. I told Bri. Only Papa and Bri, though. No one else. I couldn't keep it to myself. I had to tell someone. I'm sorry."

What did she read on his face? Bewilderment? Resignation? Relief? He stood up and rubbed his eyes. The tiniest grin flickered on his lips, and he shrugged. "Well, I guess I'm about to see your father. I don't have much of a choice now, do I?"

She wasn't sure if she saw pleasure or betrayal in his eyes.

David Hoffmann seemed taller and thinner to Ceb, his eyes darker and deeper set, his face almost gaunt, his black hair peppered with more gray. He wore a pair of blue cords and a dark-blue cardigan. He had an elegant manner about him, even in casual dress, even today, in spite of his evident fatigue.

Ceb had always liked David. When Ceb was a teen, David had been the youth leader at church. His honest manner, his stories of being an atheist and the way he had found God had intrigued young Samuel Cebrian. David had a sharp mind, and he was never afraid of Sam's questions—unlike some Christians, who had tried to defend God and failed miserably.

Now David was holding out his hand. Ceb hesitated, then gave him his left hand, and David shook it powerfully. "It's good to see you." His first words seemed stiff and nervous. Then David let go of his hand and hugged Ceb hard. The older man's words caught in his throat, as if he were holding back tears. "Sam. I didn't think I'd ever see you again."

It caught Ceb off guard, and he stiffened involuntarily. He remembered that David, the American, was always giving bear hugs. But crying? That he had never seen. He stepped back awkwardly. *"Bonjour, David."*

Ophélie broke the silence. "Papa, Ceb helped me back from the Red Cross. I was ill, I mean …"

"She fainted," Ceb said. "She should never have been out today. She needs to be on medical rest for at least a week." He could almost feel his hand writing out a prescription. "Since you're here, David, I'll be going."

"No! Please stay," Ophélie said quickly. "I need to rest, but you and Papa could … talk …"

"Off to bed with you, *chérie*," David said, motioning toward her bedroom. "Sam and I will be fine."

Smooth David, Ceb thought, unperturbed. For some reason, he felt a flood of relief at the thought that he had an afternoon before him to talk with David Hoffmann. He wondered if God had given him Ophélie today. And if so, perhaps her father was just a bonus, thrown in for good measure.

Going into the kitchen, David said, "Your parents are well, you know."

"Yes, Ophélie has caught me up on my family." His words were flat. "Did she tell you I'm on the streets?"

David poked his head around the corner and met Ceb's eyes. "She confided it to Gabby. Is there anything we can do for you?"

"No. I've got everything I need."

Silence.

When David brought out two steaming mugs and seated himself on the couch, Ceb felt his body begin to relax. They talked easily, sipping the coffee. There were no cloudy sentiments to get in the way as there had been with Ophélie.

David explained his work with Muslims, his travels, the courses he taught. Listening to him, Ceb sat forward, imagining David in his many roles. "Tell me about Eric," Ceb asked suddenly. "Is he really leaving for Algeria in three days? Ophélie told me about the young woman who was kidnapped by her family."

"A very sticky situation. I've got two more days to try to change Eric's mind. To convince him that I can get the job done."

"You can't send Eric!" Ceb stopped abruptly, realizing the anguish that David felt. Then he said, "Good grief, I'd go to Algeria before I'd let Eric go." He was silent, contemplating his words. Then he blurted out, "I need something to do, David! I'm going crazy without work! I'll go to Algeria. Yes, let me go."

It took David a minute to register this sudden confession. Then he spoke matter-of-factly. "Sam, I know we could get you a real job right here in Montpellier."

"With 12 percent unemployment in this city? How?"

"It wouldn't be too hard for a guy like you."

"Samuel Cebrian is dead, David. I'm just plain ol' Ceb."

"I don't care who you are," David said forcefully, a frown creasing his forehead. "I've known you forever, and there's nothing that Samuel—or Ceb—couldn't do if you put your mind to it."

It felt like a dare, and that was what he needed. Someone to dare him to do something impossible. "Let me go to Algeria then." Ceb pronounced the words, but they seemed to come from somewhere outside of himself. He said it again, more forcefully. "Let me go! I know Algiers. I can speak the language. And what is there to lose? If I get killed, nobody will have to grieve. They've grieved for me already. I'm dead as it is. Let me do it, David! I'll leave this weekend. Or tomorrow if you want. I've still got my passport. Look at me. I look like the terrorists. They won't suspect an old cripple." He was standing now, bending down over David.

Measuring his words, David said, "I appreciate your offer. But, Sam, it's a delicate mission. The Christians could be in great danger with one wrong move. It calls for both daring and diplomacy."

Ceb's face broke into a smile. "That's me, David! You know it!"

David's wary expression did not change.

"Are you saying you need someone to go who believes in God? I won't blow your cover, David. You know me better than that. I'm not afraid. Let me go. Look at me and tell me honestly if you can think of anyone better suited for the job."

David stared at him and said nothing.

Ceb felt this was an opportunity made just for him. Maybe this God of his youth *was* still around. He sat back down in the overstuffed chair. Now was the time to use his best skills to convince David Hoffmann that his idea was not as outlandish as it sounded. A rescue mission in Algeria. It was impossible and absurd, and suddenly Ceb wanted to be a part of it as much as he had ever wanted anything in his life.

Mme Ploussard took Ophélie's temperature. "*Ooh là là!* It's 103! Dear child, you must stay in bed. I saw your father—such a handsome man he is—and he told me how sick you were. So I promised I'd make you some soupe and tisane. Tisane with honey and lemon. You just sip this and you'll be back to new in a day or two."

"*Merci, Mme Ploussard,*" Ophélie whispered.

"And you will never believe who I saw with your father, Mlle Duchemin! Why, it was that wild man. Poor man." She whispered. "He has a scarred face and a withered hand! *Ooh là,* these homeless. But I said to myself, and then I told André, that I was sure that M. Hoffmann would know just what to do with him. After all, he's a priest, isn't he? Your father." She paused and scratched her head.

"But I have never exactly figured it out—how M. Hoffmann, being a priest and all, has a wife, a daughter, and sons. Now how in the world did that happen?"

Ophélie woke in a sweat, knowing the fever had broken. She sat up in bed and listened. Everything was still, yet the dream flashed vividly in her mind. All of her life she had understood things that baffled others, little flashes of intuition that became for her glimpses of God's plan. Why He let her see them she did not know. But at different times throughout Ophélie's childhood, adolescence, and adulthood, God had spoken to her through a vision. And this dream reminded her of those other dreams, realistic, communicating truth.

In her dream, Eric was running down a dirt road. There was the sound of an explosion, and debris littered the road. He entered a farmhouse, screaming, "No!" Then he bent down. When he looked up, his hands and face were bloody, and it was no longer Eric. It was Ceb.

She remembered now that her father had come and talked with Ceb even as she slept. She slipped out of bed, glancing at the clock. Almost ten at night. The apartment was empty. Her father had left a note on the kitchen counter.

Didn't want to wake you, sweetheart. Very good talk with Samuel. He has proposed an interesting solution to our problem. I'll call you tomorrow.

Was this what the Lord was telling her? Had Ceb offered to go to Algeria? What a relief it would be to her father and Bri if Eric stayed in Montpellier. She wanted her kid brother to be safe. Perhaps God had given her the dream to prepare her for what was coming.

It seemed impossible that Ceb would leave, yet she felt sure of this dream, just as she had felt on other occasions. But she shook with fear, remembering Ceb's words to her. *You should find somebody else to send. Who's got nothing to lose, nobody to care about.*

Her soul ached, and she wanted to scream, *It's not true! I love you. Come back for me!* Instead she got out of bed, opened the wooden chest, reached down through the quilts, and pulled out the perfume bottle. Cradling it in her hands, she whispered, "Oh, Ceb. If only you knew how much I care."

22

He came into the room like someone used to being in control. He was tall and muscular, his hair thick and black, cropped short, his eyes shadowed under bushy brows that joined in the middle. His eyes traveled up and down Rislène's body as if he were sizing up a fine racehorse. He didn't smile, but his slight nod let Grandmother Namani know that he was pleased with what he saw.

"Hello, Rislène," he said stiffly, reaching for her hand and kissing it lightly.

She lowered her eyes, her cheeks burning, and said, "Hello." It took extreme concentration to keep from trembling all over. *Please, God ... this can't be happening.*

Grandmother Namani spoke. "This is Yassir. He's from a fine family in Algiers and has offered a sizeable dowry. He has been to France and is open to returning there in the future. Is that not right, Yassir?"

"It is something we will talk of later."

Grandmother smiled. "I will leave the two of you to get acquainted."

"We will have all of our lives for that," Yassir stated. "I think it a wiser use of time to discuss arrangements for the wedding. There seems to be a need for urgency." His eyes bore into Rislène, and there was a hint of accusation in his voice.

Grandmother Namani raised her eyebrows, then smiled. "As you wish. Yes, I have already begun making plans. Since weddings are forbidden during the holy month, we shall hold the ceremony immediately after Ramadan is finished, on the fourth of March. It will be a lovely way to end the fast. Will this be satisfactory for you, Yassir?"

"Satisfactory, yes. A feast. People must not be afraid on the night of our wedding. You will work with my mother to ensure the best foods available. This is imperative."

"Of course."

Rislène shrank back from the conversation, feeling invisible as they discussed plans and strategy. The only thing she could do was repeat again and again in her mind, *Hurry, Eric. Oh, God, please make him hurry.* Four weeks until the wedding. Surely he could get here before then.

But she had learned something that deflated her hopes even as they began to swell. Ever since the Air France plane had been hijacked at the end of December, there had been a ban on all air and boat travel to and from Algeria. Her family had been on one of the last flights into the country. How could Eric get in? How could she get out?

She stood stiff in her place, letting the conversation between her grandmother and her arranged husband-to-be drift in and out of her thoughts. A verse she had written out just yesterday floated into her mind. *After you have suffered for a little while, the God of all grace … will Himself perfect, confirm, strengthen, and establish you.*

Later that morning, after Yassir left, Rislène took the eyeliner and toilet paper and scribbled another message.

Eric, today I have met Yassir, the man who is to become my husband. The wedding date has been set for March 4, as soon as Ramadan ends. I'm terrified. I don't know how you will get into the country, but someone must get me away from this place before Ramadan ends. Please, please hurry. Time is so short. Rislène.

She tucked the paper into the pocket of her skirt and slipped out of her room. She had a strategy of her own, and she prayed it would work.

"Grandmother, please let's go to the market." She wore a bright smile. "I want to help you choose the foods for my wedding! Let's see what is available and plan accordingly. I agree with Yassir. It must be extravagant!"

Nazira regarded her suspiciously. "Why the sudden change in disposition?"

"I've met my future husband. He seems strong and wise. I know we will grow to love each other, and he said we will talk of returning to France. Just think, Nazira. Don't you long for it?"

"*Ah oui!* It's all your fault that we're here, holed up in the middle of hell."

"But if I find favor with Yassir, he will agree to take us both back. We must plan the perfect wedding."

"And what about the red-haired boy?"

Rislène pouted, then laughed. "It could never work. We're too different. I see it now." She came to Grandmother's side and warmly interlaced her arm in the old woman's. "Grandmother, you were right to bring me here to remind me of the strength in our family. I want to go back to France to be with my parents and brothers and sisters. I'm sure Yassir will understand. Surely he'll want to leave this place."

Grandmother Namani beamed. "How wonderful that we have our old Rislène back. I knew it would not take long. Come along then. To market. And then we'll work on the bridal gown. It will make Ramadan pass more quickly, won't it, girls?"

They reached the market after noon. With Ramadan beginning, people slept late into the morning, shopped in the afternoon, and stayed up well into the night feasting. Grandmother had remarked that Algerians spent more money on food during Ramadan than during the rest of the year. Fasting and feasting went hand in hand.

But Rislène wondered if terrorism would change that usual rhythm. It was almost as if the smell of fear and death permeated the market today, obliterating the aroma of rich spices. Fewer people crowded around the stalls. Rislène went to the exact spot where she had stood four days ago, but she did not see Madira. She picked up an avocado. "Look, Grandmother! These will be perfect for an *entrée*. And the couscous."

Her words sounded joyful and carefree, but her eyes betrayed worry. She turned away from her grandmother, scanning the crowd. Then she felt a hand on her sleeve. Her heart beating wildly, she turned around to see Madira, her face all but hidden behind her veil.

"I've moved my booth over here," she whispered without looking at Rislène.

Rislène followed the woman's subtle gesture. "Grandmother! Look! The oranges and olives. Perhaps we could order them early."

She followed Madira, retrieving the toilet-paper message concealed in her pocket. Before they arrived at the booth, Rislène managed to slip the note into Madira's hand. Now she picked up oranges, examining them carefully.

"They are the finest quality, as are the olives, grown on our farm just outside of Algiers. What can I get you?" Madira's eyes communicated hope and warmth.

"It's not for today. It will be in four weeks, at the end of Ramadan. I'm getting married." Rislène motioned for her grandmother to join her. "We want to have a big feast. Can we order in advance?"

Madira met Rislène's eyes without a hint of concern. "This might be possible. Can you tell me the exact date?"

"It will be March 4," Grandmother Namani said. "And it will be a grand occasion! Can you promise me that your products will be available?"

"Yes, if you will give the number expected at the wedding." Madira hesitated, then added, "I have a friend who does catering for weddings. With a month's notice, she may be able to help. Would you like me to mention it to her?"

"Oh, yes!" Rislène enthused. "Wouldn't that be wonderful, Grandmother? Someone who caters."

"We'll see." Grandmother turned to Madira. "How can we best get back in touch with you?"

"I am here every day."

"Good. We'll return. I'll have the exact count ready for you by next Tuesday."

"Very good."

"Good-bye and thank you," Rislène said, smiling with a wave of relief as Madira's kind eyes sent back the message: *Everything will be okay.*

❈

Jala limped into the kitchen, leaning heavily on a cane. Her thick black hair fell down her back without its usual sheen. There were dark circles under her eyes. Her name meant "shining light," but today her eyes were dull. She closed them but could not shut out the pain in her legs where the shattered glass had cut her in Monday's explosion. Despite cleaning and changing the bandages regularly, the gash in her left leg had become infected. It should have had stitches. She let herself down into a chair, wincing with the effort. More than anything, she did not want El Amin to see the terror in her soul.

At first, all those years ago, she had not believed that her husband was involved with the terrorists. Eventually she could deny it no longer. She had gathered her children around her and prayed to Allah for safety. She had forced herself not to think of what he might be doing in the weeks that went by with him absent. But it broke her heart. He never spoke of these things, but life went out of him. At times, upon returning home, his eyes were glazed over with exhaustion. And behind the fatigue she saw the horror, the repulsion. El Amin was a good man. What had become of him?

She knew he loved her passionately, devotedly. He used to admit it, in their intimate moments. He would easily risk his life for her and his children. But he was caught, with no escape. And so she had not been surprised at his reaction when he learned of her injuries in the explosion. A hard look, with a terrible sadness behind the eyes. A strong embrace. But no words. He was slipping away, and there was nothing she could do. One way or another, she would lose him to this war. Perhaps it would be the government who imprisoned or murdered him. Perhaps it would be in a raid.

She leafed through the newspaper, refusing to read the headlines of other massacres. But she paused to read an article written by a woman journalist. It expressed what Jala felt in her heart, and her eyes welled up with tears as she read the words.

> *In the beginning of this sacred month of Ramadan, I cannot keep quiet before the events in Algeria. I must protest against the assassins and the fanatics who are causing such evil in the name of our religion.... We must remind the world, and especially the Muslims, that this month where the divine revelation came down from heaven is supposed to be a month of asceticism, of internal piety, of goodness toward all creatures and of moral perfection.*

If Algeria was to survive, it must once again be the women who rose up for reform. But today, weighed down with worry and physical fatigue, Jala did not know if she had it in her to keep fighting.

El Amin heard his wife in the kitchen and joined her at the table. Without a word, she slid the newspaper over to him, her expression filled with a tired anger. His eyes skimmed the front page, then focused on one article.

> *In the middle of the night while a sleepy village lay in darkness, terrorists raided the farm of humble farmers,*

dragging whole families from their beds and slitting their throats. Several were decapitated.

In a neighboring village, raiders entered a school building and, while the schoolchildren looked on in horror, slit the throats of two teachers.

A journalist was killed when he opened the door to his apartment and a bomb exploded, leaving the apartment in debris.

Twelve peasant farmers were hacked to death in a mosque at the end of evening prayers. The village imam received two bullet wounds and died shortly after the massacre.

All of these attacks occurred on the heels of Monday's explosion, what is being called the bloodiest act of terrorism since the start of the conflict in 1992. On Monday morning, a car bomb exploded in front of the police commissioner's office, killing 38 and injuring 256 ...

Jala rested her face in her hands, not looking at him. "What do you have to say for yourself, El Amin? Tell me, what can you possibly say?"

"It is not us, Jala! The Groupe Islamique Armé is responsible. You know it as well as I do. They are targeting the rural villages that have turned away their support and are now backing the military."

El Amin's eyes were dark and gloomy. In the area south of Algiers known now as the Triangle of Death, the little villages were helpless. The government promised increased measures of protection in these isolated regions, which made El Amin laugh bitterly. And who could prove that the government's secret service was not staging these massacres itself? Some had occurred within sight of a military base.

But all of this seemed unimportant when he thought of his wife, her arms and legs wrapped in gauze. She had been there Monday morning. Jala might have figured among the thirty-eight dead. Now she regarded him with fire in her weary eyes.

"I'm taking the children. We're leaving this country."

"Jala, where will you go? We have no family in France. You won't be allowed in. Please, Jala, you must stay!"

"Stay! Stay in a country where madmen hack teachers to death, and young girls are dragged off to terrorists' camps to be gang-raped? Where I come close to losing my life while standing in line at the post office! Stay?" Her voice was hysterical, her cheeks bright red. "Do you care about your children, El Amin? What is school for them now? It is brainwashing, indoctrination! It is nothing to do with the Islam we know and love. They are trained for bloodshed from the time they are six years old. You know it's true! It happened to you! I won't let it happen to them!"

She grasped El Amin's shirt and yanked on it. "Let me try to leave, El Amin. Otherwise we will all die." She calmed herself then and looked up at him, eyes overflowing with tears. "I don't know who you are anymore. I don't know what you are doing. I don't want to know. I only want to leave."

The muscle under his left eye twitched uncontrollably. El Amin clenched his teeth, his whole soul filling with anger. Slowly he pulled Jala to him and wrapped his arms around her. What could he say?

Inshallah? But what was Allah's will? A hazy confusion engulfed him. He had absolutely nothing to promise his wife or children except more bloodshed and death. Ramadan had come, and his wife wore scars to prove her words were right. He silently begged Allah that Jala would not see how terrified he was.

In the middle of the Algerian night, one hundred miles southeast of Algiers, two cars, both with headlights turned off, stopped outside of a small shack surrounded by tufts of dry vegetation and fine sand.

Hussein stepped out of his car and walked the short distance to the red Renault. The driver of the second car got out, and the two men walked for fifteen minutes in silence. They found the small cave even without the aid of a flashlight. Tonight the moon had smiled down to light their way.

The musty smell of wet rock and dripping water rose in their nostrils as they walked back into the empty cavity. Hussein handed some scribbled notes to the other man, who produced a flashlight and turned it on, shading the sudden light with his hand. He studied the sheets of paper and cursed under his breath.

"You want us to raid the house, kidnap the girl, and bring her to you? It will never work. She will disappear forever. She's better off just marrying the guy. I have enough problems without this."

Hussein's voice was steady. "I'm not asking you to supply me with men. I only want you, El Amin. You, I trust."

"Jala was injured in the explosion on Monday. She could have been killed! And my men are watching me, Hussein. I'm sure of it. I can't help you."

"We know when the wedding is planned—after Ramadan. We have four weeks. Your mother has had contact with the girl."

El Amin kicked at the sand. "My mother! Can she not leave well enough alone? For five years I've kept the terrorists away from the farmhouse. If they ever knew about you Christians, do you think any of you would survive? They would behead you all. They brag about it among themselves, and I can only cringe and pray to Allah that they never discover my parents' allegiance."

Hussein understood the internal battle that El Amin fought. He had known this man for years, knew what he was involved with. More than once El Amin had appeared at his house late at night, begging Hussein to get word to his parents to change their church meeting to another time and another home. He could not go to them himself; it was too dangerous. And Madira and Abdul never knew that the information came directly from their son.

Hussein did not betray El Amin's confidence. He understood quite well the great need for El Amin to remain anonymous. Politically and religiously, they differed in every way. But deep in their souls, Hussein and El Amin both were fighting for the ones they loved. And they both lived lives of secrecy.

"So David's boy is coming over for the rescue," El Amin muttered. "How does he think he'll get into the country, with all the airports and ports shut down?"

"He's coming through Morocco."

"He's crazy."

"He loves the girl, and he's about to lose her forever."

"I suppose we should thank Allah that someone still has the notion of chivalry and love. All we know here are barbaric acts, treachery, and fear."

"Will you help us, El Amin?"

A minute passed in silence, then another. Finally El Amin spoke. "Yes, I will help you."

"Good. I'll contact you when the boy arrives."

"Jala will relay the message if I'm not there." He reached out his hand in the darkness, and Hussein shook it. As they walked to the opening of the cave, El Amin asked, "How are my parents, Hussein?"

"Fine. You know how they rejoice during Ramadan. With all the parties at night, they can pray without arousing suspicion."

"They must be careful!" El Amin responded, a rough urgency in his voice.

"They are careful, and their God protects them. They worry for you."

"They cannot know. I'd rather them worry. Anything else would be much too risky. Good night, Hussein."

"Good night, El Amin. God be praised that Jala's life was spared. You'll be hearing from me soon."

"So be it then. *Inshallah.*"

23

It had all happened so suddenly that no one knew quite what to say when they gathered at the Hoffmann house the morning of February 3. David welcomed Ceb warmly, Gabriella made coffee, and Eric stood with his hands in his pockets, not meeting Ceb's eyes.

As he began to talk, Ceb felt his confidence rising. If there was one thing Samuel Cebrian could be, it was persuasive. He had that charismatic personality, that strange, forceful energy that made every plan and strategy sound like an adventure, a game of chess where one must simply move one's pawns to the right place on the board and the game could be won.

Ceb watched Eric's expression soften, his tight jaw relax, as Ceb eloquently explained why he was the man for the job. "Don't I look the part of a crazed terrorist, with my long hair, scarred face, and this hand of mine with only stubs for fingers!"

He waved his right hand in front of Eric. No one would doubt, despite his lighter skin, that he had been a part of the war that ravaged Algeria. No one would suspect him of anything else.

Afterward Ceb listened to Eric and David describe Rislène's past and present predicament. They reported the latest news received from Madira and Abdul. Ceb smiled to hear the names of the couple who had worked for his parents when they lived in that farmhouse in Algiers thirty years ago. For only a moment, he lost the thread of the conversation and let his mind wander to scenes from his childhood with his bosom buddy, El Amin Charfi.

"... a map of the area where Rislène is staying," David was saying. "You'll have help from Hussein. You remember Hussein?"

Ceb shook himself back to the present. "Yes, of course."

When the information had been given, all eyes turned to Eric.

"Well, son, what do you say? The final decision is yours."

Before Eric could speak, Ceb made his last plea, carefully planned, like the defense lawyer's final argument before a jury.

"Eric, this is my chance to do something worthwhile. You will be giving me what I need. A mission. You know I'm not afraid of bombs or death. I'll bring her back to you. I swear it." Then he played his final card. "You have a lot of people who need you, Eric. But me, I've got nothing to lose. Please, let me try."

He felt the irony in his words. He would go to Algeria to keep Eric safe and bring Rislène back so that this young couple could live out their love. But what he'd said was a lie. He had everything to lose. For the first time in three years, he cared deeply about someone.

He had seen Dominique's phone number written on the message board in Ophélie's kitchen the other day. Once again he thought bitterly that Dominique was the kind of man she needed. By the time he got back, surely Ophélie would have realized it too. Cruel irony! For the first time in so long, he felt he had a chance at a new beginning, another destiny. He wished he could see Ophélie one more time before he left. He wanted to tell her to wait for him, that he was lying when he said he had nothing to lose. And yet he was too afraid to risk the emotional strain and vulnerability. He felt much safer risking physical danger. That he could handle. He *must* go to Algeria. There really was no choice after all.

Then Eric's voice spoke out softly, breaking into Ceb's thoughts. "All right, Ceb. You win. You can go."

When Bri called to tell her the news, Ophélie swallowed hard and nodded. So it was true. Her vision had been a sneak preview of God's plan. Ceb was leaving, and here she was, sick in bed, unable to teach, so weak that all she could do was cry.

"Do you want me to come over?" Gabriella asked.

"No. No, I'll be all right. I'm going to Lodève tomorrow to spend the weekend with Mama and Moustafa. Thanks for telling me, Bri." She hesitated, then asked one last question, "When does he leave?"

"Tomorrow morning at eight."

An hour or so later the buzzer sounded, loud and aggravating. For a moment Ophélie contemplated ignoring it. Instead she pulled herself out of bed, down the hall, and across the den.

Picking up the intercom, she said, "*Allô?*"

She could barely distinguish the voice at the other end through the static.

"Filie, it's me. Ceb. Can I come up?"

Without saying a word, she pressed the button to open the door. She leaned against the door and let the tears come in a flood of relief. Ceb was here. She unlocked her door, then made her way back to the bedroom, discarding her nightshirt and pulling on a pair of jeans and a blue V-neck sweater. Hearing his knock, she called out, "Come on in. It's open."

She met him in front of the sofa. His hazel eyes were lit up with hope, and for a moment Ophélie saw wild, sweet Samuel there, passionate and charming, a disarming smile on his lips. She felt the electricity in the moment, some magnetic force pulling them together. There was a slight sound, and then each took a step toward the other. Suddenly she found herself in Ceb's arms. He was holding her so very tightly, kissing her hair, and she couldn't say anything except, "You came. I can't believe that you came."

He helped her to the sofa and sat her down softly. "Filie," he whispered, grasping her hand tightly. "Sweet Filie." His brow wrinkled, his eyebrows went up in an innocent concern.

He's in control again, she thought. How he needed to be in control. He was her friend, her protector, her doctor, sitting beside her, stroking her hand. But what was it she saw in his eyes? Was there something more?

They talked for a long time about everything and nothing, cuddled together on the sofa, he refilling her coffee, she leaning so comfortably against his broad shoulder. At last he explained his plan to leave for Algeria the following morning. His voice was excited as he spoke of strategy. It made her insides fill up warmly to see his enthusiasm.

Without thinking, she murmured, "Sam, I'm so glad you've come back."

In the space of that simple phrase, she felt him distancing himself. He sat up straight, took his arm from around her shoulder, and stared at her. "No, Filie. I'm not Sam! Can't you understand?"

It was a plea, but she had no chance to reply. He hurried on. "I buried my first life on that mountain. That was one destiny. Now I have another. I can't go back. All I can do is create another self with all this pent-up energy. Don't ask me to go back and grieve the past, Filie. It's a scar now, healed over, however imperfectly, like my hand. I've gotten used to it now."

He held out his right hand and examined the stubs. "If they told me tomorrow that they could make it whole again, through months of surgery and pain, do you think I would accept it? I couldn't. Not again."

"But you have to grieve, Ceb," Ophélie whispered, pronouncing his name carefully. "Otherwise the pain and remorse will eat you alive on the inside. You've begun, but you can't quit midway through."

"Don't talk to me about grief!" he snapped. He swung his fist and knocked over his mug, spilling the coffee. "What right do you have to talk to me about grief? What have you ever lost?" He leaped to his feet, his face contorted and furious, and began to pace about the room. "I have to go," he said after a moment. "I don't want to hurt you, Filie."

"No, Ceb, don't leave yet." Ophélie suddenly felt unbearably cold, as if the gust of death had swept through the apartment, transforming the warmth and kind conversation of five minutes ago. She was shivering, her sweater pulled over her jeans, her knees hugging her chest.

Ceb sank down into an armchair and waited, but the boiling rage still glimmered just beneath the surface.

She stared at him, tears streaming down her face. "I'm sorry," she managed, and slowly got to her feet. "You can go. But please hear me first. I'm sorry. I had no right … please forgive me, Ceb." She was shaking, her teeth chattering from cold and fear as she stared at this angry man. "Good-bye, Ceb."

She didn't know what pushed her to go to him, to kneel down in front of him and take his face gently in her hands as if she were speaking to a child. Tenderly, still crying, she pushed the hair off his forehead and kissed him there. He didn't move, but his expression softened.

"You do care, don't you? You really do care about me." He wrapped his arms around her, and they held each other, letting the silence speak.

When he was calmer, she whispered, "Do you believe in anything anymore, Ceb? What happened to your faith?"

He laughed. "You mean what have I done with God? Oh, Filie, He hasn't been a part of my existence for a long time. Long before the accident. My life was full of so many other things."

"I know."

"And then since the accident ... well ..." He shrugged. "What do you think? I blamed Him for it all. I said if this was how He punished me for my backsliding, then He wasn't a God I was interested in. I thought about it a lot, Filie. Really. And it came to me that Christianity is hopelessly superficial.

"When something good happens, Christians say, 'Praise God for this wonderful answer to prayer!' And when tragedy strikes, they say, 'Oh, Satan is really raging!' It's never God's fault. He always gets off the hook. I decided either He's in perfect control and is just cruel, or He doesn't have ultimate control and so things go wrong. I chose the latter, to keep my sanity. But a weak God doesn't interest me much."

"Maybe it's not Christianity that is too superficial," she answered. "Maybe it's you."

He chuckled. "I should have expected it. Filie to the rescue—defending her personal Savior. Her almighty God!"

"Scripture talks a whole lot about suffering, Ceb."

"Yes, I know. Good ol' Job. Blame it on the devil."

"Not just Job. The message of Jesus and of Saint Paul is that it's through trials that our faith is made strong."

"You're sounding like a religious tract, Filie. Shame on you!" He shook his head. "Your faith is part of you, your personality. It comes naturally. But not for me. I tried God once. In the end, He didn't work for me."

"It doesn't seem like *your* way has worked very well either," Ophélie whispered. Her eyes were fixed and intense, her attention totally focused on his every word. She saw a gradual feeling of discomfort come over him, and then he stood.

"Enough theology for today. I have to go." He walked briskly to the door.

Ophélie sprang to her feet, pushing past the dizziness that tingled in her head. She grabbed his arm. "Go? Where could you possibly have to go?"

"I have to get ready for the trip. I have things to prepare," he said.

Desperate, Ophélie whispered, "Ceb, please. I only want to help you."

He stared at her, anger in his eyes. "You can't help me. You're my past, and I won't go back there. I won't!"

"Ceb, I'm not your past! I'm now. I'm your future. You've been off on some strange tangent for so long. But it's time to come back to the present."

"No, Filie. If you try to force me back into society, you'll only be disappointed. I don't fit there. Don't you understand? I wouldn't come back as the brilliant young Dr. Samuel Cebrian you remember. He doesn't exist anymore. I'd come back as a murderer—a man who killed his wife and child." He turned toward the door. "I was wrong to see you again. It's best if you leave me alone!"

"You aren't a murderer, Ceb," she said, as he opened the door. "You're a coward! That's what you are."

All through the afternoon that one little word nagged him, echoed in his mind, angered him. How dared she call him a coward! At least there were action and power in the word *murderer*. But coward! *Coward* was the opposite of everything Samuel Cebrian had been. Coward was lethargy, resignation, helplessness, giving in.

All day he cursed Ophélie for pronouncing that judgment on him. Blasted woman!

But all day it came back, like the strains of a haunting melody. A coward. Yes, she had seen it, dared to say what he could never admit. He was running away from his past. He had said it himself. *Samuel Cebrian does not exist anymore.*

She was right.

It was as if in admitting it, something broke through Ceb's mind, coming from the back of a dark cave toward the light. He curled onto the mattress in a corner of his squat, like a frightened child recalling his bad dream, and let the memories come.

Samuel looked out the window of their chalet in the chic ski resort of Méribel. It was the last day of vacation and the snow was perfect, pristine, and sparkling in the early-morning sun like a million diamonds.

"Come on, Annie, let's stay just through noon." His voice was insistent. He had always been able to persuade her.

She nodded, giving in once again to his powerful personality.

They were on the slopes by nine a.m. when the first chair lift was set in motion. By noon they had made every run on that side of the mountain. The sun was suddenly obscured by graying clouds.

"We still have time to do Val Thorens," he said, adventure in his eyes.

"What about Marion?"

"We'll get her lunch and put her back in ski school for the afternoon," he said. "She'll be fine. Don't worry." He pulled Annie close to him and kissed her hard. "Please, *chérie*, just two more hours. Then we'll head home."

He heard himself insisting, remembered the way she had laughed halfheartedly and acquiesced.

The storm had come in suddenly, so that they found themselves at the top of the farthest mountain range, racing down the slopes with hail pelting their goggles like little hard pebbles.

Sam skied the way he did everything in life—fast, dangerously. Fortunately, Annie was an expert skier as well. But when they reached the chalet, after having retrieved Marion, Annie fell into Samuel's arms, exhausted.

"Why must you always beat yourself, go ever higher, outrace the storm?" She tousled his hair and tossed their ski clothes into the suitcase. "Someday you're going to kill yourself."

But she had been wrong, dear Annie. His impulsive urges had not killed him.

There she was before him again, begging him not to leave in the middle of the snowstorm. "Sweetheart, it's too late. We'll leave tomorrow, no harm done. We're all tired. Let's have a nice dinner and a good sleep and we'll leave in the morning."

But again he had pushed, forced his way. He had no desire to get home on Sunday afternoon only to be at the hospital at five the next morning to start a grueling week. He wanted a full day to rest.

Thinking of it now, Ceb rested his forehead in the palm of his left hand and wept. What had he been thinking? What incredible force possessed him so that he went beyond all reason to have his way?

He remembered frantically packing the car, watching the snow pile up on the suitcases before he could get them into the trunk. It was madness to leave now! In an hour it would be dark. They must be down the mountain before dark. Urging them to hurry, pushing them on, he saw himself in retrospect driven by his sole determination, ignoring the fear in Annie's eyes.

"*Chéri*, please, it isn't wise. Please."

Fighting his anger, forcing his voice to remain calm. "Get in the car. It will be fine if we leave now."

He scooped up little Marion, hugged her in his arms, and said, "Ready for an adventure, partner? We're going home in a snowstorm. It'll carry us all the way to Montpellier!"

Marion had laughed as Annie helped her fasten her seat belt.

The chains on the tires helped, but from the moment he started the motor and inched forward, Samuel knew he was wrong. It was no time to be heading down the mountain. Not another car was in sight.

But he was a surgeon. He was always in control of the instruments. The car was in his hands. They were safe.

It was on the third hairpin turn that the car began to slide, and he saw Annie's terrified stare. He remembered the panic that swept through him as the car slid swiftly toward the sharp embankment. He clutched his ears to shut out the sound of little Marion screaming, "Papa! Help me!" And the sensation of falling, falling.

The self-hatred welled up inside of Ceb, his head pounding, his heart pounding too. Why? What was it that pushed him to kill them? He had murdered them by his wild, driven spirit, as surely as if he'd held a gun to their heads and shot them.

The ski patrol had found the car two hours after the accident. Annie and Marion were dead. Later the coroner claimed they had died instantly, but Ceb often wondered if the man had said that to ease Ceb's guilty conscience. Perhaps they had really frozen to death, in the midst of innumerable broken bones and unbearable pain.

The rescuers had thought he was dead also. Three weeks later, when he emerged from his coma, the doctor had simply said, "Dr. Cebrian, you have an incredible will to live."

Then followed the months of physical therapy where he again pushed himself beyond what anyone thought he could do. It was his way of doing something with the grief. He would come back. He would be a surgeon again, even if he had to operate with a mangled right hand that had only three fingers.

Nine months after the accident, he went back to work. His staff and colleagues cheered him. Even his critics expected the *homme à tout faire* to somehow pull one more magic trick out of his hat.

But at the operating table, 283 days after his accident, Samuel Cebrian's luck ran out. He panicked. The left hand, the one he had retrained through meticulous, grueling therapy to compensate for the right, failed him. He couldn't control its tremor, and his eyes glazed. Fortunately Professor Voisin, his mentor, had insisted on being there with him during this first surgery, just in case ...

He had known from then on that he would never operate again. How headstrong and foolish! His brilliant career came to an abrupt, painful halt, smashing against the side of another mountain.

Slipping, slipping into a long, numbing depression, he abandoned everything—his house, his family, his career. He searched for oblivion. And found it as a homeless man on some forgotten street in one of France's largest cities. He had no more family, no future. At night he gulped bottles of cheap whisky and stared at his mangled hand and cursed his existence.

Samuel Cebrian died on the mountain with Marion and Annie. This strange new man was just Ceb, a pitiful beggar with a withered hand.

There was really nothing to get ready. Ceb stuffed a change of clothes into a torn khaki duffel bag along with his passport. He flipped open the document and looked down at the picture of the young, confident professional. He hardly recognized his own face anymore. His eyes searched the squat for anything else to take. He opened the drawers of the knobless chest and withdrew a handful of francs and his papers. By the time he got back from Algeria—*if* he got back—this place would be taken by some other SDF. *So let him come,* he thought. *Help yourself to my little slice of heaven.*

Ceb had agreed to sleep at the Hoffmanns' house that night so that David could take him to the airport early the next morning. His plane out of France would land in Morocco, where he'd be met by a string of Christians who would eventually deliver him to Algiers.

These were the details with which he needed to fill his mind. Strategy, planning. But all he could hear was that word *coward.* He still felt such a heaviness in his soul. *Oh, Filie!* Why couldn't she just let him hold her? Why did she have to play teacher? If she only knew how close he had been to telling her what he felt … *He hasn't been a part of my existence for a long time.* That was another lie. God was somewhere just out of reach. Ceb could feel Him coming back.

Lord! I don't have time for theology, he whispered, slinging the duffel bag over his shoulder and going down the stairs. *I just need You.*

24

All Friday afternoon she cursed herself for her foolishness. Why had she lectured Ceb, called him a coward? Couldn't she have just stayed by his side, content to talk about things that didn't matter?

Ophélie, sweetheart, not everybody wants to probe as deeply as you do. Her mother had said it a hundred times in the past. Well, her mother was right.

But there was something that had come from the disastrous argument with Ceb. The realization that what she had seen in his eyes was not love. He cared for her as an old friend. But he was a keg of dynamite, ready at the slightest provocation to explode. Maybe he was right. Maybe this trip to Algeria was just what he needed. At any rate, what he needed wasn't Ophélie.

She put on a CD and let the room fill with music. Above the strains of the orchestra she heard the buzzer sound. "Again?" she said out loud, angrily. Then her pulse increased. Was Ceb coming back one more time? She glanced at her watch. Seven thirty.

And then it hit her. Dominique! She had a date with Dominique that she had forgotten to cancel. She picked up the intercom.

"It's me, Ophélie. Dominique."

"Dominique, can you come up, please? I'm not quite ready."

She ran her hands through her hair. It was dirty and uncombed. She still wore the same jeans and sweater that she'd thrown on that morning. She hurried to the bathroom, ran a brush through her hair, and applied a little blush to her pale cheeks. *Oh, God, I feel so raw tonight. I'm going to burst into tears if I don't watch out. Lord, help.*

She went to the door and opened it. Dominique stood there with a bouquet of red roses in his hands.

It was awkward to say it, but in the end it would make things easier. "Dominique, I've been sick with the flu. And then there's all this stuff about my brother leaving for Algeria, and now Ceb has decided he should be the one to go. I forgot about tonight. I should have called to cancel. I'm so sorry." For some reason, she giggled. "Look at me. I haven't washed my hair, and I'm wearing the ugliest thing in my wardrobe, and I'm so weak I feel like I'll faint—"

Dominique held up a hand, grinning. "Enough. A guy can take a hint! It sounds like you're begging for a little rest."

"I really am sorry." An idea flashed in her mind. "Why don't we just get a pizza or something? I've got some lettuce in the fridge and a bottle of red. I could whip up something." But even saying it made her feel tired.

"No way, *mademoiselle*. You'll do absolutely nothing. Leave it to me. I'll be back in thirty minutes." He started to go out the door, then turned around and, still grinning, said, "Will that give you time to wash your hair?"

She stuck out her tongue at him and teased, "Just you wait and see."

She wore a simple red wool dress that flattered her figure and made her cheeks come alive with warmth. Her long mahogany hair, still slightly damp, glistened in the candlelight. She regarded the meal that Dominique had prepared and felt her appetite, gone for several days, suddenly returning with a force.

"It all looks delicious."

Dominique poured the wine and raised his glass. "To Ophélie, who looks beautiful even with dirty hair, and stunning when it's clean."

She rolled her eyes, laughed nervously, and touched her wineglass to his. "Thank you, Dominique. Thank you for all this. For being patient with me. It's lovely."

Handel played in the background. Dominique reached across the table and took her hand. She squeezed his with a smile. She felt suddenly very glad that he was there.

He had washed the dishes and was now stretched out beside her on the sofa. "What are you so worried about tonight, Ophélie?" He put his arms around her in a gentle hug.

She stiffened immediately and then chided herself for not being able to relax in his embrace. "Not worried. Just pensive."

He touched her temples softly. "But something is tormenting you in here. I can't get to it; you've locked yourself away from me. What am I to do? Can't you see that I want to understand? I truly do."

She bit her lip. "I'm too different, Dominique. I don't know what else to say. We see life so differently."

"Please don't think I'm criticizing you, Ophélie. Your philosophy seems simplistic to me, and yet I know there is profound truth in it for you. But if you had lived on the streets, seen the hopelessness, the people on the edge of society who can never really integrate, maybe you would understand why I say it is too simple. I've heard the SDFs begging God for mercy, imploring Him in tears, confessing sins, and promising to do better. But nothing ever changes. You know what I believe? We're each climbing, doing our best, getting better. There's no one way to go. Not just one path. Our lives are wanderings, in and out."

"I don't agree," she said. She struggled with the thought, seeing the cynicism creep over his face. Then she brightened. "It's like you— Dominique the street mediator. Your job is to take the government's high and lofty ideas and translate them into everyday talk, to meet the homeless and represent the government in a way they can understand, so they'll accept the help that is available. Isn't that what you do?"

He smiled. "More or less. If you simplify it, that's my goal."

"Well, Jesus did the same thing—lived among humanity to show us what God was like so that we could accept His help and love. He was a mediator."

Dominique reflected on her words, wrinkling his brow. "An interesting analogy. But too narrow. I can't believe that."

"Can you think about it at least?"

"If that would make you happy, Ophélie, I'll do it. I'll think about it."

It was the second time that day she had sat on this couch in a man's arms. She liked being close to Dominique. He was strong and kind and sure of himself. And stable. There. She'd said it. Ceb was an accident waiting to happen. Dominique had a different type of control than Ceb.

The conversation dwindled, and he pulled her to himself and kissed her tenderly on the lips. She took in the smell of his aftershave, the incredible softness of the kiss, closing her eyes, feeling a fire kindle within her. And then the kiss was over.

She stared at him. He hugged her against him, his eyes bright and dreamy.

"I know you, Ophélie. Nice and slow. So I better stop myself while I can." He held her tightly against him. "I don't want to make you afraid. I don't want anything to mess this up." He took her face in his hands. "Do you understand?"

She could only nod and murmur, "Thank you."

As she walked him to the door, he bent his head down and kissed her again. "I'll call you soon," he whispered as he left.

She wondered if it was the mixture of wine and medicine, or if this was perhaps just a dream. He had brought her roses, fixed her dinner, cleaned everything up afterward, and listened to her talk. He had held her tenderly and kissed her, and then, amazingly, he had stopped, respecting her wishes without her even having to voice them.

It had been quite a day. Sweet Dominique. *Le médiateur de rue.* He was a very good man. She fell asleep with a smile on her lips.

Early Saturday morning Mme Ploussard was planted by the window in her usual place, staring out to the open square below. "You were already asleep last night, André, so you missed it all! Mlle Duchemin's guest!"

"You've already told me that the homeless man came back again, Evelyne! With your running commentaries, *bon sang*, I haven't missed a detail in twenty years!"

"I'm not talking about that homeless man, André! He left Mlle Duchemin's apartment yesterday afternoon. But then another man, a nice-looking *Frenchman*, arrived. Brought her roses and a bottle of wine and stayed for hours! For hours, André."

Eyes shining, she turned from her perch at the window and sat down beside her husband. "But he didn't spend the night, no, he didn't! You were fast asleep, but I saw it all. He left just like a gentleman should, well before midnight. *Ooh, là là!* Finally, a respectable man for poor Mlle Duchemin! I have a good mind to go over there and see how she's doing."

André took his wife's hand and squeezed it tightly. "You will do no such thing! It's eight o'clock in the morning. She's probably still in bed. Leave her be. And fix me a cup of coffee, won't you?"

Mme Ploussard waddled into the kitchen, muttering under her breath, "After that Arab girl and that homeless man, well, it was about time for her to find *un homme respectable.*"

Ophélie awoke with a start and a funny, hollow sensation in her stomach. Not hunger. Emptiness. She glanced at the clock. Eight fifteen. Ceb had already left for the other side of the Mediterranean.

She slipped out of bed and sank to her knees on the throw rug and prayed for God's protection on him and Rislène and the other Christians, and all the people in that land who were victims of circumstance.

"And bring Ceb back, dear Lord. Please bring him back."

She did not add *for me*. That was no longer the question.

After a light breakfast, she pulled on jeans, a bright-red turtle-neck, and a faded sweatshirt, picked up her overnight bag, and folded her coat over her arm. With a quick check of all the windows, she let herself out the door, locked it behind her, and took the elevator down. Two days with Mama and Moustafa in Lodève were just what she needed.

The farmhouse that stood before her was big and rambling and unchanged. Ophélie breathed in deeply, relishing the crisp February air in the countryside. She needed to tell her mother what had been going on in her life for the past two months. Though she talked with her mother every week, there was so much that she hadn't truly shared with her. She owed Mama that. Dear, beautiful Mama, still slim and striking, still strong of body and soul. There were few people she admired as much. They had always been close, almost like sisters. Her mother was, after all, only seventeen years her senior.

But for matters dealing with men, Ophélie was more apt to confide in Bri. Sharing too many heartaches with Mama only made her worry. And Mama had enough worries of her own right now, with Moustafa having just been let go after twenty years of faithful service at his job.

"*Coucou*," Ophélie called out, letting the heavy oak door swing open wide. She was greeted with silence. "Mama? Moustafa?"

She hung her coat on the back of the leather couch, walked through the hall that was lined with framed photos. She took the steps upstairs two by two. "Mama?"

Her mother poked her head out of a bedroom, brushing a wisp of gray hair behind her ears. She wore a broad smile and came to her daughter, wrapping her in a warm embrace.

"Sweetheart! How are you?" Instinctively, she put her hand on her daughter's forehead. "Doesn't feel like you have a fever."

"Fever's gone, Mama. I'll be fine. A little air from Lodève and I'll be back to normal."

"Your room is ready. Moustafa's out back."

"How is he?"

"He's doing just fine. Gardening, woodworking, fixing this old place up." She laughed. "He says except for the fact that we don't have much money to live on, he thinks he could get used to this idea of early retirement."

"Are you going to make it okay?"

"Ah, let's not talk finances right now. Get yourself settled, then go out back. Moustafa is anxious to see his girl."

"You think you could find time to take a walk with me this afternoon?"

"There's nothing I'd like better," she said, and Ophélie knew that she meant it.

The phone sounded loudly from the Hoffmanns' kitchen, jarring Eric from his discussion with his father. It was too early to have word from Algiers.

"Let me get it, son."

For five minutes his father listened to the voice on the other end of the phone line. His face was ashen when he came into the den, his dark eyes glazed with tears.

"What is it, Papa? Bad news?"

"Tragic news, Eric," he choked out. "Samira died last night."

Eric collapsed in an armchair, pulling his hands over his face. Samira, dead! This vibrant young Arab woman, so sincere and ardent in her faith. Dead!

"They say she just gave up," his father said softly. "After the attempted suicide, she stopped eating. The family allowed Pastor Varak to visit when they realized how desperate her condition was. She told him she just wanted to be with Jesus. Life here was too hard."

Eric thought of Rislène. She had met the man who was destined to become her husband. Did she feel the same hopelessness as Samira? Perhaps not yet, but what if Samuel did not get there in time? Why had he not gone himself?

"Was I wrong to stay, Papa? What will happen to Rislène? Do you believe that she'll get out?"

What could his father say? Samira had been whisked away and married before the Christians could react. And now she was dead.

Papa sank into a chair. His face was drawn and tired, the stress he was under obvious in his physique. He had lost weight and appeared gangly and worn. "Eric, have you thought about what needs to happen next, when Rislène returns?"

He noticed that his father pronounced the word *when* with conviction.

He shrugged. He had to admit that all his thoughts and prayers were centered on having Rislène safe.

"She won't be any safer here than in Algeria if her father gets hold of her," Papa said with difficulty.

This was true. Eric swallowed hard.

"Are you ready to marry her, Eric?" There was no joy in the question, no happy anticipation. It was a matter of business, a deal that must be made to protect the client.

Marry her! Of course he would marry her! That was his deepest desire. "Of course I'm ready, Papa."

"When?"

That was it, then. If Rislène were to be protected by marrying a Christian, it would have to be done quickly. Eric felt his legs go weak. Was he ready to marry a nineteen-year-old? He had no job. She had years of schooling ahead of her, and his next year at the Fac would be the most difficult. And at the end of the year, to qualify to teach high school in France, he had to participate in nationwide exams where only the top 10 percent succeeded.

But he loved her, of that he was sure, loved her courage and her determination and her quick smile. He loved her heart of compassion and her passionate faith. He closed his eyes and thought of her coal-colored eyes and her smooth skin with its soft, perpetual tan, of the way she twisted her thick black hair onto the nape of her neck or let it fall loosely on her shoulders, of the way her slim figure danced underneath a sheer summer frock.

Rislène!

But to live with her, to be her husband, to take on that enormous responsibility ... the thought left his heart ramming into his ribs. He was an idealist. He had imagined carefree moments together and a long engagement. Now the truth slapped him in the face. If he wanted Rislène, he would have to take her now.

He was not sure how long he had been silent. He looked up at his father. "I'm ready to marry her, Papa. Will you help me get all the papers in order? We can at least do that much, can't we?"

Papa answered with a slow nod of the head. Eric thought he saw a mixture of sadness and relief in his father's deep-set eyes.

One of Ophélie's favorite things about this region of France was the panoply of trails to discover. Today she and her mother decided to go on a walk in the neighboring village of Saint-Guilhem-le-Désert. As they stepped over ancient boulders and peered inside the twelfth-century abbey, Ophélie explained her volunteer work, her dates with Dominique, the way she had met up with Samuel Cebrian, and his pleas for her to keep his identity secret from his parents.

In the damp interior of the abbey, where Saint Guilhem's bones were kept, Ophélie ended her monologue quite abruptly. They stared at the crypt, a somber silence in the air.

At last her mother stated thoughtfully, "Samuel has been through a hell we cannot understand. I'm so deeply grateful that he is alive. Give him time, Ophélie. He'll come back. You've started the process. God will finish it."

For Anne-Marie, faith was real and practical. She trusted and God worked. For all its simplicity, her faith had been tested and held firm through many heart-wrenching circumstances.

Ophélie had often wished she had inherited some of the simplicity of her mother instead of the agonizing, questioning temperament that came directly from her father. She knew her mother wished her daughter would not take life quite so seriously. *I wish it were that easy to put into practice*, Ophélie thought.

They stepped from the abbey into the blinding sun of the Midi and the quick chill of the mistral. The naked trees resisted the wind, stubby knobs thrust to the sky. Without a word the two women turned from the abbey and started a hike up a tiny trail, what was called "the postman's route," past houses built directly into the Cévennes mountains that dated back to the Gallo-Roman period.

"Mama, you know what?" Ophélie asked suddenly.

"Mmm?"

"I love you a lot." She squeezed her mother's arm.

Mama squinted in the sun and smiled. "Which is another way of saying case closed for today, *n'est-ce pas?*"

"You're right, Mama. No more men talk today. Just lots of prayers."

"That you will have, sweetheart. I assure you of that."

25

Ceb wanted to flee. Or throw up. Something was suffocating him, pushing down on his chest, making his breath come in panicked gasps. The woman standing before him was like a fuzzy photo, her smiling face contorted.

"Water, please," he whispered.

She led him to an old brown leather couch. He sat down and buried his head in his hands, a lump in his throat. For a moment he was unable to catch his breath.

The two-hour flight into Morocco had been uneventful. Three nights traveling in five different cars with five different drivers through mountain and desert into Algeria, the deathly silence and the fear, this Ceb had handled with no problem. The drive through the Algerian countryside was fine; after all, it was not the first time he had been back since his family's mass exodus with the rest of the pied-noirs in 1962.

But stepping inside the farmhouse where he had spent the first six years of his life, he was not okay, in spite of the warm welcome he received from the Charfis. The house smelled the same, a mixture of strong coffee and sand. The long cherry dining-room table was the same one his mother had adorned with her finest linen and crystal when receiving family and friends on special occasions. The old chiming clock above the buffet was the one he used to watch attentively, waiting for the time to leave for school. The same crystal bowl Mama had received as a gift for her service to the children of the village still sat on the dining-room table as a silent reminder of the past.

How was it that returning to the house where he had lived as a child suddenly seemed like the hardest thing he had ever done? Memories sprang at him unguarded, as if he had walked into a black cave and now hundreds of bats were flying in his face. Perhaps they were harmless, but they scared him to death. Hadn't he just allowed himself to remember the details of the car accident? Now did he have to replay his childhood as well?

"Samuel, you need to rest."

The gentle voice of Madira Charfi, his mother's maid and dearest friend, unnerved him completely. He followed her into a bedroom and, without any resistance, lay down on the bed. This was not the time for weakness. He needed strength and courage for the task ahead. But all he could do just then was cry into the pillow like a frightened child. For the time being, he had nothing left in him. Within moments, he fell asleep.

❀

The phone call from David Saturday explaining in veiled language that someone would be coming in the next few days had in no way prepared Madira to see Samuel Cebrian. She had expected Eric, or perhaps David himself. But Samuel! At first she had not recognized him, not until he said, "Hello, Madira. It's me, Sam." She had stared deep into the hazel eyes tinged with red and let out a sharp cry. Impossible! Samuel Cebrian, lost for three years, stood before her in the last place on earth she would have expected to find him.

His sudden emotion had prevented them from any conversation, and now he slept. Madira wadded her apron in her hands and looked for something to do. In a few hours it would be light, and she would begin preparing for market. She would meet with Rislène and her grandmother to discuss food for the wedding. When Samuel woke up, she would find out more details about the planned escape and could scribble a note to Rislène.

Everything felt numb. Eliane's lost son was asleep in her farmhouse in Algiers. Did Eliane know it? Madira wondered if bright, enthusiastic Samuel Cebrian still existed somewhere underneath the scruffy beard, the straggly hair, and the scars.

Her brow furrowed, she tried to pray, but all she could think was, *Samuel Cebrian is here. One sheep is returning to the fold. And what about the other, Lord? What about my boy, El Amin? What about him?*

❖

In the woods beyond the mountain village of Sidi el Kebir, an hour south of Algiers, El Amin wrestled with his thoughts. He wanted out. Out of this war, of murder, of brutality. They had said they were fighting because the government was against Allah. They had known in their viscera that Algeria needed to be an Islamic state. They had fought for Allah, and it was a holy war, a jihad. Was not this the ultimate honor?

But El Amin remembered peaceful years, before he had been indoctrinated by radical Islam, years when he had wanted to serve Allah, but the desire was not fueled by hate.

A sound startled him from his thoughts. Was it just a small animal in the dry leaves? He listened attentively. No, it sounded like a child's muffled sobs. El Amin glanced behind to make sure that his men had not followed him. "Who is there?" he whispered. "I won't hurt you!" He pronounced the words, then stared down at his machine gun in shame.

He stumbled upon a boy crouched behind an olive tree. The child's hands were bloody, his eyes filled with horror. He could not have been more than ten. He shrank from El Amin and began to run. El Amin caught him by the arm and covered the boy's mouth with his hand. "Shh! Please! Don't scream. I will not harm you."

The fear in the boy's eyes did not lessen.

"I didn't kill these people. I want to help you. What is your name?"

Wide-eyed, the child mumbled, "Nassim."

"What happened, Nassim? Can you tell me what happened?"

Nassim's big black eyes filled with tears. "Bad men came to our house three nights ago. They grabbed my mother and said, 'Your son works for the military. He is an infidel!' Then they slit her throat." Nassim looked down at his bloodstained hands. "My father and brother too. Then they left me there, sitting in the blood of my family."

A glaze came over his eyes, and El Amin was sure the child would faint. Instead, he looked El Amin in the eyes and asked, "Why didn't they kill me? I wish they had killed me too. Now I have no one."

Suddenly he grabbed El Amin by the hand. "Please, sir. Allah has sent you here to kill me. I don't want to live without my family. Kill me, please!"

El Amin's mind whirled. What could he do with this kid? Jala! He would take this boy home to Jala. She would keep him until he could figure out what to do.

"Nassim! Listen. I want to help you. I'll take you home to my wife and children. You'll live there. Things will be different." It was a rash, impossible promise.

The boy began to shake. "No!" he screamed. "Kill me. It is Allah's will! I want to die!" In a rush of adrenaline the boy raced past El Amin, back toward the farmhouse, screaming, "Kill me! Kill me too." Seconds later El Amin heard the *pat, pat, pat* of gunfire.

"No!" he cried, racing after the boy. But he was too late. Nassim lay motionless at the feet of one of his men.

In a rage El Amin grabbed the young guerilla and shook him. "Why did you do that?"

The young man shook free of El Amin's grasp. "Why?" He laughed. "Easiest job I ever had. The kid begged me to kill him. What's the big deal?"

El Amin realized that all five of the men were staring at him, puzzled. He could not afford to be suspected by his own men. He walked away, mumbling, "Nothing. Let's get out of here."

He could not let himself look back at the upturned face of the young boy, eyes wide open, staring lifelessly at the sky.

Grandmother had come from her house to take Rislène to the market, but Nazira didn't feel like going today. Her stomach grumbled, and the sight of all that food would just make the fast all that much harder. She was in a foul mood. What a rotten job, always watching her sister, the crybaby who spent so much time in the bathroom that Nazira wondered if she had a perpetually upset stomach. Served her right!

But maybe there was hope. Maybe once Rislène was married, they could all go back to France. Any person in his right mind could see that staying in Algeria was a dead-end road. And she meant *dead*. She picked up Rislène's copy of the Koran and flipped through the pages. Several pieces of toilet paper floated to the floor.

Stupid girl, keeping toilet paper in her holy book! She really must be desperate.

Absentmindedly Nazira bent down to pick up the paper. That was when she noticed the thick, dark writing on the plies of pink.

She read them with difficulty. It looked like Rislène had taken something, not a pen or colored pencil, but … an eyeliner? Yes, an eye pencil. She had scribbled down some sort of strange proverb. She retrieved the other paper that had whisked itself under the bed. Narrowing her eyes, she began to understand. Bible verses! Yes, here it said Matthew, and this one said Isaiah. Those were names from the Bible, she was sure. So that was Rislène's little trick! Eyeliner pencils and long stints in the WC to write Bible verses.

Cursing loudly, Nazira ripped the toilet paper in several pieces and headed to the WC. Then, her hand poised above the toilet, she refrained from flushing away the evidence. No! She must keep this for Grandmother to see. Dear sweet Rislène was not as naive and submissive as she appeared. Nazira cursed again and tucked the pink toilet paper into the pocket of her skirt.

It had worked! Madira was waiting for them at the market, and Grandmother had made the order for oranges and olives. And now, as Rislène returned to her uncle's home, her hands burned to open the note that Madira had slipped to her while Grandmother was examining the fruit. She only needed to get to the bathroom to find out the news.

Nazira met them at the door, her eyes defiant and blazing. "Come in, Grandmother. I have something interesting for you to see."

Her sister's cold, angry words sent a chill through Rislène's body.

"Liar!" Nazira yelled and slapped her across the cheek forcefully. "She's a no-good liar, Grandmother! Look what I found. Bible verses written on toilet paper with the eye pencils I gave her. And hidden in the Koran. Can you believe it? The blasphemy! And all along pretending to be coming back to Islam. Traitor. Double traitor!" She lifted her hand to slap her again, but Rislène covered her face.

"What does this mean, Rislène?" Grandmother's voice was firm.

She made no reply, glad that Madira's note was tucked safely away. *Oh, God, please don't let them find the other pieces of toilet paper that are hidden in the back of the armoire.*

"She hides in the bathroom to write Bible verses, Grandmother. That's what it means!"

Grandmother began to shake Rislène. "What else are you up to? What else?"

Tears streaming down her face, Rislène whispered, "Nothing, Grandmother. It's just a few Bible verses. You've taken everything else away from me. What harm can a few Bible verses do?"

"Plenty! Get rid of them now!" Grandmother Namani nodded to Nazira, and Rislène watched her sister take the crumpled pink paper and drop it into the toilet.

"Flushed away, Rislène, like a bunch of excrement." Nazira laughed. "That's all your religion is. Excrement."

"See what else she has hidden, Nazira," Grandmother ordered, and within moments Nazira had emptied the armoire. Shreds of pink toilet paper lay all over the floor. While Grandmother held Rislène's hands, Nazira pulled the sheets off the bed and searched under the mattress.

Silently Rislène prayed, *Oh, Lord, please, please give me a chance to read Madira's note.* So far Grandmother only suspected her of writing Bible verses. She still had no idea that she'd had contact with any Christians.

Nazira picked up the bright-yellow gourd and examined it closely. "Why did you buy this gourd, Rislène?"

"A child was selling it. She seemed so sad."

"I saw that child last week," Grandmother Namani broke in. "She asked me where you were." Her eyes narrowed. "Do you know that child?"

"No! Of course not! I'd never seen her before!"

"Hey, and there was a woman at the market in this neighborhood selling gourds the other day. You talked to her, too," Nazira accused. "The woman who sells oranges and olives!"

Grandmother slapped Rislène hard, pushing her down on the bed. With a yank, she ripped Rislène's blouse, exposing her shoulder. "What else have you hidden, child?"

Her grandmother's voice was rough and cruel, and a holy anger burned in her eyes. She shook Rislène forcefully. Instinctively Rislène clutched at her skirt. They could beat her senseless, as long as they didn't find the note.

"Strip down, Rislène!" Grandmother ordered.

"No! Why are you treating me this way?" She pulled her arms around herself for protection.

Grandmother grabbed her arms and held them in a fierce grip. "Take off her skirt, Nazira."

Rislène kicked and struggled, but even as she did, she saw the folded piece of paper fall to the floor. She tried to cover it with her shoe, but Nazira simply laughed, picked it up, and unfolded the white sheet. She read the words on the paper out loud.

"Man arrived from France today. Escape planned for Friday February 10. Get to Madira at market by three." Nazira stared at her sister in amazement. "You had it all planned. You really did, you wench." She yanked back Rislène's hair and spit in her face.

"This Friday! The Christians are serious about getting you back!" Grandmother released her grip on Rislène and looked her straight in the eyes. "You will not leave this house until you're married. You will not be left alone for even one minute, not even to go to the bathroom. No one is coming to 'rescue' you, Rislène. I'll call the *imam* today! Under such circumstances, I'm sure he will agree to let the wedding take place during Ramadan."

Grandmother left the room, slamming the door as she kicked several shreds of toilet paper under the bed.

She had been so close. They had worked it all out. That was why Madira had been so insistent that Rislène and Grandmother return to examine the produce on Friday afternoon. Friday afternoon she would have been free, if only ... if only she hadn't left those verses in the Koran. Usually she was careful to conceal them all in the armoire when she went out of the room.

Why, God, why did You let Nazira find them?

Someone had come from France to get her. Was it Eric? It didn't matter. She felt utterly helpless. She could not warn them that the plan had been discovered. By the time they realized that she was not coming to meet Madira, she might already be married. There was absolutely nothing she could do.

Abide in Me.

Well, yes, she could still do that. She could trust. She could pray. She could recite Scripture in her head. Hadn't God done everything up until now anyway? Surely He hadn't run out of ideas, even if Grandmother Namani's plan seemed invincible. Help was on the way. God could still come through for her.

For after you have suffered for a little while, the God of all grace will confirm, strengthen, and establish you.

Three more days. It seemed her whole life would be determined in the course of three short days. Two destinies, she thought. France and Eric, or Algeria and Yassir. Two destinies, but just one Lord. No matter what, there was only one Lord.

※

"I must speak with the police chief! It's urgent!" Grandmother Namani's voice rose hysterically. It was her third attempt to get through to the authorities. Her afternoon had been spent on the phone making frantic calls to Yassir's family and the imam, pleading and arranging for a wedding in three days' time. She felt completely spent, but she needed to sound convincing to the police chief. It helped that he was a personal friend of the family. Grandmother Namani wanted her residence guarded, with no chance of anything else going wrong. Rislène would not escape!

"Yes, what is it?" A gruff voice came on the line.

"Hello, Inspector Zandine. This is Mme Namani. I have a problem. My granddaughter has converted to Christianity. She was brought to Algeria, and we've arranged a wedding to a fine Muslim man. But there are Christians in Algiers secretly trying to arrange an escape. Christians, Inspector! The imam has given me permission to have a private ceremony Friday night at my house. I need some of your men to come guard the house."

His voice calmer, the police chief spoke. "Mme Namani, with all due respect to you and your family, this is a private matter. Not something for the police. We don't have time for such a thing."

"The police are not interested in locating Christians? Please, Inspector Zandine, you must send someone!"

"And you think these Christians will be violent?"

"They are desperate to rescue my granddaughter."

The police chief was silent for a moment. She heard him shouting orders to someone in the background.

"Mme Namani? Yes. When exactly is this wedding scheduled?"

"Sunset Friday night."

"You understand that I cannot spare any officers, but I'll send a few of our young men in training over late Thursday morning. They'll stay until your granddaughter is married. Will that be satisfactory?"

"Yes. Yes. Thank you very much, Inspector Zandine." She quickly gave the police chief instructions to her house and hung up the phone, feeling immensely relieved.

Late in the night, Hamid would bring Rislène back to her house, and she would lock her granddaughter in the bedroom until it was time for the ceremony on Friday. Quick and simple. There would be no time to prepare an elaborate feast. But it could not be helped. The family honor was at stake, and that was what mattered most. *Inshallah.*

The small, thick man with the flat nose and the broad smile shook Ceb's hand forcefully. "Samuel! Samuel Cebrian! Well, of all the people I thought I might see, I never considered you." He nodded. "But David was right to send you. The perfect man for the job. Fearless Sam!" His eyes rested briefly on Ceb's maimed hand, then stared out the window of the Charfis' farmhouse.

"You were always up to no good, weren't you?" Hussein ran his hand across his brow. "Remember the time you were staying with Ophélie and me out at Lodève? Oh, you couldn't have been more than nine, ten tops. And you stole all those chickens from the neighboring farms. Wrung their necks, plucked the feathers off, cut 'em up, cooked them, and sold them at the market the next day, barbecued and all, and made four hundred francs." He slapped his leg. "And no one ever suspected a thing. Sweet, charming Sam, our visiting friend from Montpellier."

"Yeah." Ceb nodded, a grin flickering across his face. "Anne-Marie and Moustafa were gone for the day, and Filie was at a friend's house. But when she found out, she was furious. I think that was the only time she ever really got mad at me. Livid. Righteous anger. Thank goodness you were there to placate your little sis."

"My little sis." There was a catch in his voice. Hussein cleared his throat. "How is she? Do you ever see her?"

"Yeah, I've seen her recently."

"I hear she's still single, lovely, caring for others."

"True, that's Filie." He cocked his head to the side.

Hussein laughed, but it sounded forced. "My little sis."

Ceb felt something tingle inside, seeing the hurt and love in Hussein's eyes.

The stocky man continued, "You and Ophélie were very close as teens."

"Oui."

"And now?"

"Now?" Ceb asked, surprised. Then he sighed. "She's helped me want to live again."

There was an uncomfortable silence. Hussein pursed his lips. "Please give her my love the next time you see her." He hesitated, then added, "And don't let her get away from you again, Sam."

Ceb had thought that Algeria would be nonstop action. War, risk, adventure, violence. Not memories. Not more thoughts to torment his soul. He had thought it would be a new beginning, not a long, painful step back into his past.

His had been a carefree childhood, chasing his friend El Amin through the orange groves. He remembered lining up his array of tiny green soldiers on several large stones that he had perched precariously one on top of another. Across the path that represented an ocean, El Amin had crouched with his gray plastic men, preparing a sneak attack. Even at six, Ceb had thought that El Amin was a master military man.

"I'll be a general one day," the Arab boy had bragged.

He was not a general now, thought Ceb, watching his childhood friend pace in the sand before him, angrily spitting out olive seeds. He was a terrorist, a fervent member of the fractured FIS. Ceb wasn't one bit surprised.

The reunion had been awkward when Hussein had driven him out to the desert in the middle of the night and left him there with El Amin. They had regarded each other from a distance, like two dogs, each sniffing the scent of the other to see if it was enemy or friend. Finally El Amin had crooned, "Samuel Cebrian. What do you know? And I thought you were dead."

"I was," he stated simply.

"Yeah. I was sorry to hear about Annie and Marion." He cursed. "Rotten world we live in." Another long silence. "Why'd you come back here?"

"To have something to do."

El Amin grimaced. "I've never known you to be at a loss for things to do."

Ceb changed the subject. "How's Jala? The kids? You've got four, don't you?"

"Yeah. They're okay. Jala got banged up pretty good in a bombing last week."

Ceb stared at El Amin, and he knew the Arab saw the accusation in his eyes.

"It wasn't us, Sam. It's such a mess over here. You can't begin to understand."

They were supposed to be making plans to rescue the Algerian Christian named Rislène. Instead they relived their childhood and adolescence, confiding easily in one another, knowing full well that their paths might never cross again. For El Amin it was a sudden, incredible relief to have this long-lost friend show up at a time when he most needed an impartial, objective observer. He could not share his thoughts with another Algerian. That was to risk death. Already suspicion had been aroused.

"Do your folks know you're here, Sam?"

"No. They don't even know I'm alive. Not yet."

"Will you go see them?"

"Maybe. Sure. If I get out of this place in one piece, I plan to go see them."

"What put you on the streets? What made you give up? Was it *their* deaths or something else?"

"It was the complete loss of control in my life. No wife, no child, no job, nothing."

There was a faraway look on his face, and El Amin felt a piercing hurt for his childhood friend.

"So I let Samuel Cebrian die, El Amin. He's gone. I'm Ceb now. Just Ceb."

El Amin contemplated his words. "So why did you come back here?"

"I thought it was for the adventure, the risk. To have something to do. But I don't know anymore."

"I'm out of control too, Ceb," El Amin admitted, standing up and hurling an olive pit far off into the sand. "In a different way, I have lost control of my life. I'm living with too many secrets, and someday I'm going to slip."

"Do you see your parents?"

"No. Never. Much too dangerous."

"What do they think?"

"They think I'm a lunatic. They fear I will betray them." He felt the tears welling up in his eyes, tears that had not been allowed to surface for so many years. Anger, grief, hurt. "I've spent these last years protecting them, and they'll never know it. They can't know it. It is much safer for all of us if they believe I hate them. But it's not true." He covered his face with his hands, letting the tears moisten his palms. "I love them more than this, than what I believe in, but ..." He couldn't continue.

Ceb's hand on his back brought comfort. "I'm so afraid for them," El Amin whispered finally. "The hatred the militant Muslims have towards the Christians is terrifying. But it doesn't really matter. They could just as easily be slain in town. It almost happened to Jala. When I think of my family, Jala and the kids, Mama and Baba, my sisters. If I take one wrong step, they'll be the first to go. I'm trapped and I'm petrified. Trapped in hell."

For a long time the two men said nothing more. The only movement was El Amin nervously running his hand through his thick black hair. It was Ceb who spoke at last.

"Could you get out of here? Come to France?"

There was utter desperation in El Amin's voice. "I'd be sought out there just like here. No hope, no escape."

"Doesn't your religion teach assurance of paradise if you die in a jihad? That seems like hope."

"I used to believe it, but I don't know what I believe anymore. Surely Allah must weep at the massacres, at the senseless cruelty. If he doesn't weep, does he gloat? And then what kind of god is he?"

"Who can say, El Amin? I decided that my God was too weak to make things right, so I abandoned Him."

"Even if I abandoned Allah, I couldn't abandon the war. It's impossible." He drew a circle in the sand with his finger. "I'm stuck right here in the middle of it all. You know what I think, Sam? I think it is all up to us. I don't think your God or mine cares about helping. We're just thrown out here to do the best we can. Fate decides in the end what will happen. It's a rotten deal. We need help!"

"I used to believe that help had come."

"And now?"

Ceb shrugged. "I just don't know anymore."

26

The weekend in Lodève with Mama and Moustafa had helped Ophélie turn her thoughts away from Ceb. But now it was Wednesday morning, and every Wednesday morning for the past five weeks she had spent with Ceb, rediscovering her old friend. With Ceb in Algeria, she wondered if anything still compelled her to go to the Red Cross. She thought of the men and women standing in line waiting for coffee. She thought of their stories and of the courage that many displayed. Then she thought of Jean-Marc smiling at her, wearing that old red sweater, proud to have followed her advice and thankful that someone cared enough to want him to be warm.

I do care, Lord.

A shiver went down her spine. Was it her subconscious warning her not to care too much? Hadn't Dominique been right? The SDFs would not change.

For a moment, Ophélie let herself imagine what it would be like, working beside Dominique, sharing this life together. But not just with the homeless, sharing *their* life too. He was a kind, strong man.

Who doesn't share my faith. Like Bachir.

She felt another shiver and pulled on a bright-blue turtleneck with jeans and a sweater. There was much to be done at the Red Cross, people to be helped. And afterward, a visit to see Jean-Marc and Lassie and the puppies would do her good. She smiled at the prospect.

Show me how to care for these people as You do, Lord, beyond the
limits of human love. Show me how to be Your hands and feet today.

When she entered the squat, she found it strangely quiet and deathly
cold. She reached back and knocked on the door again. "*Coucou,*
Jean-Marc. It's Ophélie."

At first glance, he was nowhere in sight. Then she saw him and
smiled to herself. He had fallen asleep, sprawled out behind the puppies' cage.

The puppies made no noise as she approached. They too seemed
to be sleeping, piled on top of each other. Then she saw that they were
not asleep, but lying there pitifully, eyes open, tongues out, looking
too weak to move. Lassie was sitting beside Jean-Marc, whining and
licking his face.

"Jean-Marc, have you been feeding these puppies?" she asked,
nudging the sleeping man, letting a stern tone creep into her voice.

Jean-Marc did not answer. She nudged him again before she
realized the truth: he was not asleep. His hand was frigid, and she saw
that he must have fallen, because he was twisted awkwardly beside
the cage, with one hand on the latch, as if his last movement was an
attempt to free the puppies from their prison.

Ophélie screamed, staggered back, feeling the bile rise in her
throat. "No, it can't be. It can't be." She couldn't bear to look at him
again but backed into a corner and vomited. Then she made her way
to a chair and sat down, resting her head on the filthy table.

"I didn't know how horrible your life really was," she whispered.
"I didn't want to know. I didn't want to feel your pain. Not really.

I don't think I believed Dominique when he said that many of you died on the streets with no one to care." She felt too weak to move, as if she was fighting delirium, sitting in a squat and talking to a corpse. She wished Ceb were there to tell her what to do.

Dominique. She must find Dominique. "I'll be back for the puppies. I promise I'll take care of them, Jean-Marc. And Lassie, too. That's one thing I can do." She closed the door and fled down the steps into the narrow alleyway, weeping as she went.

Dominique held Ophélie close as she cried. In between sniffles, she managed to say, "Now I see how awful your job is. They really die, don't they?"

Dominique did not respond but bent down and gently touched the dead man's hand. "You were a good man, Jean-Marc. I'm going to miss you." He hesitated, then, with a look of sorrow in his eyes, turned Jean-Marc on his back. At that moment, Ophélie saw Dominique's soul. His was not just a job. *Médiateur de rue* was his vocation. He loved these people. He was devoted to them, even when it meant picking up the body of a dead old man and carrying him to an unmarked grave.

"I'll keep Lassie and the puppies," she whispered with difficulty. "I promised it to Jean-Marc. Please, let me do that. If they live, I'll keep them for him. It's the least I can do."

Dominique looked back at her. "It's a good idea, Ophélie. I'm going to get help. If you think you can handle the pups, I'll let you." He sniffed. "I'm so sorry it had to be you who found him."

"It had to be me so that I could finally understand."

It happened often, this battle within herself, this seeking to be free of something and freed to something. It was the dark side of Ophélie's personality that few people saw, the ever-spiraling tyranny of guilt and fear, and the terrible, terrible solitude. Today again she found herself literally crying, begging the Lord to stop the vicious circle of self-condemning thoughts. After a while, sitting on the couch in her den, she felt the late-afternoon sun that came through the French doors from the balcony touch her face, as if God were reaching out a tender finger through the rays of the sun and personally wiping away each tear.

She picked herself up off the couch, relishing the warmth of the sun through the glass. "Let this be a new beginning," she prayed hesitantly. "Whatever it takes. I give You Ceb and Dominique, as I've given You every other man in my life. As I gave You Bachir. You know the pain."

The phone rang shrilly, interrupting the last sentence of her prayer. She hurried to answer, out of breath. "Yes?"

"Ophélie, I've made you dash to the phone."

A smile spread across her face. "Bri! No, that's okay. Just having an argument with the Lord."

"Ah, who's winning this time?"

"He is, fortunately."

"Do you want to talk about it?"

"No," she said too quickly. "I'll be fine. What's up?"

"We've heard from Algeria. Ceb arrived safely and has met up with Hussein and Abdul and Madira. Rislène has been in contact with Madira, and the escape is planned for Friday. It's rather tricky, so I thought you'd want to know so you could be praying."

"Of course. Oh, thank the Lord!" She let out a long sigh. She could imagine Ceb's mind planning each step, each procedure, like an operation, his hand ready for the scalpel. For now, he was safe.

"Yes, thank the Lord," Gabriella said. "Are you sure you're okay?"

"I'm better now. But exhausted, empty."

"I'm so sorry about your friend."

"He was beginning to be my friend, Bri. I feel so rotten about it."

"I hear you're taking care of his puppies?"

"Yes. Eric helped me get them from the squat. It was the least I could do."

"Listen, Ophélie. You've done a lot. Get yourself a cup of tea and take a break for a little while. It's okay to just be sad, you know. Will you do that for me, please?"

Ophélie glanced at the papers strewn over her desk, waiting to be graded, and shrugged. "I promise, Bri. And *merci*." She hung up the phone and let the tears come again. He always knew what she needed, this loving God.

With Janine's help on Wednesday night, Ophélie bathed all five puppies, fluffed their fur with a hair dryer, and gave them plenty of warm milk and a fancy brand of puppy food. They devoured every bite. Lassie, bathed and dried, walked over to the cage and whined.

"Here you go, sweetie," Ophélie said, opening the cage door. "You don't have any more milk, so they won't be bothering you. But go on. Give them a little loving." Ophélie reached in and took Hamlet by the scruff of the neck and laid him beside Lassie. The black mutt gently nuzzled her offspring, then licked him all over and seemed very content to do it. Next out was Cleopatra, who was easily holding her own with her four brothers. She nipped Hamlet on the ear, then pounced on Lassie.

"She's got more energy than the rest of them put together," Janine commented.

"What would you expect from a girl named Cleopatra?"

"Cleopatra? That's great. What are the others' names?" Janine smiled as Ophélie told her. "I think they're going to be okay, Ophélie." She reached into the cage and picked up Saint X and held him to her cheek. "What a cutie you are! Black with four white paws. And now you smell fresh and clean." Janine scratched him behind the ears, and Saint X responded with a tiny tongue licking her cheek. "I've always wanted a puppy, Ophélie. Can I have him?"

Ophélie stared at her, surprised. "Really? You'd like to take Saint X?"

"Yeah. When he's ready."

Ophélie smiled. "That'll be great. He's already got his shots and everything, thanks to Ceb." She stuck her arm in the cage and caressed the runt. "Anyway, I'm going to keep Le Petit Prince for myself."

Later in the evening, the puppies were snuggled close to Lassie and all were asleep. Janine was sipping a cup of decaf, sitting cross-legged on the couch. "What are you studying with your class these days?"

"*Le Bourgeois Gentilhomme.*" Ophélie pulled her knees to her chest in the overstuffed chair.

"Molière! Perfect! That was the first play I acted in, when I was fourteen. *Ah! La belle chose que de savoir quelque chose!*" Janine recited, then set down her cup and comfortably stretched out her legs. "Mama hates it that I'm spending more time at your church."

"I'm not surprised. She thinks she's losing you."

"All she's doing is making me lose my mind! That woman! She reminds me of M. Jourdain!"

"M. Jourdain of *Le Bourgeois Gentilhomme?*"

"One and the same. The man who only seeks position and fame and to be with *les gens de qualité.*"

Ophélie laughed. "I take it your mother doesn't think the congregation of the Eglise Protestante Evangélique are 'people of high standing.'"

"Sorry to say it, but she thinks you're too nice, and she can't stand the fact that true French would mix with pied-noirs and Arabs. It infuriates her!" Janine rolled her eyes. "Hopeless case."

"I could have sworn I saw Simon at church two weeks ago."

Janine colored. "You did. He went to check it out. Mama and Simon are afraid I'm getting into a cult."

"They *are?* I mean, I can understand that from your mother, but from Simon?"

"Don't worry. It's just his paternal instincts coming out. Anyway, he told me he was very impressed, and that your church is definitely not a cult."

"*Ouf!* Glad he came to that conclusion," Ophélie said with a hint of irritation in her voice. Her eyelids were growing heavy, but unfortunately Janine seemed to have settled in for a late-night discussion.

"I really like the church, Ophélie. I haven't wanted to admit it, but it's true." Her eyes were bright, her bobbed hair swinging softly around her head as she talked. "I know we've had this conversation before, but what exactly is wrong with reading my horoscope? Or sleeping with a man that I care about?"

It was the last thing Ophélie felt like doing, getting into a discussion about Christian values. Wearily she said, "Janine, I love you dearly. And you know I'm thrilled that you like the church. But I don't have the strength to answer your questions tonight. I'm sorry. Call me a rotten friend."

Janine laughed. "No, I'm the rotten one. I was the one who said you needed to lighten up, and here I go asking you questions. Anyway, I know what your answer would be."

"You do?"

"Sure. You'd pick up the Bible, open it, point to some verse, and say, 'Obedience.'"

For some reason, Janine's assessment made Ophélie burst into laughter. "You're right, Janine," she said. "You're absolutely right."

She was back in Jean-Marc's squat, and the smell was overwhelming. She gagged and turned to run out, but then something soft and fragrant drifted into the room, transforming the darkness and cold and terrible stench into something bright and airy. In the corner, Jean-Marc woke up and smiled at her....

Ophélie sat up quickly in bed. She glanced at the illuminated numbers of the clock on her bedside table. 2:33. She felt like she had been wrestling something, someone. Staring down beside the bed, she saw that it was only the sheet and blanket that lay in a heap on the floor.

A verse of Scripture floated into her subconscious. *We are a fragrance of Christ to God among those who are being saved....* She blinked, tried to clear her mind, but the question was there:

Had she brought any pleasant smell at all to Jean-Marc's squalid surroundings?

Ophélie felt a wave of despair wash over her.

All at once, she found herself on her knees amid the tangled bedcoverings. "Oh, God, I have tried so hard to bring hope to my students. And to Janine and Simon and the rest of the troupe, and to the homeless, too. Show me what You want me to do next, Lord. Please."

She climbed back into bed and fell asleep thinking of a little red runt of a puppy and an empty bottle of perfume tucked away in an old wooden trunk.

27

The dress was bright blue, made of a fine silk and covered with gold embroidery that swirled all over the material in luxurious fashion. A thick gold belt, a gift from Yassir, outlined the bride's thin waist. But for all its beauty, the wedding gown itself was almost hidden underneath dozens of strands of pearls that hung around Rislène's neck, the shortest hanging just at the base of her throat, a bright amethyst embedded in the midst of the pearls. Strand after strand cascaded down her body. She felt pulled down by the weight. Or perhaps it was merely the heaviness in her mind.

Grandmother Namani placed the bridal cap on Rislène's head. It resembled a gold crown studded with jewels. Small gold charms dangled from the bottom of the crown, lying flat against Rislène's forehead. Underneath and held in place by the heavy crown, Rislène's bridal train of a crisp white material rose in a point. It too was embroidered with gold trim. The rest of the train was appliquéd with delicate golden symbols and billowed behind her, reaching almost to the ground.

Her thin frame quivered underneath the wedding attire, her eyes turned to the floor. Her grandmother had forgotten her anger and now excitedly adjusted the dress and train.

"You will be a beautiful bride," she exclaimed, as if Rislène were as excited as she about the wedding. She embraced her granddaughter. "Ah, my dear child. You'll see! You'll be happy. Yassir is a good man. And he has offered a handsome dowry! *Hamdulillah!* Allah be praised!"

Grandmother Namani brought out a pair of earrings. They too were made of intricate strands of pearls interlaced with gold. Rislène stood obediently as her grandmother attached them to her earlobes. What else could she do? She was back at Grandmother's house, and two of her uncles guarded her room. Three other men, whom Rislène suspected of being with the police, were stationed outside the house. Even in the bathroom, Rislène was obliged to leave the door cracked while Nazira stood by, counting the seconds.

And now she wore the wedding gown that had been handed down from generation to generation in the Namani family. Tomorrow, February 10, the day she should have been escaping this prison, she would be married and entrapped forever. Married to Yassir. He was strong and striking, ten years her senior, with cold, serious eyes. Rislène could suddenly understand Samira's act of attempted suicide as she contemplated a life with a man she had laid eyes on only once. A man who expected her to bear him many sons. And even if they did eventually move to France, what good would it do her? She fought the nausea welling inside.

She had been to the hammam that morning for the required ceremonial washings for a bride. Back at her grandmother's house, several aunts and cousins had made a paste of crushed henna leaves, which was put on the palms of her hands and then covered with cotton and tied in place with a scarf. Tomorrow the skin on her palms would be a beautiful red tint. It was the custom. And in a few minutes the salon stylist would come to Grandmother's house to prepare Rislène's hair. Everything, though rushed, would be ready for the celebration tomorrow.

The imam had agreed to a small ceremony at dusk, followed by a modest meal. Then Rislène would move to Yassir's family's house, where the newlyweds would finish out the month of Ramadan. Later, he promised to take her on a trip outside of Algeria.

"Please let me talk to Mother," Rislène begged as Grandmother Namani inspected the wedding attire. "I need her advice. I am so afraid. Please."

"You may have all the advice you want from her after you are married. Now you must undress. The gown fits you beautifully, Rislène. You see, even this shows that it is the will of Allah that you marry Yassir." Grandmother Namani smiled, but her large, wrinkled face betrayed signs of worry. "Hurry up now. The call to prayer is in fifteen minutes."

The apartment in Montpellier was filled with people celebrating the end of the day's fast. Altaf's three sons and youngest daughter had invited several friends for the meal, and now they laughed and danced in the living room.

The telephone ringing at ten thirty at night meant that something unusual was happening. Her husband hurried to answer it, and Altaf quietly followed and stood outside the bedroom listening. His gruff voice dropped to a hushed tone, and she was sure it was his mother on the other end, talking about Rislène.

"A planned escape? Tomorrow?" The whispered questions were filled with rage. Silence. Then Youssef gave a short cry and said, "This is wonderful news, Mother! Not escape, but a wedding. Tomorrow! And such a large dowry ... Of course you did the right thing. And the house is well guarded? ... Yes, of course, we will come for the real celebration after Ramadan. Very good. Good-bye, Mother."

Altaf scooted away from the door, picking up an empty tray and carrying it back to the kitchen. She met her husband in the hall.

"Who would call at such an hour?" she asked innocently.

"Adida's parents. Checking to make sure she is here. They expected her home earlier."

Altaf nodded. She hid her alarm as her husband joined the young people in the den, his somber face now breaking into a broad smile. She needed to talk with Mme Hoffmann! Hadn't Mme Hoffmann promised that Rislène would be brought back to France? Something had gone wrong. How could there be a wedding tomorrow, before the end of Ramadan? But Youssef's words left no doubt. Tomorrow Rislène would be married to a man she didn't even know!

Mme Namani leaned against the doorpost, observing the young people dancing. "I'm tired, Youssef. I'm going to lie down."

Her husband came to her and kissed her forehead in an unusual display of affection. "You have worked hard to prepare this feast. Rest and pray. I'll join you soon."

As music blared from the other end of the house, Altaf slipped into her bedroom and closed the door. She fell on her knees and closed her eyes, trying to pray. But all she could imagine was Rislène dressed in the elaborate Algerian wedding gown that had been in the Namani family for generations. She must be terrified.

And I have never even met this man. He will marry my daughter, and I don't even know his name.

"Allah! I beg you to protect my daughter. All I want is her happiness. That is all, for her to be happy. What should I do? What should I do?"

El Amin woke up in a sweat, eyes wild, heart beating erratically. The dream had seemed so real. Many Muslims had dreams and visions during Ramadan. It was when Allah spoke clearly to his chosen people. El Amin had never really had a vision before, but this he could not mistake. It was such a disturbing vision!

The man standing before him was dressed in white. Or not exactly white, but an incredible brightness. He was walking toward El Amin with hands outstretched. His eyes were a blazing fire that made El Amin recoil in horror. This man was reading every evil thought and action that he had ever committed! There were so, so many. Unable to bear the scrutiny of the eyes, El Amin had turned his attention to the man's hands. Pierced hands, wounded, bloody. Almost in spite of himself, he fell prostrate before the blazing figure, sobbing, "I'm sorry! Forgive me! Forgive me, Jesus!"

"Go quickly. Your parents need you."

Had the man truly spoken?

Wait, wait, don't leave. I have questions!

He was running after the disappearing figure, screaming at the top of his lungs. And then he was awake.

"What's wrong, El Amin? Why did you scream?" Jala's groggy voice was punctuated with concern. "Look at you. You're drenched."

"What time is it?" he asked, unable to focus on the clock by the bed.

"Ten till five. Morning prayer is soon."

El Amin grabbed Jala's hands, then pulled her to him and clung to her fiercely. "I have to go now, Jala. My parents are in danger."

"Your parents? But you've always said that *seeing* them would put their lives at risk."

"Something has happened." He jumped out of bed and began to dress.

Jala followed him, grabbing her robe. "What do you mean? What has happened? You're scaring me, El Amin. How long do I have to live with terror in my soul?"

His heart softened, and he knelt before her. He searched her eyes. Could he trust her with his vision? Dare he burden her with his thoughts?

"I can't explain why, but I just know I must see them. Jala, I love you! Pray for me. Pray that Allah will show the way." He scribbled an address on a piece of paper. "If I don't return by tomorrow, go to this address. They will know what to do."

"El Amin! Why are you saying this? You have never acted like this before!"

"I am telling you because I want you to know that I love you with everything within me. And I want you to know that whatever happens, you will be taken care of."

"El Amin! Don't go!"

"Shh! I must. I love you, Jala. I'll be back tomorrow."

"Tomorrow," she whispered, tears streaming down her face.

He thought that she had never looked more beautiful.

Altaf left the apartment before dawn while the rest of the household slept. She pulled her hijab over her hair and stepped outside. The morning was cold, with a bitter wind, but all she noticed was a numb feeling in her heart as she hurried along the sidewalk to the bus stop. A number 9 bus came shortly, and she climbed aboard, looking around, afraid she was being followed. By whom? Her own children? But she was the only passenger.

Twenty minutes later, her legs seemed to propel her along in a panicked rush toward the Hoffmanns' house. The sky was still pitch dark when she pounded on the door, shivering with a cold that had nothing to do with the weather.

Mme Hoffmann, tying the belt of her robe, opened the door and was unable to hide her surprise. "Mme Namani! Come in," she said. "Is something the matter?"

She clutched the red-haired woman's arm. "Last night Youssef received a call from his mother. Rislène is getting married today. I heard him say it! They must have feared a rescue for the imam to give permission for a wedding to take place before Ramadan ends." She closed her eyes. "All I want is for Rislène to be happy. That is all I ask of Allah."

When the phone rang at the Charfi farmhouse at six a.m., Madira was just stepping into the kitchen to prepare breakfast. She was humming softly to herself, trying to ignore the knot in her stomach. Today she and Samuel Cebrian were going to market to rescue Rislène. Samuel sat at the dining-room table that had belonged to his mother, deep in conversation with Abdul.

"I'll get it!" she called out, drying her hands on a towel and going down the hall to the bedroom. The knot in her stomach tightened. Who would be calling at this early hour? *"Allô?"*

"Madira! It's Gabriella." Gabriella's voice sounded strained.

"Gabriella! How are you?"

"Oh, Madira. Not so good. There are no more oranges available. At all. The olives are not of good quality. Instead, today—today," she insisted, "there will be crescents and pearls. Pearls, Madira. Today!"

"Today! But that's impossible. I'm going to market in a while with the oranges and olives, everything for the celebration after Ramadan."

"I'm afraid that the client tasted the olives and was very unhappy with the quality."

Madira's mind reeled. What had happened? Pearls! That meant a wedding. Today! She felt as if she had been punched in the stomach. *No, Lord! We have it all worked out.*

Gabriella's voice softened. "I am sure, Madira, that the olives are still in season somewhere."

"Yes, Gabriella. Still in season somewhere."

Soft-spoken, kind Madira came into the room, her face drawn and pale. Ceb noticed at once that there were tears in her eyes.

"What is it, *ma chérie?*" Abdul asked, alarmed, going to his wife's side.

"That was Gabriella. She says Rislène is getting married today."

"Today!" The two men exchanged glances. "Impossible."

"No, it is true. Pearls! Today."

Ceb had learned their coded language and listened with fear as Madira explained the conversation. Evidently the imam was allowing the wedding because Grandmother Namani had learned of the planned escape.

Abdul's voice remained calm, even though his brow was furrowed. "The first thing we must do is pray. As surprised as we may be by this news, our heavenly Father is not surprised or confused." He took his wife's hand and then reached across the table for Ceb's. "Would you join us, Ceb?"

Without saying a word, Ceb grasped hands with Abdul and Madira. He was glad that their eyes were closed so they could not see the tears in his own. Over the past four days what had impressed him most about this couple was the simplicity of their faith. On two occasions, ten or twelve other believers had gathered at this farmhouse for late-night prayer vigils. Ceb had not joined in these times of worship and prayer, but he had felt strangely drawn to them, like a little boy hiding outside the door, wanting to be part of something that was just beyond his reach. These people believed that God was present and at work in the circumstances of every day, just as Ophélie, Eric, Gabriella, and David believed. As his parents believed. Just as he had believed as a teen.

But the problem for Ceb was that he had never really seen God at work in his life. And in truth, he knew it was because he had never waited long enough to find out what God was up to. He was too busy with his own plans. He had always identified with the apostle Peter, the reckless man who constantly tripped over his own feet.

How many times had the Lord reprimanded Peter for trying to work things out on his own? And yet this burly fisherman who had denied his Lord had also loved Him with every part of his being. He had eventually learned to listen to the Christ.

But I never have.

Abdul's voice was a fervent whisper as he petitioned God almighty to direct them, to give them wisdom, to intervene in the situation, to protect Rislène. He quoted Scripture with ease, weaving it into the fabric of his prayer like a skillful tailor. When he said amen, Madira began to pray, her soft voice breaking at times.

A tingling sensation came over Ceb, a feeling of incredible depth, as if he were being drawn closer to something strong and bright and good. The room was suddenly silent, and without knowing why or how, he began to pray. "Dear God, this may sound crazy, but I know You are here and I know You hear the prayers of these good people. I have been so far away for so long, I don't feel worthy to pray to You. But I want to help. Please show me how ..." His voice cracked. "And forgive me for all the hatred that is bottled up inside ..."

He could not continue, but let his voice drift off, still basking in the paradoxical sensation of lightness and depth, feeling himself being pulled so gently toward something that was true. He didn't want to open his eyes. He didn't want to move.

Somehow Abdul and Madira must have understood that it was a holy moment. They held his hands and kept silent, in spite of the urgency of the situation, until Ceb opened his eyes and whispered, "Thank you. It's going to be all right now."

El Amin's heart lurched within him as he walked up the dusty driveway to the familiar farmhouse surrounded by olive trees. His car was hidden two kilometers away. Dawn was breaking, with its pinks and purples and blues spreading across the sky, and something was breaking inside of him as well. Was it a new beginning or simply the end? He hesitated at the door, then knocked lightly.

There was a long silence before he heard his mother's soft voice. "Who is it?"

He cleared his throat, looked around. "It's me, Mama. It's El Amin."

There was a sharp cry, a fumbling with a lock, and the door opened. For an instant he thought he read fear and doubt in her eyes—but then she took his arm and pulled him inside, quickly closing the door behind them. She reached with her hand to touch his face. Her fingers hesitated, as if she might not find her son standing there, but only empty air. "El Amin?"

Several seconds passed. "I'm alone, Mama," he said. "Don't be afraid."

Then her arms were around him, and her tears were moistening his shirt. "El Amin. My son. You are here."

His face was harder, lined with fatigue. He looked as if he had not shaved in several days, and his black hair needed to be cut. He was muscular, every ounce of his body enwrapped in strength. Gone was any boyish look that Madira had known. Her son was not a boy. He was a terrorist. But for that moment, she did not think of him this way. What miracle had brought him to her door? Was it God's answer to their prayers? Or were other terrorists looming in the olive groves?

Whatever the situation, Madira willingly basked in the present. Her son, whom she had not seen in five years, was standing beside her, one arm around her shoulder, the other around Abdul's.

Thank You, Father. I didn't know if I would ever see him again. Thank You.

Ceb sat at the table, his face full of questions. El Amin strode over to him and shook his hand. Not a word passed between them. El Amin motioned to his parents to sit down, then he began to speak.

"Please don't be afraid, Mama and Baba. I come as a son who loves you. I have always loved you and wanted to protect you from harm. But I couldn't let you know. Only Hussein knew. Hussein, and now Ceb."

"Ceb knows?"

"We're working together to free Rislène."

The shock and relief that Madira felt was mirrored in Abdul's eyes. El Amin continued, "But I am here right now because your God spoke to me in a dream. Your Christ came to me this morning with outstretched hands and said that you need me. It was such a strong, intense light. It seemed real. I can't stay. The less you know about me the better. But I am not your enemy. I will always protect you, no matter what it takes."

Madira was weeping softly, but she wore a radiant smile on her face.

Abdul continued grasping his son's hands, unable to speak. At last he managed, "The Christ spoke to you? He told you to come here?"

El Amin turned his eyes down. "He held out His pierced hands, and His eyes knew all about me. I had to come. I could do nothing else."

"Praise God that you have come," Madira said, taking her son in her arms again. "Praise God."

It was a miracle. In her house were two lost sons. God had wrapped them in His love and brought them to her door. Why, she could not say. Nor for how long. But for this moment, she would soak in the joy.

It was almost as if they had stepped back in time. At any minute, Eliane Cebrian might call out from the back of the house, "Madira, can you help me with these curtains?," and she would turn to the two small boys and send them outside to play.

Lost and found, waiting and renewal. The fabric of life was constantly unraveling and being patched back up. Long ago Madira had learned that she had no control over life's circumstances. But prayer was the thread that God used to stitch lives back together. And standing before her were two young men who had been sewn up in her prayers for a very long time.

El Amin gathered his thoughts, trying to make sense of the dream that had propelled him to his parents' house. So the Arab girl was to be married today, and there was no time to lose. It was good that he had hooked up with Ceb in the early morning. But was that the reason for the vision? He could not think it was. The Christ had spoken of his parents' need, not the girl's. Couldn't this God communicate clearly?

No, Rislène was not the reason that he had come running to see his parents after five years of secrecy. It was for their safety. He fully believed that their God was telling him that their lives were in danger. Why else would their God speak to him, a Muslim? And why had it hurt him so terribly to look into the eyes of the Christ? He remembered the feeling of shame and disgust that had washed over him, as if truth were staring him in the eyes.

Truth! What was he saying? This God did not have ultimate truth. But this God did have the key to his fears.

His mother's face looked so serene and joyful. She brought them breakfast, and he knew she simply wanted to hold him, to talk to him, to ask him a hundred questions about Jala and the children. But she didn't dare intrude. So as he ate, he talked of each child and of Jala, and he watched his mother trying to picture every thought and word.

"Jala sent this for you." He handed his mother a photograph of the six of them, taken sometime last year.

"They are beautiful, the children." She never said that she longed to see them, to cradle the baby in her arms. His mother was a woman of peace and control. But she held the photo gently, as if the faces smiling out at her were real flesh and blood appearing right in front of her in the farmhouse.

El Amin had tasted the spice of home for a mere thirty minutes, and now he had to leave. It was time to disappear from their lives without the faintest idea when he would see them again. A day? A year? A lifetime? It was time to leave with Hussein and Samuel, without ever knowing why the Christ had summoned him to his parents' home in such a dramatic way.

He hugged his father and felt tears sting his eyes. Then he took his mother in his arms, softly kissing her wet cheeks. "I must go. Never forget that I love you. I'm sorry I came like this."

"Don't be sorry," Madira choked. "It is the happiest moment of my life. I know you are well. I know Jala and the children are well." She glanced down at the photo. "Thank you for coming, El Amin. Thank you for explaining why you never came before."

"A day doesn't go by without my thinking of you."

"It is the same for me."

"And for me as well, my son," his father said, meeting his eyes.

"Good-bye, Mama and Baba. May your God protect you."

"And may He do the same for you."

⁜

Ophélie knocked on Eric's studio door three times before he opened it. When he did, she let out a sharp breath, shocked to see the tears streaming down her little brother's face. He was clutching his old guitar, and the look in his eyes was like madness.

She took the guitar from him and set it by his desk, grabbed him in a fierce hug, and held him without saying one word. Minutes ticked by, and Eric's grip on her didn't lessen. Then she pulled back and looked him straight in the eyes. "Don't give up, Eric," she said. "Don't you dare give up hope."

They sat down on his bed, and Eric buried his head in his hands.

"I just sit here and imagine what's happening to Rislène at this very moment, how terrified she must be. How can they force her to marry a man she doesn't love? It's like a nightmare, Ophélie. I can't make it stop. I can't even pray."

Ophélie let him cry, didn't try to comfort him with meaningless words.

After a moment he looked at her. "I'm afraid I'll never see her again. My faith has vanished into thin air. And if that is how I feel, what must Rislène be feeling? How can she hold on to her faith?"

Ophélie stood and reached a hand to her brother. "You're not staying here alone. Come on, Eric. Get your coat. I'm taking you to Papa and Bri's."

As if in a trance, he obeyed her, pulling on his jacket and then picking up the guitar.

A nightmare. Yes, he was right. Once again, thoughts of the whole horrible debacle with Bachir pelted her. She forced them away. This was not the day to remember that tragedy. Today she must believe in a God of miracles. For Eric and herself.

Ten minutes later, Bri came out to the car and led Eric into the house as if he were a small child. He was still clutching the guitar.

Ophélie drove toward school, thinking of her brother and the beautiful Arab student whose chair would be empty again today.

28

Ceb sped through the quiet streets at the wheel of Abdul's car, with El Amin giving instructions, and felt the adrenaline pump through his body.

They had decided to go to Hussein's apartment. A coded phone call while at the Charfis' had assured them that he would be waiting for them. Then they would go to the Namani residence.

Ceb wanted to hear more about El Amin's vision, only in part because it distracted them from the impossible task toward which they drove.

"I remember years ago David Hoffmann telling us that Christ often appears to Muslims during Ramadan. He had amazing stories of men and women he knew who converted to Christianity, all because of a vision."

"They were foolish."

"Perhaps. But why do you think the vision came to you?"

"It was for my parents. To warn them, so they would be safe."

"Maybe He wasn't coming to warn your parents. Maybe He came for you."

El Amin's brow twitched nervously. "And what makes you the prophet of truth all of a sudden? I thought you abandoned this God a long time ago."

"I did. But then I came here and lived with your parents for five days. They are good, strong people, El Amin. And Hussein too. They risk their lives every day for the love of Christ."

"And I do the same for Allah!" El Amin retorted angrily. Then he sighed. "But I cannot fault them. Their love for their God is as radical as mine for Islam. Only they move mountains with prayer. We do it with violence."

The household was brimming with activity. Rislène watched the movements in a numbed stupor. Time was running out. The ceremony was planned for sunset, when the fast would be broken. She found herself quivering uncontrollably. She had not let herself imagine her first night with Yassir. She felt such repulsion and fear. She had been prepared to be without God's Word, prepared for suffering and persecution, prepared to hold on to her faith in the midst of mockery and trials. But she was not prepared to become a stranger's wife and share his bed.

Jesus, please make him be kind to me. Please help me not to hate him. I am too weak and terrified. I can't do this. Please don't make him hate me for my tears, Lord. Please save me. Please.

The wedding gown and its elaborate trimmings lay across Nazira's bed, ready for her to wear. Rislène had always thought the gown beautiful. She remembered touching it when her older cousin had married years ago and imagining herself in it. Now the sparkling stones and bright-gold trim seemed like taunting treasures, entrapping her in a life she had no desire to lead ... a life so far from Eric.

"There's no use to cry." Nazira's voice was irritated. "You're a spoiled brat. Think of it. Yassir is from a prosperous family. He's smart and handsome. You're lucky, Rislène. Quit crying."

"You take him, if you think he is so wonderful!"

"I hate you, Rislène! Father and Mother have always loved you more. Everything for beautiful, bright Rislène. I hope you are miserable for the rest of your life. It serves you right." Nazira picked up the wedding gown, then threw it back on the bed. "I'm a good Muslim. All I want is to obey Allah. Yes, I would gladly marry Yassir!" She turned and fled from the room, leaving Rislène to dry her tears.

Hussein had observed the Namani residence several times in the past weeks. It was a rather large house by Algerian standards, squeezed in between two other residences. From the exterior, all that distinguished it from the adjoining houses was a beautifully crafted wooden door and a gold knocker of Fatima's hand, a symbol of protection seen often in the Muslim world. Hussein had not been inside, but he knew the typical layout of these homes. There were no windows on the exterior, but the front door led into a courtyard that opened to the sky. In this way, Algerian women were hidden from outside view, but light came into the home from above.

Today there was much activity surrounding the house. People were coming and going, carrying baskets of fruits and vegetables. Two young men dressed in police uniforms stood just outside the front door, machine guns by their sides. And somewhere behind the house's high walls was a young woman whose future lay in his hands.

"The only way to get her out will be messy," El Amin had declared as the three men observed the house from a distance. "I have guns. We'll have to kill the men, snatch the girl, and run like the wind."

"We will not kill," Hussein stated emphatically. "We must find another way. What about tranquilizers?"

Ceb nodded. "Yeah, El Amin. Could you get tranquilizers? How many police are inside anyway?"

"Two outside, but who knows how many inside, plus all the men in the family." Hussein shook his head. "This won't be easy."

El Amin spoke angrily. "Impossible. My men don't use tranquilizers. And there's no telling how many men in the family will be armed. I tell you, if we can't shoot, we'll be dead."

Hussein sighed and rubbed his eyes. It had seemed feasible to rescue Rislène when their plan was to take her at the market, in the midst of a crowd of people. Feasible to create confusion as Rislène and Ceb ran to the waiting car. But this ... this did not look feasible.

The sun was high overhead, and the brisk chill of the February morning was fading into a warmer noontime.

Hussein smiled suddenly. "I have an idea," he ventured. "I've got a couple of old police uniforms at home that I've used on certain occasions. El Amin, you and I could try to get in dressed as police."

"And what about me?" Ceb questioned.

"You'll be busy outside, creating confusion on the street. Something that will disrupt the ceremony."

"Yes!" El Amin said excitedly. "A bomb!"

"A small car bomb," Hussein clarified. "Something that makes a lot of noise but won't harm anyone."

Ceb nodded. "Yes. I can set off the bomb and then find cover on another street. You bring the girl out, and I'll take off with her."

"If we can get into the house, it just might work."

Ceb furrowed his brow. "But if you're seen, the two of you, won't your cover be blown? What about your work?"

"You know, Ceb," Hussein said, patting the Frenchman on the back, "I take my work one day at a time. This isn't how I had planned it, but then, my work rarely goes smoothly. And God is with us. He's been with me so many, many times."

"And what does your wife think?"

"She believes as strongly as I that God has called me, has called us, to this life. We wouldn't change it, Ceb. Every day Jesus' love spurs us on. We would not change it."

"And what about you, El Amin? What will happen when they find out a Muslim terrorist disguised as a policeman aided in the rescue of a Christian?"

El Amin shrugged. "It's good not to ask too many questions, Ceb. Otherwise I'd go crazy. All I can do is follow my heart."

They walked back to where the car was parked on a side street a block from the Namani home.

Hussein drove away with a prayer in his heart. *Protect us, Lord.* He thought of the two men riding with him. A fundamentalist Muslim and a homeless Frenchman. *Unite us for good, Lord. And uniforms. Help me find the police uniforms, please. No time to waste.*

The message relayed by phone calls around Algiers was short and to the point: "No more oranges available. Olives still in season. Please confirm if you are still interested."

Abdul and Madira spread the message to those in their house church. Each believer understood. *No more oranges* meant that plans had changed. *Olives still in season* meant that prayer was their only recourse. And *please confirm* meant simply that an emergency prayer meeting was being called for that evening at the farmhouse.

Hussein pulled boxes out from under the bed and emptied the contents of each on the floor, hurriedly tossing clothes to the right and the left.

"Hussein! What are you doing?" Dounia asked, coming into the bedroom. "What are you looking for?"

"They're here somewhere," he answered. Moments later he pulled a police uniform out from under a pile of clothes. He kissed it softly, whispering, "Thank You, Lord," and handed it to his bewildered wife. "Dounia, if ever you've ironed quickly and neatly, please, my love, do it now." He emptied the last box, and another uniform, this one neatly folded, slid onto the floor.

"Where did these come from?" Dounia asked, dumbfounded.

"Shh. No questions now. Only prayers. Our God has provided, and we must hurry."

Ten minutes later, he and El Amin were dressed in the uniforms. Dounia wrapped a long white turban around Ceb's head, tucking his straggly hair underneath.

"You look better," Hussein commented, grinning to break the tension. "And here. This should fit you. Its owner was a tall man, like you." He tossed a long tunic to Ceb. "It'll be some disguise at least."

Ceb held the white material in his hands, a baffled expression on his face. "What am I supposed to do with it?"

"Wrap it around your body, you nut!" El Amin laughed. "Here, let me help you."

The men left the apartment with Dounia standing at the door, a thousand questions on her face.

"Don't worry, my love. Only pray. Pray!" Hussein kissed her quickly on the lips. He did not let himself think of when he might see her next.

"All right. Let's review the plan," Ceb stated, feeling the blood pumping in his ears as they walked briskly to the car.

"Hussein and I will try to get through as police guards. It should work—those guys stationed outside the house are just officers in training." El Amin shot a look at Hussein. "Do you have the letter?"

Hussein nodded.

El Amin continued. "Ceb, you'll be out around the corner. Wait until Hussein comes back outside. That will be the signal that all is ready. Then light the fuse. If you do it right after the prayer time, the streets should still be empty. I'll grab the girl and bring her to the other car where you'll be waiting, a block away. And then it's up to you to race out of there to my parents' place. She'll hide in their

cellar until we've worked out how to get you two back across the sea."
He stroked his chin. "If I'm not with you, are you sure you can find
their house?"

Ceb had been studying the city maps for the past five days.
"Yeah, no problem. I'll get her there. But what about you? How will
you get out?"

"Don't worry about us," Hussein broke in. "You came for Rislène.
That's your job."

But Ceb was worried. He was worried about everything. *Oh,
God. I need You like I've never needed You before. I know it's downright
rotten of me to ignore You for all these years and then come begging. But
please, God, get us through this thing safely. I want to take this girl back
for Eric. For You. I swear I do. And I want to live ...*

He closed his eyes and pictured Ophélie in her apartment. *Give
me a chance to see if she wants me, God. Will You please just give me the
chance?*

The police cap was pulled far down, almost hiding his eyes, and El
Amin was glad for his beard. He walked briskly to the door of the
Namani residence, heels clicking. "The chief radioed you needed
extra help—rumor of an attack."

The policeman shrugged. "I haven't heard it."

"Here's the message we received." El Amin thrust a sheet of
official-looking paper into the policeman's hands. His men had used
the trick a hundred times.

The policeman examined it cursorily. "I don't doubt it. These people are paranoid. A wedding in the middle of Ramadan. It's enough to incur the wrath of Allah! Come on in. Both of you."

The officer led El Amin and Hussein into the inner courtyard, which opened to the sky. He nodded. "You take the far stairwell, and you the one on the right. If you see anything suspicious, let me know."

"When's the ceremony taking place?" El Amin asked.

"Sundown." The officer looked at his watch. "Thirty minutes at most, I'd say."

El Amin glanced at Hussein, infinite relief in his eyes. They weren't too late.

He could hear the grandmother talking excitedly in the kitchen, barking orders to family members who dashed in and out of rooms, arms laden with food and flowers. The smell of couscous was enticing, and the sun was low in the sky. El Amin marched into the kitchen, saluted Grandmother Namani, and then spoke in a whisper. "I must talk with the bride."

"Impossible!" Grandmother Namani whispered back vehemently. "No man is allowed to see the bride before the ceremony."

"Do you want your granddaughter married?"

"Of course!"

"Then let me talk to her. I must warn her what to do in case there is a problem. Police regulations, you understand."

Grandmother Namani eyed him angrily. "She's in there." She indicated a room down the hall on the right. "And make it quick."

El Amin was perspiring heavily when he knocked on the door. It opened, and a roomful of women giggled and fluttered to the other side of the room, hiding the bride from his view. "I'm sorry to bother you," he said curtly. "A simple matter to discuss with the bride. Police regulations."

The women didn't budge.

"I have the grandmother's permission," he added crossly.

The young bride came to him, dressed in an elaborate wedding gown. Her eyes were red and swollen.

"Mlle Namani," he said sternly, "I have requested a moment with you to explain police procedures in case we encounter difficulties." There was anger in his voice. He spoke loud enough for the other women in the room to hear. "Our men are tired and busy with other matters. I want this wedding to take place without incident. During the ceremony, if there is any problem, I will receive a signal. You are to come with me, and I'll get you to safety. Is this clear?"

The bride nodded, her eyes turned to the ground.

"The ceremony will begin shortly." His face was hard and jaw set. "You understand, Mlle Namani?"

She did not look up, but mumbled, "I understand."

He walked out of the room, sweat seeping through every part of his uniform in spite of the crisp afternoon air. He felt a greater fear here than when he had been involved in terrorist attacks. Now he was on the other side.

No, not the other side. A third possibility, something that had nothing to do with this war. His mission was not to destroy, but to rescue. It was a completely different demand. Save, rescue, no shedding of blood. Peaceful.

It was his parents' way. Peaceful, with prayer. It went against all his training. He was a master of force and violence. This he knew how to control. But a peaceful rescue? Only the God of his parents could engineer such a thing.

Across the town came the call on the loudspeaker. Time to pray. Every man fell to his knees. Suddenly El Amin was unsure of his prayers. Did he invoke Allah's help for a plan that would surely infuriate the Muslim god? He saw the Christ again, as he had in his vision, hands outstretched. Once again he felt the terrible shame and guilt in his heart and then the peace.

God of my parents, I don't know why I am here. And I don't know why You appeared to me in the dream. I'm afraid. I have no one to turn to. Please, God of the Christ, save this girl. Save us all. He could not help adding, *Inshallah.*

Rislène felt dizzy and sick. This wedding was going to happen, and the police were here to make sure of it. The officer who spoke to her was wiry, muscular, and handsome but with a cruel look in his eyes. His words had been filled with reproach.

The clock in the hall ticked relentlessly, and the house suddenly fell into shadows as a cloud obscured the sunlight.

"It won't be long now, Rislène. Sunset is almost here," Nazira taunted. Strand after strand of pearls was lifted carefully over Rislène's head. Now they hung around her neck, cascading down the front of the wedding gown. So heavy. Everything seemed so very heavy. Rislène did not think she could even muster the strength to put one foot in front of the other and walk into the living room where the wedding would take place.

Grandmother rushed into the room, her puffy face flushed under a bright-yellow scarf. "The imam is here. Hurry up, Rislène! Get your wedding veil on. Go on, Nazira. Help your sister. The ceremony will start as soon as prayers have been said."

A wave of nausea and panic washed over Rislène. She tried to think of a Bible verse, any verse, but she felt so incredibly hot and dizzy. She knelt with Nazira to pray.

It's too late, Lord. Too late.

Ceb parked Hussein's old Citroën a little past the Namani residence on the opposite side of the street. There had been no time to find a discarded car in which to place the dynamite, so Hussein had insisted that his car be used, after having removed the license plate. El Amin's car was parked one street away. All was quiet as darkness fell across the city. Ceb's palms were sweating. *Hurry up, Hussein.* If the bomb went off now, it would merely create disturbance. But in fifteen minutes, after prayers, the streets would come alive with people.

One of the young policemen glanced his way as Ceb got out of the car. *Where was Hussein?* Suddenly the stocky Arab came out the door and called the other policemen over to him. It was time!

It was the simplest of bombs. Three sticks of dynamite and a jerrycan of gas. He had only to light the long fuse and get out of there. Ceb struck the match and held it to the fuse. It flamed immediately. Thirty seconds was all he had. He walked quickly down the street, not daring to look back.

❊

The imam was a small, silver-haired man with a long white beard. He motioned for Rislène to come beside him with Yassir, who was dressed in a white robe. The groom looked regal and determined. Rislène concentrated on each movement. *One foot in front of the other. One at a time.*

The faces of the Namani family looked on. There were thirty people crowded into the room. The ceremony might be rushed and short, but the meal afterward would be festive, Grandmother had insisted. Rislène's aunts, uncles, and cousins were all there.

The imam was speaking softly, invoking Allah's blessing on the ceremony. Rislène's legs felt like jelly. She was sure she would faint. *Too late, too late*, her mind taunted. *Too late!*

The noise startled everyone in the room. An explosion so loud it sounded as if it had happened in the next room. Several people sprinted to the door. "A bomb! A bomb in the street!"

"Marry them quickly!" Grandmother Namani insisted, glaring at the imam. "Don't stop the ceremony now! Marry them!"

"Are you crazy? Get all the women and children to the middle of the house." It was the cruel policeman calling out orders. "All armed men outside."

The policeman grabbed Rislène's arm tightly. "You come with me." He motioned to Yassir. "I'm taking her out back. Guard the door!"

"No!" screamed Rislène. "Stop it! Help me! Let me go!" Perhaps, she thought desperately, if she stayed in the house, whoever had set off the bomb would come to rescue her.

"Go with the man," Yassir commanded. She saw then that he held a pistol in his hand. "I'll find you shortly."

It was a nightmare. Women screaming, children crying, and this strong man dragging her after him, outside. They stepped into the night air. She heard the sounds of a siren in the distance. She looked around to see Yassir watching them from the back entrance.

The hold on her arm was so tight. And now the man was talking to her. "Hurry, Rislène! Hurry! We have no time to lose." Her mind was foggy as they dashed down the street, she tripping on the long veil and scrambling to her feet. Then he stopped beside a car. "Get in! Quickly!"

"What are you doing?" Yassir was running after them, eyes flashing. He reached them before Rislène could get into the car and pulled her away, menacing the policeman with his gun. "This isn't where you said I'd meet you."

The policeman lunged at Yassir and struck him forcefully in the face. Yassir reeled backward and fell to the ground, and Rislène screamed.

"Be quiet! And get in the car, Rislène!" A turbaned man—the driver of the car—was speaking. "We're here to rescue you. Hurry up!"

How did he know her name? Confused, she stumbled into the backseat, the policeman helping her stuff her wedding gown into the car. He climbed in beside her and was turning to pull the door shut when a shot rang out. Yassir, on his knees, had fired his pistol. The policeman fell across Rislène's lap.

The driver leaped from the car, ramming his head into Yassir's ribs before he could fire another shot. They both fell sprawling to the ground; then the driver scrambled for the gun and brought it down forcefully on Yassir's head. He groaned, then lay still.

The turbaned man rushed back to the driver's seat. "Shut the door, Rislène. Hurry!"

"Is he dead? Oh, dear Lord, did you kill him?"

"He'll be fine," the driver assured her. "Better off than we'll be if we don't get out of here fast."

The car sped off in the night as blood from the wounded policeman soaked onto Rislène's veil and tears streamed down her face.

"Lie down, Rislène!" Ceb ordered. "And take off the veil." He heard her sobbing softly. "Rislène." He turned his head to look at the beautiful young woman. "I'm a friend. We've come to take you away. I promised Eric I would bring you back, and I will."

Her face went pale, and she leaned forward. "Who are you? What are you saying?"

"We'll tell you more later. How is El Amin? Where was he hit?"

"In the chest. He's losing a lot of blood."

"Hang in there," Ceb called back to El Amin. "Hang in there."

Their plan had almost worked perfectly. Now he was racing through a town he did not know with a wounded friend in the backseat. *Oh, God, take care of him. And Hussein.*

Hussein's words came back to him. *It never works out as smoothly as planned, but God is with us.*

The man called El Amin was breathing sporadically as Rislène cradled his head in her lap. "Drive faster, please! He isn't doing well." There was blood everywhere. She pulled off her veil and wrapped it around the bullet wound in his chest.

"Hello, Rislène," El Amin said, his breath coming in gasps. "It's good to meet you."

"Shh, don't talk," she whispered. "Save your strength."

"I have to ask ... why do you believe ... in this God?"

She leaned closer to hear the wounded man's words.

In a raspy voice he continued, "Why ... would you risk losing everything for Him? I must know."

Her mind reeled. Was this man not a Christian? And if not, who was he? Why had he helped her escape?

"When He looks at you, does He see ... everything you've ever done?" El Amin's eyes bore into hers. He gasped for breath.

"He did," she whispered, frightened by the urgency in the wounded man's voice, the desperation in his eyes. "But now He's forgiven me, and when He looks at me, I'm clean. He promises me hope, eternal hope—a place where I'm safe—and love. And every day He shows me that I'm not alone. That He is here. Even in Algeria."

"That is what I seek," the man said softly, closing his eyes. "Something sure and safe. And hope for the future. For me and my family."

El Amin passed in and out of consciousness on the ride through Algiers. He had been shot before, once almost fatally. He wondered ironically why this wound had to be the worst. He was on a mission of peace and rescue. This would never qualify as a jihad, and if he didn't die in a jihad, there was no assurance of reaching paradise.

Now He's forgiven me, the girl said. *He promises me eternal hope....* Again El Amin saw the blazing eyes and the outstretched hands. The pierced hands. And then he knew why Jesus had sent him to his parents. Ceb had been right. It wasn't for them. It was for *him*. It was his last chance to see them and his last chance for a Savior.

"The pain ..." he murmured as Rislène wiped his forehead and tried to stop the flow of blood. "Pray for me. I need a Savior. Jesus!"

Ceb pulled off the road in a clump of trees, stopped the car, and leaned over the backseat. El Amin was pale, gasping for breath, his chest soaked in blood. "We'll have to get him out of the car. I can't help him like that."

Slowly he lifted El Amin's limp body from the car while Rislène supported his head. Ceb laid him on the cold ground and ripped open his shirt. It was stained through with blood.

"My God," whispered Ceb. Shot in the chest. It was a nightmare for any surgeon. And he had no instruments, no hospital, nothing but his hands. His imperfect hands.

As he bent over El Amin, the memory flashed before him. Bending over Annie, trying in spite of his unbearable pain and numerous wounds to bring her back to life. And Marion. His lips pressed against her tiny lips, his broken hand pressing her chest, begging it to pump blood again. He had tried to save them. He had tried!

"Please, El Amin. Please live. Don't stop now. You've got to live. Oh, God, let him live!"

El Amin clutched Ceb's maimed hand, gasping for breath. "I want to live, Samuel. I want to live forever. Tell me how to live … forever."

Stunned, Ceb murmured, "I … I will pray for you." Kneeling beside him, with Rislène clasping El Amin's other hand, Ceb stumbled through a prayer. "Holy God, You see El Amin. He wants You. Forgive him of his sins …"

His friend's labored breathing broke into words. "There are so many … sins. God … forgive. Mama and Baba … were right. Jesus … thank You for the pierced hands. Take me with You." El Amin groaned heavily.

"No!" Rislène screamed. "Come on, El Amin. Live!"

Ceb wrapped the bloody veil over his chest. "Live, friend. Don't give up."

A pained smile flickered across El Amin's face. "I am … alive. Tell Jala. Tell Mama. I am alive." His hand fell limp in Ceb's, and his eyes stared lifelessly to the sky.

"No!" Ceb yelled, pulling him up and cradling his head to his chest. "No!" He would not let El Amin die! Not like Annie and Marion. He worked furiously on El Amin's body for ten minutes, but it was useless.

He hugged El Amin against him. "Why, God? Why couldn't I save him?" He laid the lifeless body on the cold ground and rested his head on the bloody chest.

The Arab girl, this beautiful stranger with the strands of pearls draping down her body, touched Ceb lightly on the back. "This is all my fault. I don't even know you, and you saved me. Thank you." She wiped her hand across El Amin's brow. "I'm so sorry about this good man. You couldn't save him, but ... but Jesus could. And I believe that He did. That is what I believe." She buried her face in Ceb's arms and wept.

When they arrived at the farmhouse, Ceb parked the car out of sight of the house and cut the engine quickly. He sat with Rislène in a numbed, anguished silence. Rislène was free, but El Amin was gone. And now he had to carry his body to Abdul and Madira and explain to them what had happened.

"What am I supposed to do?" he asked, and in his mind he was addressing the Lord.

Rislène opened the door and wearily pulled herself from the car. "Come on, *monsieur*. I'll help you."

"You don't understand," Ceb said. "This is his parents' house. I have to tell his parents that El Amin is dead, but I can't."

"Then I will do it," she said. "Let me tell them. He risked his life for me. You all did. Are his parents Christians?"

"Yes. Yes, they are."

As she walked across the sandy driveway, Ceb opened the back door of the car and gently, slowly pulled El Amin out. Then he picked up his friend in his arms and trudged to the farmhouse door. His tears ran into his beard as he looked down at El Amin's peaceful face and recalled his last words. *Tell Jala. Tell Mama. I am alive.*

29

When Dominique met her at the door with flowers, Ophélie felt her heart melting again. He kissed her softly on the cheeks. There was that same enticing smell of aftershave. How could she find the courage to do what she knew needed to be done?

"Can I see the puppies? And Lassie?" he asked.

"Sure. Come on in."

He knelt down beside the cage and chuckled as he watched them nipping and playing together. "They look great, Ophélie. Thanks so much for taking them. And how are you?"

"Tired. Tired of all these emotions."

"Do you want to explain?"

She told him about Rislène and the rescue plan. "We're all waiting on pins and needles to hear what happened."

"What a story! Yes, I can imagine you feel drained."

"It's very personal for me, Dominique. I guess it's this situation that has forced me to ... to say that I haven't been totally honest with you."

"What do you mean?"

"Let's sit down." She indicated the couch. "I mean—" She bit her lip, hesitating. "I mean that I'm not interested in pursuing a relationship with you."

Dominique stared at her as if she had punched him in the gut. "Well," he said after a moment. "At least you don't mince words. May I ask why?"

"You know why."

"Not handsome enough, or smart enough."

"You know that's not it. You're wonderful. But you just aren't for me."

"It's your faith, right?"

"Right."

He scrunched up his nose. "I don't get it. How can that be such a big deal? I've told you that I respect your beliefs. You can't expect me to swallow it all."

"No, that's precisely it. I don't expect that. I don't want it."

"Now you're really confusing me. You mean that even if I converted to your brand of Christianity, you wouldn't want me? Even if we shared that in common?"

"What I mean is that it would never work for you to 'convert,' as you say, for me. That's between you and God. And anyway, we're in such different places spiritually. It would never work."

He reddened. "A lot of women have told me a lot of things, Ophélie, but not one has ever said that to me. What does that even mean?" He sounded almost angry. "That I don't have a soul?"

At once her eyes filled with tears. "Of course not, Dominique. But it won't work. Believe me, I know. I'm willing to compromise on many things in a relationship. But not my faith. I can't. I've tried that before, and it only left me miserable."

"Do you mind giving me some details of this miserable experience?"

Ophélie winced at his sarcastic tone. "His name was Bachir. He was Algerian," she said in barely more than a whisper.

"Whoa! You were in love with a Muslim?"

"He came to our church. I thought we had the same faith. And I was smitten with him."

"Smitten?"

"I had just come off of a disappointment with a boy—had a dream die." She glanced up at Dominique and brushed away the tears rolling down her cheeks. "Samuel—Ceb—had just married Annie. I finally realized he wasn't ever going to choose me. So I turned a page and started living again."

Dominique's face was pained. He reached across the couch and took her hand. "I'm sorry. I didn't realize ..."

Ophélie shrugged. "I let myself fall in love with Bachir. I told myself it was good and right. He said he was a Christian. He came to meetings and he listened to me and my ideas. Within six months we were engaged.

"My father and stepmother were adamant that it was too soon, but I had this naive dream. You see, my mother, a pied-noir, *did* marry an Arab man who converted to Christianity. Theirs is a beautiful love story—terribly hard, but beautiful. I wanted that too, Dominique. I wanted it so badly."

Ophélie stood up, walked into the kitchen, and filled a glass with water. She felt the perspiration breaking out on her face, remembered exactly the way she had felt all those years ago. She took a long gulp of water and sat back down beside Dominique.

"Bachir's parents were still living in Algeria. They had no idea he had converted—he never told them. He lied to me and said they knew, that they had agreed to the wedding, that they would come to France for it.

"We sent out the invitations, had the whole ceremony and reception planned, and then—" She took a deep breath. "And then Bachir began to beg me to come with him to Algeria, to meet his family, to have a ceremony there. He said we could have a ceremony in France *after* the one in Algeria. He wasn't making any sense. It scared me—he seemed to be changing before my eyes. He loved me—I knew that—but suddenly I saw the danger—his family was drawing him back to his Muslim roots."

Dominique's eyes bore into hers.

"I guess my father and stepmother had seen it for a while. They begged me not to go to Algeria. But I would have gone, Dominique. I would have. I loved him so much. I wanted it to be all right. I *needed* it to be.

"A few days before we were to leave for Algeria, I grew terribly ill, deathly ill. But Bachir refused to believe I couldn't travel. He was determined to take me with him. And that's when I understood that he was going to take me there forever—he didn't care how sick I was, because once he got me there, I would be his.

"In the end I refused, and he left alone. I never heard from him or saw him again."

Dominique's face was filled with pain and compassion. "I'm sorry, Ophélie," he whispered. "I really am."

"I've never been lucky in love, Dominique. And I know you're not like Bachir, or Sam. And I don't even expect you to understand." She swiped at her tears again, but they kept falling. Finally she met his eyes and said, "I'm so very sorry. If you think this is easy for me, I assure you it isn't. It's why I don't go out on many second dates. Forgive me for leading you on. It was wrong."

His face still held a shocked and pained expression. "I don't know what to say, Ophélie. Thank you for telling me your story. It makes more sense." He let go of her hands and stood up. "I guess I'd better go." He seemed momentarily disoriented, then kissed her softly on each cheek, held her to him for only a moment, and left the apartment.

Ophélie listened to Dominique's footsteps fade, then threw herself on her couch with a groan. Sometimes following God seemed so very black. She had prayed for a new beginning, but this seemed like the same old familiar pain. She went into the kitchen and boiled water for a cup of tisane. Then she put on the CD from *Les Misérables* and let the heartbreaking alto voice of Eponine reach into her soul. "I love him, but only on my own ..."

Life was just plain hard sometimes. And unfair. Was it so wrong to want someone to care about, to pray for, to hold in her arms? Dominique would maybe never understand, and Ceb was lost in Algeria. *I told You that I wanted to surrender, Lord. To do whatever it takes to be all Yours.* The teakettle whistled. *But I'm having such a hard time. So can You do it for me? I don't even have the strength to try.*

Madira Charfi washed the face of her dead son, who was stretched out on the bed in her bedroom. There were no more tears to cry. They had been spent throughout this longest of nights.

Lost and found. Lost and found and lost again. She leaned forward and kissed El Amin's forehead and then covered her face with her hands.

In all her life she would never get over this day—the day that had dawned with the distressing news of Rislène's impromptu wedding; the day when El Amin had appeared at her door and proclaimed his love for them and his association with Hussein and Ceb. The long, unbearable afternoon of waiting. The prayers. The night falling and the Christians coming to the farmhouse, one by one.

And then the knock at the door. There stood Rislène, disheveled in her bridal gown, which was stained with blood. And behind her, Ceb, carrying the body of El Amin. At once, Abdul had hurried them inside. What should have been a moment of great rejoicing was swallowed up in intense shock and grief. *Why, God? Why?*

And then Rislène had spoken to all the believers gathered there, her voice smooth and sad, her eyes brimming with tears. "You have all risked your lives for me, prayed for me. And El Amin"—she met Madira's eyes—"El Amin sacrificed himself. I don't know why. He was a Muslim, and yet ..." She had cried softly for a long time, and no one had dared to speak. Then, clearing her throat, she said, "But he wanted Jesus ... and he found Him."

Madira thought of Ceb, eyes glazed, energy spent, who had stood slowly to his feet and walked over to her, placing a gentle hand on hers. "I have lived with you for five days, and I have seen Christ here. God brought me off the streets of France to Algeria to call me back to Himself. He reveals Himself in so many different ways." He took her hand and squeezed it tightly. "And Christ did this for El Amin. In a vision that brought your son back to you. We talked of the vision and of what it could mean. And at last, he understood. He chose Jesus." Ceb ran his hand through his beard. "His last words were *Tell Jala. Tell Mama. I am alive.*"

Madira looked down at her son and wondered at this day. She had thought he would die in one of the grisly massacres, but he had died bringing life to another. And she had seen him, had those few moments of joy with him, a gift from the Lord. The *why* was still on her lips, a *why* for a life snuffed out, for a wife left to raise four young children alone. But the years of doubt and hurt for her son had been healed. El Amin had loved them, protected them in the way he thought best. And if what Rislène and Ceb said was true, he had found the truth at last.

This morning she had tasted heaven. Two lost sons reunited in this house. And tonight, with one of them already in God's presence, she tasted it again. "Only a short while, my son. Only a blink of an eye, and we'll be together again. Forever."

There had been no time for long good-byes. Madira had helped Rislène take off the bloodstained wedding gown, insisted that she wash up, and given her a long, brightly colored floral dress to wear. When Hussein showed up at the farmhouse in the middle of the night, Ceb knew that they must leave at once. There had been time only for a fervent hug to Abdul and Madira, a whispered *merci* that got choked out through tears, and a short, silent vigil at the bedside of El Amin. Then he and Rislène had hurried to the car and left. Now the young woman slept in the backseat.

"How did you get out?" Ceb asked Hussein as the Arab sped through the night.

"I heard the shot and came running. I found Yassir knocked out and disappeared down an alley before the rest of the family came looking. Hid out till the town started partying, then showed up on the doorstep of a friend's place, changed clothes, and borrowed his car."

"It almost worked just right."

"Yeah. Almost. It was my fault. I dragged El Amin into it."

"Maybe you should be thankful that he's free. He told me he was stuck. No way out."

"He was. His men were beginning to wonder about him."

"How do you know?"

"I can't tell you how, Ceb. I just know."

"Are you stuck too, Hussein?"

"No, Ceb. God never runs out of ideas. I'm not stuck."

"And what about El Amin's wife and kids?"

"I'll go see them tomorrow. With Dounia."

"I thought my life was hard as a surgeon. Or an SDF. But, Hussein, you work in the middle of hell. Why?"

"I think you understand why."

"Yeah, maybe. But it terrifies me. What is this God going to ask of me next?"

"Something way too hard for you to do on your own. That's for sure." He stopped the car. "Look, all the papers are here. Passport. Visa. She shouldn't have any trouble. When you get to the airport in Morocco, someone will have your tickets. I'll call David and let him know they should expect you in two days."

"I don't know what to say, Hussein. A simple *merci* somehow seems to miss the mark."

"Take care of yourself, Ceb. God be with you."

"Yes, I think He is, now."

The two men shook hands. Then Ceb tapped Rislène on the shoulder. "It's time to go."

Her eyes fluttered open, and she asked, "Where are we?"

"Far away from Algiers. We'll be at the Moroccan border in a few hours."

She broke into a broad smile. "Oh, thank You, Lord. And thank you, Hussein! Is it really true?"

"It's true," Hussein said. "Go on with you now. Your next chauffeur is waiting just over there." As if on cue, someone stepped out of the shadows. Ceb and Rislène made their way to him.

"Don't forget to give Ophélie my love," Hussein said softly.

"I won't."

"And the rest of them too."

When Ceb looked back, Hussein's car was already out of sight.

Rislène had slept through two different trips in the car, but once they crossed the Moroccan border, she was wide-awake. "Is it really true, Ceb? Will he be there at the airport waiting?"

Ceb chuckled. "I kinda think he will, ready to greet his bride."

"His bride," she pronounced in amazement, then laughed. "Yes, with my hair all braided and henna on my hands. And a dress three sizes too big for me. I must look awful."

"You look all right," he said. "In fact, you look great."

She blushed self-consciously. "So, Ceb. Tell me about yourself. Who are you anyway?"

He chuckled again. "You don't know what a hard question you've just asked. And my only response is, I'm not sure."

"What are you not sure about? Can't you tell me something about yourself? We've got hours to get to know each other."

Slowly he related bits and pieces of his story as they drove through the countryside.

Much later, Rislène shared the fear and horror of her experience in Algeria. Ceb listened transfixed as she explained her idea for the toilet-paper Bible.

"Not a bad idea," he commented.

"So you see, God had prepared me for each thing. I didn't know it until the time came, and then it seemed so impossible. But He was there. Every step of the way."

It struck Ceb suddenly that he had been prepared too, long ago. He had not been able to accept it back then. But this God was redeeming the time. Ceb could not deny His existence anymore. Neither could he explain the reasons why things happened. But he knew, as surely as Abdul and Madira, Ophélie and David and his parents and this beautiful Arab girl knew, that God was real and that He was indeed at work down here on earth.

It was the longest hour of his life, waiting for the plane to arrive. Eric had butterflies fluttering in his stomach and had already been to the bathroom three times. He felt immensely grateful that his parents and Ophélie were there with him in case he did something silly like pass out.

And then he saw her coming down the ramp that led from the plane. She might have been walking down the aisle of a church. She wore a brightly colored long dress, fastened with a gold belt, and her hair was braided extravagantly. She looked disheveled but radiant, holding the hem of the dress in one hand so that she wouldn't trip, her eyes wide and her smile even wider.

His knees wobbled as he tried to move forward, and his mouth went dry. He heard her cry "Eric!" and then watched her break into a run, her dress flowing out behind her, and a crowd of people looking on.

It might have been a second or an entire day before he at last managed to move his legs, and then he was holding her in his arms and laughing and squeezing her so tightly. "Rislène," he murmured, searching for her lips and pressing his so softly against them.

He vaguely heard the sound of whistling and hands clapping as he lifted her off the ground and into his arms. "I'm so glad you dressed for the occasion," he whispered. "We're going to the *mairie* to be married."

"We are?" she asked, stunned. "When?"

"Right now," he said. "Didn't you know? All the papers are ready. City hall, here we come."

"But ... are you sure, Eric? You don't have to rush into it if you're not sure."

He put his fingers over her mouth. "Shh, my love. God didn't bring us this far just for me to get cold feet. I'm sure." Then he set her down and took her face in his hands. "But are you sure?"

"Dear Eric! Marry me! Marry me now. I've never wanted anything more in all my life."

Ophélie was standing behind David and Gabriella, quietly observing Eric and Rislène's happy reunion. Ceb felt drawn to her as never before, something that was close to an aching down deep in his heart. He walked across the crowded airport, his strides purposeful and directed, and caught her up in his arms.

"Filie! Filie!" He held her at arm's length, his eyes shining and bright, then squeezed her to his chest again.

She let him hold her and didn't speak. Perhaps she was weeping.

"Filie! I'm so glad you're here." Then he whispered into the nape of her neck. "You were right. I had to surrender to Him. And once I understood that, nothing mattered at all anymore." He realized how tightly he held her and released his grasp. "Do you understand, Filie? Does it make sense?"

Her face was shining with tears, and the sweetest smile rested there. "Oh, yes, Ceb. I understand surrender. How well I understand it now."

Ceb needed to speak the next words, needed her to know. "Filie, thank you for never giving up on me." Then he could not remember the next line. He had repeated it again and again in his mind, but the words did not come. There was nothing else to say. Nothing to promise her except that he was, at last, God's. Suddenly he felt terribly vulnerable.

"Hussein sends his love to you, your folks." He was sweating now. "It was so awful, Filie. El Amin …"

"Shh. It's okay. Abdul called Papa."

His chest was burning. He could talk about God, about Algeria, about anything else under the sun, but he could not pronounce the most important words. He felt an awkwardness in the silence and turned to watch Rislène and Eric. "Thank God it worked."

"Thank the Lord, yes. And thank you, Ceb."

"Mmm."

"I'm going to the *mairie* with them. I'm going to be Rislène's *témoin*."

"They're getting married now? Today?"

"*Ah oui.* Right now at city hall. We'll have the church wedding later, but for her safety, they need to be officially married at once."

"Of course. And you're the bride's witness?"

"Yes. You can come along if you want."

Now they were so far from what he had wanted to say that he couldn't imagine getting back. "I have things I must do. Will you just keep praying for me, Filie, that He shows me what is next? It's as if—" He couldn't think of the comparison at first. "It's as if I have a new destiny—a new beginning. Does that make sense?"

She nodded.

"I don't know where this will lead. But thank you, Filie." He pressed his lips against her forehead and caught a handful of her hair in his hand. "With everything I have, I thank you for caring enough to point the way."

He backed away, waving. Eric saw him leaving and ran to catch up with him. He shook his hand, pumping it hard.

"Thank you, Ceb. How can I ever thank you?"

Ceb shrugged, overcome with emotion. "It's I who must say thanks." Then he hugged Eric hard, turned, and left. Suddenly he knew exactly what he had to do next.

�֍

Eliane Cebrian was slicing tomatoes for lunch, standing in front of the kitchen counter with the window that looked across her yard. Several new subdivisions had sprung up in the past five years, making it hard for her to distinguish the pointed rock called Pic Saint-Loup far in the distance. It was the tallest mountain peak in the region, and her children had often climbed it with Rémi when they were young.

The sun outside was warmer today than in the past week. The *méteo* had announced clear skies for Tuesday, the fourteenth of February, and it looked to Eliane as if it had been right. A beautiful day. She smiled to herself as she thought of little Catherine snuggled close to her yesterday, opening her baby mouth and displaying the barest hint of her first tooth.

Directly outside the kitchen lay the backyard, large by French standards and surrounded by a low stuccoed wall. Across from the yard was an open lot, the only one left in the subdivision. This morning a man stood in the middle of the tall grass on the unoccupied lot. He bent down and touched the dirt. Perhaps it was the new owner, though he didn't look like someone who would be buying a lot in Prades-le-Lez. He had reddish-brown hair and wore a tattered coat and threadbare jeans. She frowned, wondering if a homeless man had somehow wandered into the subdivision. He lifted his head and stared at her from fifty yards away.

Eliane gasped.

She let the knife fall from her hand. It bounced on the cutting board, sending a spray of tomato juice before it landed on the tile floor. "Samuel!" she said, but the word hung in her throat, caught by a sudden tightening there.

He met her eyes, and a half smile formed on his lips. Then he waved one hand at her, like he used to do as a kid. He stepped onto the stuccoed wall and hopped over into the backyard.

Eliane raced to the back door and swung it open, her vision blurred by the tears welling up in her eyes. "Samuel!"

"*Bonjour, Maman,*" he said softly, stooping down to kiss her on the cheeks. The bristle of his beard pricked her cheek, and she relished the feel. Then he caught his mother in a strong embrace and whispered, "I'm home."

And so Samuel Cebrian did indeed come trotting across the field, just as Eliane had always imagined, right back to her. It felt so natural to have him there as she cried into his worn jacket, and the sun warmed them both.

The fierce blue of the February sky reminded Ophélie of a day last month in this same park where she had met Ceb and then talked for hours in the café. She soaked in the bright, strong afternoon with the tiniest of breezes. A flowering bush reached toward her with its fluorescent-pink blooms, as if daring the sun to fade them. On this Tuesday afternoon the Jardin des Plantes was crowded. Two young women jogged side by side. A student, his blond hair pulled back in a ponytail, took a textbook from his backpack and, flattening himself on the length of the bench, began to read. Several Arab women, their heads covered with bright scarves, pushed strollers and chatted animatedly.

Eric and Rislène were married. Ophélie could hardly believe it, even though she had been there an hour ago as the required witness. By the state, they were officially married, and that was all that mattered in France. What an incredible relief.

The young couple, giddy with fatigue, had not known what to do next, but Ophélie had already figured it out. "Stay at my apartment for this week," she had told her brother after the call had come in the night from Abdul, informing them of Rislène's upcoming arrival. "I'll take a few things to Bri and Papa's and stay there."

Eric had been immensely relieved. "Thanks, sis. You're the best."

"My pleasure. Just don't forget to feed the dogs."

Together she and Eric had rushed around all morning, turning the apartment into a honeymoon haven, complete with roses and champagne and a skimpy silk camisole that she had purchased for the bride.

And now they were married.

Ophélie didn't want to go to Papa and Bri's. Not just yet. She needed to think. To digest so many things. The incredible goodness of God to have Rislène back and married to Eric. It wouldn't be an easy road ahead for them, but with love and the Lord, they would do fine.

And Ceb. Ceb's arms around her, strong and alive, and his eyes full of passion and purpose. Oh dear God, how good that had felt! He had said thank you and told her he was surrendering to God. What wonderful news. Every prayer answered.

Well, not every prayer. She admitted it. She had wanted to hear him say *je t'aime*. I love *you*, Ophélie Duchemin. But there had been nothing in his attitude to hint at anything but true gratitude to her for helping point the way back.

She had not dared speak of Jean-Marc after she had heard the news of El Amin. She wondered even now how Ceb would handle these tragic deaths. He had seemed so fragile last week and so strong just hours ago. Ceb! Samuel! How this hurt.

And Dominique. Good, kind, and patient Dominique. Friday night she had dismissed him from her life. So why did she want to grab him back today? Her heart felt so confused. She walked in the park for over an hour. Dominique and Ceb. Both of them gone.

Jesus, this is hard. Death and life and love and a thousand questions. This is very hard.

30

The *volets* were wide open, and the Montpellier skyline was outlined in the orange of a waning afternoon. Rislène snuggled close to Eric and ran her hand through his coarse hair. How could it be that this was her husband? Her *husband*! Only weeks ago she had hidden in this apartment, terrified of her future. And now here she was with Eric, free. Free! Free to love him, free to be a Christian, free to pursue whatever she wanted.

It scared her in a completely different way. There was so much she wanted to learn about her husband—how to make him happy, what his dreams were for their future.

"Eric." He had dozed off but now reached for her hand. "Are you afraid, Eric?"

"Of what?" he answered groggily.

"Of everything. The future. Us. Are you afraid it was a big mistake?"

He sat up and pulled her into his arms. "Let me show you how afraid I am." He kissed her tenderly, then laughed. "Yes, I'm afraid. I'm afraid I'll never have enough days to show you how much I love you and how incredibly thankful I am that you are my wife."

Sweet Eric! He seemed so absolutely carefree. But images of the past days kept haunting her thoughts. "I didn't think I would get away from there, Eric. It was so awful. I was only minutes away from being trapped forever."

He took her face in his hands, and his expression sobered. "Listen, my bride, and listen well. Papa asked me if I was ready to marry you when you came back. It did scare me. It scared me because so much is uncertain. But Papa and I talked. He married Mama quickly too. He told me I had to be patient, to give you time to trust and heal. That's what I want to do. There's no rush now. You're safe. I promise you, sweet Rislène, you are safe."

Safe. She nestled close to him. *Good Lord, thank You that he understands. He knows that waking up from a nightmare doesn't necessarily mean that the bad memories don't still frighten me.*

Then, reading her mind, he added, "Whenever you want, I'll call your parents. No hurry. Just whenever you want."

"It may take me a while to get used to this, to you." She blushed. "I keep seeing my family and the imam and Yassir. And then El Amin shot and dead. All that seems so close."

"You're safe, Rislène."

"Why did I get to live and El Amin die?"

"I don't know."

"It was my fault."

"No. No, don't say that. El Amin knew what he was getting into. It's not like he'd never held a gun. It was an accident. A terrible accident."

"Can you please just hold me? I just need to be held."

"That, my dear, will be my pleasure."

She began to cry softly, then harder, as she clung to Eric's neck. It was over. The long nightmare was over.

"I tell you what, André! Mlle Duchemin is a sweet lady, but she is playing with fire!"

"Now, Evelyne, *du calme*! It won't help your blood pressure to get upset."

"Can you imagine? Her handsome brother moving into her apartment with his Algerian bride! The nerve. The absolute nerve."

There was a knock at the door. Mme Ploussard looked at her husband crossly, then waddled across the room and peeked through the peephole. "*Ooh là là!* It's her! It's her," she whispered frantically.

"Mlle Duchemin? Don't worry, dear. I'm sure she didn't hear a thing."

"No, not Mlle Duchemin. The girl. The *Arab* girl!" She took a breath, tried to wipe the deep frown off her face, and opened the door. "Yes?"

"*Bonjour, Mme Ploussard.* My name is Rislène. I'm Eric's new wife. Ophélie—Mlle Duchemin—has told me so many nice things about you and your husband. Since we'll be living here all week, I just wanted to say hello and bring you some flowers. We received so many from friends after our marriage."

She was smiling and holding out a bouquet of bright-red and yellow tulips.

For a moment Mme Ploussard could not get a sound out. Then she grunted, blinked, and reached out her hands for the flowers.

"*Merci. Merci beaucoup.* How thoughtful."

M. Ploussard padded over to the door. "Well, *bon sang*, Evelyne. *Les tulipes!* Your favorite flower."

"Well, good-bye, and nice to meet you both," the Arab girl said.

"Yes, yes, of course," Mme Ploussard stammered. "*Enchantée.* Very nice to meet you too."

Four days at his parents' home in Prades-le-Lez passed in a blur for Ceb. He slept fitfully. He found it hard to sit still. There was a nagging in his brain, something that pushed at him, just beyond his conscious memory. His family was discreet. They did not bombard him with questions. There were no big get-togethers, just a quick visit from his sister and his brother one afternoon.

His mother and father went about their days as if it were the most normal thing in the world that he was there. At times his mother came into a room and found him there, touching a pillow, caressing an old armoire. She just smiled, and every once in a while commented lightly, "Let me know if there is anything I can get you, dear." But he knew that beyond the forced insouciance they were wondering, *Will he just up and disappear again?*

It would be nice to stay here for a while. To rest in the comfort of his old room. But it was that beckoning, that feeling of drivenness. Was it from God or just his old restlessness? It was so hard to tell. He longed to see Ophélie. A dozen times a day he thought of calling her, just to talk for hours about nothing and everything. But he couldn't—not until this other thing was done. On the fifth day he announced to his parents, "I'm going to Méribel tomorrow. I called Bernard, and he has a room free. He'll meet me at the train station."

His father cleared his throat and wiped a napkin across his mouth. "Would you like me to come with you, son?"

"No. Thanks, Papa. It's something I have to do alone. But it's okay. I swear that I'll be okay."

He knew it took a lot of courage for them to say good-bye. He read the fear in their minds. If he returned to the scene of the accident, would it send him spiraling back into a dark depression? He could not answer their unasked questions. But he was not afraid to go back now. The God of the universe was on his side.

Bernard was in his early fifties, a man who had grown up in a little valley at the base of the Alps. Years ago he had bought a spacious chalet in the town of Méribel, perched at the highest point in the village with a breathtaking view of the Alps and only a minute's ski to the slopes, and turned it into a popular hotel. It was considered by many as the most chic resort in all of the French Alps. It was where François Mitterrand skied.

For years Samuel and Annie had rented an apartment at Bernard's for a week each winter. When little Marion was barely two, she put on her first pair of boots and skis just outside the lobby of the chalet.

"It's good to see you again, Samuel." The mountain man took Ceb's hand and shook it forcefully.

"Thanks, Bernard. Thanks for finding room for me on such short notice."

"No problem. Stay as long as you want."

For three days Ceb sat in the cozy apartment with the ceilings that rose steep and fell down low, and the windows that looked out on every side to white snow and ski lifts and figures bundled in brightly clad snowsuits. He ate the croissants that Bernard's wife, Geraldine, brought to his door each morning and drank cups of strong black coffee. In the afternoons he walked through the town and remembered every restaurant, every shop that he and Annie had frequented. He stood for hours by the ski school and in his mind heard Marion's delighted squeals as he pushed her on a plastic sled.

Then, chilled to the bone, he came to the bar in the chalet and drank a *vin chaud* with Bernard. One cup after another of the hot spiced wine, until his head was spinning and he was laughing like old times at Bernard's slightly off-color jokes. He drank until he could no longer see in his mind's eye the cup of hot chocolate that his daughter sipped, leaving a foamy brown mustache on her face.

It was on the fourth night at the chalet, his mind blurred by the vin chaud, that he said to Bernard, "I'm ready now. Do you have a shovel?"

"Sure."

"I need to borrow it. And the truck."

"Ground will be awfully hard, Sam. You want some help?"

"No. No help. Thanks."

Ceb drove Bernard's truck past the site of the accident, continuing two hundred feet farther down the road until he found a place to park. It struck him again that if only he had made it around two more hairpin turns, the car would not have fallen over the side, tumbled down fifty feet to the next piece of road, and crashed into the side of the mountain, but would have merely skidded into a wide embankment. If only.

He found the site as surely as if it were marked with a permanent spot of blood and began digging with the shovel and ice pick until he had carved out a small hole a foot deep. He went to the car and retrieved his backpack. From it, he lifted a simple stone cross two feet high, one he had found at a flea market in Prades-le-Lez. He set it in the ground, piled the frozen dirt around it to hold the cross in place. Then he retrieved a bouquet of roses, red and yellow, from the truck and placed them at the foot of the stone cross. He brought out a photo of a bright-eyed little girl whose head was covered in silky brown curls. He pressed his lips to the photo, then set the photo by the flowers. The pain in his chest pierced him so deeply that for a moment he could not catch his breath.

How I miss you, Marion. My baby, gone forever. He placed the photo of Annie beside Marion's and wept hot tears for her, for them. In his anger and hurt and confusion, he had tried to bury his past on this mountain, to deny the horror of what happened. But today he was choosing to accept it and move forward. He wasn't a coward, and he hoped to high heaven that he wasn't a murderer either. He had found God's forgiveness in Algeria, but now, what he needed more than anything else was to forgive himself.

Do You hear me, God? I choose to go on!

The next morning Ceb put on ski boots, struggling with the buckles, then kicking off the snow and snapping the boots onto the skis. He pulled his red ski hat down over his face and fumbled with the gloves. He wondered briefly if he could hold the pole in his right hand.

He rode the ski bubbles to the very top of the mountain, leaning forward in the seat and reaching as if to touch the thick snow that weighed down the evergreens. He had always loved the contrast between blue sky, green trees, and white snow. Simple, bright, vibrant.

On this tall peak, he was alone with the mountain. He raced downhill, bending his knees and swiveling his hips as he encountered each mogul, for a time oblivious to everything but the dizzying speed and the icy wind on his face. If he had dared to look to the side, he thought that maybe Annie would still be there.

He came to a wide-open basin and stopped, peering out toward the splendor of the snow-capped peaks in the distance. He could tell that the top of the basin, which fell away almost perpendicularly, was icy, still in shadows. He hesitated, then pushed off the edge and flew down the center of the basin, constantly on the verge of losing control. He didn't care.

A little-used slope veered off to the right, marked with the black diamond indicating the most demanding slopes. Here was another challenge, a slope he had never skied before. It advanced at a steep grade, twisting precariously with little room to zigzag and slow the speed. The trees gathered in around him, tickling his face as he sped forward.

And then the path opened before him. Not another skier in sight, only far-off peaks and snow. He swished to a stop and looked down. Just beside the path, the mountain disappeared into a staggering, jagged cliff. Even as he peered over, a few loose rocks bounced off the side and tumbled hundreds of feet below. It would be so easy to simply ski off the side of the mountain into nothingness.

The Alps had always stolen a part of his heart, but they would not take his soul. That belonged to Another. He stared at the white expanse and the precipitous drop. His breath came in gulps, the clean air puncturing his lungs with a welcome chill. Ceb looked toward the valley. It really was an accident. He hadn't meant to kill them. *Please God. Annie and Marion aren't here to forgive me. They can't. You have forgiven me, God. Please help me to forgive myself.*

It was starting to snow. Ceb clutched his arms around himself and felt the snow touch his beard. "Thank You, Lord," he choked out. "Thank You for this new beginning. You can bring good out of bad. I won't go back. Take me forward. I'm Yours."

Now the snow fell more heavily, but still soft in its touch even as its intensity increased. The flakes on his face were a gift from God, this eternal whiteness that gently, softly stacked itself on his parka and skis. He wouldn't need to come back again. In the best possible way, it was over.

When he got to the bottom of the slope with the crowds of skiers and the alpine village in front of him, he was free. He was not a murderer after all.

Eric and Rislène were going to live with the Hoffmanns until they could get an apartment through student housing. Ophélie was glad to be back in her apartment, glad to have the puppies and Lassie there to keep her company.

Ceb had gone to his parents' house and then on to Méribel, according to Bri. Ophélie wondered if he could handle going back there. But apparently it was something he needed to do.

Her morning at the Red Cross had not gone well. She kept seeing Jean-Marc's face in every homeless man who came to look through the clothes. And when Dominique had stopped in for a cup of coffee, the tension and awkwardness between them had been evident to everyone. She wasn't sure she could keep going back.

But she had an idea of something she could do, a simple way to help the SDFs. Tonight she would start. Spread out on the floor of the den were copies of the New Testament, photocopied sheets of paper with the addresses of the shelters, phone numbers, maps of Montpellier, and several used phone cards that still had some units left on them. She had ordered a stack of tracts that spoke of hope in Christ and seemed tastefully done. And on a quick trip to the store she had bought chocolate bars, granola bars, small boxes of crackers, packets of instant coffee, washcloths, toothbrushes, and tubes of toothpaste.

This was what she could offer the homeless. A little plastic bag filled with a few necessities, a few nonperishable food items, and all the information necessary to find a place to stay the night. And God's Word. This was the hope that she would hand out at stoplights.

She could not bring Jean Marc back. And perhaps she could not face the pain of seeing Dominique and Ceb. But this she could do. The next time an SDF approached her at a traffic light, she did not have to turn her eyes away and be ashamed. God had given her an idea of how to be the hands and feet of Jesus to the hurting, even if she never left her car.

31

The grave was hidden amid the orange groves, the freshly turned ground outlined with small flowering plants. Within weeks they would blossom and spread until El Amin's grave would be completely covered. No terrorist would be able to find it or learn what really happened to this man. This fact brought some comfort to Madira as she stood in front of the grave, one hand resting on the shoulder of El Amin's son, Mehdi. Jala and her three girls stood off to the side, listening as Abdul read Scripture. It had become a daily ritual, a simple Christian ceremony that Jala had not objected to.

El Amin's wife had not cried at first when Hussein and Dounia brought her to the Charfi farmhouse last week to see her husband's body. She had sat by El Amin through the night, speaking softly to the man she loved and who was no more. The following morning she had seemed relieved in a strange sort of way when Hussein, along with Abdul and Madira, related the last day of El Amin's life.

With tears streaming down her face, Jala told them of El Amin's dream and of his conviction that he must see his parents. She had cried only briefly, and Madira marveled at her strength and quiet dignity. For years this woman had suffered silently the fear and uncertainty of a husband involved in terrorist activities. She even wore scars from where she had been caught in the bombing three weeks earlier.

Madira and Abdul could see that she was terrified. And so they opened their home to their son's wife and four children, promising shelter until Jala could decide what to do next.

"If his men ever find out that he was helping Christians, they will murder us—I know they will," she had confided. "We must leave Algeria!"

The underground church was working on a way to get Jala and her children to France. Until that time, they would stay with the Charfis.

Abdul knelt in the soft dirt, offering a prayer to God. It was a bittersweet reunion, thought Madira. God had taken her son and given her back a daughter-in-law and four grandchildren. This was a sweet miracle, a balm for the wounded heart. It was such a hard life. But Madira's wound was pure and clean. No more wondering and anguished prayers. El Amin was resting in the arms of Jesus. This she believed with her whole being.

"Grandmother, can I put my flowers on Baba's grave?" the youngest child, Rachida, inquired.

"Of course," she answered. Madira's eyes met Jala's and communicated, she hoped, love and understanding. Nothing was settled in Algeria. But it was settled in Madira's heart. In one way or another, all the children had come back home. God be praised.

Rislène came downstairs as the doorbell rang. She hesitated, looked up the stairs, and called, "Eric, she's here." Then she opened the door.

Her mother stood there, her scarf covering her hair and coat pulled around her. They met in a warm embrace.

Inside the house, Mme Namani took her daughter's face in her hands. "Rislène, tell me you are happy."

"I'm very happy."

The wooden staircase groaned with the sound of footsteps, and a moment later, Eric came into the den.

"Mother, I would like you to meet my husband, Eric."

The worried eyes of her mother studied the lanky young man for a long time. She held out her hand, and Eric took it. Then Mme Namani smiled. "I'm glad to meet you. Take good care of my daughter, please."

"I promise you I will."

Rislène brought out cups of coffee. They sipped in silence. It seemed her mother was satisfied simply to watch her daughter's every move, to observe that she was indeed well.

"Mother, I'll be finishing school. Eric and Mme Hoffmann and Ophélie will all help me review for the *bac*. And next year I plan to attend university."

"This is good. Your father will be proud."

Father had refused all contact with Rislène, and Grandmother claimed she was banished from the family forever, but at least she had Mother. Mother would relate the news, and someday, maybe …

"Nazira is staying in Algeria," her mother stated matter-of-factly. "She is marrying Yassir this summer. We'll be going to the wedding."

Hearing Yassir's name made a chill run through Rislène. This memory was too close. She tried to imagine Nazira married. She seemed so very young. "I'm happy for Nazira, and for all of you, Mother."

She read her mother's unspoken thoughts. If only … But the words were too difficult to pronounce. Someday perhaps there would be communication with the rest of her family. But not now. Rislène was not sure what to do with the aching inside. Life's choices were hard. Sometimes unbearable.

"You'll come back to see me, won't you, Mother?"

The older woman stood abruptly. "Yes, I will." She addressed Eric. "Thank you for taking care of Rislène. We shall all speak again. Soon. I promise."

Rislène kissed her mother on the cheeks, then held her for a long moment. She felt the stiffness in her mother's posture melt away.

"I'm glad I was able to meet you, Eric. I pray you will be a good husband for Rislène. May Allah be with you both always."

"He is, Mother." Rislène whispered through the catch in her throat. "I assure you, He is."

Dominique stepped inside the minivan to inspect it once again. A 1991 model, white. The interior had been refurbished with two benches hooked to each side of the van. The benches lifted up to reveal storage space for blankets, coats, and sleeping bags. Installed directly behind the driver's seat were a small refrigerator, a stovetop, and a white metal cabinet. Dominique opened the cabinet, examining neatly organized rows of medicines.

After many months of red tape, this project had come through. Now there was a means to reach the most remote SDFs with food and medical supplies. The goal was to penetrate the darkest corners of the homeless world. In the past eighteen months, Dominique had seen twenty people die on the streets. He thought of Jean-Marc. These people called Dominique their guardian angel, but all too often he wasn't there when they needed him most. Maybe the van would get help to some in time.

Guardian angel. The words made him think of Ophélie Duchemin. Now there was an angel. A woman of convictions, smart, and savvy. At least she wasn't one of those women who'd say anything just to get his approval. Her talk of religion intrigued him. *Médiateur de rue.* He chuckled to himself to think of Jesus Christ having the same job description as him. What a strange comparison. But behind the humor, there were questions for Ophélie. It might take a while, but he wasn't going to give up on her.

The men's shelter was empty in the middle of the day, and Dominique slipped into his office, to the desk piled high with papers. When the buzzer sounded insistently, he ignored it. But by the fourth ring, Dominique set down his paper and went to the front door.

At first he didn't recognize the man who was standing there. Then he saw the long scar on his forehead. "Ceb! Come in."

Ceb had trimmed his beard, and his hair was shorter and clean. His jeans were worn but not tattered, and the green sweater he wore was spotless. He looked transformed.

"Good to see you again, Ceb. I hear you went to Algeria."

Ceb nodded.

"Glad you got out alive."

Ceb laughed, a hint of nervousness in his voice. "Alive. Yes."

"How long have you been back?"

"Ten days."

"I suppose you heard about Jean-Marc?"

"Yes, Janine told me. Awful. Senseless."

Dominique wondered why Ophélie had said nothing. Surely Ceb had seen her. He motioned for Ceb to have a seat at one of the round metal tables where the homeless men ate breakfast. "Can I get you a cup of coffee?"

"*Oui*, coffee sounds good." He rubbed his hands together. "Still a bit brisk out there."

When Dominique set down two paper cups of steaming liquid, Ceb began to talk. "I came back to thank you, Dominique, for all you're doing here. All you did for me. I'm off the streets." He paused to let the words sink in, and Dominique nodded. "And I want to volunteer to help out as a medic, anything you need, free of charge. Maybe I could keep what happened to Jean-Marc from happening to someone else."

Dominique scooted back in his chair, traced the outline of his beard with a finger, and smiled. "Well, if that's the case, Ceb, then I have something to show you."

They stepped outside and went around the back of the building where the minivan was parked. "This little baby was just fixed up last week. Take a look inside."

Stepping inside the minivan, Ceb examined the interior, opening each cabinet and shelf, picking up bottles of medicine and turning them over in his hands. A smile spread across his face. "It's not bad, Dominique. Not bad at all. Congrats. You worked hard for it."

"Yeah. Took it out last night for the first time. We've got two social workers to man it, and I'll go out when I can. All we lack right now is a nurse. Or a doctor." He looked at Ceb. "We could use you, for hire, not volunteer, if you could get your papers together. The city's willing to pay part-time minimum wage for a medic. What do you think?"

"I told you I'm not looking for pay." He scratched his head. "Do you really think it's a possibility?"

Dominique contemplated the question. He didn't want to give false hope. And what did he have to prove that Ceb was truly off the streets? He had been wrong before. Still, he had the feeling that Ceb was on the right track.

"I think it's worth a try," he said at last. "You're just the kind of guy they're looking for—a reformed street person coming back to help others. Of course, it doesn't hurt that you're a doctor. Let me see what I can do."

They stepped out of the van, and he pulled the door closed and locked it.

"Bring me your papers tomorrow, Ceb. And plan to stick around. You can make the rounds with us—a tour of Montpellier's inner streets."

"*Merci*, Dominique. *Merci de tout coeur.*" He held out his maimed hand, took Dominique's, and shook it forcefully.

Dominique watched Ceb leave. Everything about the man's manner seemed more confident. *I think you're gonna make it, Ceb. I think you're getting your life back.* What was more satisfying for a *médiateur de rue* than to know that an SDF had gotten off the streets? He'd even come back to say thanks.

But a question still hammered in Dominique's head. What about Ophélie Duchemin? Where was she in all of this?

The puppies were seven weeks old and getting too big to stay in the cage. They had long since been weaned from Lassie. Janine had already claimed Saint X. One of Ophélie's sisters had agreed to take Cleo, and her mother and Moustafa wanted Jean Valjean. Bri had called yesterday to say that Eliane Cebrian would be happy to take Hamlet. That left Ophélie with Lassie and the Little Prince. She had decided to keep them both.

She wondered if Ceb was back from the Alps. What was he doing? She couldn't bring herself to call up and ask to speak to him. This was something she had to get over. In a few months, she told herself, she could see him at a family function and be able to control these crazy emotions. In a few months. But not yet.

Lassie nuzzled her hand, and Ophélie stroked the dog's black fur absentmindedly. She was supposed to be working on a new play. The idea had come to her back in mid-January when she had sat in the Jardin des Plantes, hoping to see Ceb. Now she wasn't sure if it was truly inspired or if she was just forcing something to keep her mind occupied. She had talked to Simon about it, the story of two unemployed people who fall in love, and he'd seemed interested. It was a story for these times. Jotting down ideas for the play was good therapy, but tonight she was having a hard time concentrating on anything.

She went into the kitchen and leafed through a cookbook. She'd invited Simon, Janine, M. and Mme Dufour, and her father and Bri for dinner next week. She hoped that in an informal setting, the Dufours and Simon would talk openly about their fears about the church. Janine had seemed pleased with the idea.

Ophélie put down the cookbook and picked up Hamlet, scratched the puppy behind his ears, then set him back on the floor and walked into her office. She picked up the phone, started to dial the Cebrians' number, then hung up the receiver. Maybe if she just started to write, the ideas would come and the thoughts about Ceb would leave. Work, pray, cry. Anything but listen to these crazy feelings. Ceb was okay, and he didn't want her in his life.

And if she didn't have the creativity to tackle the play, there was always a stack of papers she could grade. What was her problem?

Loneliness. That was it. Life was getting back to a familiar routine, and she was scared. Ceb was starting over. Eric and Rislène had a brand-new life in front of them. But for her, it seemed, it was the same old status quo.

Ceb walked into the Galeries Lafayette without knowing why. Often he and his homeless friends had spent the days sitting outside the chic department store, keeping warm inside the mall. But today he had come shaven and well dressed, looking for something tangible and important and just out of reach.

The possibility of helping with the minivan excited him, sent that old familiar adrenaline pumping. Work!

But hold on a minute, he told himself. *You spoke of surrender. Hadn't you better check it out with the Almighty?*

It was a good idea, but all he really wanted to do was to check it out with Ophélie. Call her up and ask her opinion. Call her up and talk for hours. Filie. Beautiful Filie.

But what about Dominique? They hadn't spoken of Ophélie. Ceb hadn't dared give the street mediator the opportunity to pronounce the words he dreaded. "Yeah, I've been spending quite a lot of time with your friend Ophélie lately. She's wonderful." It would hurt too much. And deep inside Ceb still wondered, *Doesn't Filie deserve someone strong and stable like Dominique?*

He detested these insecure thoughts. He wanted to feel in control.

Surrender. Surrender.

He wandered in and out of the makeup booths, ignoring the smiles of the models, their eyes heavy with mascara and lips painted in thick, strident colors as they offered advice on lipstick, lotion, and perfume. Everything was neat and orderly and clean. Aisle after aisle of scarves and earrings and pocketbooks and jewelry. An English pop song played in the background. What was he doing, standing in the middle of the women's department in an upscale department store? What did he possibly hope to find? He felt terribly out of control. He had survived the death of his wife and daughter, survived the streets, escaped with Rislène from the horror in Algeria, but when he thought of telling Ophélie what was really in his soul, he panicked. He couldn't do it, he was sure. That was why he was here. He needed something to communicate what he could not say. A scarf? Makeup? Ridiculous. Better a book of poetry.

And then he saw it, across the aisle, high up on the shelf. He laughed out loud. It couldn't be! He bought it immediately and left the store, walking back into the crowded mall with a boyish grin on his face.

32

Ramadan was over, and the last night had erupted into a feast of partying and eating. But Grandmother Namani did not feel like celebrating. Her old body ached with a despair that she never let anyone see. Rislène was lost forever to the family, and how Grandmother loved Rislène! But tears were not allowed tonight. Fortunately, there was plenty of work to be done. She and her son Youssef had decided that Nazira would marry Yassir. The family honor could be saved, and the child was excited at the prospect. The child! She was only a year younger than Rislène. It would work out well.

Yassir had not been pleased at first. Nazira did not share her sister's beauty, but his family was equally determined to find a solution to the terrible disgrace that had befallen them. In the end he had agreed to the marriage. Now when Yassir came to the house to see Nazira, he seemed proud to be with the girl whose eyes betrayed complete infatuation and loyalty.

Grandmother Namani sighed heavily and began to go through the ceremonial washing, washing the hands, touching the forehead, repeating the words that she had repeated daily for nearly seventy years. Duty, duty. But the family honor would be saved. This mattered most. An elaborate wedding would hush the whispers and turn back the stares of neighbors who gossiped about the strange disappearance of Rislène. *Inshallah.*

The eruption of violence during the month of Ramadan had only added to the confusion and despair in Algeria. It broke Hussein's heart to observe it. Not only did his people live with the threat of daily bombings, but also the food supply was dwindling. On some days Dounia returned from market practically empty-handed. He looked out the den window at the black sky. For this moment everything was quiet, almost tranquil. The celebrations of the conclusion of the fast had ended yesterday.

Dounia came from the children's back bedroom and joined him at the window, resting her head on his sturdy shoulder and putting an arm around his waist. "Malika told me tonight that all her friends at school talk about is death. And it's not just at school. Behind every locked door, families whisper about the murders that aren't even mentioned in the newspapers. The young people don't talk about music and movies—they talk about death!"

As Hussein listened to his wife, he heard the deep exhaustion behind her words. Algeria! The land that he loved seemed destined for self-destruction. Was it surprising, when young boys thought more about becoming terrorists than about their future? What future? For 5,000 *dinars*, minimum wage, a teenager was ready to kill a neighbor or blow up a bridge.

Dounia sighed and shook her head. "All we want is a normal life, a roof over our heads, enough to eat, and something to smile about. Will it ever be, Hussein?"

What did he have to promise his three precious children, those gifts from God who slumbered in their bedrooms? How could their dreams be peaceful when their waking hours were filled with stories more horrible than the worst nightmare? *We have hope in Christ*, he told them each day. Did they even believe him anymore?

Hussein took his wife's hand in his and, still staring into the darkness, he began to pray. "Dear Lord, we are here to be salt and light in the midst of this devastation."

He thought of El Amin, and his eyes misted over. Death and life. Yesterday he and Dounia had visited Jala at Abdul and Madira's house. What was God's answer for them? What was God's answer for Dounia and him, for their children? No easy answers.

"We can only reaffirm, Lord Jesus, that we believe You are in control and You are sovereign. We won't try to understand it tonight. Help us remember Your many miracles in our life. Erase the doubt. Give us courage for tomorrow. We love You and we trust You, Lord Jesus." His voice faded into a choked-out *Amen* as he held Dounia against his chest.

The mistral was blowing, causing the stoplight to jiggle on its wire. Ophélie pulled her car to a stop at the busy intersection. She noticed the young man immediately, a cardboard sign in his hand, his eyes expressionless. Quickly she reached over to the floor of the passenger's seat and picked up one of ten small plastic sacks that lay there. Today she knew what to do for this man.

As he approached the car, she rolled down the window. "I have only this to offer. Please take it. There is information in it, and food."

The young man's eyes narrowed, registering suspicion and then surprise.

"Please," Ophélie insisted as the wind gusted through the car.

The light turned green. He grabbed the bag and murmured, "*Merci, m'dame.*"

"God be with you," she whispered, almost to herself. It felt right and good.

Ophélie stood before her class wearing a pale-blue sweater and jeans. Her lips felt dry. She licked them twice, cleared her throat, and smiled. *"Bonjour, tout le monde."*

It was the last class of the day, and she was glad. For some reason, she felt completely drained. It had been a very long week. Her eyes scanned the room of twenty-two teenagers until they rested on Rislène. She was there in class again, with her quick smile, her thick black hair twisted into a French braid, and her slim body tucked into jeans and a sweatshirt.

"Want me to drop you off?" she asked Rislène after class.

The young woman flashed her a smile. "No, I'm meeting Eric at the Fac for coffee. Thanks though." They kissed on the cheeks, and Rislène left the classroom.

Ophélie sat down at her desk, nibbling on a pencil, thinking of Eric and Rislène and Ceb. They were the cast in a play she had not written. They had learned their lines, were acting out their lives, had found their way home.

God, I am so lonely. Ophélie placed her head in her hands. Thoughts of Ceb distracted her from writing, from teaching. From the Lord. But what else could she do? She'd been honest with the Lord about everything. Very honest. Did new beginnings always take a while to get used to?

Surrender. Abide. Oh, yes, she could do that.

It was time to go home. She got up, locked the door to her classroom, and left the *lycée*. A young man was sitting on the steps. He looked vaguely familiar, a face from the Red Cross. Maybe tomorrow she would find the courage to go back.

The man stood and looked at her as she hurried down the steps. "*Mademoiselle*," he implored. She turned and saw the stringy hair, caught the stench of alcohol on his breath.

"Can I help you?" she asked.

"Ceb told me I'd find you here. He wanted to show you something."

Ophélie swallowed hard. "Ceb?" she said weakly.

"*Oui, mademoiselle.* He's waiting for us at the van. Could you come?"

"Ceb? Waiting?" She hurried beside the SDF, taking the steps two at a time.

Several other homeless men whom she recognized from the Red Cross joined them. "Look over there, Mlle Ophélie. We've got ourselves a special van. Free food, blankets, coffee. And a doctor who gives medicine. Dr. Ceb! Can you believe it?"

A white minivan was parked in the lot not far from her car. "When did this happen?"

"Just this week," one of the men confided proudly. "Go on in."

The backdoor to the minivan opened, and Ceb stepped out. She almost didn't recognize him. He had on a doctor's white lab jacket over his jeans. His reddish-brown hair was short and clean, his beard trimmed, and there was a certain confidence in his stance. And the eyes. She couldn't meet his eyes.

He came to her with a wide smile on his face. "Hello, Filie." He kissed her three times on the cheeks and then took her hands, his hazel eyes twinkling with excitement. "Come look around."

A chill went through Ophélie, and she blinked. "Ceb?"

He seemed not to notice the question in her voice as he held her arm and pointed out the different features of the van. "Dominique's baby. I've been hired as the doctor. What do you think?"

She shook her head in wonder. "It's incredible, Ceb. It's what you both wanted. What you dreamed of."

"You were right about second chances, Ophélie." He turned quickly, as if that one phrase had revealed too much. "Have a seat. I'll get you some coffee." Back still turned, he said, "I've been staying with Mama and Papa."

"Yes, I heard."

"It's been good these past weeks." He hurried on as if he were afraid of her questions. "I've had time to think, you know. I went back to the Alps, to the accident." His voice cracked almost imperceptibly.

"I'm sure that was hard."

"Hard, yes, but good." Now he was sounding like Samuel the surgeon. Everything was fine, everything in control. He seemed a million miles away. "Got some papers in, and with Dominique's help, I'll be working with the van twenty hours a week." He looked at her for the first time when he pronounced Dominique's name. "I'm thinking of starting a practice downtown, maybe what they call a roaming doctor, making daily rounds at the shelters. It won't pay much, but it's what I want to do."

Determined, happy Samuel was back. This was not Ceb, and this was not the conversation she had imagined.

"Oh. I'm so glad." Why did her voice sound so flat?

He motioned for her to sit down on one of the benches and brought her a cup of coffee. He paced awkwardly in the small cubicle, seeming suddenly unsure of what he wanted to say.

"I've been thinking about you, Filie...."

She acknowledged it with a smile that she hoped did not seem too eager.

"Thinking you'd be a big help here with the mobile van. I could use an assistant for the paperwork. I thought maybe on Wednesday mornings, if the Red Cross could spare you, you could help me out. I know you're busy." He fumbled with his hands.

An assistant. Her face fell, and the hammering in her chest slipped from anticipation to brutal reality and disappointment. She measured her words. "It's wonderful what you're doing, Ceb. But I ... I really don't think I would be much help." She stood to go, barely able to keep from shaking, her emotions raw and wild. His assistant. Did he not see how that hurt?

"Do you have to go, Filie? Couldn't you stay for the afternoon?"

"No, Ceb. I'm sorry. I have ..." Her hands were clammy. She felt suddenly dizzy. "I have things to do."

Ceb shuffled to his feet, looking down, looking like the insecure SDF of two months ago. It startled her, momentarily bringing her back from her emotions.

"Please don't go, Filie. I have a problem. I need to talk to you about a problem."

A problem! She didn't have the strength to stay and hear about his problems. This was torture. "I'm sorry, Ceb. I'm late. I have to go. I have people coming over tonight." She stepped out of the van and hurried to her car, pausing only to call back, "It's a great thing, Ceb. I'm very happy for you."

She unlocked the door and slipped into her car, but before she could start the ignition, there was a tapping on her window. She looked up to see Dominique smiling down at her. She let out a little cry. "Dominique! You scared me!" She rolled down the window.

"Sorry, Ophélie! Where are you going so quickly?"

"I-I'm late. My parents are coming for dinner. Janine too," she stammered.

"I see Ceb's shown you the van. What do you think of it?"

"It's super. You did a great job getting it. And working things out for Ceb. Amazing."

"Do you have time for a cup of coffee? Fifteen minutes?"

Her head began to throb as forcefully as her heart. "Look, Dominique. That's kind, but I thought I had made things clear."

"Perfectly clear. Just one question. Janine has been telling me about a study she attends at your church. A study for, how did she put it ... for those who are seeking." He grinned. "I might like to come someday."

"You would?" Ophélie narrowed her eyes. "Are you just saying this for me?"

"No, I promise. I'm intrigued." He shrugged, then laughed. "I seriously want to attend. And if you're there, well, so much the better."

"Dominique, please."

"Hey, don't worry. How are the puppies?"

"They all have homes. They're doing great. Lassie too."

"Good. You sure you won't join me for coffee?"

"I really have to go."

"I understand. Good-bye, Ophélie. See you soon." He leaned down and through the open window kissed her on the cheeks.

Soon, she thought. Maybe even at church. *You just never know about people.* On an impulse, she called back to him. "I can't have coffee, but if you're free tonight, I'd love for you to join us for dinner."

Dominique smiled. "I'd like that. I'd like that a lot. What time?"

"Seven thirty."

She hurried home. She had a meal to get ready for Simon, the Dufours, Janine, Bri and Papa. And Dominique. Somehow it seemed he would fit right in.

"Well, Ophélie, you are certainly a fine cook. *Délicieux*," Mme Dufour exclaimed, wiping her mouth with a cloth napkin. "Such a talented young woman. Teacher, playwright, gourmet chef. *Ooh là là.* And Sunday school teacher."

"*Merci*, Mme Dufour. I'm so glad you liked the dinner," Ophélie said, ignoring Mme Dufour's last comment.

"It really was delicious, sweetheart," her father added.

"I couldn't have done it without Janine's help. She's the talented one." Ophélie gave Janine a wink.

"Well, yes, Janine has always been the talented one in the family," Mme Dufour continued, speaking of her daughter as if she were not in the room. "And such a good heart! Working with the homeless. And she's told me how much she adores your little church."

The two friends exchanged glances. Up until now, the evening had been light and cheery, but now Mme Dufour seemed ready for a lively conversation. She had barely taken a breath. "And I certainly wouldn't dream of putting pressure on her to be at the Catholic church. I've always told her to try different things. Isn't that right, Georges?"

M. Dufour merely grunted.

"Anyway. I think the church sounds just perfect for Janine. She says she has found a purpose in life. And good friends. Well, *tant mieux.*" She turned to David. "Although I must admit I find it a bit, shall we say, unusual to see Arabs in the church. But we must keep an open mind, *n'est-ce pas?*"

"That's always a good idea," David commented, and Bri nodded politely.

"That's right, Mama," Janine said quickly. "A great idea."

"And why anyone would think of your church as a cult, well, I can't imagine for the life of me!" Mme Dufour set her napkin on the table and sighed. Janine raised her eyebrows, Ophélie suppressed a giggle, and Simon sat back in his chair and gave a deep belly laugh.

It was after midnight when Ceb parked the van and stepped outside. He locked the doors and rubbed his hands together. It was not that he had forgotten he'd told his mother he'd be home for supper. But he just couldn't do it. Home was with the street people, helping them. Keeping busy tonight so that he didn't have to remember Ophélie's eyes turning away from him, and then watch her from the window of the van as she talked to Dominique. *Too late. Too late.*

There were still lights on in her apartment. He stood in the dark for half an hour, staring up at the tall building, wishing that she would appear on the small balcony and wave down to him. When the doors on the ground floor of the residence opened, Ceb drew back into the shadows and observed the Hoffmanns, a few people he didn't recognize, and then Janine and Dominique, who were talking animatedly together. They didn't even glance toward the white van parked around the corner.

Blowing on his hands, Ceb retrieved a small plastic bag from the van. When the others were out of sight, he walked the short distance to the apartment building and pressed the intercom button with a prayer on his lips. *God, please, give me one last chance.*

The dishes were stacked beside the sink. The leftovers were covered and placed in the refrigerator. It had been such a pleasant evening. And Dominique had fit in so well. She was glad he had accepted the last-minute invitation.

Lassie and Le Petit Prince were curled in a corner of the office on a small throw rug. Ophélie yawned and gave each of the dogs a pat. She glanced at her backpack on the floor in her office. It was stuffed with papers to grade. Well, that could certainly wait until tomorrow. The buzzer sounded from below. Someone must have forgotten something. She smiled. Probably Janine. She was always leaving her purse. Ophélie picked up the intercom and pressed the button without listening for a voice. She left the door slightly ajar and returned to the kitchen, humming to herself.

A minute later there was a soft tapping on the door. "Can I come in?"

Ophélie turned around to see Ceb standing in the entranceway, a shy grin on his face, his brow wrinkled.

"Ceb!" she choked out. "What are you doing here?" Then she recovered from her shock. "Yes, come in."

"Sorry to stop by so late. I wanted to wait until your dinner guests left." He held a small plastic bag in his maimed hand.

"Oh, you should have come up. It was just Papa and Bri, and Janine and her parents. And Simon, the play's director."

"And Dominique."

"Oh, yes, Dominique came too." Her throat felt so tight. "Would you like to sit down?"

"Thanks, Filie." He took a seat on the couch and motioned for her to join him.

Ceb leaned forward, started to say something, then sat back and licked his lips. "I'm not good at this. I've rehearsed it enough times, but—" He ran his hand through his hair. "It was simply a pretext today. What I said about an assistant. I didn't know how to say what I've been wanting to tell you for so long. So I brought you this." He reached into the plastic bag and handed Ophélie a small rectangular box wrapped in red and gold paper.

"A present for me?"

Ceb smiled. "Yes, go ahead. Open it."

Ophélie removed the wrapping paper and found a pale-pink and blue floral box with the word *Essentiel* written diagonally across the box. She stared at it in wonder. Then she laughed. Opening the box, she lifted out a small curved white bottle with a pink opaque top and the same pink cursive writing on the bottle.

"I can't believe they still make this," she said. She unscrewed the top, lifted the bottle to her nose, and inhaled. It was not a fine perfume, yet its delicate fruity fragrance pleased her. She splashed some on her neck and wrists.

Instantly Ophélie felt a tightening in her chest. It was as if she were seventeen again, that same teenager who had loved a boy, who had wanted the cheap bottle of perfume to mean more than it could possibly mean to Samuel Cebrian. She looked up at him, a hundred questions racing in her mind. What in the world was Ceb trying to tell her now? Her head was pounding, and she realized that she was terrified to hear his next words.

"This time I mean it," he whispered, as if reading her thoughts. "I need to tell you that my problem is you." He scooted closer to her on the couch. "Filie, it's true I want your help. But not with the van. I want you. I'm so afraid to ask you. You saw what I had become. You brought me back from the grave. I can never tell, my dear Filie, if it is love I read in your eyes or just that deep compassion. For so long I've wanted it to be love. For love is what I feel for you. I love you, Filie. And I only dare mention it because I have started over. Could you accept me now?"

Ophélie was crying and could not stop. His words seemed like a foreign language or something she had written in a play. For how many lifetimes had she longed to hear them? He put his arms around her and held her very tenderly.

When she finally could speak, she whispered, "Ceb, what do you mean can I accept you? Love you? Perhaps I hid it well. How could I let you see, when I was sure you were only wishing for something else?" She took his face in her hands and looked him in the eyes. Those bright-hazel eyes! She chose her next words carefully. "I love you, Samuel 'Ceb' Cebrian. I love you for everything you are and have been through."

He kissed her on the lips quite naturally. Then he kissed her hair and her cheeks. They began to laugh softly, then harder until their eyes shone with tears. Ceb took her hands in his. Suddenly, reading each other's thoughts, they whispered in unison, "*L'essentiel est invisible pour les yeux.*"

As if on cue, the red puppy padded into the den.

"I love you, Filie," Ceb murmured as he held her tightly against his chest. There were no more words for the longest time. She felt the truth in the strength of his hands.

Epilogue

Eliane and Rémi's house in Prades-le-Lez was brimming with activity. They had expected thirty people for the annual Christmas get-together, and they had not been disappointed. To Ophélie, it was a thing of wonder, this Christmas Eve. She sat cuddled up beside Ceb in front of the large stone fireplace. Her husband of three months rubbed his bearded cheek on hers, and the prickly sensation made her smile. Her husband! They were starting something new and good and challenging. And Ophélie read it on every face. This year, there was a special joy and a conviction that it was so very right. Ceb had come home. Home to her.

The night before, they had taken the minivan into centre ville to give a party for the SDFs. Outside the little square of Notre Dame des Tables, several skinny dogs had burrowed through the scraps of food that overflowed the trash cans by the *crêperie* on the corner. Pigeons approached cautiously, occasionally finding a crust of bread that the dogs had missed. When the white minivan pulled up beside the church, a group of men and women had already gathered. Word of a party had traveled quickly.

Rislène and Ophélie had ladled out the hot cider spiced with cinnamon and cloves. Ceb distributed gifts. Janine cut slices of her *bûches de Noël*, placing them on paper plates along with other homemade treats. Dominique gave out the plates to eager men and women. A bonfire glowed inside one of the trash cans, and people took turns warming themselves beside it.

Eric had played his guitar as Ophélie and Janine handed out blankets, and soon a crowd of more than a hundred of the city's homeless were huddled together, singing in hoarse, raspy voices. *Christ, the Savior, is born. Christ, the Savior, is born.*

Now Eric was strumming the guitar in the Cebrians' living room while voices softly sang. Ophélie observed Rislène, who with tranquillity and deep pride in her eyes was watching her husband's fingers pick the strings of the guitar. Eliane kissed Rémi on the cheek, then turned toward Rachel, who was cradling little Catherine in her arms. Catherine had taken her first steps just yesterday.

This was heavenly peace, thought Ophélie. This luxury of being surrounded by family. Mama and Moustafa were sitting next to Bri and Papa. For tonight all worries were erased from their faces. Worries about jobs and finances and racial tensions.

Jesus has come! Rejoice! Rejoice! It is a holy moment. We are all here. We are celebrating the incarnate Christ. He has come, and life will never be the same. It was both a summing up and a beginning. *God with us. Again.*

... a little more ...

When a delightful concert comes to an end,

the orchestra might offer an encore.

When a fine meal comes to an end,

it's always nice to savor a bit of dessert.

When a great story comes to an end,

we think you may want to linger.

And so, we offer ...

AfterWords—just a little something more after you

have finished a David C Cook novel.

We invite you to stay awhile in the story.

Thanks for reading!

Turn the page for ...

- **A Historical Note**
- **Discussion Questions**
- **About the Author**

A Historical Note

The Algerian Civil War, which began in 1991, is estimated to have cost between 150,000 and 200,000 lives. The war effectively ended with a government victory, following the surrender of the Islamic Salvation Army and the 2002 defeat of the Armed Islamic Group. However, low-level fighting still continues in some areas.

In 2006, the Algerian government passed a law that required all Christian groups to declare themselves to the government for surveillance, which ultimately would result in the denouncing of Christians, putting their lives in great danger. Therefore, Algerian Christians continue to meet clandestinely in house groups, receiving occasional visits from believers in other countries. Literature, Bibles, DVDs, and financial support for the Christian pastors are still smuggled into Algeria in small quantities. Rislène's story, although fictional, resembles the story of many young North African women who have converted to Christianity.

The homeless situation in France shows no signs of letting up. Each year men, women, and children die on the streets, alone, refusing the help of the agencies created to help them. It is my prayer that you will find a way to help the persecuted church around the world (www.opendoorsusa.org) and the homeless in your area of influence. Your concern and prayers will make a difference, even if it means just handing out a bag and a smile at a traffic light.

Discussion Questions

1. In chapter 1, Ophélie admits that she feels awkward when a homeless person greets her at a traffic light. How do you respond to people begging for money or food?

Later in the novel (chapter 14), Ophélie wonders who she is coming to help at the Red Cross, the homeless or herself. Have you ever done some type of charity work to feel better about yourself, to ease guilty feelings? What was the result?

Then, at the end of chapter 30, Ophélie makes a decision about what she can do for the homeless who approach her on a daily basis. What do think about her idea? Would you be willing to try it?

2. Think back on the several scenes that describe the prejudice felt by the French toward the Arabs (Mme Ploussard's gossip about Rislène in chapters 4, 6, and 8; and Mme Dufour's disapproval of inviting Arabs to church in chapter 10). Have you ever felt this way about a different minority, or have you ever been the one who was described in derogatory terms? Share your experiences.

3. How much do you know about the persecuted church throughout the world? Have you ever tried to put yourself in the place of Christians who are persecuted for their faith? Have you had any personal contact with persecuted Christians? Does the thought of being persecuted for your faith frighten you? Why or why not?

4. At the beginning of chapter 12, Ceb thinks about his adolescence. Can you relate to an experience of having tasted faith and then turned your back on it, or has someone you care about deeply been through this experience? What happened next? Is it wrong to pursue a high-level career, to be on the fast track? Discuss.

5. At the end of chapter 12, Ceb thinks about Ophélie as his friend. Have you ever been in a place where you needed a friend to help you come back from despair, or have you ever helped a friend in this way? What was the outcome?

6. Look at the scene at the beginning of chapter 14 where Rislène feels that her circumstances are too hard and that she has not been prepared for what she is enduring. Why does she change her mind? How has she been prepared? Have you ever been in a situation that seemed too hard for you only to see as you moved forward that God had prepared you to face this battle through lessons learned in the past? Share your experiences.

7. Discuss the theme of lost children in the novel. (Consider Ceb's mother, who practically closed off her emotions when her son disappeared. Think also of the plights of Rislène's mother when she has to leave her daughter in Algeria, and of El Amin's mother, who wonders if she will ever see her son again.) Can you relate to these women's grief? Share your experiences and what or who you found to help you through a difficult time.

8. Think about Ophélie's different interactions with Ceb that ended

in heated exchanges: in chapter 16 when he reluctantly accepted her invitation to shower and have lunch at her home, and in chapter 23 when they conversed about faith and grief. Have you ever tried to help a needy person, perhaps someone close to you, and gone about it all wrong? What happened? Were you able to make things right eventually? What would you do differently today if faced with the same situation?

9. Look at this conversation between Ophélie and Gabriella in chapter 18:

> "*Oui.* I understand that God must teach us humility and total dependence on Him. But even for me it's hard. And how in the world can I help Samuel understand that God can use such deep hurt for good?"
>
> "You can't, Ophélie. Trying to give spiritual answers for another person's tragedy falls on deaf ears. Or enrages. I have found that all I can do is to trust God as I live out the pain in my life and pray that God will reveal Himself to another in his own trials. It is wonderfully freeing, you know. Giving it back to God. He's big enough."

Do you agree or disagree with Gabriella's thoughts? Discuss.

10. Throughout the novel, Algerian women are portrayed as strong behind their veils. What do you think of Altaf Namani and her actions during the novel? What about Grandmother Namani? Nazira, Rislène's younger sister? Jala, El Amin's wife? Dounia, Hussein's wife?

11. Consider this passage from chapter 25:

> Ceb had thought that Algeria would be nonstop action.
> War, risk, adventure, violence. Not memories. Not more
> thoughts to torment his soul. He had thought it would be a
> new beginning, not a long, painful step back into his past.

Have you ever experienced the need to go back in the past before
being able to move forward in the present? Did it end up being necessary? Why or why not?

12. In chapter 24, Ophélie compares Dominique's work with that of
Christ's:

> "It's like you—Dominique the street mediator. Your
> job is to take the government's high and lofty ideas and
> translate them into everyday talk, to meet the homeless
> and represent the government in a way they can under-
> stand, so they'll accept the help that is available. Isn't that
> what you do?"
>
> He smiled. "More or less. If you simplify it, that's
> my goal."
>
> "Well, Jesus did the same thing—lived among
> humanity to show us what God was like so that we could
> accept His help and love. He was a mediator."

What do you think about this metaphor?

13. Discuss the pros and cons of marrying someone who does not share your beliefs. Can it work? Is it okay to date a person from a different religion? Think about Ophélie's struggle in this matter with Dominique and the possibility of Rislène being forced to marry a Muslim man.

14. Read this scene from chapter 26:

> It happened often, this battle within herself, this seeking to be free of something and freed to something. It was the dark side of Ophélie's personality that few people saw, the ever-spiraling tyranny of guilt and fear, and the terrible, terrible solitude. Today again she found herself literally crying, begging the Lord to stop the vicious circle of self-condemning thoughts. After a while, sitting on the couch in her den, she felt the late-afternoon sun that came through the French doors from the balcony touch her face, as if God were reaching out a tender finger through the rays of the sun and personally wiping away each tear.
>
> She picked herself up off the couch, relishing the warmth of the sun through the glass. "Let this be a new beginning," she prayed hesitantly. "Whatever it takes. I give You Ceb and Dominique, as I've given You every other man in my life. As I gave You Bachir. You know the pain."

Have you ever wrestled with these types of thoughts? Have you cried out to God? What was the outcome?

15. Throughout the novel, Ceb is portrayed as a man who needs action and control. When does he ultimately relinquish control of his life and why? How does he come to accept forgiveness and to forgive himself?

16. Look at Gabriella's conversation with Ophélie in chapter 26:

> "I hear you're taking care of his puppies?"
>
> "Yes. Eric helped me get them from the squat. It was the least I could do."
>
> "Listen, Ophélie. You've done a lot. Get yourself a cup of tea and take a break for a little while. It's okay to just be sad, you know. Will you do that for me, please?"

Do you have a friend who will give you this type of advice? If not, think about some people in your life who might serve in this role. Also consider how you might fulfill this role in someone else's life.

17. Discuss the symbolism in the novel: To whom does the title *Two Destinies* apply and why? What does the perfume bottle *L'Essentiel* represent in the novel? What other symbols or metaphors stuck out to you?

18. Discuss the themes of surrender, abiding, second chances, and new beginnings that occur throughout the novel. Think of how these themes apply to Rislène, Eric, Ceb, Ophélie, El Amin, and Hussein.

19. If you have read *Two Crosses* and *Two Testaments*, discuss how the characters from the first two novels changed and matured over the years.

About the Author

Elizabeth Goldsmith Musser, an Atlanta native and the best-selling author of *The Swan House*, is a novelist who writes what she calls "entertainment with a soul." For over twenty-five years, Elizabeth and her husband, Paul, have been involved in missions work with International Teams. They presently live near Lyon, France. The Mussers have two sons and a daughter-in-law. To learn more about Elizabeth and her books, and to find discussion questions as well as photos of sites mentioned in the stories, please visit www.elizabethmusser.com.